D1552626

BLUE RAVENS

GERALD VIZENOR

BLUE RAVENS

———————— HISTORICAL NOVEL ————————

WESLEYAN UNIVERSITY PRESS

⟩⟩⟩ ⟨⟨⟨

MIDDLETOWN, CONNECTICUT

WESLEYAN UNIVERSITY PRESS

Middletown CT 06459

www.wesleyan.edu/wespress

© 2014 Gerald Vizenor

All rights reserved

Manufactured in the United States of America

Designed and typeset in Parkinson Electra

by Eric M. Brooks

Wesleyan University Press is a member of the
Green Press Initiative. The paper used in this book meets
their minimum requirement for recycled paper.

Library of Congress Cataloging-in-Publication Data
available upon request

5 4 3 2 1

*Ignatius Vizenor was born May 4, 1894,
son of Michael Vizenor and Angeline Cogger,
on the White Earth Reservation in Minnesota. He was
a dapper dresser, wore a fedora, and fought for a nation that
once inspired natives in the fur trade. The surname Vizenor
was derived from Vezina in New France. Private Vizenor
was killed in action on October 8, 1918,
at Montbréhain, France.*

*Ignatius Vizenor was buried at
Saint Benedict's Catholic Cemetery on the
White Earth Reservation. The military coffin was sealed,
and no one at the funeral could account for his entire remains.
Thousands of soldiers were harrowed in the soil that
early autumn at Alsace, Lorraine, Champagne,
Ardennes, and Picardy in France.*

Raven created the world for his amusement
and people were the most amusing
of all animals to him.

In the Company of Crows and Ravens
JOHN MARZLUFF, TONY ANGELL

〉〉〉 〈〈〈

Blue is not aggressive and violates nothing;
it reassures and draws together. . . . The same is
true in many other languages: *bleu, blew, blu, blau*
are reassuring and poetic words that link
color, memory, desire, and dreams.

Blue: The History of Color
MICHEL PASTOUREAU

〉〉〉 〈〈〈

The French early gained the utmost
confidence of the Ojibways, and thereby
they became more thoroughly acquainted
with their true and real character, even during the
comparative short season in which they mingled
with them as a nation. . . . The French understood
their divisions into clans, and treated each clan
according to the order of its ascendency
in the tribe.

History of the Ojibway People
WILLIAM WARREN

Today a bird flew near our battery during the chaos.
It seemed stunned and no wonder when man has so
upset the order of life. What a blessing will it be
when mother nature has the running of the
universe to herself again.

The Diary of Elmer W. Sherwood
EDITED BY ROBERT H. FERRELL

⟩⟩⟩ ⟨⟨⟨

Houses are eviscerated like human beings
and towns like houses. Villages appear in crumpled
whiteness as though fallen from heaven to earth. The
very shape of the plain is changed by the frightful heaps
of wounded and slain. . . . Turn where you will,
there is war in every corner of that vastness.

Under Fire: The Story of a Squad
HENRY BARBUSSE

⟩⟩⟩ ⟨⟨⟨

Touching war memorials, and in particular, touching
the names of those who died, is an important part of
the rituals of separation . . . thus testifying that whatever the
aesthetic and political meanings which they may bear, they
are also sites of mourning, and of gestures which
go beyond the limitations of place and time.

Sites of Memory, Sites of Mourning
JAY WINTER

Contents

Roman Beaks

1907

Aloysius Hudon Beaulieu created marvelous blue ravens that stormy summer. He painted blue ravens over the mission church, blue ravens in the clouds, celestial blue ravens with tousled manes perched on the crossbeams of the new telegraph poles near the post office, and two grotesque blue ravens cocked as mighty sentries on the stone gateway to the hospital on the White Earth Reservation in Minnesota.

My brother was twelve years old when he first painted the visionary blue ravens on flimsy newsprint. Aloysius was truly an inspired artist, not a student painter. He enfolded the ethereal blue ravens in newsprint and printed his first saintly name on the corner of the creased paper.

Aloysius Beaulieu, or *beau lieu*, means a beautiful place in French. That fur-trade surname became our union of ironic stories, necessary art, and our native liberty. Henri Matisse, we discovered later, painted the *Nu Bleu, Souvenir de Biskra*, or the *Blue Nude*, that same humid and gusty summer in France.

The blue ravens were traces of visions and original abstract totems, the chance associations of native memories in the natural world. Aloysius was teased and admired at the same time for his distinctive images of ravens.

Frances Densmore, the famous ethnomusicologist, attended the annual native celebration and must have seen the visionary totemic blue ravens that summer on the reservation. Her academic studies were more dedicated, however, to the mature traditions and practiced presentations of art and music than the inspirations of a precocious native artist.

President Theodore Roosevelt, that same year, proposed the Hague Convention. The international limitation of armaments was not sustained by the great powers because several nations united with Germany and vetoed the convention on military arms. The First World War started seven years later, and that wicked crusade would change our world forever.

Marc Chagall and my brother would be celebrated for their blue scenes

and visionary portrayals. Chagall painted blue dreams, lovers, angels, violinists, donkeys, cities, and circus scenes. He was six years older than my
brother, and they both created blue visionary creatures and communal
scenes. Chagall declared his vision as an artist in Vitebsk on the Pale of Settlement in Imperial Russia. Aloysius created his glorious blue ravens about
the same time on the Pale of White Earth in Minnesota. He painted blue
ravens in new reservation scenes perched over the government school, the
mission, hospital, cemetery, and icehouses. Many years later he blued the
bloody and desolate battlefields of the First World War in France.

Chagall and my brother were the saints of blues.

Aloysius was commended for his godly native talents and artistic portrayals by Father Aloysius Hermanutz, his namesake and the resident priest
at Saint Benedict's Mission. Nonetheless the priest provided my brother
with black paint to correct the primary color of the blue ravens. The priest
was constrained by holy black and white, the monastic and melancholy
scenes and stories of the saints. Black was an absence, austere and tragic.
The blues were totemic and a rush of presence. The solemn chase of
black has no tease or sentiment. Black absorbed the spirit of natives, the
light and motion of shadows. Ravens are blue, the lush sheen of blues in
a rainbow, and the transparent blues that shimmer on a spider web in the
morning rain. Blues are ironic, the tease of natural light. The night is blue
not black.

Augustus Hudon Beaulieu, our cunning and ambitious uncle, overly
praised my brother and encouraged his original artistry. Our determined
uncle would have painted blue the entire mission, the face of the priest,
earnest sisters, the government school and agents. He had provoked the
arbitrary authority of federal agents from the very start of the reservation,
and continued his denunciations in every conversation. Our uncle easily
provided the newsprint for the blue ravens because he was the independent publisher of the *Tomahawk*, a weekly newspaper on the White Earth
Reservation.

Aloysius never painted any images for the priest, black or blue, or for the
mission, and he bravely declined the invitation to decorate the newspaper
building with totemic portrayals of blue bears, cranes, and ravens. He understood by intuition that our uncle and the priest would exact familiar representations of creatures, and that would dishearten the natural inspiration

of any artist who created a visionary sense of native presence. My brother would never paint to promote newspapers or the papacy.

Blue ravens roost on the fusty monuments.

Aloysius was actually a family stray, but he was never an orphan or outcast in the community. He had been abandoned at birth, a newborn ditched at the black mission gate with no name, note, or trace of paternity. My mother secretly raised us as natural brothers because we were born on the same day, October 22, 1895.

We were born in a world of crucial missions unaware of the Mauve Decade and the Gilded Age and yet we created our own era of Blue Ravens on the White Earth Reservation. That same year of our birth Captain Alfred Dreyfus was unjustly convicted of treason and dishonored as an artillery officer in France, and Auguste and Louis Lumière set in motion the cinematograph and screened films for the first time at Le Salon Indien du Grand Café at the Place de l'Opéra in Paris.

Two Benedictine Sisters, Philomene Ketten and Lioba Braun, embraced the forsaken child at the mission gate and named him in honor of the compassionate priest. Aloysius was my brother by heart and memory, by native sentiment, and our loyalty was earned by natural scares, and covert confidence, always more secure as brothers in arms than by the mere count and conceit of our paternal blood descent.

Father Aloysius was solemn and solicitous in the presence of the boy who would bear his first name, and the name of a saint. The priest was an honorable servant, and he was much adored by the native parishioners of the reservation mission. Yet, to appreciate his consecrated name in the dark eyes of a forsaken native child would never be the same as a ceremonial epithet on a monument or holy façade.

My mother was not pleased that her second son, my brother by chance, was named in honor of the priest. She respected the priest, the dedication of the sisters, and the mission, but she considered the name too much of a burden on the reservation. The situational caution of that priestly name was soon alleviated, however, when my aunt named her son, born a year earlier, Ignatius. The priestly name was delayed because he was not expected to survive the year. Only then were the honorable namesakes of two priests and two saints acceptable to the mission and to our native families.

Aloysius was never an easy name to pronounce. The teases and ridicule of his saintly name were constant at the government school, such as, Alley boy, wild son of the mission priest. Mostly the parents of the teasers were members of the Episcopal Church and dedicated critics of the Catholic Mission. Aloysius practiced the artifice of silence and the politics of evasion, similar to the rehearsal of a wise poker player, and he studied the strategies of counter teases. He would pause, turn aside, and declare, "Mostly, the son of tricky saints." Only the priest, the sisters, and my parents knew that my brother had been abandoned at the mission.

Aloysius was delivered a second time, in a sense, a few days later at our house near Mission Lake. My mother raised us as twins, nurtured us as a timely union, and taught us to perceive the natural motion of the seasons, and the subtle hues of color in nature. She was an artist at heart and might have painted her children blue and united in flight over the reservation. Those early insights and memories were the start of my natural sense of creation stories and family. We were not the same, of course, natives and brothers are never the same, but we became intimate and loyal friends by experience and confidence. We were driven by the same intense curiosity, by a sense of empathy, wonder, the natural surprise of intuition, and always by the tender tease of our mother. She experienced the world through our adventures, and so she teased every scene, gesture, pose, and story.

Our parents were born near Bad Medicine Lake, north of Pine Point and west of Lake Itasca, the source of *gichiziibi*, the Great River, or the Mississippi River. Many generations before the treaty reservation two great native families, and only two, lived on the north and south shores of Bad Medicine Lake.

Bigiwizigan, or Maple Taffy, the ironic nickname of a dubious native shaman, created stories of mistrust about Bad Medicine Lake because there was no obvious source of the water. The cunning shaman used the mystery of the lake to sway his stories of unease and medicine mastery.

Bad Medicine, about five miles long, was cold and crystal clear, and the sources of water were natural springs. Our native ancestors created by natural reason the obvious origin stories of the water, and were secure on the north and south shore, the only native families who dared to live near the lake.

Honoré Hudon Beaulieu, our father, was born on the north shore of Bad Medicine Lake. He was also known as Frenchy. Our mother was born on the south shore of the lake. These two families, descendants of natives and fur traders, shared the resources of the lake and pine forests. My father was private, cautious, but not reticent. He was native by natural reason and disregarded the federal treaty that established the White Earth Reservation. Honoré refused to honor the boundaries and continued to hunt, trap, fish, gather wild rice and maple syrup in the manner of his ancestors.

Honoré shunned the federal agents.

Margaret, our mother, was carried in a *dikinaagan*, or native cradleboard, and remembers the scent and stories of maple syrup. The two families of the lake came together several times a year to share the labor and stories of gathering wild rice and making maple sugar. Our parents met many times at wild rice and sugar camps. More natives were conceived at sugar camps than any other place.

Honoré was a singer and woodland storier, and in his time created scenes about resistance to federal agents and the native police. He refused to relocate and shunned the summons to receive an assigned allotment of land according to the new policies of the federal government. He was a fur trade hunter and never accepted or obeyed any government. My father continued to hunt, fish, and cut timber near Waabigan, Juggler, and Kneebone lakes, as his ancestors had done for many centuries.

Honoré had earned the veneration of many natives for his resistance to the government, and for his integrity as an independent hunter and trapper. Politicians and federal agents cursed his name, and yet they had never visited or heard his stories. The native police ordered and threatened him several times, but only our mother and the contract of a timber company convinced him to accept an allotment. Our father never located the actual land that was allotted in his name, an arbitrary transaction, but he agreed to move with his pregnant wife to a new house near Mission Lake, and at the same time he was hired by a timber company to cut white pine near Bad Medicine Lake.

The federal agent selected the new teachers at the government school. Most of the teachers were from Connecticut, Rhode Island, and Massachusetts in New England. The agent never hired a native teacher. He always wore a black suit, and the teachers were secured in layers of white muslin with creamy flowers. The classroom was unnatural, a drafty box of distractions, the pitch and duty of an awkward hem and haw civilization.

The teachers roamed and droned for hours at the chalkboards. The autumn wind soughed with the stories of native shamans in the corridors. Native word players cracked in the cold beams, and the ice woman moaned at the frosted windows. The ice woman murmured seductive stories to lonesome natives in winter, and we were the lonesome ones in school. She whispered a temptation to rest in the snow on the long walk home at night. She gathered the souls of those who were enticed by her treachery.

The ice woman was a better story than the presidents.

Every winter day we cracked and moved the thick clear chunks of ice on the schoolroom windows, and pretended to melt the ice woman and other concocted beasts and enemies of natives by warm breath, touch, and natural motion on the windowpane. Sometimes we told stories that the government teacher was the ice woman but we never dared tease her to rest overnight in the snow. Actually we never mentioned the name of the ice woman. Our stories were only about the natives who had been tempted by the ice woman and froze to death.

The federal agent ridiculed the ice woman stories and blamed the deaths on alcohol. Only the clumsy son of the assistant agent dared to name the teacher as the ice woman. He knew nothing about native stories of shamans or the ice woman. We turned away and shunned the stupid student because natives needed the most creative stories of the ice woman to survive the winter, and we needed even better stories to survive the federal agents and barrels of commodity salt pork.

Summer in the spring was our natural liberty.

The only memorable experience on the reservation was nature, the rush of the seasons, summer in the early spring, the fierce autumn wind out of the western prairie, the gusts and whispers in the mighty forests of white pine. Our every moment outside of school was a sense of fugitive adventures. We shared the notions of chance, totemic connections, and the tricky stories of our natural transience in the world. We were delivered by stories, and our best stories were nothing more than the chance of remembrance. My brother was delivered by chance, we learned years later, and that clearly demonstrated our confidence in stories of coincidence and fortuity.

Margaret, our mother, never revealed the mission secret that my brother was a reservation stray, a newborn of obscure paternity, and apparently that we were not related by blood, until that early summer when we were drafted and departed by train for military service in the American Expeditionary Forces in France.

Our mother was a herbal healer and insisted that her son the artist use only natural paint colors. She provided the natural blue tints that my brother used to paint ravens. Blue was not a common native pigment, so the blue ravens were doubly distinctive. The pale blue tints were made with crushed plum, blue berries, or the roots of red cedar. My mother boiled decomposed maple stumps and included fine dust of various soft stones to concoct the rich darker hues of blue and purple. The synthetic ultramarine powder from traders was not suitable for painting.

Most of the blue ravens were abstract, with huge dark blue angular beaks and almost human eyes. The curves of the wings were broken in flight, and several feathers were painted with elaborate details. Some ravens were turned upside down in flight, as ravens turn over, cant, bounce, and play in flight with other ravens over the mission and post office.

My brother painted blue ravens as sentries at the stone gate of the hospital, and that troubled the priest more than a naked woman, even more than the stories that my brother was the son of the priest. The giant claws of the abstract raven were painted dark blue, with faint veins and the broad traces of human hands. Two claws were curved with cracked fingernails. The two blue sentry ravens wore masks. The huge beaks were outlined and distorted, and turned to the side of the ravens.

Aloysius truly painted abstract scenes by inspiration not by mere duplication or representation, and yet the priest was concerned that he had painted the images of demons in the ravens. My brother had never seen the haunting images of raven masks with monstrous beaks worn by medical doctors during the Black Plague in Europe.

Aloysius was curious, of course, but my brother had already established his own expressionistic form and style, abstract blue ravens in the natural world, and the chance associations of material scenes in cities. Later he had created blue ravens of war, and he would continue to create his inspired scenes of blue ravens over the parks, statues, and bridges over the River Seine in Paris.

No one on the reservation would have associated the abstract blue ravens with the modern art movements of impressionism or expressionism, or the avant-garde, and certainly not compared the color and style of the inspired raven scenes on the reservation with the controversial painting *Les Demoiselles d'Avignon* by Pablo Picasso. Yet, my brother painted by inspiration the original abstract blue ravens at the same time that Picasso created *The Brothel of Avignon*, the translated title, in 1907. Picasso was swayed by the notion of primitive scenes. The five naked women were pitched to the viewer, angular, gawky, excessive, abstract, and two women wore masks, the obvious influence and deliberate conceptual imitation of primitive art that had been exhibited at the Musée d'Ethnographie du Trocadéro in Paris.

Aloysius accepted the crown of chance, an uncertain destiny and saintly name, and became a soldier and artist in the American Expeditionary Forces in France. We served together as scouts in the same division and infantry regiment, and survived the unbearable memories of shattered blue faces in the brush, broken bodies, small bare bones in the muck, and solitary tremors of hands and hearts in the ruins of war. The eyes of soldiers at the end turned hoary with no trace of rage, sense of solemn touch, shimmer of blood, or praise of irony.

We were brothers on the reservation, brothers in the bloody blue muck of the trenches, slow black rivers, brick shambles of farms and cities, brothers of the untold dead at gruesome stations. Bodies were stacked by the day for a wretched roadside funeral in the forest ruins. We were steadfast brothers on the road of lonesome warriors, a native artist and writer ready to transmute the desolation of war with blue ravens and poetic scenes of a scary civilization and native liberty.

>>> <<<

The Italian Aloysius of Gonzaga, a sixteenth-century saint, was castle born and encouraged by his mighty father to become a soldier. He was a warrior only in name. Aloysius the original renounced his inheritance to become a priest and vowed chastity, poverty, and obedience, a comely ritual of conceit, monotheistic separation, and ancestral agony.

Father Aloysius Hermanutz was born in the ancient Kingdom of Württemberg in 1853. He studied to become a Benedictine priest and dedicated his godly service and obedience to the care, conversion, and education of natives for some fifty years at Saint Benedict's Mission on the White Earth

Reservation. Aloysius, my brother, continues his saintly name in the marvelous artistry of a painter, not in the doctrines of monotheism, obedience, and the noticeable pain of priestly courtesy.

Saint Aloysius envisioned his own death at age twenty-three on June 21, 1591. Aloysius Hudon Beaulieu was drafted with me and other native relatives at the very same age and in the same month some three centuries later as ordinary infantry soldiers of the American Expeditionary Forces in the First World War.

The chance connections of soldiers and saints.

Ignatius Vizenor and many of our other cousins enlisted or were drafted that same summer to serve as soldiers in the ironic name of the Great War. Ignatius was the namesake of Father Ignatius Tomazin, and more notably of Saint Ignatius of Loyola.

Ignatius, our cousin, was the firstborn of Michael and Angeline Vizenor. He was raised with four brothers and two sisters. Joseph, the last born, was elected many years later as the manager of the Minnesota Chippewa Tribe in Minnesota. Ignatius and his brother Lawrence, who was a year younger, were privates in the American Expeditionary Forces in France.

The Beaulieu and Vizenor families praised and raised large godly families, a legacy of the fur trade and that premier native union with spirited descendants of New France. The families were mostly devout but they became cautious Roman Catholics after the First World War and the Great Depression. Absolute devotion to a church or a saint was more uncertain after the massive death and destruction of an unspeakable world war and the absolute desperation of extreme poverty.

Many native fur trade families came together with new and obscure traditions, the union of blood and treasure to honor and defend France. A disproportionate number of natives enlisted and others were drafted to serve in the military, and their reservation families invested in patriotic war bonds to cover the cost of the American Expeditionary Forces.

Peter Vizenor, or Vezina, and Sophia Trotterchaud raised fourteen children, including Abraham, Henry, and Michael who married Angeline Cogger. Peter was a native hunter and fur trader at the time the reservation was established in 1868. Two of their children married and raised twenty more children. Abraham Vizenor and Margaret Fairbanks, for instance, raised five boys and six girls on the reservation. Henry Vizenor and Alice Mary Beaulieu raised nine children on the reservation and then the family moved to Minneapolis at the end of the Great Depression.

Clement Hudon Beaulieu and Elizabeth Farling raised ten children and were removed by the federal government from Old Crow Wing to the new White Earth Reservation. Augustus Hudon Beaulieu, the firstborn, founded and was publisher of the *Progress*, and later the *Tomahawk*, the first weekly newspapers published on the reservation. Clement Hudon Beaulieu, the eighth child and namesake of his father, became a priest in the Episcopal Church. Charles Hudon Beaulieu served in the Civil War and was promoted from private to captain in the Ninth Minnesota Volunteers. Theodore Basile Beaulieu, the youngest of the ten children, married three times and raised six children with his first wife Anne Charette, two children with his second wife Maggie Pemberton, and four children with his third wife Anna Tanner.

These first native families of the fur trade and the reservation begot a new nation, and their sons and daughters served with honor and distinction in every war elected, concocted, and declared by politicians in two centuries. Most native soldiers were born on federal reservations, served with others in integrated companies, and were not yet recognized as citizens at the time of the First World War. Natives of the fur trade served to save one of the nations of their ancestors. France established many war memorials, but never a memorial to honor the natives of the fur trade.

Ignatius of Loyola was the mastermind of the Society of Jesus, otherwise named the Jesuits. Basque born more than four centuries ago he waived nobility, his knightly fortune, and by vows of poverty and chastity became a hermit, priest, and theologian. Ignatius was inspired by many reported visions of the saints, sacred adventures, and holy figures, and these marvelous ethereal contests in his dreams determined the stories of his divine service. He was canonized and declared the patron saint of soldiers.

Ignatius Vizenor was never secure with a saintly name.

Father Ignatius Tomazin was the first priest delegated by the abbot of Saint John's Abbey to establish a mission at the White Earth Reservation. Federal policy at the time favored the mercy and politics of the Episcopal Church over the secretive papacy of Rome. Father Tomazin was a testy immigrant from Ljubljana, Slovenia, with a great vision of political resistance, and he spoke the language of the native Anishinaabe. He was provoked and criticized by Lewis Stowe, the nasty federal agent, who had been appointed by the Episcopal bishop Henry Benjamin Whipple. Stowe was actually the agent of the bishop, not the federal government, and he maligned Father Tomazin.

The Catholic natives on the reservation defended the mission priest and united to resist the arbitrary authority of the agent and the policies of the federal government to designate a minority religious functionary.

Father Ignatius Tomazin, in February 1879, accompanied a delegation of five principal native leaders, Wabanquot, or White Cloud, the head chief, Mashakegeshig, Munedowu, Shawbaskung, and Hole in the Day, the younger, to discuss the crucial issues of native liberty on the White Earth Reservation with federal officials in Washington.

Father Tomazin was eventually removed from the White Earth Reservation because he rightly goaded the federal agents and chosen Episcopalians. The feisty priest protected native political liberty. Some thirty years later he served as the pastor of a church in Albany, Minnesota. Tragically the nasty parishioners of that mingy and disagreeable community challenged the priest, beat and cursed him in the parish house, and chased him out of town. Father Tomazin, then in his seventies, was badly wounded in spirit, and deceived by his own resistance, wandered to Chicago and "jumped to his death from the sixth floor of a hotel," according to the *New York Times*, August 27, 1916.

Ignatius, our coy, courteous, and elegant cousin would not survive the saintly names or priestly patronage. He was born premature, so tiny as an infant that he was swaddled in an ordinary cigar box. Partly to overcome the constant teases and tedious stories of his hasty birth and chancy presence he became a fancy dresser on the reservation. He wore smart suits, ties, and a dark fedora, but his courage and costumes were not enough to survive the horror of the First World War. Ignatius was killed in action on October 8, 1918, at Montbréhain, France, and buried in Saint Benedict's Cemetery on the White Earth Reservation.

>>> <<<

Aloysius revealed his visions in the creative portrayals of blue ravens, and the abstract ravens became his singular totem of the natural world. He was convinced that his totemic associations were original, and there were no other blue raven totems or cultures in the world.

Aloysius forever soared with ravens and never wholly returned to the ordinary world of priests, missions, communion of saints, the strains of authenticity, newspapers, manly loggers, salt pork, or the mundane catechism, recitations, and lectures on civilization by lonesome missionaries, teachers, and federal agents. He became a blue raven painter of liberty.

My brother actually inspired me to become a writer, to create the stories anew that our relatives once told whenever they gathered in the summer for native celebrations, at native wakes, and funerals at the mission. Our relatives were great storiers, and natural leaders with many versions of stories and reservation scenes, and for that reason they were associated with the crane totem, the orators of the early Anishinaabe.

Frances Densmore, the musicologist and curious explorer of native cultures, recorded native songs and stories on the reservation. She was mostly interested in the translation of the songs and oral stories. My interests were in the actual creation of the songs and stories, and the totemic variation of stories, not in the mere concepts and evidence of culture. The specialists forever collected native stories and concocted a show of conceptual traditions. The culture was ours, of course, and the show was never the same in the studies by outside experts. Similar stories were told over and over with many personal and communal variations at native festivals, funerals, and summer celebrations. The heart and humor of native stories and cultures are never in the books of outsiders.

Aloysius inspired me to create visionary stories and scenes of presence, stories that were elusive and not merely descriptive. The scenes of blue ravens in court, ravens balanced on the back of a black horse, and seven blue ravens perched in a caboose were memorable. He created abstract ravens in motion, the very scenes of his visions and memory, but words were too heavy, too burdened by grammar and decorated with documented history to break into blue abstract ravens and fly. My recollections of the words in stories were not the same as artistic or visionary scenes, not at first. Dreams are scenes not words, but one or two precise words could create a vision of the scene. That would be my course of literary art and liberty.

Frances Densmore visited the reservation that summer and indirectly provided me with the intuition and the initial tease of visionary songs and stories. Yes, we were twelve-year-old native amateurs at the time, so the actual memory of my inspiration is much clearer today. Densmore recorded hundreds of native singers on a phonograph, a cumbersome machine that recorded sound directly onto cylinders. We had heard the songs of shamans and animals, of course, but we had never heard the immediate recorded tinny sound of a human voice.

Densmore recorded singers and the song stories, the situation, cultural significance, and descriptive meaning of the song. The stories of the songs inspired me, and by intuition the actual creation of written scenes and stories became much easier for me.

Densmore, for instance, recorded this song by Odjibwe, the traditional native singer, *little plover, it is said, has walked by*. Only eight words were translated, nothing more. The song scenes were active and memorable because the listeners understood the story. The song story is what inspired me to create the presence of listeners in the story.

The song dancers imitated the natural motions of the plover, elusive motions to distract intruders and predators. The little plover was alone, always vulnerable near the lakeshore. That sense of motion was portrayed in my three written stories that were inspired by the native song of the plover dance. The listeners and readers must appreciate the chance of the plover.

My first three stories were neatly written on newsprint, and my brother painted two blue abstract ravens for the cover of the plover dance scenes. The first stories were gathered by my mother but were lost in a house fire, never folded or signed on the corner. The fire destroyed the early box camera photographs of my brother and me when we sold newspapers at the station, when we worked in the livery stable of the Hotel Leecy, and the only photographs of us as soldiers in the American Expeditionary Forces. Ignatius was the first to leave for the war, and we were pictured arm in arm at the train station.

The first story was about the cocky little plover with the most sensational wounded wing dance, so impressive that the evasive motion of the plover dance was easily perceived and imitated by envious dancers and predators.

My second story was about the plover with an irregular hobble, an intricate dance that feigned a broken foot and a wounded wing. The elusive dance was so decisive that the plover could only reveal the artistry of the dance to escape the envies of a predator.

The third story was about a plover with a variety of trivial vaudeville performances, feigns, guises, blue raven masks, acrobatic, and deceptive plover dances that entertained and completely distracted and deceived the intruders and predators. The most evasive plover dances were the crafty and clumsy practice of tricky entertainment.

My first three written stories were visionary, and the stories demonstrated by specific metaphors of three plover dances the actual and familiar experiences of natives on the reservation. My last story was the dance of the trickster plover of liberty.

Native saints and secrets were blue, the blue of creation and visions of motion, not deprivation, the conceit of sacrifice, or the godly praise of black and tragic death. Blues were the origin of the earth and stories of creative energy. The mountains emerged from the blue sea and became that singular trace of blue creation and the hues of a sunrise.

Blue morning, blue seasons, blue summer, blue thunder, blue winter nights, and the irony of blue blood. Blue snow at night, blue shadows in the spring light, blue spider webs, and wild blue berries were natural totemic connections. Some nations were blue, coat of arms blue, blue flags on the wind. The chances of native stories, memories, conscience, and the sacred were a mighty blue. Blue ravens were the saints forever in abstract motion, and the traces of blue were eternal in native stories. Blue ravens were the new totem of native motion.

OGEMA STATION
1908

Aloysius painted seven gorgeous blue ravens seated as passengers in a railroad car. The enormous wings of the spectacular ravens stretched out the windows, bright blue feathers flaunted at various angles. The passenger train seemed to be in natural flight that summer afternoon over the peneplain. Great blue beaks were raised high above the windows, a haughty gesture of direction, or a mighty military salute.

The Soo Line Railroad a few years earlier had laid new tracks and built new stations at Mahnomen, Ogema, and Callaway on the White Earth Reservation. The passenger trains arrived twice a day from Winnipeg and Saint Paul. Every afternoon in the summer we heard the steam whistle in the distance, that evocative sound of a new world as the train stopped at the Ogema Station.

Winnipeg, Thief River Falls, Mahnomen, and Waubun were familiar places in one direction of the railroad line. Detroit Lakes, Minneapolis, Chicago, Sault Ste. Marie, and Montreal were not familiar in the other directions. We envisioned many other places, marvelous railroad cities. Places without government teachers, federal agents, mission priests, or reservations.

Blue ravens were our totems of creation and liberty.

Aloysius told the priest that the blue ravens were the only totems that could convey his native vision. No other totems were as secure as the blue raven, not even the traditional crane totem of our ancestors. The stories of native totems were inherited and imagined, but the blue ravens were original and abstract signature totems. My brother created totems as a painter in almost the same way the first totems were imagined by native storiers, by vision, by artistry, but not by the tricky politics of shamans and warriors. The first totems were painted on hide, wood, birch bark, and stone.

The priest would never associate with the creation of native totems. Nature was a separation not an inspiration of holy faith or godly associations.

The priest glanced at the blue ravens and then turned away in silence. He seemed to regard the personal creative expressions of my brother as a private and necessary confession or sacrament of penance.

Augustus, our favorite uncle, celebrated the visions of a thirteen year old, or any totemic vision that provoked the priest, and hired us to paint blue ravens and other totems on the outside of the tiny newspaper building. His praise was conditional, as usual, so we returned with our own strategies and agreed to paint the building if he would hire us to sell his newspapers. Our uncle paused to consider our adolescent tactics, and then consented but with more conditions. He would pay only a penny a copy for the newspapers we sold, and we must find new customers and ways to increase the circulation of the reservation weekly.

We painted the newspaper building white a few days later but not decorated with blue ravens. The paint was thick and lumpy, not an impressive cover. The next day we started our first positions as newspaper hawkers, news salesmen with a commission. No one, not even our younger cousins, would work for only a penny a newspaper. The venture, however, was worth much more than the mere penny income.

Augustus was a heavy drinker, at times, and that was both a problem and an advantage. He was more critical of the federal agent when he had been drinking, and that troubled Father Aloysius. Our uncle was always generous when he drank alone or with others, but he seldom remembered promises. One night we easily persuaded our feisty publisher to pay the cost of two train tickets to promote the weekly newspaper at every Soo Line Railroad station between Ogema and the Milwaukee Road Depot in faraway Minneapolis.

The *Tomahawk* sold for about three cents a copy by annual subscription, and everyone on the reservation who wanted the paper had already subscribed, so we decided to hawk the newspaper to strangers on the train at the Ogema Station. The trains arrived twice a day and we earned about ten cents in a day.

Hawking the *Tomahawk* was easy because there were no other newspapers published in the area, and because we were directly related to the publisher. I tried to read every issue of the newspaper and to memorize a few paragraphs of the main stories, enough weekly content to shout out the significance of the news stories.

I actually learned how to write by reading the newspapers we sold, by memory of selected descriptive scenes, and by imitation of the standard style of journalism at the time. I learned how to create scenes in words, and to imagine the colors of words, and my brother painted abstract scenes of blue ravens. Most students at our school had learned how to mimic teachers, to recount government scenes, federal agents, and native police, but we were the only students who hawked newspapers with national stories and learned how to write at the same time.

The *Progress* was the first newspaper published on the White Earth Reservation, and the news was mostly local, including a special personal section on the recent travels, experiences, and events of reservation families. The newspaper reported that our grandmother, for instance, traveled by horse and wagon to visit relatives in the town of Beaulieu. The *Progress* published reservation news and critical editorials about the ineptitude of federal agents and policies of the federal government.

Major Timothy Sheehan, the federal agent, and native police confiscated the very first edition of the *Progress*, the newsprint and the actual press, and ordered my relatives to leave the reservation. Agent Sheehan must have thought he was the deputy of a colonial monarchy. Augustus was publisher of the *Progress* and Theodore Hudon Beaulieu was the editor and printer at the time. The first edition of the *Progress*, critical of the federal agent and the policies of reservation land allotment, was published on March 25, 1886.

Our relatives refused to leave their homes and newspaper business by the order of a corrupt political agent, and instead sought sanctuary at Saint Benedict's Mission. Father Aloysius Hermanutz, the mission priest, provided a secure refuge for some of our relatives, and protection from the arbitrary authority of the federal agent. The Episcopal Church had been active in the selection of the agent and dominant in the administration of federal reservation policies. The native police had refused to arrest or remove our relatives from the reservation.

The obvious constitutional issue of freedom of the press was decided a year later by a federal court. The court ruled in favor of my relatives, who had a right to publish a newspaper on the reservation, or anywhere in the country, without the consent of a federal agent. The native and constitutional rights of my relatives and other citizens were restored on the White

Earth Reservation. The second edition of the *Progress* was published on
October 8, 1887.

Augustus Beaulieu changed the name of the weekly newspaper to the
Tomahawk in the early nineteen hundreds, and the content of the newspaper changed, along with the name, from local reservation stories and
editorials to national and international news reports. The readers must have
wondered what happened to the local stories, and at the same time marveled at the publication of national news stories. Straightaway the reservation became a new cosmopolitan culture of national and international news.

White Earth became a cosmopolitan community.

The readers of the *Tomahawk* could not understand how the publisher
was able to gather so much news from around the world every week. The
national news was seldom timely, never daily, but the readers were not concerned because most stories on the reservation were seasonal. Sometimes
national stories were read a month or two later as current events, and in this
way national news was always current on the reservation. The sense of time
was created by native stories, not in the urgent political reports of newspapers. Later, the *Tomahawk* published on the first page regular editorial and
news stories and by Carlos Montezuma, or Wassaja, one of the first native
medical doctors.

We learned much later that natives on the reservation were more liter-
ate than the general population of new immigrants, and natives read more
newspapers because the federal government established schools on reservations. Federal assimilation policies forced most native children to learn
how to read and write long before national compulsory education. We were
required to attend the government school on the reservation, and too many
native students were sent away to boarding schools.

Augustus subscribed to preprinted or patent inside newspaper pages, the
actual pages were printed somewhere else and delivered to the reservation
for publication. Theodore Beaulieu, once the actual printer and editor of
the *Progress*, was superseded by the patent inside pages of the *Tomahawk*.
Many newspapers were published around the country with the same patent
stories of national and international news reports and advertisements. The
pages of the patent inside were selected editorial tours of world news, not
local native issues or reservation rumors, but a parcel of disaster reports and
other stories from obscure and marvelous places.

"Everyone knows the strange old stories of the reservation," our uncle declared. "The *Tomahawk* needs new strange stories, and the newer and stranger the outside stories the better for reservation readers."

Augustus was right, but in time we became better at creating our own strange native stories of the reservation than hawking the content of some faraway story by a writer who constructed the news of the world for hundreds of weekly newspapers. The patent inside pages displayed national advertisements. Mostly the advertisements were for fast medicine cures. Some blank sections of the newspaper were reserved for local promotions.

"Paxtine Toilet Antiseptic for Women" was a regular patent advertisement in the *Tomahawk*, but the use of a douche remained a mystery. We were callow about the need and the actual usage, so we never hawked the douche promotion to women at the Ogema Station. We were not hesitant, however, to declare the news, wave our newspapers, and shout out about other advertisements.

"Ladies can wear shoes one size smaller after using Allen's Footease, a certain cure for swollen, sweating, hot, aching feet." We never sold one paper with that announcement, so we learned to hawk discreet news and to avoid any laughable promotions of patent medicine cures.

The Hotel Leecy, the largest and "most commodious hotel" on the reservation, was advertised on a side column in almost every issue of the *Tomahawk*. The hotel served daily communal meals with seasonal fish, game, and vegetables, and provided a livery stable. John Leecy, the proprietor, allowed us to ride free on the horse carriage between the hotel and the train station because we always promoted the hotel to arriving passengers. Leecy admired our ambition and hired us a few months later to feed and groom horses in the hotel livery stable.

Aloysius painted two blue ravens perched on the back of a roan stallion owned by John Spratt. Two years later he invited us to work in his harness shop. That was a very good job at the time, one of the best, because we continued to care for horses and at the same time learned about the harness business. We learned how to forge and fashion metal, but later we returned to work in the livery stable at the Hotel Leecy. Daily we encountered travelers and government bureaucrats who stayed at the hotel, and every visitor talked with us about horses and the future. No one ever talked to us about the forged parts of a harness. The blue ravens my brother painted and my tricky stories would become the crucial totems and portraits of our future service in the First World War.

The Leecy, Hiawatha, and Headquarters were the only hotels on the reservation, and there was a summer boarding house in the community of Beaulieu. Louis Brisbois, the proprietor of the Hotel Headquarters, rented clean rooms, according to the newspaper advertisements, and the "tables are always provided with fish, game and vegetables in their season." Aloysius sold Brisbois a blue raven perched on the peak of the hotel, and he invited us to work in the kitchen for food and money. The invitation was very tempting, the food and pay, but we were more interested in horses at the time, and naturally we were loyal to our uncle and to John Leecy.

The Pioneer Store, established by Robert Fairbanks, and many other merchants and traders in groceries, lumber, and sundries, advertised in every issue of the *Tomahawk*. The Motion Picture Theater, the first and only theater on the reservation, was promoted on the back page of the newspaper. Movies were shown twice a week. The tickets cost ten cents on Tuesday and twenty cents on Saturday.

Augustus treated us to our first movie, short scenes about trains and cowboys, but the tiny theater was musty, crowded, and the actors were crude and dopey. The cost of a single movie ticket was about the total income for a day of newspaper sales at the station, so we saved our money to travel on the Soo Line Railroad to Winnipeg, Minneapolis, or Montreal.

I started to write scenes and stories that summer, and imitated the newspaper style of the patent insides. Later, the government teachers corrected my style, and they would not believe the sources of my literary inspiration. My first written scenes were tightly packed with descriptive, imitative, derivative images and analogies. Most of my scenes were not yet original expressions or even creative enough to be considered unintended irony or mockery.

Aloysius painted blue ravens posed as the engineer of the train, as haughty passengers, and enormous ravens seated in the caboose, perched on the water tower, and blue ravens waiting at the station. Later he painted ravens with blue bluchers, blue women with raven beaks, and the station agent with blue wings. I wanted to write in the same way that he painted.

Together we sold an average of ten copies of the *Tomahawk* two or three times a week at the Ogema Station. We earned a total of about thirty cents a week, and after three months of hawking the newspaper that summer at the station we had earned less than two dollars each. Not enough to buy two train tickets to Winnipeg or Minneapolis.

The Feast of Good Cheer was our deliverance.

Aloysius sold several portrayals of blue ravens on newsprint but together we sold only four copies of the *Tomahawk* to relatives at the fortieth anniversary of the treaty settlement of the White Earth Reservation on May 25, 1908. Naturally there were pony races and music by the native White Earth Band. Augustus raised his whiskey bottle and praised our success as hawkers of his newspaper. We smoked a peace pipe for the first time that summer at the reservation anniversary, and we ate with the adults at the Feast of Good Cheer.

Soo Line Railroad tickets were more expensive than the cost of travel on the old Red River Oxcart Trail that ran four hundred miles from Winnipeg or the Selkirk Settlement through the reservation near the trading post at Beaulieu and White Earth to Detroit Lakes and the final destination in Saint Paul, Minnesota.

The deep ruts of the oxcart wheels were evident on the entire route north to south across the reservation. Aloysius was always ready for an adventure. We were eight years old the first time we walked several miles in the old wagon ruts on our way to another world. The weather turned out to be the adventure, however, not the route of the oxcarts. A severe thunderstorm, lightning, thunder, and heavy rain, changed the rutted course of our adventure to rivers. We took cover under a huge white pine and waited for the storm to pass. The oxcart wagon ruts overflowed, natural tributaries of an obsolete time, and our great adventure ended with stories of a memorable thunderstorm.

The new railroad, station, and the weekly newspaper became our sense of the future, although later we actually earned more money mucking out the livery stable at the Hotel Leecy. Yes, at the time the muck of horses provided a better salary than hawking newspapers with patent cosmopolitan news stories about the nation and the world.

Aloysius painted two solemn blue ravens seated on a bench at the railroad station in Mahnomen. The huge beaks of the ravens were covered with dark blue spots. A copy of the *Tomahawk* was on the bench next to the blue ravens. The banner headline was a single word, SMALLPOX. Wisely we never hawked that scary headline of the newspaper, and there was no reason to reveal the actual story that smallpox had been reported at Munroe House in Mahnomen. The Minnesota Board of Health had released the same report that "smallpox was increasing" in the state.

That afternoon we announced instead that the "Japanese landed more than thirty thousand troops in Wonsan, Korea," and expected to "advance on Vladivostok" in Russia. We sold three papers with that headline, and four more copies with the report that "annuities due under the old treaties will be paid to the Mississippi and Lake Superior bands by Agent Michelet." The annuity payments started on Monday, May 29, 1908, and each person received $8.40 in cash. Naturally our families were there for the carnival of treaty payments. Our relatives danced and told stories about the fantastic new worlds of railroads and automobiles.

The Great White Fleet was news that week in the *Tomahawk* so we hawked the story at the station. President Theodore Roosevelt had ordered the fleet to sail around the world for about two years to demonstrate the naval power and mastery of the United States. The great fleet left San Francisco on July 7, 1908. Not one paper was sold in the name of the ironic pale peace voyage.

Aloysius painted blue ravens on the mast of ships and named the Great White Fleet the Great Blue Peace Fleet. The chalky color code of the fleet was an obvious contradiction of sentiments. The color of peace was not the same as the notion of naval power. The Blue Fleet would have been a more humane and enlightened color in Australia, New Zealand, Philippine Islands, Brazil, Chile, Peru, and San Francisco. The blue ravens represented a greater sense of peace than the voyage of dominance around the world by sixteen white battleships of the United States Navy.

William Jennings Bryan was nominated for president at the Democratic National Convention that summer in Denver. Clearly there was no need to shout out that story because the mere mention of his name sold nine copies of the *Tomahawk*, more than any other person, place, scandal, or political story. Bryan ran three times for the presidency. He never won the electorate but he was greatly admired by natives on the White Earth Reservation.

The next train arrived later that afternoon from Winnipeg and we hawked the newspaper story about an absurd prison sentence. Emma Goldman, considered the antichrist of anarchism, touched the very hand of an army private and that single touch became news around the world. The private was sentenced to five years in prison. The train passengers were apparently not interested in the story and turned away. We hawked the name of Emma Goldman down the aisle of the passenger car but the ironic news of a soldier and the touch of a great anarchist was not good enough to read on the train.

The passengers were particular about news stories, and the greater the stories of shame, coincidence, and native victimry the more newspapers we sold at the station. The travelers wanted to read about adventures, crime, war, storms, cultural turndowns, political corruption and rebuffs, and the ironic survival of ordinary people.

These newspaper stories about public experiences were our best tutors. I imagined these scenes later and created my own ironic stories. We were persistent, persuasive, and pretended to be at the very center of the worldly stories that were published that summer in the *Tomahawk*.

The Ogema Station was built near the grain elevator at the very edge of the woodland and the peneplain. The new station faced west, warmed by the winter sun, but in the summer the platform was not shaded. The Soo Line Railroad provided a residence for the agent and his family in the two-story station. The observation site and ticket office were located in the bay window near the main tracks, and a second building to store freight was attached to the side of the station. The railway mail and "wish book" cata-logue orders were stored in the freight house. Montgomery Ward shipped the famous Clipper steel windmills to farmers. Many years later several houses, the entire precut materials, planks, windows, doors, siding and shingles, were ordered by mail from Sears, Roebuck and Company cata-logue and shipped by train to the Ogema Station.

The station agent was a stout, silent, serious man who sat in the bay win-dow and waited for the next train from Detroit Lakes or from Winnipeg. He encouraged and protected our newspaper business and allowed us to board the trains to hawk copies of the *Tomahawk* to passengers. The sound of his whistle was absolute and we never abused his trust. His wife provided water on hot summer days, and sometimes she would make sandwiches. The sta-tion agent, his wife, and our mother were very close friends. They had once lived near Bad Medicine Lake.

The Mogul engine sounded the whistle and came to a slow stop at the station. The building and platform shuddered from the weight and coal-fired rage of the mighty engine. Steam shrouded the station windows. We waited inside to avoid the heat. Patch, the assistant agent, a smartly dressed native in uniform, greeted every passenger with a salute. He wore gray work gloves and his military coat was properly buttoned, even in the heat and humidity of the summer.

Patch Zhimaaganish, our good friend, was not paid for his service and dedication, but the station agent was sympathetic and allowed him to prac-tice the manner and courtesy of a railroad conductor. Patch was the only boy to survive in his family, and so his given name was a tease of fate. The translation of his surname was "soldier" in the language of the Anishinaabe. His mother tailored a dark brown uniform for him with bright brass buttons and told her son to find a future on the railroad. So, he reported early every day to the station agent and proudly carried out his unpaid railroad duties with dignity.

Patch was taught to play the bugle by his grandfather who served as a bugler in the Civil War. His grandfather was badly wounded, lost a leg, and was given the nickname *zhimaaganish*, or soldier, when he returned from the war. That nickname became a surname when the reservation was cre-ated by treaty in 1868.

Patch Zhimaaganish was an ecstatic singer with a rich baritone voice. The government teachers praised the soldier but the students only mocked his manly voice. He sang native dream songs when the trains arrived at the station, and sometimes he sang in the rain and to the sunset. The Soo Line Railroad agents at other stations on the line told passengers to listen for the great voice of the young agent at the Ogema Station. Patch was honored for his voice, dream songs, and for his courtesy.

In the sky
I am walking
A bird
I accompany.
The first to come
I am called
Among the birds
I bring the rain
Crow is my name.

Aloysius painted an abstract portrayal of a soldier in uniform, and with two blue ravens at his side. The ravens with enormous beaks pecked at the bugle and buttons on his coat. Patch never had a father or a brother, so he was grateful for our attention and especially for the picture of the blue ravens. The students at the government school teased him as a stupid student, and more so in uniform, and gave him a new nickname, "Niswi S," or "Triple S," for Simple Simon Soldier.

Patch Zhimaaganish was a dedicated volunteer conductor at the station, a singer, bugler, and the soldier of his name. We became close friends that summer because he served the railroad agent and we hawked newspapers to passengers at the Ogema Station. Later we were mustered together and served as soldiers in the First World War in France.

› 3 ‹

GATEWAY PARK
―――――― 1909 ――――――

The Soo Line train arrived on schedule that afternoon and we boarded as passengers on our first adventure south to the great city of Minneapolis. Augustus bought our tickets as he had promised a year earlier. We were dedicated to the promotion of the newspaper during the year and that pleased him more than our hurried mission as painters. The white paint had already started to blister and crack on the sunny side of the newspaper building.

Augustus emerged from the steam of the engine, a great man on our reservation, and gave me a brown envelope with money for the hotel and other expenses on the journey. Aloysius was given a new book of art paper. He touched the smooth white paper, and then we both hugged our uncle on the steamy platform. We were about to leave the reservation for the first time and without permission of the federal agency regime.

Honoré, our father, had not been home for more than three weeks. He was cutting timber near Bad Medicine Lake. Our uncle told us not to worry, because no agent would dare to confront him or anyone in our family about government permission to leave the reservation. He had shunned the authority of the federal agent and every agent since the federal court had decided in favor of the constitutional right to publish the *Progress*. Augustus would never solicit favors or permission from any agent of the government to leave the reservation.

Margaret, our mother, our uncle, Patch Zhimaaganish, the eager soldier and conductor, and the station agent and his wife were there to wave as the engine slowly pulled away from the station. My heart beat faster with the mighty thrust of the engine. Aloysius convinced our mother that we must present the original totemic paintings of blue ravens to curators at art museums and galleries in Minneapolis.

Patch saluted and then he removed his gray gloves and waved until his hand vanished in the distance. Suddenly we realized that our friend, the good soldier, should have joined us on the train to the city. That would not happen, however, for another nine years, when we were drafted at the same time to serve with the American Expeditionary Forces in France.

We packed thirty folded copies of the *Tomahawk* to hawk at stations on the way, but the tout and trade was reversed. The sound of the engine and the whistle was the same but every station was an adventure. We left the train for a few minutes at each station rather than board the passenger car to promote the newspaper and the Hotel Leecy on the White Earth Reservation.

I sold only five copies in one direction and twelve copies on our return to the Ogema Station. Aloysius painted blue ravens in scenes at every station, blue ravens with beaks under wing, and with great feathers that shrouded the passengers.

The Soo Line Railroad stopped at stations in Callaway, Detroit Lakes, Vergas, Ottertail, Henning, Parkers Prairie, Alexandria, Glenwood, Eden Valley, Kimball, Annandale, Maple Lake, Buffalo, and other towns without stations. We remembered every town on the railroad line, and we announced the street names and counted every house and building as the train approached the Milwaukee Road Depot in Minneapolis.

Eden Valley and other country towns moved slowly through the windows of the passenger car, one by one, surrounded by farms. The towns were built by migrants and fugitives from other worlds of stone and monarchies.

Chicago, our uncle said, was built twice with white pine trees cut down from our reservation, and we wondered at the time about the timber that built the houses in Minneapolis. We were native migrants in the same new world that had created the timber ruins of the White Earth Reservation.

The slow and steady motion of the train created our private window scenes, woody, churchy, junky, curious domains, and yet the steady rows of the newcomer towns were treacherous. Aloysius painted giant blue ravens perched on white pine stumps, beaks agape, and tiny houses decorated with bright blue leaves afloat in the pale sky. We were eager captives in the motion and excitement of railroad time. We sat first in window seats that faced the motion of the train through the late summer woodland and towns. Later we moved to the opposite seats and watched the new world pass slowly with the steam and smoke behind the train. We decided then that we would rather be in the motion of adventure, chance, and the future.

The Mississippi River rushed with great energy and memory over Saint Anthony Falls and created a spectacular spirit world of mist and light around the many flour and lumber mills near the Milwaukee Road Depot. The waterfall spirits had started out as a cold trickle at the source of the Great River and months later became a misty light in the city.

The riverfront was overrun with railroad tracks, engines, and boxcars. We had never seen so many railroad tracks and engines in one place. The engine smoke and coal power of the mills poisoned the air and the river. The *gichiziibi*, the great native river at the headwaters in Lake Itasca, became a hazy and murky shame of greedy commerce in the cities.

Blue ravens were hard to imagine in the heat, smoke, and commotion. Only my words could describe our adventures, the roar of machines and deadly scenes on the riverfront, a spectacle no native totem, animal, fish, or bird could easily survive. I wrote about our first experiences on the river, and my report was published a few months later in the *Tomahawk*.

Aloysius was inspired, however, by the majestic curves of the Stone Arch Bridge over the Mississippi River below Saint Anthony Falls. He painted a row of three blue ravens perched on the bridge with enormous wings raised to wave away the poison coal-fire smoke and hush the strange whine, clack, and other machine sounds along the river.

The Milwaukee Road Depot was enormous, a great mysterious cavern of massive railroad engines. The building was granite with a great tower. We were already transformed by the city, only thirty minutes after the train moved slowly through the alphabetical street names, and then into the sooty, smoky rows of warehouses and railroad tracks.

Indians, are you Indians?

The station agent asked about our reservation when we only wanted to check our bundle of newspapers. He was in uniform, pressed his hands on the counter, and examined our clothes. Our mother made new white shirts and dark trousers for our journey. My brother stared back at the man but refused to answer his question. Not a glare, but a stony stare, and the appropriate response to his inquiry. My brother waited for the agent to continue, and then turned away. We were natives on the road, traveling without permission of the federal government, and we had good reasons to worry that the station agent might notify the federal agents.

Augustus was our champion only on the reservation. He had visited the city many times, and he arranged for us to stay at a hotel managed by one of his close friends, but he could not protect us once we left the reservation.

The station agent leaned closer, over the counter.

No, we are artists on our way to the museum.

What museum?

The Minneapolis Society of Fine Arts, said Aloysius. He had read about a collection of art in the new library. My brother showed the station agent several paintings of blue ravens perched at several stations between Ogema and the Milwaukee Road Depot.

Where is that?

North of Detroit Lakes.

No, the museum?

The Minneapolis Public Library, said Aloysius. The station agent tested our knowledge about the public collection of fine art that was located at the time in the city library.

Artsy books?

No, original art at the library. The station agent was wary, we were not old enough to be artists, and he had no conception of creative art. So, we told stories about the train stations and recent news reports in the *Tomahawk*.

What are these newspapers?

Our family newspaper, said Aloysius. The *Tomahawk* is owned by our uncle, Augustus Hudon Beaulieu, and we are hawking the newspaper to people in small towns, people who have never heard of international news.

No, not on a reservation, said the station agent. He turned away and refused to believe that natives could publish newspapers on reservations. Luckily there was no way to overcome his mistrust, so we told him that the newspaper was an experiment in the distribution of national news stories, an unusual investment by the bishops of the Episcopal Church in the newsy prospect of education, assimilation, and civilization. The choice was strategic, but even so the testy station agent might have been a Roman Catholic.

Gateway Park near the train depot became the second scene of blue ravens in Minneapolis. That afternoon the sun shimmered in the perfect rows of pruned trees. Aloysius painted several abstract ravens over the pavilion, one enormous blue beak above the arcade and classical colonnades on each side of the entrance. We had never seen so many warehouses, so many motor cars, electric streetcars, horses, carriages, and so many great stone and brick buildings.

The Minneapolis Police arrived on patrol wagons drawn by horses. Two were parked near the construction site of the new Radisson Hotel. Every major street was obstructed with carriages and motor cars. The Model T Ford was the most common, of course, but there were cars that we had never seen on the reservation, such as the Pierce Arrow, Stanley, Hudson, and the practical Mason Delivery Wagon.

Commission Row, the center of wholesale groceries, vegetables, fruits, and perishables, was one of the few quiet places in the city that afternoon. The white and brown horses were harnessed to empty wagons. The deliveries were done and the horses were waiting to return to the stable.

Nicollet House, an old hotel with four stories, was across the street directly behind the park pavilion on Washington and Nicollet avenues. The entrance was spacious and shabby, and it was the first time we had ever been in a grand hotel lobby. Many dignitaries had stayed there over the years, and we sat in the very same leather chairs as the ordinary and grandees. Oscar Wilde, the poet and playwright, who we later learned more about from a trader on the reservation, was pictured alone in the lobby. He posed for the photograph with long hair, and he wore a heavy fur-trimmed coat.

Oscar Wilde had lectured about decorative art at the Academy of Music near Nicollet House. The *Tribune* newspaper review of his lecture was framed and mounted near his photograph. "Ass-Thete" was the headline of the review dated March 16, 1882, thirteen years before we were born. The reviewer noted that Wilde was "flat and insipid," and from "the time the speaker commenced to his closing sentence, he kept up the same unvarying endless drawl, without modulating his voice or making a single gesture, giving one the impression that he was a prize monkey wound up, and warranted to talk for an hour and a half without stopping."

Actually, as we read, we thought his lecture was learned, more than a jerky vaudeville lecture. We could not understand at the time his traces of irony. Wilde lectured, for instance, "The truths of art cannot be taught. They are revealed only—revealed to natures which have made themselves receptive of all beautiful impressions by the study of and the worship of all beautiful things." Reading the story for the first time at the hotel we understood only the first part of his lecture, "art cannot be taught." Rather, and

·we agreed, art can be "revealed," and that was an obvious description of the inspired blue ravens painted by my brother. Aloysius wanted to meet the great Oscar Wilde but he died when we were five years old.

〉〉〉 〈〈〈

Minneapolis was a commercial center of great lumber and flour mills built on the shores of the river. Most of the lumber came directly from the reservations, White Earth, Red Lake, and Leech Lake, and the grain was delivered by railroad from the plains. Our father was a lumberjack, a timber cutter for the agency mill on the reservation. Honoré continued to cut timber with older men because he could not survive in the new reservation communities. He was a calm and quiet man. The white pine was his natural destiny, not his investment or enterprise.

Aloysius created a blue raven totem in the timber ruins of the reservation. We were cosmopolitan natives by words, by preprinted stories in the *Tomahawk*. The city was our new world, but we were not worldly by experience. Yet we pretended to be cosmopolitan natives overnight on Hennepin Avenue.

Minneapolis, we learned later, had grown by more than a hundred thousand people in the past decade, a wealthy city of immigrants and newcomers. We were fourteen years old at the time and knew just about everyone in our reservation community. Our uncle was absolutely right that the mind and heart must change to live with so many people. The city was abstract but not aesthetic, rather a strange and exciting creature of fortune and politics. That summer the river city was an unwashed window after a storm, and a noisy scene in constant and unnatural motion.

Aloysius created the aesthetic scenes with blue ravens, the natural presence of great abstract totems. The city was no sanctuary or state of creation for traditional native totems, no natural site or marvelous estate for bears, wolves, plovers, migratory sandhill cranes, kingfishers, or even the stories of the ice woman.

〉〉〉 〈〈〈

Hennepin Avenue was already famous for the great theaters, hotels, and restaurants. Every building, every hotel was impressive as we walked up Hennepin Avenue from Gateway Park past the Bijou Theater and the Pence

Opera House that had been converted to a rooming house. We might have stayed there, but our uncle insisted that we stay at the more secure Waverly Hotel on Harmon Place near the Minneapolis Public Library.

Napa Valley Wine Company, located in the next block, had sold wine "continuously for the last twenty years." We were too young to enter the establishment, so we read the advertisements in the window and pretended to be wine enthusiasts. "Our house is the only one in the wine and liquor line in the city catering to the family trade, which has no bar."

Father Aloysius used sacramental wine at services in Saint Benedict's Mission Church. Luckily one of our older cousins was an altar boy. He was obliged to share the taste of red church wine from the Beaulieu Vineyards in Napa Valley, California. We were rather conceited about the sacramental wine that was bottled in our family name. Naturally we used that coincidence, the relations of a surname wine, to our advantage when we first arrived as infantry soldiers in France.

Napa Valley Wine could be ordered by telephone, and that was very modern at the time. We knew about telephones because our relatives had established the first system in Callaway on the White Earth Reservation. Telephones were cosmopolitan at the time, but not the party line conversations. Simon Michelet, the contentious federal agent, ordered reservation telephone lines to the government schools in Mahnomen, Beaulieu, and Porterville. The Napa Valley Wine advertisement explained, "Ladies can visit our establishment as unconcernedly as any dry goods store."

Early the next morning we visited the three great dry goods stores on nearby Nicollet Avenue. Aloysius was inspired by the fortune and display of clothing in the stores, the great bay windows, and naturally he painted blue ravens in every display window of Dayton's Dry Goods Company, Donaldson's Glass Block, and down a few blocks at Powers Mercantile Company. We did not have enough money to buy anything, not even a paper napkin or a handkerchief, but we tried on shirts, coats, hats, and my brother painted me as a grandee in an enormous raincoat. The black sleeves became great blue wings that reached over the counters. The blonde clerk waved her hands and told us to leave, but when she saw the painting by my brother she was much more friendly. Aloysius painted the woman in a fedora and a brim of blue raven feathers over a train of light blue hair.

Aloysius paused at his reflection in every window.

The West Hotel was a great cruise liner afloat on a sea of shiny cobble-stones, and surrounded by new theater buildings on Hennepin Avenue and Fifth Street. The Masonic Temple, a secret mountain of sandstone with decorative carved emblems, was only a block away. As the streetcars turned the corner in front of the hotel the trolley wheels sparked, a magical ritual at the foyer of the hotel.

The doorman was courteous, raised his hand and inquired about our business in the hotel. We were young, native, and not properly dressed for the entrance, but we were not skanky. Aloysius told the doorman that our uncle was the publisher of a newspaper, and then announced that we were there to paint blue ravens.

What is the name of the newspaper?

The *Tomahawk*.

Surely not a newspaper?

Yes, and with international news.

How the world changes.

We only want to see the hotel lobby.

The West Hotel lobby was luxurious and lighted by an atrium. The blue settees inspired my brother to paint blue ravens in every cushy seat, claws crossed as moneyed gentlemen, and disheveled wing feathers spread wide over the padded backs and arms, and across the marble floor of the huge lobby.

Rich ravens in shiny blue shoes.

Mark Twain, the great writer, had stayed at the West Hotel on July 23, 1895, in the same year that we were born on the White Earth Reservation. In a leather-bound book near the registration counter we discovered photographs and news stories about his visit to Saint Paul, Duluth, and Minneapolis.

The *Minneapolis Journal* reported that he suffered from a carbuncle on his leg, and had declined the invitations of admirers to visit the Minneapolis Public Library and Minnehaha Falls. "To the casual observer, as he lay there, running his fingers through his long, curly locks, now almost gray, he was anything but a humorist. On the contrary, he appeared to be a gentleman of great gravity, a statesman or a man of vast business interests. The dark blue eyes are as clear as crystal and the keenest glances shoot from them whenever he speaks." Twain entertained an enthusiastic audience for ninety minutes that night at the Metropolitan Opera House.

Mark Twain left traces of his marvelous irony in the grand lobby of the West Hotel, and surely he would have told memorable stories about native totems and blue ravens from the White Earth Reservation.

Aloysius painted blue ravens on streetcars, a conductor with blue wings, blue ravens in dance moves on the cobblestones in a rainstorm, and dark blue eyes reflected in the bay windows of the West Hotel.

Hennepin Avenue was crowded with streetcars, motor cars, and horse-drawn wagons and carriages. The sounds were strange, unnatural, strained machines, and engines so loud we could barely hear the most familiar sound of the steady clop clop clop of horses on the cobblestones. We walked past great stone buildings, theaters, and restaurants, on our way to the Waverly Hotel.

The Orpheum Theatre was a majestic dominion of murmurs, theatrical recitations, ironic pronouncements, acrobatics, the lively tease of vaudeville, and the memorable voices of great lectures and plays. The theater that late afternoon was empty but not lonely. No one was at the ticket window so we entered the great auditorium without a ticket or a story. Everywhere we could hear the rich and evocative voices of actors in the balconies, the secrets, shouts and moans in the cluttered dressing rooms backstage.

Aloysius declared the theater his second home of visions and fantasy. He selected a seat in the front row of a side balcony and painted blue ravens in a stage play. The ravens of the theater turned a wing and raised their beaks to the audience. The only real play we had ever seen was the shortened government-school production of *Hamlet* by William Shakespeare.

The Waverly Hotel rented rooms by the week, but the manager was a friend of our uncle so we paid only five dollars for two nights. "Electric lights, bath, and telephone" were advertised in theater programs and newspapers. The hotel was located near the public library.

We walked past several restaurants on the way to the hotel and later read the advertisements, "Superb Cuisine at Café Brunswick," and "Schiek's Café Restaurant," but the menus were too expensive and ritzy. So, we ate meat, potatoes, and corn at a nearby cafeteria for students. That first night we lingered in the tiny lobby of the hotel and found a program of events scheduled earlier in the summer at the Orpheum Theatre. Aloysius imagined the grand performances from our special seats in a side balcony. The program listed matinee admission to the gallery for fifteen cents. We were two months too late for the performances.

"Scotch Thistle," a musical program directed by Theodore Martin, was advertised in the May 1909 program of the Orpheum Circuit of Theatres. Miss Charlotte Parry and Company presented "The Comstock Mystery" that same month.

"Master Laddie Cliff," featured in another program, was "England's famous little Comedian and Grotesque Dancer." Another program announced the "First American Tour of Three Sisters Athletas, Direct from New York Hippodrome." The sisters were "Extraordinary Lady Gymnasts." "The Kinodrome New and Interesting Motion Pictures" reported that the pictures were about a "Ring Leader" and a "Jealous Hubby."

Naturally, we were excited to read the programs and would have attended every matinee performance. We were more interested in the Lady Gymnasts than the Kinodrome. The movies we saw on the reservation were trivial and flimsy. The stories in the movies were monotonous, more about agents than the ice women or the dance of the plovers.

4

CARNEGIE TOTEMS

1909

The Minneapolis Public Library was only ten years old that summer of our migration, a massive stone building with magnificent curved bay windows. The turrets on two corners resembled a baronial river castle, but the books inside were never the reserved property of the nobility.

Andrew Carnegie, the wealthy industrialist and passionate philanthropist, donated more than sixty million dollars to build public libraries, and more to establish schools and universities around the country. A slight portion of his great treasure acquired from the steel industry and other investments was used to construct the Minneapolis Public Library.

Carnegie was a master of steel, stone, railroads, and the great bloom of libraries. More than two thousand libraries were built in his name, but he would not give a dime to build even a bookrack on the White Earth Reservation, our uncle explained, because the federal agents were not reliable and the government would not promise to support the future of books for natives.

Carnegie was a new totem of literacy and sovereignty. The libraries he created were the heart and haven of our native liberty. No federal agents established libraries on reservations, and not many robber barons constructed libraries and universities.

Aloysius painted a huge blue raven, our great new totem of honor and adventure, in one of the turret bay windows of the library. The beak of the raven almost touched the sidewalk and stairs near the entrance. My brother never painted humans, but some of his great ravens traced a sense of character, a cue of human memory. Carnegie was portrayed as a stately blue raven with a bushy mane and great beak in the turret windows.

We could not believe that the books were stacked on open shelves and available to anyone. We walked slowly down the aisles of high cases and touched the books by colors, first the blues, of course, and then the red and black books. In that curious hush and silence of the library the books were a native sense of presence, our presence, and the spirits of the books were revived by our casual touch. Every book waited in silence to become a totem, a voice, and a new story.

The books waited in silence, waited for readers, and waited for a chance to be carried out of the library. *The Last of the Mohicans* by James Fenimore Cooper was tilted to the side. The novel was illustrated by Frank T. Merrill, and in one picture a couple with fair skin watched a native wrestle with a bear. The couple was dressed for a dance, and the native wore leather, fringed at the seams, and three feathers on his head. The book waited to be recovered by a reader, but not by me or by my brother. That novel was introduced by our teachers at the government school, along with that nasty poem *The Song of Hiawatha* by Henry Wadsworth Longfellow, but we were never obliged to remember the loopy cultural fantasies of literary explorers. The elaborate frontier of *The Last of the Mohicans* was a snake oil story.

Augustus teased the reservation native police with the name Chingachgook, and he sometimes used the name Natty Bumppo, both characters in *The Last of the Mohicans*, in stories about the missionaries and federal agents. So, we had a tricky sense of the characters in the novel by the time our teachers wrote the names on the chalkboard.

Aloysius touched *The Call of the Wild* by Jack London.

Augustus celebrated our thirteenth birthday with two new books. Our uncle always celebrated our birthdays with books, first picture stories and then literature. The new books were wrapped in the current edition of the *Tomahawk*. He gave me a copy of *The Call of the Wild*, and Aloysius received a copy of *White Fang*. Augustus knew we were inspired by native totems and animal stories, and he knew we would talk about these scenes in the novels. My uncle was a teaser, and he teased and coaxed me to become a creative writer, to create stories of native liberty, and a few years later gave me a copy of *Moby-Dick* by Herman Melville.

Jack London was a great writer but he was mistaken about dogs and natives. Buck was a natural healer and would never return to the wolves, never in a native story. London was not aware that wolves were native totems, and not the wild enemy.

London made *White Fang* more human and never understood the native stories of animal healers. The real world of nature that we experienced was always chancy, and sometimes even dangerous, of course, the weather can be dangerous, but not evil and not as violent as the human world. London worried about the animals he had created in an unnatural way, and he might have sent them to some church. The notion of redemption was monotheistic, and that was not natural or native. London was a political adventurist in fiction and never understood native stories, animal totems, or the dream songs of native liberty.

Jack London would not survive on the reservation.

The card catalogue listed every book in the library. Aloysius looked through the cards in the drawer for his name and found a book about Aloysius Bertrand, a French symbolist poet, and Saint Aloysius Gonzaga. Beaulieu was listed many times, a winery in California, and as a reference to a place in France, Beaulieu-sur-Mer, a commune near Nice and Monaco.

The *Manabozho Curiosa*, that ancient Benedictine manuscript about monks, sex, and animals was not listed in the card catalogue. Naturally, we avoided the word "sex" when we asked the librarian about the *Manabozho Curiosa*. She had never heard of the manuscript but thought a copy might be found in the Rare Book collection at the University of Minnesota Library.

Aloysius opened several art books on a huge oak reference table and together we brushed the images with our fingers, touched the painted bodies of soldiers, women poised near windows in soft natural light, darker scenes of animals and hunters, and distorted images of humans and houses. Most of the old images portrayed a civilization of pathetic poses and contrition, and the great shadows and slants of divine light by master painters.

The ancient blues were muted.

Yes, the bright flowers, pristine fruit on a table, and exotic birds, seemed at the time to be more authentic than our actual memories and experience of the natural world. The reds, yellows, and greens were bright, the blues faint. The images of exotic birds were realistic studies, an obsession of godly perfection in bright plumage. The painted birds were steady pictures, similar to the portraits of warriors and politicians.

The best of nature, and our sense of nature, was forever in motion by the favor of the seasons. The overnight bruises, creases, crucial flaws caused by the weather, and every wave, ruffle, gesture, and flight were wholesome. The ordinary teases, blush, and blemish of character, were a natural presence, and yet the birds, painted flowers, and fruit that we touched in the giant art books were bright, perfect, ironic, and unsavory.

Ravens would never peck at a pastel peach.

Aloysius slowly backed away from the reference table, looked around the library, and then he painted three blue ravens with massive claws over the modern art images in the books. The wings of the ravens were painted wide and shrouded the table and chairs with feathers.

A young librarian waved a finger and cautioned us not to touch the books. She praised the blue ravens that my brother had painted, and then explained that painting was not permitted in the library. Yes, we pretended to understand the unstated caution, that only the bookable and bankable arts were favored and secured, not the original blue ravens and native totems.

Aloysius painted with two soft brushes and a thick, blunt cedar stick that was roughened on the end. One brush was round, soft, and pointed. The other was a wide watercolor shadow brush. His saliva, and sometimes mine, was used to moisten the blue paste.

Aloysius had made his own paintbrushes. He carved the wooden handles from birch, molded the ferrule sleeve from copper, and the tufts were bundles of squirrel hair for several of his brushes. He used sable hair for the brushes with a fine point.

The new images were much richer and the hues of blue more evocative on the professional art paper. The blue ravens on the newsprint were strong, abstract, and the lines and shadows were in natural motion, never distinct as portraiture, but the ravens were enlivened on the new paper. My brother had created a book of paintings on our first visit to the city.

My first creative impressions were short descriptive scenes, only a few words, more precise than abstract. Every spontaneous scene was more obvious in my memory than in my written words. My original scenes were composed in short distinct sentences, only single images or glimpses of the many scenes in my memory. My words seemed to contain a natural vision of motion, but the actual practices of a writer were not the same as a painter.

My heart is a red raven and rises on the wind.
The eyes of nature are in my stories.
Cars move with great explosions.
Curved windows bend our smiles.

Winter is an abstract scene in the autumn.
The ice woman is natural reason.
City men strut in black coats and tight shoes.
Horses wait for motor cars to pass.
Books are silent stories.
White pine lives in memory.
History is overgrown and chokes the trees.

The sound of a pencil on paper is similar to the sound of a
watercolor brush but the words create scenes in the head not
the native eye. My written words came together with painted
blue ravens in the heart, the intuitive eye, and memory.

Aloysius continued to paint blue ravens in the library reference room. My brother spit in the blue paste and painted grotesque beaks that carried away the pastel fruit, the shadows of librarians at the window, blue soldiers, and the art books.

Gratia Alta Countryman, Head of the Minneapolis Public Library, was summoned to the reference room because my brother would not stop painting. She watched him move the thick brush over the paper, and then she leaned closer as he brushed the blue raven beaks with the softened cedar stick.

Gratia, we learned later, was the very first woman to direct a major city library. She was raised on a farm, graduated from the University of Minnesota, and initiated book stations for laborers and immigrants, and she seemed to appreciate that we were native newcomers in search of adventure and liberty. My brother was the painter, and the stories were mine.

Carnegie was surely impressed with her philosophy of free libraries and enlightened dedication to the public access of books on the shelves. We were impressed that so many books were at hand, and touchable without permission. The books were not concealed, and instantly summoned for review. Books were federal prisoners at the government school.

Gratia rested her heavy hands on the reference table. Her wrists were thick like a native or peasant, her hair was parted on the left, and her narrow nostrils moved with slight traces of breath. She leaned closer to my brother, and with a comic smile asked him to paint a blue raven with a copy in claw of *The Wonderful Wizard of Oz* by Lyman Frank Baum.

Aloysius turned to a new page in his art book, spit in the tin of blue paste, and briskly painted the abstract portrayals of Scarecrow and the Tin Woodman protected by the enormous wings of a blue raven on the reference table. He continued to paint an outline picture of the orphan Dorothy Gale and Toto depicted as a reservation mongrel on the back of a fierce raven with a huge dappled blue beak.

Gratia raised her peasant hands in praise and laughed out loud in the hushed reference room. Several readers turned and stared at the head librarian. The younger librarian was anxious, of course, but she did not raise her finger or comment on the laughter or the saliva and blue paint in the library.

Aloysius had never read *The Wonderful Wizard of Oz*, but the story of the fantastic adventures were told by several teachers at the government school on the reservation. We resisted the peculiar scenes of wicked cackles and godly virtues because they were not recounted in any native experiences. Stories of the ice woman were much more urgent and memorable. Yet, our slight resistance to the Scarecrow and Tin Woodman must have encouraged the actual memory of the story. So, in a sense the cockeyed wicked scenes became a creative rescue years later at the Minneapolis Public Library. My brother remembered a crude summary of the wizardly story and portrayed the characters in a speedy abstract painting. The head librarian was very impressed by his talent and invited us to her office in the turret with the curved bay windows.

Gratia served milk and cookies, and explained that she was always prepared to serve children treats and books because they are the future readers and patrons of the library. She had established the first reading room for children. Luckily we had entered the main section of the library.

You boys are not children, of course, but we must share the cookies, she said, and turned toward the windows. The reflection of her face was curved and her nose and ears were elongated.

Gratia was apologetic that she had never visited a reservation, but she mentioned Frances Densmore who had studied native songs of the White Earth Reservation. She was surprised to learn that our uncle published a weekly newspaper.

The Minneapolis Society of Fine Arts was located in the library, but the collection of paintings was not open to the public. Aloysius was downhearted that the art collection was not available because that was the primary purpose of our visit to the city. My brother wondered where he could see art, meet artists, and present his blue raven paintings.

Gratia suggested that we visit art galleries to see the work of other painters. She named the Golden Rule Gallery in Saint Paul, and the Beard Art Galleries in Minneapolis. She was certain that we would be inspired by many of the artists who exhibited their work at these galleries. She warned us to be aware that the trendy and new abstract painters were not current or popular in the galleries.

Blue ravens were totemic not mercenary.

Saint Paul was another strange and distant city. The saintly names of missions made sense, but sainted cities were not sensible. Cities were enterprises, sprawling, noisy, and scary places, and not the centers of saints.

The Beard Art Galleries were located on Hennepin Avenue near Lake Street. We boarded the streetcar, sat at the back, and counted the city blocks to the gallery. The conductor pointed to a building on the other side of the street. There, displayed in the bay window of an ordinary storefront were three paintings, a woodland landscape, a bowl of unsavory fruit, and a bright portrait of three Irish setters with feathery tails.

Irish setters were not bound for museums.

Aloysius was worried for the first time about his vision of blue abstract ravens. He had created raven scenes on the train, in parks, on the streets, department stores, hotels, and at the library. The Irish setters and fruit bowl were obstacles to visionary art and he refused to enter the gallery. Suddenly he was distracted and vulnerable in the commercial world of gallery art.

The Irish setters were aristocratic posers, haughty pedigree portrayals, plainly favored over natives and the poorly. So, we walked slowly around the block, and then continued several more blocks west to Lake Calhoun, or the Lake of Loons, which was a native descriptive name. The lake was renamed to honor John Caldwell Calhoun, the senator and vice president. We rested on the grassy lakeshore and created stories about mongrel portraits and landscapes of white pine stumps in the gallery window.

The actual paintings in the gallery window were good copies of a concocted nature, but not abstract native totems or chancy scenes of liberty. We watched the sailboats swerve with the wind and then walked back to the gallery.

Our faces were reflected in the gallery window, and at that very moment a yellow streetcar passed through the scene of our reflection, a throwback to abstraction and native stories. The muted aristocratic setters mingled with passengers on the streetcar. That scene became the most distinctive story of our two days in the city. We told many versions of that story to our relatives. The Irish setters, native faces, and the slow motion of the streetcar that afternoon became a chance union of abstract creation.

The Beard Art Galleries became an abstract scene.

Aloysius pushed open the door with confidence, and we were surprised by the art inside the gallery. There were no bright fruit bowls or setters with feathered tails. The strain of art in the window was deceptive, and we decided that the display was only selected to entice passengers on the streetcars.

The cloudy walls were covered with original art, gouache, oil on canvas, and watercolors on paper, mostly natural water scenes, evocative barns and country houses, railroad stations, sailboats, glorious summer sunsets, autumn maples, and winter landscapes. The trees and outlines were precise images, and the colors were intense and clean. The emigrants who moved to the cities must have been heartened by the romantic and picturesque landscapes.

Three framed distinct watercolors were displayed on sturdy oak easels near the entrance of the gallery. Aloysius moved closer and reached out to touch the magnificent images of misty scenes, and then held back with his hands raised above the easels. The three watercolors, *Snowy Winter Road*, *Summer Afternoon*, and *Woman in the Garden*, seemed to reach out to touch and enchant my brother and me.

Snowy Winter Road was a watercolor of giant trees on a curved country road. The trees were covered with heavy wet snow, a natural bow to the season. The entire scene was muted but the snowy trees, and the morning light, shimmer in the gallery and in my memory.

The *Summer Afternoon* watercolor was a subtle diffusion of light and the waft and scatter of colors on a sleepy afternoon, a misty secret scene of lacy trees in praise of nature and memory. We could hear the sound of birds and insects in the scene, and the slight glint of dragonflies over the lily pond.

The Japanese *Woman in the Garden* wore a traditional kimono, and she was crouched near a garden of lilies. We were touched by the subtle motion and magic of the visionary watercolor scenes. The elegant curves were natural, erotic, and magical.

Aloysius was captivated by the *Woman in the Garden*.

Harmonia, the gallery manager, a lanky, intense woman with short blonde hair pointed directly at my brother, but not at me. She wore a dark gray pinstripe suit, bluish necktie, and black-and-white oxford shoes. Naturally, we were distracted by her manly costume and hardly noticed her severe gestures.

Keep those dirty hands in your pockets, she shouted, and then shooed me toward the door. Aloysius lowered his hands and stared at the manager. She, in turn, folded her arms, raised one long pale blue finger, and stood directly in front of the three easels.

The Irish setter in the window, how much?

The setters are not for sale.

The *Woman in the Garden*, how much for that watercolor? Aloysius moved behind the easels and read out loud the name of the artist. Yamada Baske, how much for the Japanese *Woman in the Garden*?

Very expensive, what do you want?

Aloysius told the gallery manager that we wanted to meet the watercolor artist named Yamada Baske. She turned in silence, rocked on her oxfords, and waited for us to leave the gallery.

Aloysius announced that our uncle owned a newspaper, and he would surely buy the *Woman in the Garden*. Suddenly her manner changed. She cocked her head to the side, smiled, and pretended to be friendly, unaware, of course, that the newspaper was published on the White Earth Reservation. Yamada Baske was Japanese, she said, and he taught art in Minneapolis.

Aloysius revealed that he was a watercolor artist. She smiled and again folded her arms with one finger raised as a gesture of doubt. One of our teachers at the government school raised her finger, but the gesture was more about derision than doubt. My brother opened his art book and presented several of his most recent abstract blue ravens, but not the ones he had painted earlier that day at the library.

Harmonia slowly turned the leaves of his watercolor book, examined each blue raven, and then announced that Yamada Baske, or Fukawa Jin Basuke, was an instructor at the Minneapolis School of Fine Arts. Naturally we were surprised to learn that the art school and the Society of Fine Arts were located on the same floor of the Minneapolis Public Library.

The same conductor was on the return streetcar and asked us about the art gallery. Aloysius told him about the window display, the bright fruit and red setters, and then described the watercolor scene of a beautiful Japanese woman in a garden of lilies.

What does she look like?

Her face was turned to the lilies.

So, why was she beautiful?

The elegance of her hands and feet crouched by the lilies, my brother explained to the conductor, but he was not convinced. We were touched by the mood and subtle hues of the watercolor. The *Woman in the Garden* was the only picture that was enticing and we wanted to be in the garden scene with that sensuous woman.

Yamada Baske was standing at an easel with a student when we entered the studio. He smiled, bowed his head, and then turned to continue his discussion on the techniques of painting subtle hues of color, traces of reds and blues in watercolors. Baske told the student that the wash of blues was a natural trace of creation, a primal touch of ancient memories. The blues are a procession, he explained, and the turn of blues must be essential, the epitome and trace of natural hues of color.

Aloysius was inspired by the chance discussion of colors, the hues of blue, and once again he flinched and turned shy. My brother was a visionary artist, and that was a native sense of presence not a practice. He had never studied any techniques of watercolor as a painter. So, when he heard an art teacher describe his own natural passion as a painter he became reserved and secretive.

The contrast between visionary, mercenary, and gallery art was not easy to discuss with a learned painter. My brother created blue ravens as new totems, a natural visionary art, and for that reason the scenes he painted were never the same, and are not easily defined as a practice by teachers of art. There were no histories about blue ravens, no learned courses on new native totems. My brother was an original artist, and the images he created would change the notions of native art and the world. His native visions cannot be easily named, described, or compared by curators in art galleries.

Aloysius mounted several of his blue ravens on the empty easels in the studio. Yamada Baske studied the raven pictures from a distance, at first, and then he slowly moved closer to each image on the easels. He described the totemic images as native impressionism, an original style of abstract blue ravens.

Baske was reviewed as an impressionist painter, and exhibition curators observed that he had been trained in the great traditional painting style of the Japanese. Later, in the library, we read that his watercolors conveyed a traditional composition, "but rendered with the airy, misty technique of the impressionists. In some ways this reflects completion of a circle of influence given that the impressionist movement was deeply influenced by Japanese art, particularly watercolors and Ukiyo-e woodblock prints."

Aloysius created blue ravens, an inspiration of natural scenes and original native totems, and one day his watercolors would be included in the stories told about abstract and impressionist painters. My brother would create the new totems of the natural world in visionary, fierce, and severe scenes.

Baske was truly impressed by the pictures of the blue ravens. He moved from easel to easel, and then mounted more pictures to consider. He commented on the mastery of the blue hues, the subtle traces of motion, the natural stray of watercolor shadows, and the sense of presence in every scene of the ravens.

The blue ravens are glorious, visionary, a natural watercolor creation, said Baske. He raised one hand and waved, a gesture of praise over the blue ravens on the easels, and then he turned to my brother, smiled, and bowed slightly.

Aloysius opened his art book and painted a raven with wings widely spread over the studio easels, misty feathers tousled and astray, beak turned to the side, a blue raven bow of honor and courtesy. My brother presented the watercolor to the artist of the *Women in the Garden.*

Baske mounted the blue raven on a separate easel. Young man, he said, you perceive the natural motion of ravens, and only by that heart, by that gift of intuition, and distinctive sensibility create the glorious abstracts of impressionistic ravens.

Aloysius was moved by the curious praise, of course, but he was hesitant to show his instant appreciation and sense of wonder. The blue ravens were in natural flight, and the studio was silent. We heard only our heartbeats and the muted screech of streetcars in the distance. The mighty scenes of new totems were gathered on the easels. No one had ever raised the discussion of blue ravens to such a serious level of interpretation or considered the abstract totems with such critical sensitivity.

Aloysius invited the artist to visit our relatives on the White Earth Reservation. Baske smiled, bowed, and accepted the invitation. He walked with us down the stairs to the entrance of the library. Outside he paused, turned to my brother, handed him a tin of rouge watercolor paint, and suggested that he brush only a tiny and faint hue of rouge in the scenes of the blue ravens. Baske told my brother that a slight touch of rouge, a magical hue would enrich the subtle hues of blues and the ravens.

Baske was a master teacher.

My brother painted blue ravens over the train depots on our slow return to the Ogema Station. He practiced the faint touch of rouge, the hue on a wing or in one eye of a blue raven, and a mere trace of rouge in the shadows.

5

PEACE MEDALS

1910

Odysseus arrived as usual on horseback that early summer but his familiar songs were faint and unsteady. In the past summers we could hear the sonorous voice of the trader at a great distance. His hearty songs were gestures of amity on the reservation.

Mine eyes have seen the glory

Aloysius listened for the trader and created blue ravens as a present, an original totem of native respect. The scenes were finished by the time the trader arrived and raised his cowboy hat, as he had for more than ten years, to the banker, federal agent, newspaper editor, priest and nuns, and then dismounted at one of three hotels, the Leecy, Hiawatha, or the Headquarters. Most of his lively summer songs were familiar and reminiscent of the American Civil War.

Glory, Glory Hallelujah,
His truth is marching on.

That summer my brother painted a raven perched on a blue-spotted saddle. The raven and the saddle were in magical flight over the train station. Aloysius always created an original painting to celebrate the coming of our great friend the singing trader, and later my brother carved the fantastic image of a blue raven on a wooden pendant.

Old John Brown's body lies moldering in the grave,
While weep the sons of bondage whom he ventured all to save;
But tho he lost his life while struggling for the slave,
His soul is marching on.

Odysseus traveled and traded with natives in many parts of the country, from Santa Fe, Navajo Mountain, Oklahoma, and Omaha, to Pine Ridge, and, of course, the White Earth Reservation. He raised his white cowboy hat, smiled, and waved to everyone on the wooden walkway as his two horses walked slowly past the government school, the mission, the post office, the new house of our uncle, Theodore Beaulieu, and past the Chippewa State Bank.

Odysseus arrived that summer at the livery stable with a dislocated shoulder and a broken ankle. One shoulder was hunched forward, and his right ankle was badly swollen. He winced with pain as he tried to unsaddle the horses. Finally he moved on one foot to rest on a hay bale. One boot was fastened to the saddle horn.

Aloysius loosened the cinch, and together we heaved the heavy saddle over a wooden horse. The brown leather skirt of the saddle was decorated with precious silver peace medals. Odysseus wore a similar peace medal on a thick leather band around his neck.

Calypso, the blue roan mare, had carried the wounded trader more than forty miles from the headwaters of the *gichiziibi* at Lake Itasca to the Hotel Leecy. She ambled past two other hotels directly to the very best livery stable on the reservation, a natural choice of horses and traders.

Calypso was the spirited companion of the trader and she remembered the way after so many summers on the same trail from Onigum on the Leech Lake Reservation, to Cass Lake, Bemidji, Lake Itasca, and the headwaters of the *gichiziibi*, the Great River in the language of the Anishinaabe. Calypso ambled that memorable summer on the old trails near Bad Medicine Lake, the village of Beaulieu, Bad Boy Lake, and at last to the popular Hotel Leecy on the White Earth Reservation.

Bayard, the bay mare packhorse, was loaded with marvelous and exotic trade goods, precious stones, turquoise, silver jewelry, magic mercury, flamboyant cloth, spirit bones, peyote, absinthe, cigars, and white, red, and bright blue bird feathers from Florida, Mexico, and South America. We untied the two bundles cinched on the sides of the packhorse, and then provided feed and water for both horses in separate stalls. We were lucky to be working at the livery stable that summer when the trader arrived. The past summer we hawked newspapers at the train station and the trader commonly stayed at the Headquarters Hotel.

Augustus understood our reasons to leave the newspaper and work in the livery stable. Month by month we hawked fewer copies of the *Tomahawk*, and the newspaper had lost subscribers. Radios were more common on the reservation and could be purchased, along with guns, sewing machines, bicycles, entire houses, and even motor cars, by mail order from Sears, Roebuck and Company. The sound of radio news was more communal, the necessary gossip and native stories of the reservation, and many readers missed that ordinary hearsay as a community service of a newspaper. Our uncle was worried about the decline of subscribers to the *Tomahawk* but he was involved in many other enterprises on the reservation.

Augustus forever teased us about the stench of muck chucker stable boys. We were determined to learn more about horses, even though horses were spooked and out of place in the new world of motor cars and trains. Horses were spirited, loyal, and most of the new motor machines were unreliable and noisy. We loved horses, the shiver and nudge of horses, and sometimes stayed in the stable overnight. At the same time we had been to the city and were excited by gasoline engines, electric street cars, washers, and the hearty promises of new machines.

Calypso was a native blue healer.

Odysseus needed a reliable livery stable, and the two horses walked directly to the Hotel Leecy. Mostly the trader needed the doctor to treat his shoulder and broken ankle. Aloysius asked John Leecy, the proprietor of the hotel, for permission to deliver the trader by wagon to the White Earth Reservation Hospital.

Odysseus was a giant compared to my brother and me, and his head, neck, arms, hands, and feet were enormous. He was friendly, brawny, darker and much larger, maybe even smarter, than anyone on the reservation.

Odysseus was fully licensed by the federal government to trade with natives on reservations, and he had every right to stay at the hotel. The federal agent, however, was suspicious and refused to recognize the trader, and the agent never greeted native visitors from other reservations.

The trader leaned to one side in the back of the wagon, and smiled even in agony, but he never said much to us on the way to the hospital. The road was rough near the entrance to the hospital, the horse lurched twice, and we worried that the sudden motion of the wagon would cause more pain in his shoulder and ankle. The trader turned and smiled in silence.

The White Earth Hospital was constructed and expanded many times by the Episcopal Mission. Bishop Henry Benjamin Whipple and the federal agents competed with the Order of Saint Benedict and hurried to build a school, sawmill, and the first flourmill on the reservation. Native men were hired, and families moved closer to the schools, but the choices of native solace were regularly undermined by the federal government. The federal agents and clergy shunned native healers, brushed aside shamans, and derisively named them the causes not the healers of disease. The White Earth Hospital was the only trustworthy medical sanctuary on the reservation.

Misaabe, his son Animosh, and five mongrel healers were on duty at the entrance to the hospital. Damon Mendor, the medical doctor, trusted shaman healers and sniffer dogs trained to detect diseases. The doctor seldom relied only on the common practices of hospital medicine, and the nurses never doubted the diagnosis but forever waved the mongrels away to avoid dirty nose prints on their uniforms.

The word *misaabe* meant "giant" in translation, and *animosh* was a "dog" or mongrel in the native language of the Anishinaabe. Misaabe, a miniature man not much higher than the reach of the mongrel healers he had trained to detect diseases, was an obvious ironic reservation nickname. Misaabe tutored the most perceptive mongrel healers in the history of reservation medicine. Animosh was raised with mongrels.

The native nurses, dressed in white from cap to sturdy shoes, could hardly support the giant trader out of the wagon and into the hospital. The scene was comical as he hopped between the two nurses and the mongrel healers to a vacant treatment room. The nurses were tiny at his side, but their voices and directions were not weak or hesitant. The nurses waved the mongrels out and at the same time ordered the trader to remove his shirt.

Odysseus removed only one thick sock and revealed the monstrous swollen ankle. The nurses told us to immediately fetch the doctor who was out fishing with friends that afternoon at nearby Bad Boy Lake.

Doctor Mendor, who had been drinking more than fishing, tied his horse to the back of the wagon on the return to the hospital. The doctor, who served three reservations in the state, was acquainted with the trader, and he seemed to appreciate our basic description of the wounds. We learned much later that the good doctor traded peyote for medical care.

Biitewan, the new federal agent, dismissed native healers, and he was aware of bad health and poor nutrition, decayed teeth, diseases of the lungs, and ruinous alcoholism on the reservation, but had no obvious concern about peyote. The agent was concerned only about federal health services and that the trader, who was licensed but not a resident of the reservation, was treated as a native at the White Earth Hospital.

Biitewan, a descriptive native nickname, meant "foamy" in translation. The agent forced his words, and foam collected, soured, and curdled at the corner of his mouth. No one on the reservation, not even the priest who was a native speaker, revealed the actual translation of his nickname. Biitewan was told that his native name was sacred, a word that described the rush of water, or a great wave.

Odysseus removed his shirt in the end but not the peace medal around his neck. He held the medal in his hand as the doctor and two strong medical assistants pushed his shoulder back into place. We heard the bones move, thump, crunch, and smack. The doctor pushed the trader back on a bench, examined his ankle, and then pressed his fingers deep into the swollen flesh to feel the bones. The trader was silent, and in great pain.

Odysseus wore a wide blue sling to protect his shoulder, and the nurses packed his ankle in chunks of ice. The doctor could not determine if the ankle was sprained or a bone was broken, so the trader was ordered to remain in the hospital for several days. The trader resisted, the doctor insisted, and the trader agreed but only if he could sleep on the porch at night.

Aloysius told the trader that we had cut most of the ice that winter on the lake. The ice, buried in straw, was stored near the hospital and had slowly melted. We returned the wagon to the livery stable, watered and fed the horses, and then walked back to the hospital. The trader had eaten dinner and was seated on the screen porch in an oversized leather rocker. His ankle was wrapped in a blanket packed with ice and raised on a bench.

Odysseus described the scene of the accident at the headwaters of the Mississippi River at Lake Itasca. The lake was cold, as usual, and the breeze carried the scent of red pine. That chilly morning the flies were slow to move. Calypso, startled by the sight of an animal or snake, whinnied, lurched, and reared back. The trader lost his balance and landed hard on the rocks.

Calypso nosed me, pushed me awake, the trader explained and then mimicked his horse. The nurses were amused by his gestures. Calypso leaned forward and lowered her head, he said, and waited for me to mount. My shoulder was dislocated, and my ankle was swollen badly.

Aloysius told the trader stories that we had heard many times from our father about the Fleury sur Gichiziibi, an ancient monastery established near the headwaters many centuries ago by wayward brothers of the Order of Saint Benedict. The monks created the *Manabozho Curiosa*, a mysterious erotic manuscript that described sex between monks and animals, and especially the mongrels with two feathery tails.

Honoré, our father, explained that the ghosts of the monks wandered in the woods near the headwaters and frightened animals and birds. The ravens circled and croaked over that spooky place but never perched in the red cedar, and never landed near the headwaters. Sometimes the howl of wolves was a strange tremulous sound, and even chickens, rabbits, and skunks were nervous, weird, and bouncy near the headwaters.

Calypso was spooked by the ghosts of the monkery.

Odysseus smiled, saluted, but said nothing about the ghostly monks. He was a mighty storier that night, and no one, not even the spirits of the shamans and monks, would have dared tease or voice a word of distraction. The trader told stories about his names, the peace medal he wore around his neck, and the dance of the dead in memories of the American Civil War, his service as a cavalry soldier, and his experiences as a trader, that night on the screen porch of the hospital. We were enchanted by the great stories of his adventures. The doctor, nurses, and three other patients gathered around the shimmer of the lantern to listen. Yes, that was a special moment on the hospital porch. The trader was stimulated by the audience, the northern night sky, and by the weather, a gentle summer breeze. Every gesture of the trader created a huge shadow on the porch.

〉〉〉 〈〈〈

Odysseus Walker Young raised the peace medal and told stories about his three names. Aloysius, the doctor, nurses, and several patients in turn leaned closer to examine the silver medal, an image of General Ulysses S. Grant. The name of the president was not embossed on the medal. Grant is pictured on the front of the medal with twelve curved words around his image: *United States of America, Let Us Have Peace, Liberty Justice and Equality.* The earth, a tablet, and farm implements were embossed on the back of the medal, and with these words and the inauguration date of President Grant: *On Earth Peace, 1871, Good Will Toward Men.*

Odysseus was born in the leap year 1864, on February 29, the very same day that President Abraham Lincoln nominated Ulysses S. Grant for promotion to Lieutenant General in the Army of the United States. A year later, on April 9, 1865, General Robert E. Lee signed the documents of surrender in the village of Appomattox Courthouse that ended the bloody Civil War. Grant, a great soldier, was later elected the eighteenth president of the United States.

Odysseus was named in honor of the heroic literary character and the famous general who ended the Civil War. Jefferson, his father, and his grandfather had been steady traders at Ganado, Keams Canyon, Tuba City, and many other native posts on the Navajo Reservation. They had obtained in trade several peace medals issued by many presidents including Thomas Jefferson, James Madison, James Polk, Abraham Lincoln, and Ulysses S. Grant.

Odysseus explained that his father, Jefferson Young, had read a translation of *The Odyssey* by Homer and favored the Greek name in the epic poem to the Latin Ulysses. Odysseus said his father revised familiar classical myths. He created his own versions and adventure stories to serve the moment around a campfire, and in the marvelous union of native storiers at trading posts.

Jefferson, as his son the trader explained that night on the screen porch at the hospital, taught him how to chant and sing on the road, to create memorable stories, and to privately praise the tricky arts of the native tease and irony. Natives trusted him as a trader because he was a singer and a creative storier.

Odysseus, for instance, could chant sections of *The Odyssey* and of *The Red Badge of Courage* by Stephen Crane. Teachers at the government school had read out loud selections of the same two books, but not with the same dramatic mastery as the great renditions of the trader.

Jefferson was the saint of irony among natives and traders, but not among federal agents. Odysseus praised his father for his humor, courage, and generosity in the company of natives, and then chanted a few poetic lines about the sense of place and family from *The Odyssey*.

So, as welcome as the great show of life again in a father is to his children, when he has lain sick, a mighty trader, suffering strong pains, and wasting long away, and the hateful spirit of the dead has brushed his shoulder, but then, and it is welcome, the gods set him free of his sickness, and a welcome was heard in the desert and forest now for my father.

Odysseus was an enchanter and a teaser among natives and traders, and we were captivated that night by a master storier. The doctor lighted a narrow cigar. The nurses were teary, not so much by the descriptive mastery of scenes but because of the emotive sway and natural pace of the chant. Later, he told us that he had revised a few lines in the heroic poem, and created the reference to the "mighty trader," the mention of "shoulder," and the view of his father in the desert. His stories were created for the moment, for the trail, for the wagon, for the porch, and always with some local rumors, personal notices, and situations.

Aloysius painted a blue raven with enormous wings.

The stars were brighter that night of the new moon, and every star shimmered in the leaves of early summer. The nurses and patients waited on the porch to hear more stories, the dramatic sway of memory and descriptive scenes of literature.

Odysseus reached over his head with one hand to touch the stars, and to tease the shimmer of light. His hand cast a shadow across the porch. Then he turned to the nurses, smiled, and recited poignant war scenes from *The Red Badge of Courage* by Stephen Crane.

When the youth awoke it seemed to him that he had been asleep for a thousand years, and he felt sure that he opened his eyes upon an unexpected world. Gray mists were slowly shifting before the first efforts of the sunrays. An impending splendor could be seen in the eastern sky. An icy dew had chilled his face, and immediately upon arousing he curled farther down into his blanket. He stared for a while at the leaves overhead, moving in a heraldic wind of the day.

So it came to pass that as he trudged from the place of blood and wrath his soul changed. He came from hot plowshares to prospects of clover tranquilly. . . .

The American Civil War endured in memories, the sublime scenes forever wanted in a chant or chorus of honor, and the slightest trace of death, or gesture of gruesome disability, torments the soldiers, the sole survivors of disunion, national duty, and the lonesome families, without grace, cover, or ordinary dignity. The bloody bodies of so many young men have never withered in memory, and were summoned to stories over the years as the clover of tranquility.

Dead soldiers were the clover of tranquility.

Aloysius painted scenes of abstract blue ravens in natural motion, the traces of visual memory, and especially the mighty stories and recitations of the trader. The Civil War stories were unbearable scenes, stories of misery and heartbreak at the time, and yet the poignant recitation by the trader that night inspired me to create stories of soldiers. My perception and recollection of those stories that so enchanted me on the porch of the hospital that summer night were written several years later. My stories were mostly silent at the time, waiting at night for a clever origin, and almost ready to be created as scenes of memory.

Odysseus was conscientious about his ancestors, and included them in most of his stories. Captain Charles Young, for instance, a graduate of the Military Academy at West Point, was a direct relative. The trader recounted that night on the porch the service of Captain Young in the Ninth Cavalry Regiment and later the acting Military Superintendent of Sequoia and General Grant National Park. He paused and raised the peace medal as a gesture of respect when he mentioned the name of President Ulysses S. Grant. The world of generals and presidents always seemed more congenial when the trader told personal stories about his relatives. The nurses were pleased, only the doctor turned away.

Odysseus was entrusted with a middle name in honor of a career soldier, Sergeant William Walker of the Third South Carolina Volunteers. The trader recounted that night how the eminent soldier had rightly incited others to resist duty and renounce the military over the lower wages paid to freedmen. The soldiers had been promised equal treatment when they enlisted in the Civil War.

Sergeant Walker was convicted of mutiny at a court-martial and was unjustly executed by a military firing squad on February 29, 1864. Odysseus was born on the very same day, a great legacy of coincidence and a cruel injustice. The United States Congress voted four months later to provide equal pay for black soldiers. There were two great epochs of memory on the day of his birth—the execution of Sergeant William Walker and the executive promotion of General Ulysses S. Grant.

Odysseus raised his peace medal once more and recited the glorious words of the Thirteenth Amendment to the United States Constitution, the Abolition of Slavery. The trader declared that the amendment was ratified on December 6, 1865, less than two years after the tragic execution of Sergeant William Walker.

Neither slavery nor involuntary servitude, except as a punishment for crime whereof the party shall have been duly convicted, shall exist within the United States, or any place subject to their jurisdiction.

The nurses and patients shouted out their devotion to abolition and then saluted the trader who was disabled by a shoulder sling and an ice pack. The trader was always a memorable storier, but that night on the porch he was at his very best, a glorious raconteur. The spiritual strength of his entire body seemed to arise in his sonorous voice, as a whisper, chant, and the mighty shouts of justice.

Jefferson declared that he would forever remember the soldier and so named his second-born son in honor of Sergeant Walker. The black soldier was executed only because he protested the injustice of slavery and the inequity of military pay. He should have been honored not executed. So, that night on the porch of the reservation hospital the soldier was honored by name, remembrance, and stories.

Odysseus was born at home, one of seven children, in South Carolina. He was a direct descendant of freedmen, exceptional soldiers, traders, and storiers. Madison, his favorite uncle, served as a Buffalo Soldier in the Tenth Cavalry Regiment, and he fought in the Apache Wars. The Young freedmen, soldiers and traders, were strong, dark, ambitious, and winsome. Jefferson and Odysseus were secure on the trail and honored by natives because of their songs, stories, and their trade integrity.

〉〉〉 〈〈〈

Aloysius painted more than seven original scenes that night of blue ravens in the war, blue ravens perched on the porch with the nurses, and one blue raven with huge wings. A trace of red rouge was on the cheek of the soldier. My brother presented the watercolor paintings to the trader that night, and once more the nurses were teary.

Biitewan, the unaware federal agent, arrived at the hospital to inquire about the cause of shouts and laughter heard from a distance. No matter the weather the agent always wore a white shirt, necktie, vest, and dark suit, and so he was dressed that night for a federal investigation of humor, chant, and native irony. No one, not even the ice woman, would have invited the agent out that night. Chance, humor, and native irony were weakened by the mere presence of the agent. Nonetheless, and with his bony thumb hooked over a watch chain, he was convinced that his political appointment as a federal inspector and reservation agent endowed him with the rights of cultural intrusion and personal inquiry. The man was not evil, or even a dopey federal monster, but his presence was a nuisance, and a deadly distraction. Foamy was an irretrievable trespasser on native reason and stories. Mostly he was the actual sources of the ironic stories, but never as a participant.

The nurses shunned the agent on every occasion because his dreary, niggling manner was a curse in the hospital. Patients lost their spirit to live in the presence of government agents.

The covert mission of the federal agent that night was an inquiry into the misuse of federal funds to heal a trader and others who were not natives of the White Earth Reservation. The doctor, nurses, and patients turned away when the agent intruded on the porch stories. The trader, however, teased the agent with ironic flattery, comments on his shirt, vest, and watch chain. You are a proper federal man, said the trader, to wear a white shirt, necktie, and vest only to interrogate an old wounded trader on a summer night.

Odysseus invited the agent to participate in a song about peas, or peanuts, that had been popular in the south during the Civil War. The trader had encountered the agent on another reservation and knew that he was born and raised near Macon, Georgia, and many of his relatives were veterans of the Confederate States Army.

Biitewan had no personal contact with natives, and he had no appreciation of the history and vicious termination of natives in Georgia. The Indian Removal Act of 1830 and the Trail of Tears were of no concern to the provincial agent. The appointment of federal agents was always political, and any sympathetic experience, comments, or knowledge of the abuses and removal of natives from homelands would likely complicate a nomination for government service on a reservation.

Odysseus teased the agent with ironic stories about the black panthers and the cruel removal of natives in Georgia. Nothing remains in your greyback rebel birthplace, said the trader, to show the world that elusive natives and black panthers are worth more than a pocket of loam or gold dust. The trader waved and chanted that natives lost their homeland and stories to southern thievery.

Biitewan smiled slightly, a haughty gesture, unaware of the ironic analogy of natives, blacks, and panthers, and turned to the doctor for an accounting of the medical services provided to the trader. Nothing but ice for a swollen ankle, the doctor shouted, and the Beaulieu boys cut that ice last winter on the lake, and the ice is native and free to melt on the ankle of the trader, or on anyone in need of an ice pack. The trader smiled, the doctor cursed, and the nurses snickered when the agent officiously announced that the lake was federal trust land, and the ice was under his jurisdiction.

Odysseus raised one hand, gestured to the greyback agent, and started to chant the words of "Goober Peas." The nurses and patients returned to the porch to participate in the tease of the federal agent.

> Sittin' by the roadside on a summer's day,
> Chattin' with my messmates, passing time away,
> Lying in the shadow, underneath the trees,
> Goodness, how delicious, eating goober peas!

Everyone on the porch, even the doctor, encouraged the agent, who had never taken part in any native ceremonies, family wakes, or reservation activities, to join the trader, nurses, and patients in the first chorus of "Goober Peas." The Union was blue, the reservation was blue, the trader was blue, the ravens were blue, and the war continued with blue ironic stories.

> Peas! Peas! Peas! Peas!
> Eating goober peas!
> Goodness, how delicious,
> Eating goober peas!

The porch humor was memorable that night, and the dreary greyback agent never quite realized at that moment that he had been deliberately distracted with a dippy southern song of the Civil War. The trader was our captain storier that night, a trader of deliverance on the reservation. Yet the ironic participation of the antsy agent was a draw because he soon returned to fidget with his watch chain and continued the hospital inquiry.

6

PEYOTE OPERA

—————— 1912 ——————

Odysseus was sentimental at times about the old traders and chantey music. His trail stories and songs about soldiers and war were picturesque, slightly romantic, original by every recount, but never mawkish. Even so the winsome trader was teased for the first time last summer about the many songs he chanted from the American Civil War.

Foamy, the federal agent, mocked the popular war lyrics and reminded the trader that the War Between the States was ancient history. We were astonished by the taunt because no one had ever observed the agent at play. Augustus, our uncle, was convinced the agent had taken to government whiskey.

Glory, Glory Hallelujah.

Odysseus raised his white hat, gestured to the testy agent, and then turned to several students near the government school and sang a few lines from "Alexander's Rag Time Band" by Irving Berlin. The students were silent, but the agent shouted the same lines right back at the trader.

Come on and hear! Alexander's ragtime band!
It's the best band in the land!
So natural that you want to go to war.

Foamy never seemed to grasp the tricky tease of native stories, or the creative run of irony. Honoré, our father, said the agent had no sense of natural reason or presence, and no totemic associations in the world. Foamy was separated by name and disconnected by war and culture. He abided with the wrong sides, against emancipation and natives, and against the Union in the American Civil War. His new teases and greyback taunts were no more trouble than slow water over the smooth stone at the headwaters.

Calypso raised her ears, neighed, and ambled past the vested agent, the mission, post office, the bank, the gray wooden walkways, and straight into the livery stables at the Hotel Leecy. Bayard the packhorse waited in the shadows to be unloaded. The trader stacked the huge bundles of goods in a locked cage at the back of the stables, and then whispered to his horses. We listened every summer, year after year, but we never heard or understood what the trader told his loyal mares.

Odysseus walked with a limp.

John Leecy had invited the trader to display his curious merchandise in the hotel lobby that Sunday. Naturally, we were there early to assist the trader and to watch natives and others negotiate the unstated prices of exotic goods. Expensive cigars in sealed boxes, decorative feathers, cloth, jewelry, and many other curious wares were stacked on large tables in the hotel lobby.

Odysseus traded secret reserves of peyote and absinthe by discreet names. Night Visions and Morning Star were the names for peyote. The French absinthe was mentioned only as *la fée verte*, or The Green Lady. Only the doctor and our uncle were aware that the trader carried absinthe and peyote. The Green Lady became very expensive that summer because the heady spirit had been banned as a poison by the Department of Agriculture.

Augustus bartered for cigars, absinthe, and mercury.

The bank manager bought snowy egret feathers. The wispy crown feathers and other exotic bird plumage were very expensive, more than the price of gold. The trader presented oriole, common tern, snow bunting, northern flicker, cedar waxwing, and, of course, snowy egret feathers. Rumors spread that the banker, a distant relative, used reservation deposits to buy feathers for a white woman. He fancied one of the government teachers, but she had never been seen in an aigrette or any other fashion feathers. The banker actually bought the feathers for his fancy grandmother.

My mother said women were the enemy of sacred birds, and likewise men had been the enemy of the beaver centuries earlier. The decorative plume trade decimated the showy birds, and our ancestors in the fur trade brought the beaver close to extinction. Natives and most of our relatives once hunted beaver for no other reason than the fashion of expensive felt hats in Europe.

Odysseus insisted that he only sold dead egret feathers that were gathered by the Seminoles in the Florida Everglades. Augustus doubted that the egret feathers were dead, or shed in a natural way, and then rescued by natives, and he was not convinced that natives would have better protected the snowy egrets or any other totemic birds. He reminded us that our ancestors and fur traders slaughtered sacred totems for the money.

Augustus reported in the *Tomahawk* that the New York State legislature passed the Audubon Plumage Bill. The trade in bird plumage was banned in the state. The plumage laws were ignored on the reservation, and the secret trade continued.

Augustus never revealed his use of quicksilver.

Aloysius painted several blue raven scenes, and the ravens were encircled by traces of white plumes. The snowy egrets were portrayed as faint outlines with enormous blue crown feathers, and the eyes of the egrets were touched with a trace of red.

Catherine Heady, the prudish literature teacher, was there to buy calico and cotton lace. She gestured with a tight smile, but never said a word to students outside of school. The trader measured a length of lace for the teacher, touched his gray hairy cheek with the cloth, and then invited her to do the same. The teacher blushed and turned away.

Foamy bought a square yard of red velvet for a chair cushion, and the testy negotiations lasted for more than an hour. The trader met with other customers, and then returned several times to bargain over the price of velvet. Finally, the price was settled quickly when the doctor arrived to secretly barter for a sack of peyote. The agent was not aware that the trader carried the magical cactus.

Odysseus complained to the doctor that his ankle had not healed, and he was not able to walk without some pain. He was treated at the hospital two years earlier, and we were there to hear his marvelous stories. The trader handed the doctor a small canvas sack of peyote. Luckily we heard the doctor direct the trader to meet that very night at a site near Bad Boy Lake.

John Leecy loaned us a horse that afternoon, but we were too late to follow the trader to the secret location near the lake. Most peyote ceremonies started at sundown, so we waited and listened near the lake. We were too young to use peyote, and we had no obvious need to be healed at the time, but we were curious about visionary stories. There were several cabins in the woods, so we slowly ambled around the lake and listened for any sound of the ceremony. Finally, several hours later we heard an eagle whistle and the fast sound of drums.

The peyote ceremony was held in a wigwam in the woods a short distance from the lake. The mongrel healers circled the horse when we dismounted in the dark, so we walked to the nearby cabin and tied the horse to a post. Misaabe, the old healer, invited us into his tiny cabin, and at the same time the mongrels pushed through the rickety door. We had been there only once last summer. The cabin was dark, lighted by a tiny kerosene lantern, and the oil was scented with cedar.

Misaabe sat naked on a plank bench near the cook stove. He seldom wore clothes in the summer, and only covered his body in winter, and when he was on duty with the mongrel healers at the hospital. Doctor Mendor paid the old healer for the services of the mongrels at the hospital, and always brought food, sometimes even dog food, and chocolate when he gathered nearby for a peyote ceremony.

No other public health doctor had promoted the mongrel healers on the reservation. The mongrels detected by the scent of urine, bare skin, bad breath, sweat, and by muscle tension various diseases. The mongrels were not shy about pushing their noses into the crotch of a human, and they had learned how to quickly pitch the hem of a dress and sniff the genitals of a woman. The doctor was amused by the disease detection practices of the mongrels, but the nurses tightened their dresses and sidestepped the mongrel healers.

Liver, kidney, pancreas, thyroid, and stomach diseases were detected and treated by the doctor, but most tumors were not treatable by ordinary medicine. Surgery was dangerous and the last resort. The mongrel healers detected and now and then healed the most serious diseases.

Misaabe trained the mongrels to sing, smile, nudge, nuzzle, and heal the patients in the hospital. Some patients resisted the healing energy of the mongrels because they could not accept the natural spirit of animals, and because they could not imagine the presence of a disease.

Misaabe once told a federal surveyor, a man who had marked and divided reservation land into government allotments, that the ice woman caused his tumors. He encouraged the surveyor to locate by imagination the tumor in his body as a chunk of ice and then slowly day by day concentrate on the location and melt the ice away. The man could not imagine a chunk of ice in his body. He could not create or envision a scene or story to survive.

Misaabe and his mongrels healed serious diseases of more natives than the hospital doctors. Most of the government agents could not create stories, and could not imagine a disease. The ice woman stories were sources of fear and caution. That very sense of fear in stories of the ice woman could be imagined as the power to heal a disease.

Misaabe and the mongrels were natural healers. Sometimes he told natives to concentrate and imagine scenes of the ice woman and then melt the disease away with a song or story. Naturally, natives and others worried when the mongrels sniffed too closely. Any lingering scent could be the detection of disease. Harmony, a spaniel mongrel, had a nose much colder than the stories of the ice woman. The four other mongrels were distinct healers. Shimmer nuzzled and her body glowed when she sang. Nosy was skinny, tender, curious, and could heal anyone with her dark, watery eyes. Ghost Moth was so named because of his faint and misty coat. Mona Lisa was an artful healer by secretive smiles, a poser, and her gentle furry paws were crossed at rest. Misaabe named the young mongrel healer last summer when the *Tomahawk* reported that the *Mona Lisa* by Leonardo da Vinci had been stolen from the Musée du Louvre in Paris.

Aloysius sat near the kerosene lamp and painted great blue ravens in magical flight, and with abstract blue mongrels on the wing. The color blue had the power to heal in native art and stories. Misaabe used the blue ravens my brother painted to encourage natives to imagine a disease healed by blue ravens, blue totems, and by blue mongrels.

The moths bounced on the lantern, roused by the light, and left traces of wings on the globe. Gnats and other insects died on the wick. The mongrels moaned in the dark corners of the cabin. The lofty sound of an eagle whistle and the fast beat of peyote drums wavered in the distance. The peyote songs surged in the night, and we waited by the lantern for the old healer to move with the spirit of the music.

Misaabe murmured on the bench, and then chanted and gestured with his hands. His shadow became a wave of music, a natural motion with the moths, and yet he had never used peyote. The mongrels were observant, heads raised, ears turned to the music, and they watched the shadows of the great healer circle the cabin. Mona Lisa panted and crossed her paws.

Aloysius painted by the lantern.

We were secure with the moths, mongrels, and the old healer that night. The peyote music wavered and enclosed the tiny cabin. The lantern light shimmered and then fluttered with the sound of the drums. We were captivated by the music, and by the shadows of the healer. We had no need to move closer to the wigwam.

Much later we were startled by hearty shouts and the chanted names of totems, crane, raven, beaver, bear, and other birds and animals over the sound of the peyote music. The ceremony in a wigwam that night was not traditional, and not the same as the ancient native peyote practices in the desert. There were singers, peyote songs, the sound of rattles, drums, and eagle whistles, but no formal prayers, no peyote chief, no cedar man, sagebrush, and no sense of a supreme creator.

The peyote ceremony in the wigwam inspired natural visions, more individual than communal or churchy. The ceremony was dangerous, and the singers were brave visionaries. The singers were inspired by the liberation of personal and solitary visions. Later we learned that peyote created strange sensations of independence, a sense of visionary sovereignty, and the magical power of flight. The new burdens of time, masters, manners, cultures, and communal conditions were trivial in the peyote visions of magical flight. The creative stories were natural coveys, heartfelt, true scenes, and with an overwhelming native sense of liberty.

The shouts and chants roused the mongrels. Mona Lisa and Nosy circled the old healer in the cabin and waited for directions. Misaabe gestured with his lips toward the peyote wigwam and the mongrels rushed outside. We followed the mongrels into the night and recognized the voice of the chanter and trader. The mongrels nosed and bumped him back to the cabin.

Calypso neighed at the post.

Odysseus, once inside, handed each mongrel a piece of dried meat. He limped toward the lantern and sat on a rough chopping block. He raised his arms, waved his huge hands near the lantern, and reached for the shadows.

Odysseus suddenly turned to the old healer and sang "The Last Rose of Summer" by the poet Thomas Moore. We were moved by the great voice of the trader, and the mongrels turned their ears and howled with the singer. The voices of the trader and the mongrels resounded in the cabin. Shimmer nuzzled the ankle of the trader. Mona Lisa smiled and moved closer to the lantern, and she crossed her paws at the feet of the trader. Ghost Moth sat directly at the side of the trader. He raised his head in the shadows and bayed with the music.

The last rose of summer
Left blooming alone.

Odysseus told stories about the creation of the melody and then recounted the story of the great opera singer Luisa Tetrazzini who sang "The Last Rose of Summer" two years earlier on Christmas Eve on the streets of San Francisco, California. He remembered the night was bright and clear.

The trader recounted the great San Francisco earthquake, on April 18, 1906, as a personal experience. He must have read the news reports in the *Tomahawk* that more than three thousand people died from the earthquake and fire. He created a sense of natural presence in stories, more memorable than newspaper accounts, but he never experienced the earthquake or the actual outside concert by Luisa Tetrazzini.

Odysseus told stories that created an instant sense of presence and position. Time and duration were never necessary in his creative chants, and the stories he created that night were visionary peyote operas. The operas flourished as continuous dreams. He pointed in the direction of the stories he recounted to San Francisco, Montana, New Mexico, Lake Itasca, and White Earth with his eyes, a pucker and tack of his lips, and sometimes he would pause and gesture with his huge shoulders and hands. These gestures of direction created the actual and heartfelt scenes in the world of stories. Natives have always told stories with a sense of presence and direction, the natural scenes of a cultural opera. The trader was native by his stories.

Luisa Tetrazzini was sensuous that Christmas Eve. She wore an enormous hat and a white gown that shimmered in the light. The trader said she waved a stole of ostrich feathers and mounted the outside stage at the intersection of Kearny, Geary, and Market streets in San Francisco.

Odysseus arose from the chopping block seat near the lantern and his huge shadow reached across the entire cabin. The mongrels moved out of the reach of his shadow. His mighty voice teased and fluttered the lantern flame as he sang the final lines of "The Last Rose of Summer." Nosy and

Harmony moaned and moved closer to the healer in the light of the lantern. Only the mongrels dared to move as he sang.

> *When true hearts lie withered*
> *And fond ones are flown*
> *Oh! Who would inhabit*
> *This bleak world alone?*

The trader chanted and the mongrels bayed the sweet name of Luisa Tetrazzini. She was there that clear night in his song and stories, and we could hear the beautiful voice of the soprano, a pure and natural sound, the true words of withered hearts and mongrels in the white pine that summer, and at the same time in the memory of the trader on Christmas Eve. Tetrazzini was a natural presence that summer at Bad Boy Lake.

〉〉〉 〈〈〈

Aloysius convinced the trader that we had met Oscar Wilde at the Nicollet House, the old hotel, in Minneapolis. The playwright and snappy poet had long hair, and beautiful blue eyes. He wore a huge slouchy black hat, and a heavy fur-trimmed coat even in the summer. We told the trader about his lecture at the Academy of Music. The *Tribune* newspaper wrote a very critical review of his lecture on decorative art.

Odysseus leaned back on the block, smiled, touched his peace medal, and beckoned to show he understood our counter tease and story. Wilde died when we were five years old but the trader heard the sense of presence in our stories. Since we could not have actually met the playwright we imagined his presence in a story that summer night in the cabin, in the same way that the trader created the presence of Luisa Tetrazzini.

Misaabe waved one hand over the lantern, and the fidgety mongrels moaned and moved to the other side of the cabin closer to my brother. The trader shouted out his praise of our peyote opera, the visionary presence of Oscar Wilde at Bad Boy Lake.

The truth is rarely pure and never simple, the trader recited as his own words, and then paused to touch Harmony. Modern life would be very tedious if it were either easy, pure, or righteous, and peyote stories a complete impossibility. Many years later we read the original words in "The Importance of Being Earnest" by Oscar Wilde. The trader had changed "modern literature" to "peyote stories," neither new, true, pure or simple. Some of his stories were peyote operas, and the scenes were original, never recitations or liturgy.

Odysseus was a trader and told stories to create a sense of presence, and the scenes were never the same. No wonder the stories of the trader were trusted by natives. The confidence of any trader is appreciated in original trail stories.

The Matchless Mine in Cloud City or Leadville, Colorado, was a salvation of teases and stories about fancy manners, vows of aesthetics, and the descent in a rickety ore bucket with unruly silver miners for dinner, drink, and cigars. Oscar Wilde descended into the dangerous earth with men of deadly risk in search of silver, stories, and deliverance.

Wilde had lectured on aesthetics at the Tabor Grand Opera in the Rocky Mountains. He lectured and read passages from an autobiography of Benvenuto Cellini, and explained that the sculptor could not be there because he died three centuries earlier. A wild miner shouted out from the back of the audience, Who shot him?

The poet was courted by the miners to a saloon dance and read a notice over the piano: PLEASE DO NOT SHOOT THE PIANIST. HE IS DOING HIS BEST. Wilde commented that the simple notice was the "only rational method of art criticism I have ever come across." Wilde had supper in the "heart of the mountain," and the "first course being whiskey, the second whiskey, and the third whiskey."

Wilde could have easily survived by stories, even the trickery of shamans on the White Earth Reservation. My original stories created the presence of the eccentric playwright on the reservation, and his name became an aesthetic tease. The federal agent and our teachers at the government school, however, tried to conceal the name of the decadent poet who wore black silk stockings and a purple jacket.

The playwright would have survived the lusty monks at the headwaters by stories, and he would have teased the priest and nuns with bestial stories. Every mongrel on the reservation would have been at his side ready to heal the wounds of godly sincerity.

Wilde was a poser of mock revelations, and one evening, after drinking cheap whiskey with the bank manager, the postmaster, and our uncle, he entered the confessional at Saint Benedict's Mission Church. He closed the black curtain and waited to reveal his most outrageous secrets, aesthetic sex and heart booty, to the priest but he fell asleep on the hard wooden bench.

Father Aloysius nudged the poet awake that early morning and started the confession. Wilde created more stories and confessions than the priest could ever remember to absolve, the sins and sorrows of extravagance. Only a mighty act of comedy and ironic contrition could balance his universe of chance, original sins, and roguery.

The Matchless Mine was the site of his last confession, and the silver barbarians absolved his aesthetic sins forever. Wilde is the only silky poet who has ever found sacramental absolution in a silver mine.

Wilde was the utmost promise of the weird, showy, elusive, tricky, and decadent bother in a simple surname word that summer on the reservation, the perfect time and name and natural stories of deliverance on a federal and churchy colony.

7

BLUE HORSES

———————— 1915 ————————

The First World War was underway, but the news reports of faraway military encounters hardly mattered on the reservation that summer. We were curious, and the names, empires, and places of the war were strange. We practiced the accent of names in the news to hawk the *Tomahawk* at the Ogema Station.

The Hotel Leecy livery stable was not a source of international stories, but we continued to pronounce the new names in the news, Hapsburg, Archduke Franz Ferdinand, Gavrilo Princip, Ypres, Passchendaele, Marne, and many others that summer, and the names were mere captions of war in a distant colonial civilization.

The Great War became more immediate and identifiable only when we read that a German submarine torpedoed an American ship near England. The "Digest of World's Important News: Epitome of the Big Happening of the Week" in the *Tomahawk* had been our primary source of news and names to hawk the newspaper, but then, as older stable boys, we read more closely and tried to understand a world war that would forever change our lives and the culture of the White Earth Reservation.

"The American oil tank steamer *Gulflight*" was "torpedoed" near the Isles of Scilly in the Celtic Sea by the Germans, reported the *Tomahawk* on May 13, 1915. The *Gulflight* displayed the flag of the United States, and German submarines had torpedoed "seven more vessels," steamers and trawlers, from Norway and England.

President Wilson, Secretary of State William Jennings Bryan, and experts on international law "decided to suspend judgment in the case of the American tank ship *Gulflight*." Captain Alfred Gunter and two sailors died in the attack by the Germans.

A month later we read in the *Tomahawk* that a German Rumpler *Taube*, the very first monoplane, and military Zeppelins dropped several bombs on London and on the suburbs of Paris. The United States entered the war three years later, after a presidential dither in the name of international peace, and we were drafted for service in the American Expeditionary Forces.

The *Lusitania* was torpedoed and sank on May 7, 1915.

"President Wilson declared that a proud distinction might fall upon the nations of the three Americas," reported the *Tomahawk*. "In an address at the Pan-American Financial conference at Washington he predicted that great results would arise from it and that it might be influential in restoring peace to war-ridden Europe."

Augustus shouted and raved about the political milksops and maniacs of war. President Wilson was a milksop, more oratory than action, because he refused to denounce the submarine attacks, and Kaiser Wilhelm was the maniac war emperor of Germany. Our uncle published international stories about the war every week, and he ranted everyday about imperious federal agents and the obvious consequences of hesitant politicians.

The president negotiated peace by isolation, not by backbone, spirit, and power. He should have declared his outrage over the destruction of cities and libraries, and the murder of civilians. He should have considered the great visions and bravery of native warriors. The president instead announced that he was our Great White Father. He would rather capitulate in the name of peace than honor native visions and natural reason. Natives resisted colonial and federal occupation for centuries, and then natives served with the same government in several wars, and were always ready to fight again even though most reservation natives were not yet considered citizens of the United States. Naturally the federal agent saluted the president, but the agent has always been on the wrong side of native traditions and stories.

Foamy had no vision or backbone.

Robert Beaulieu, our uncle, was the first native photographer on the White Earth Reservation. That summer he collected some of his pictures for his older brother Augustus Beaulieu. He used a large camera on a tripod and took pictures of stores, the bank, the movie theater, hotels on the reservation, newspaper building, and natives at the annual celebration, but he never took pictures of traditional native spiritual or religious ceremonies. He was once the postmaster, a progressive native on the side of entrepreneurs, and he never talked about anything visionary, totemic, or traditional.

Robert photographed the Big Bear family at a maple sugar camp, and portraits of Maingans the Younger, Waweyaycumig and Nawajibigokwe, Odenegun, the native who told trickster stories to Frances Densmore, and Mary Warren English who was the native interpreter for the musicologist. William Warren, her brother, wrote the first history of the Anishinaabe. The federal agent and teachers never mentioned the native historian, but my mother owned a signed copy. The Minnesota Historical Society published *The History of the Ojibway People* in 1885.

Aloysius never painted or even mentioned his blue ravens in the presence of our uncle Robert Beaulieu. He was younger than our favorite uncle, smart, and rather distant. Actually he was vain and wore a ridiculous round straw hat on the reservation, and never told a memorable story. He cocked the straw hat to the side but it was not the right size.

We had hawked newspapers for our uncle, and later worked in the livery stable at the Hotel Leecy. Robert had no interest in our adventures, stories, or our talents. He probably considered the stable a lowly occupation. He never listened to my brother, or our mother, and he never commented on my first short local news notices and stories published in the *Tomahawk*.

Misaabe and the healers were our best friends.

Robert photographed the hotel and the bank but not his own relatives. He even posed with his bright cornet in one of his own pictures, stretched out on the ground with nineteen native brass musicians of the White Earth Band. He never took pictures of my brother or me, or our mother, not even when we were drafted with many of our cousins to serve in the First World War in France.

Aloysius carved three medallions last summer from paper birch trunks, round pendants with the raised image of ravens. The native birch was easier to carve than oak, and the bright blue paint was absorbed in the grain of the wood. The blue ravens were in natural motion, a native medal of peace.

Misaabe told my brother that the raven pendants must be carved from birch that had died by nature, not by storm, disease, or timber cutters. The spirit of the visionary ravens carved in the birch was entrusted with the memory of natural death, not with the cruel sacrifice of an ax or saw. He never mentioned lightning.

Aloysius presented the first raven peace medal to our uncle, Augustus, who was troubled that summer by his health. The second peace medal was a present to the trader Odysseus. The third medal was for the old healer. Misaabe touched the blue raven carved on the birch pendant, and then he turned the medal over and told stories about his son and the great mongrel healers. He scored the single name of his son on the back of the medal.

Animosh had been abandoned ten years ago near Bad Boy Lake. He was about three years old at the time and no one could name or remember the boy. He was stranded in a native mystery, and must have lived alone on the shoreline for several days, but he was not scared by the night. The boy told stories about the party of leaves, stones, birds, and slight waves on the shoreline. He created nicknames for the stones, the cattails, blackbirds, maple and birch leaves, and the clouds. The boy said his name was *animosh*, or dog, in Anishinaabe.

Animosh created a natural sense of presence and he was never alone. Soon he was more at home with the healer, the mongrels, and nature. The old healer taught the boy how to read and write, but he never attended a mission or government school.

Animosh told stories with a sense of presence.

Mona Lisa and the other mongrels had been abused, wounded, and wary when the old healer rescued them on the reservation. The mongrels gathered at the cabin, and many stayed for only a few days to heal their wounds. Misaabe saved many mongrels from the hands of abusers, and trained them to detect diseases, but some of the testy mongrels would rather mosey and meander than nose and heal with the old man and his boy.

Misaabe never actually described how he had trained the mongrels to become natural healers, but we learned from the doctor that the old healer collected urine and other body fluids from natives with diseases. The mongrels learned to nose and detect the scent of human maladies. The old healer described the trace and reek of disease as a brutal civil war in the body, not the scent and memory of natural death, but rather some cold treachery, a pious surrender, the sacrifice of humor. Diseases were held at bay with creative stories of trickster stones, thunder, and natural motions of the cranes.

Odysseus once invited us to participate in a peyote ceremony near Bad Boy Lake. That was our first experience with the shiver and mirage of peyote visions and stories, and it would be our last. We learned to trust our own creative sight and stories in the wild thrust of peyote visions that night, to trust the natural tease of bright colors, dreams, totems, and the touch of native mysteries.

Maybe we would return to peyote visions when we were older and not so curious about the secrets of the natural world. Yes, we understood that peyote was another sense of native presence, but we were not mature enough at the time to compare the mighty flight of peyote and natural teases of visions and stories.

Misaabe was our native teacher and the mongrels were our healers. We wondered, of course, why the old healer had not taken part in the peyote ceremonies near his cabin. Peyote customs and songs in the woods were natural attractions, but the old healer was evasive. He told us stories about a giant native who once had such intense peyote visions about moths and praying mantis he could never escape a miniature sense of his presence. He forever waved his arms as a moth to the light and walked slowly with the mantis. The giant hunted insects and soon vanished without a shadow.

Misaabe told the story of the giant native and the mantis in the faint lantern light of the cabin. The moths rebounded on the globe. The mongrels moaned over the stories, and we wondered if the tiny old healer, our teacher and best friend, was once the very native giant in his story. Misaabe might have been the giant who lost his shadow and returned to the reservation with his mongrel healers. The old healer, the mongrels, and the namesake boy rescued each other.

Odysseus arrived on the reservation that summer with a new song entitled "Unreconstructed Rebel" to tease the federal agent who had taunted him about the music of the American Civil War. When we heard the unmistakable voice of the trader we rushed out of the stable and tried to sing along but the words were not familiar.

> *Oh, I'm a good old Rebel*
> *Now that's just what I am*
> *For this "fair land of Freedom"*
> *I do not care a damn.*
> *I'm glad I fit against it*
> *I only wish we'd won.*
> *And I don't want no pardon*
> *For anything I've done.*

Odysseus told us later that the tricky lyrics of "Unreconstructed Rebel" were by Major Innes Randolph and published in *Collier's: The National Weekly*, a newsy magazine with humor, sensation, and fiction.

I hates the Constitution
This great Republic too
I hates the Freedmen's Buro
In uniforms of blue.
I hates the nasty eagle
With all his brag and fuss
But the lyin,' thievin' Yankees
I hates 'em wuss and wuss.

Foamy was the worst, the real *wuss*, a twitchy federal agent, and he never *fit* against anyone but natives and irony. He waited on the wooden walkway in front of the bank with the postmaster and our uncle Augustus. The federal agent hooked his skinny thumb over the watch chain on his vest and frowned in silence. Augustus shouted out the words with the trader, *I don't want no pardon for anything I've done*, and then applauded as the trader and his two horses ambled toward the livery stable.

Augustus bought a box of La Carolina Cuban cigars from the trader that Sunday at the Hotel Leecy. Odysseus had permission to show and trade his wares once a year in the lobby. The La Carolina cigars were special, hand rolled and expensive, and the engraved blue stamp guaranteed that the cigars were made in Cuba.

Augustus lighted a cigar.

Odysseus carried other brands that were made in the United States, but we learned later that the pricey La Carolina cigars were the very best. One cigar cost more than a dollar. We each earned thirty dollars a month at the livery stable, and with some meals, a very good salary on the reservation. One cigar would cost more than the pay for one day of work.

Father Aloysius bought a cheap box of Juan de Fuca cigars that were made by the Morgan Cigar Company in Tampa, Florida. The cigars were a present for another priest who visited the reservation in the summer. We thought the priests would smoke Idela or Belle of St. Cloud, cigars made in Saint Cloud, Minnesota. The Benedictine priests were from Saint John's Abbey, the nearby monastery.

Foamy dickered over a box of cheap cigars.

The trader also carried Perfecto Garcia cigars made in Tampa, Florida, and Happy Moment made by Winfrey and Parker in Tacoma, Washington. Camel cigarettes were popular at the time on the reservation. The advertisements promised a mild blend of Turkish and Virginia tobacco. Aloysius liked the image of the camel on the package, and he painted the camel blue when we arrived three years later in France.

Augustus secretly bought eight tiny bottles of French Pernod Fils. The absinthe had been banned as a poison three years earlier and was rare and expensive. Our uncle told us that absinthe was the glorious spirit of artists, but we could never afford the taste. The spirit was distilled and flavored with fennel, anise, flowers, and the wormwood plant. We never learned what was poisonous.

Odysseus had displayed absinthe spoons at the hotel for the past three years, including one spoon in the shape of the Eiffel Tower in Paris. The spoons were used to dissolve sugar cubes in the absinthe, and the spoons were a hint that the trader carried the forbidden spirit. Natives were scarcely the primary buyers of absinthe. The ritzy rituals of absinthe spoons and sugar cubes were not considered a manly drink on the reservation. Augustus, Doctor Mendor, the bank manager, and, we were told in confidence, one teacher at the government school bought absinthe from the trader every summer.

Foamy was not aware of the absinthe trade.

>>> <<<

Odysseus wore the blue raven wooden medal and surprised my brother that summer with a gift of rare native art. The trader presented two original paintings of blue horses. The paintings were bound in linen and carried in a leather telescope case. Yes, great blue horses in abstract flight across the plain art paper. The horses were outlines and painted with colored pencils. The native art was almost forty years old at the time. The native artists were political prisoners, and had never studied art or drawing. The blue horses were totems of native visionary artists.

Bear's Heart, the first native artist, was Cheyenne. He painted four colored horses, yellow, brown, green, and uneven blue. Each of the native riders wore a bright ceremonial headdress and carried the traditional shield of a warrior. The buoyant horses were in a row, colored horses and high riders, and with no horizon, perspective or landscape. The scene was visionary, a visual memory, and without the practiced technique of vanishing points.

Aloysius was moved by the blue horses.

Squint Eyes, the second native artist, was Cheyenne. He used colored pencils to paint four horses, brown, blue, green, and black. The two horses in the center of the painting were blue and green. The brown horse faced the viewer, and the black horse was turned away. The colored horses were in motion from the right to the left side of the paper, a natural direction in native perception and stories. The scene consisted of only four ceremonial riders and colored horses on plain drawing paper, nothing more, and that native manner of visionary art awaited the imitators and primitive modernists

Squint Eyes, Bear's Heart, Heap of Birds, Making Medicine, and more than sixty other natives were prisoners of the military at Fort Marion in Saint Augustine, Florida. Cheyenne, Kiowa, Arapaho, and Comanche warriors became visionary artists in prison. Fort Marion turned into the unintended native center of creative arts, a new academy of native visionary art.

Henry Benjamin Whipple, the Episcopal bishop of Minnesota, owned many paintings by natives at Fort Marion. He bought several drawing books from the prison artists, including "Drawings by 'Making Medicine,' Cheyenne Prisoner." Making Medicine, we learned later, had created an art book of seven paintings with many horses, red and blue, in a magical gallop above the earth.

Odysseus told my brother that Bishop Whipple wrote to President Ulysses S. Grant to praise the artists and to support the petition to release the natives from prison. Naturally, the trader remembered every story about the namesake president.

Odysseus surprised my brother once again when he ordered thirty raven peace pendants. He would pay one dollar for each pendant, and wanted a few done immediately and the rest delivered when he returned the next summer. The trader wore the medal of peace on the trail and many natives admired the blue raven. He would trade the pendants for ledger art and jewelry.

Aloysius carved medals of peace that summer.

The trader carried peyote for the doctor, and the transaction, as usual, was confidential. We never learned what was actually traded for peyote every summer at the Hotel Leecy. That night, however, the doctor and the trader wisely remained in the livery stable with their horses. Foamy had been told about the peyote ceremonies and he rode out with a posse of mounted native police to seize the mescal buttons and thwart the singers at Bad Boy Lake.

The peyote visionaries had vanished that night without a trace of breath, beat, or song. The moon was down, and the dancers rode north to the headwaters outside the federal treaty boundary of the reservation. Government commissioners, agents, reformers, priests, and churchy protectors were dead set against the use of peyote by natives, but the native ceremonies were not criminal. Foamy, though, would hound natives, the trader, and the doctor for any reason on the reservation.

8

SNOW EGGS
1915

John Leecy delivered formal invitations to Aloysius Hudon Beaulieu and
Basile Hudon Beaulieu, mere stable boys, to supper in the hotel dining room with Odysseus, Doctor Mendor, Catherine Heady, the federal
teacher, and our mighty uncle Augustus Hudon Beaulieu.

Aloysius painted blue ravens with the abstract faces of the dinner guests
that night. Naturally, the stories were timely, spirited, and ironic, and the
best stories on the reservation started with the absence of the federal agent.
Foamy was on a greyback mission with the native police to capture peyote
visionaries.

Foamy was mocked at the high table.

John Leecy poured a taster of the banned absinthe to honor the trader,
the secret bond of the boozers, and the absence of the agent. The spirit
was strong, and just enough for two salutes to ancestors and remembrance.
Aloysius watched the others and savored the scent of the spirit. We were
captivated by the conversations and stories that night at dinner.

The Green Fairy burned our tongues, but we pretended to be mature
drinkers. We were dinner guests at the high table with our employer, the
doctor, our favorite uncle, a severe teacher, and our friend the trader who
wore a medal of peace.

John Leecy served dinner in four courses, the best we had ever eaten.
We could never afford the cost of a formal dinner, but many times we ate
good food from the kitchen. Margaret Fairbanks was one of the most famous chefs in Minnesota. She was native, a distant relative, and learned
how to cook in the pricey resort hotels on the North Shore of Lake Superior. Messy was a reservation nickname because she was the messiest cook
in the state.

Messy delivered leftovers two or three nights a week at the livery stable. The hotel dining room was always crowded with hungry visitors from

around the world. Every week a few travelers on the train between Winnipeg and Minneapolis stayed over just for dinner at the Hotel Leecy.

The first course was *mandaaminaaboo*, native corn or hominy soup. Native corn is *mandaamin* and was grown by selected families in every generation to continue the tradition. The main course was fresh broiled walleye caught at Red Lake, *Gratin Dauphinois*, thinly sliced potatoes with cream, garlic, and cheese, mounds of mashed rutabaga with maple syrup and nuggets of wild garlic, wedges of cabbage with spears of carrots, radish, and chunky pepper, buttered turnips, peas, green onions, and wild rice blended with tidbits of salt pork, and mounds of freshly ground horseradish. The third course was a delicious Camembert and hard cheeses from the Marin French Cheese Company in California. Each course was served with wine. The last course was a choice of desserts, *Oeufs à la Neige*, Snow Eggs, made of meringue, vanilla custard, and caramel, and puffy warm doughnuts with powdered sugar and cinnamon. Every course was a complement of at least one good story and the start of another. We remembered every conversation and story that summer night at the Hotel Leecy.

John Leecy celebrated the great company.

Odysseus saluted his father Jefferson Young.

Catherine recited a short poem by Walt Whitman.

Augustus praised the absinthe and wine.

Doctor Mendor toasted the chef Messy.

Aloysius toasted his namesake the priest and saint.

Basile honored the mongrels and Misaabe.

My brother painted blue ravens on the napkins that night and then waited for the perfect moment, a pause in the courses and stories, to remind the company about the trader, the agent, and goober peas at the reservation hospital five years earlier, when we were only fifteen years old.

Odysseus laughed, leaned back and told the story about how he lured the suspicious and bumptious federal agent into a round of the song "Goober Peas." Confederate soldiers sang that southern ditty during the American Civil War. Foamy was uneasy in ordinary situations, and that night in the hospital he was easily duped to sing along. The trader raised his hands and sang in a loud voice, and the guests in the restaurant joined in at the end of the song,

Goodness, how delicious,
Eating goober peas!

The slight taste of absinthe was followed with fine wine, and then hard whiskey. The wine was from the Beaulieu Vineyards in Napa County, California. Father Aloysius served the very same red sacramental wine at services, and on other occasions with visitors and friends. Augustus had been invited many times to share the sacramental wine in the parsonage. The priest and our uncle seldom agreed on the mission of the church, but they freely poured the wine. There was always a good reason to gather over sacramental wine, but they drank many more bottles when they shared the same critical comments on the patronage and abuse of political power by the Episcopal Church on the White Earth Reservation.

John Leecy was worried about the economy, the lingering economic recessions, success of the railroad, and the cost of the First World War. Augustus drank more wine and waved those concerns aside. He declared loudly at the high table that the enemies of the economy and native civil liberties were the Protestants and the political patronage of the federal government on reservations. The more he drank the more intense he became about the new "federal fascists" of religion and the commissioners, agents, and government missions of the United States. Our uncle had real investments in land that he could not develop on the reservation because of restrictive federal policies.

The most memorable stories that night turned to the nostalgia of the old traders who brought exotic wares from distant and foreign worlds to barter on the reservation, and did so with humor and courage before the advent of patent inside newspapers, the telegraph, mail order catalogues, and the mighty railroads. Those marvelous stories lasted until the break of dawn.

Odysseus turned to the side and gestured with his chin and one hand in the direction of Santa Fe, New Mexico. His stories were told with gestures of an actual sense of place and presence, and natives trusted his stories for that reason. The trader traveled as a child with his father to western cities and visited pueblos and reservations in the fantastic Southwest. Jefferson taught his son how to ride, how to pack a bundle, pace his horses, sing on the trail, and how to show respect to natives and other traders.

Odysseus was a natural at the trade and was never deceptive about his wares. He could easily smile and tease his way around any tricky situation. As a boy he was on the trail most of the year with his father. Later they rode together as traders until his father died nine years ago on April 10, 1906.

Odysseus was a chosen son of the old traders, and they became his family, friends, and his best teachers. He was teased on the trail in the native way, as a gesture of favor and salutation. Odysseus told us that he had traveled as a trader in native communities for more than thirty years, and most of that time he shared the experiences and stories of the trade with his father.

Jefferson Young named his son in honor of President Ulysses S. Grant, and because he had read *The Odyssey* by Homer. Odysseus was the only boy of seven children. He was born at home in South Carolina. His tiny mother, Dovey Williams, and two of his sisters died during the influenza pandemic in 1889.

Jefferson introduced his son to the early traders who were active in Indian Territory, Omaha, Nebraska Territory, Santa Fe, Acoma Pueblo, New Mexico Territory, Arizona Territory, Navajo Reservation, South Dakota, Leech Lake, and the White Earth Reservation in Minnesota. Odysseus told many stories about the traders late that night in the Hotel Leecy.

Catherine was moved by the trade poetry.

Julius Meyer, for instance, established the Indian Wigwam in Omaha, Nebraska Territory, at the end of the American Civil War. Julius bought, sold, and traded native ledger art, curios, clothing, hides, cradleboards, peace pipes, quivers, tomahawks, and many other objects. He traveled most of the time to trade directly with natives. Julius learned several native languages, and that was an advantage for any trader. He served as an interpreter for General George Crook, and counted as his native friends Sitting Bull and Red Cloud. No doubt he survived among natives on the Great Plains because of his sense of irony.

Julius and three older brothers were Jewish immigrants and became distinguished merchants in frontier Omaha. The Meyer brothers were born in Bromberg, Prussia. Odysseus recounted that Julius traded with natives, and his brothers Max, Moritz, and Adolph sold cigars, gold jewelry, solid silverware, spectacles, penknives, guns, and many musical instruments.

The Meyer brothers established a great store in Omaha.

Odysseus described Julius the trader as a showman because he wore native clothes, a double dresser, and posed in paid photographs with eminent native leaders, such as Swift Bear and Spotted Tail. The Pawnee teased the fancy trader and gave him a native nickname that described his curly hair.

Julius, Jefferson, and Odysseus were invited more than once to native dog feasts on the Great Plains. The natives had learned to respect the curious dietary laws of the Jews and served boiled eggs to Julius. Jefferson teased the trader and the natives that the nickname for curly hair might better be related to boiled eggs.

Augustus raised his heavy glass of whiskey and declared in a loud voice, Let them eat deviled eggs. The doctor laughed, but the others at the table were silent about the nicknames. Our uncle explained later the intended irony. The French expression, "let them eat cake," should have been translated as "let them eat brioche," or bread that is light and sweet. Marie Antoinette never made that statement about hungry peasants, and the reference was more irony than contempt. So, we learned that night at the high table that the satire was in the trade stories of deviled eggs and brioche.

Julius was an energetic trader and sponsored a company of natives to attend the Paris *Exposition Universelle* in 1889. The natives lived and traveled for about a year in France. The trader had met the army scout and impresario William Frederick Cody, Buffalo Bill, several times in Nebraska Territory, but he had never seen the circus show of the Wild West until he attended the Paris Exposition.

Buffalo Bill, Julius, and the natives gathered that afternoon at the spectacular Eiffel Tower. They teased the stately attendant in uniform that the tower was an iron horse in the sky, but only the natives leaned back and smiled on the second level, the only level completed for the Exposition.

Odysseus collected paintings and ledger art by natives and especially the art by prisoners at Fort Marion. As a young trader he bought several paintings at the Indian Wigwam in Omaha. A decade later traders, galleries, and museums were in search of more native ledger art. Bishop Whipple bought several books of paintings, but since then native paintings had become valuable and rare. The artists were released from prison but not many continued painting.

Julius and the natives that he escorted to the Paris *Exposition Universelle* were invited by chance to visit an art gallery in the Luminous City. Nathan, the gallery owner, first met the natives at the Eiffel Tower, and then traveled with them to the reconstructed Bastille. Odysseus told stories about the curly haired trader and the natives as if he had attended the Exposition and gallery that summer. The Galerie Crémieux was the very first to market traditional and original native arts in Paris.

Nathan Crémieux owned the art gallery and had displayed native art for more than twenty years. Henri Crémieux, his father, and his uncle were traders on native pueblos and reservations in the Southwest and the Great Plains. Odysseus had actually met the father and uncle of the gallery owner several times at the Hubbell Trading Post in Ganado, Arizona.

Fine whiskey smoothed out the rocky details of conversations and stories that night after dinner. The candor and trail stories were entrusted to the old trader. Doctor Mendor was mostly silent that night, but never remote in his appreciation of trade stories. No one could easily escape his intense dark eyes. Catherine was caught in his gaze several times across the dinner table. Augustus was always candid, critical, instructive, and ready to comment on the tease and gist of ironic stories. John Leecy was reserved, and always the generous host of high table dinners.

Odysseus told the most stories and the others were generous listeners and drinkers. Leecy first served Wiser's, a fine rye whiskey distilled in Ontario, Canada. Much later he served Chivas Regal, an imported Scotch whisky, one of the best and most expensive in the world. Aloysius smiled and mocked the salutes, soughs, and husky murmurs over the taste of the aged mellow whiskey.

Odysseus related stories about Joseph Sondheimer, the trader in hides and furs. At the end of the Civil War the Jewish immigrant rode a white horse from Saint Louis to Muskogee in Indian Territory. He became a distinguished citizen of the territory and later the state. The natives and others voted to become the State of Sequoyah in 1905 but the petition was denied and two years later the new state became Oklahoma. Joseph bought deer, bear, beaver, otter, and other hides from natives and shipped them to markets in the east, and in Europe.

Odysseus and his father rode and traded in Indian Territory, the Southwest, and the Great Plains, and were never menaced by natives. The traders who learned to speak some native languages, who told stories with a sense of presence and irony, and who sang on the trail were not considered the enemy.

Jews were considered by natives to be the most honest traders on reservations. Joseph Sondheimer was respected for the fair prices he paid natives for hides, more than any other trader, and he even bought domestic animals that had died in bad weather. He was determined, reliable, and a trader with integrity.

Odysseus touched his nose as he told the hide story. I could smell the hide on that trader a mile away, and his house, horses, and family smelled the same, a sharp, sour stench that lingered on everything he touched and owned. We could smell the old trader in his story that night. Naturally, another sip of whiskey changed the scent and the story. Natives were more tolerant of the stench of dead animals and bundles of hides.

Solomon Bibo was a marvelous and eager trader in the New Mexico Territory. Jefferson and Odysseus visited Bibo and his native wife, Juana Valle, at Acoma Pueblo. The Jewish immigrant was born in Brakel, Prussia, and got his start as a trader with the generous support of Solomon Spiegelberg who was an established merchant in Santa Fe. Bibo was elected a Governor of Acoma Pueblo and named Don Solomono. Incredibly, he was the first outsider to be elected to the native government. Bibo, Juana and their children moved later to San Francisco, California. He ran a food store in the city. Odysseus and his father visited Don Solomono and Juana several times, and never tired of the wistful trade stories from the New Mexico Territory. The food store was destroyed in the earthquake of 1906.

Jefferson Young, one of the great traders in the history of the native west, died on the trail close by the Hubbell Trading Post in Arizona Territory. Odysseus told us that night that his father died in the early morning on April 18, 1906, the very same day as the earthquake in San Francisco. He buried his father in the desert, and then returned to grieve with his family in South Carolina.

Jefferson actually died in his sleep in the Palace Hotel in Santa Fe, New Mexico Territory. Odysseus truly honored his father with a creative and more memorable story of the desert and the Hubbell Trading Post. The trader told us later that his father suddenly could no longer ride long distances, so he boarded with his horses the Atchison, Topeka, and Santa Fe Railroad from Gallup to Lamy and Santa Fe. He died near his friends in Santa Fe.

Odysseus recounted his return to San Francisco four years after the death of his father to visit with the trader Don Solomono, and repeated the captivating scenes at the Christmas Eve concert with the coloratura soprano Luisa Tetrazzini. The old trader took another sip of whiskey and then sang a few lines from his favorite road song, "The Last Rose of Summer." Doctor Mendor and Catherine Heady were moved to tears by the mercy and memory and the music.

Odysseus leaned closer and promised that one day he would introduce us to Don Solomono and Juana. Suddenly, he turned back to the high table and continued his stories about Solomon, Levi, Elias, Emanuel, Lehman, and Willi Spiegelberg of Santa Fe, New Mexico Territory. Solomon was a Jewish immigrant and established a trade business, groceries and dry goods, near the Palace of the Governors in Santa Fe in 1846. A few years later his five brothers arrived to work in the store.

Jefferson and his son were treated as family, and always welcome at the store. Odysseus was touched by the memory of the time with his father. He told us about the spirit and generosity of Solomon Spiegelberg. During the Civil War the Confederate army actually occupied Santa Fe and seized thousands of dollars of merchandise from the family store. The Spiegelbergs at the same time rescued a slave girl who had been abused and wounded by the greyback soldiers. A month later the militia drove the Confederate soldiers out of New Mexico Territory, and the slave girl was emancipated and educated by the family.

Odysseus remembered his great father as a freedman by heart, sorrow, and ironic stories. South Carolina was a state of slavery at the time. Father and son were forever grateful to Solomon Spiegelberg for his compassion, protection, and charity.

Aloysius raised his hand and told the last story that early morning about our cousin John Clement Beaulieu and his friends who tried to out drink a mission priest. The Irish priest was a regular visitor to the reservation, and invited natives to drink for salvation and country. Whiskey inspired some priests to become instant theologians. The natives could never out drink the priest. He was the last standing at the end of the night.

So, John Clement and other natives conspired to under drink one night, tease the priest to over drink, and then bury the priest in a fresh grave at Saint Benedict's Catholic Cemetery. The priest actually toppled over drunk for the first time. The natives lowered the priest into the grave and waited nearby for the priest to awaken. At dawn the priest stuck his head out of the grave, looked around, and said, Bejesus this is resurrection morn and I'm the first to rise.

My story later that night was about the native who once again had lost his wooden leg. Pepper was a warrior in the American Civil War and wounded by cannon fire. He was held back from the direct combat areas because his loud sneezes attracted enemy fire. And even at a safe distance he became a target with a loud sneeze. As a boy on the reservation no one wanted to hunt with him because he scared the game away.

Pepper was seventeen, a short man, and even shorter when his left leg was shattered. The army surgeon immediately amputated the leg above the knee. He and the surgeon drank whiskey to kill the pain and dull the sound of the handsaw.

Pepper was given a straight wooden leg, but he always limped around and used a cane because he had hollowed out the leg, sealed the interior with a hot poker, filled the cavity with moonshine, and covered the hole with a wooden plug. The leg contained at least two large jars of drink.

The hollow limb was once again missing for several days, and then a friend found the leg in the crotch of a white pine tree. Several stories returned with his found leg. The one that lasted the longest was about the black bear who stole the leg, got drunk, and came back to steal the leg several more times. That was a much better story than the one about his woman who stole the leg at least once a week and drained the moonshine for a quiet night at the cabin.

Augustus praised my brother and his version of a family story, and my uncle praised me for another original version of the ironic native lost limb stories. Odysseus raised another glass of whiskey. Catherine was enchanted with the doctor who hardly spoke a word that night. Messy continued to laugh about my lost leg story, and shouted, True, too true. John Leecy told everyone that he was a lucky man to have so many good friends on the White Earth Reservation.

9

SHADOW DRAFT

— — — — — — 1918 — — — — — —

Augustus Hudon Beaulieu died on August 8, 1917. The news hurt my heart, but memories of his tease and confidence would last forever. He was praised for his integrity, humor, and for his dedication to native rights and liberty. Our favorite uncle was honored by hundreds of friends and thousands of readers of his newspapers on the reservation and around the state. There could have been more than a hundred reverent pallbearers that summer day at his funeral.

Augustus decried in the *Progress* and later in the *Tomahawk* the General Allotment Act that divided the treaty reservation into individual barren cuts and parcels of land. He encouraged natives to be inventive, progressive, productive, but not for the government or as the mere assimilation of native stories and culture.

"Gus H. Beaulieu Dies at Barrows."

"The call was sudden and occurred at 3 o'clock P.M. on Wednesday, August 8th," the *Tomahawk* reported eight days later on the front page. Augustus was living in Barrows, Minnesota, near the "extinct village of Old Crow Wing." Clement Hudon Beaulieu, his father, once lived there before the treaty that established the White Earth Reservation and "had long been the agent in charge of the fur trading business conducted by the American Fur Company."

On the "day of his death he and his wife and son decided to spend the afternoon fishing. Shortly after luncheon they embarked in their car and drove to a lake on the west side of the Mississippi River where as a boy he had fished often." The road was rough near the lake, "so the three disembarked a few paces from the waters edge and proceeded on foot to the shore." Augustus "had a fishing rod in one hand and a can of bait in the other, suddenly he fell forward at full length and crashed to the ground." Ella and Chester rushed to his side and tried to "revive him from a faint, for as he fell they thought he had simply stumbled." The cause of death was apoplexy, and the doctor "expressed the opinion that life had flown before the body reached the ground." The *Tomahawk* concluded that the loss of Augustus is "distinct and great to this community and to all the Chippewas of Minnesota."

Aloysius placed a blue raven medal in the coffin.

The body of our uncle was returned to his residence on the reservation, and then moved to Saint Columba's Episcopal Church for an informal service. Augustus was a member of the Catholic Church, but his brother Clement Hudon Beaulieu, the younger, was an ordained minister in the Episcopal Church. Augustus was honored in death by the two great religions on the reservation. Episcopalians and his brother, however, never mentioned the critical stories of churchy power on the reservation. Father Aloysius conducted the actual interment rites at Saint Benedict's Catholic Cemetery.

The *Tomahawk* continued to publish newspapers once a week with a new editorial writer. The character of the "editorials will in the future be as nearly alike to those of the past," wrote the editor, Clement Hudon Beaulieu, on the front page, August 23, 1917. "The *Tomahawk* now makes an appeal to all Chippewas and progressive Indians everywhere, to place supporting hands under its arms as it fights for rights both tribal and racial."

"Gladly in memory of a departed loved brother, he contributes his services as editorial writer, and with this fraternal memorial goes also affection and sympathy for his people."

Augustus, Odysseus, and Misaabe encouraged me to become a writer, but in separate and distinctive ways. The trader was precise and directed me to create stories with a sense of presence that teased and healed by adventure, luck, and irony. My uncle published some of my stories and visitor notes on the back pages of the *Tomahawk*. Wisely, he never printed my name as the author, although at the time his decision seemed punitive. Augustus did not want me to be the critical focus of newspaper stories about natives on the reservation, and my name never appeared in the *Tomahawk*.

Misaabe told stories and created shadows that converted the obvious and changed the world. The scenes in his stories resided forever in my imagination, and his marvelous presence was in every flash and faint flicker of light, and in every explosion during the war at night in France.

The sudden death of my uncle last year had obliged me to write more directly about Augustus, Odysseus, Misaabe, the *Tomahawk*, the government school, federal agent, and my family on the White Earth Reservation. Augustus told stories with precise rage, and concise irony, and he would never accept more than casual regret for the dead, and he would conspire from the grave to overturn romantic notions of eternal memory. He told me, and my brother, when we painted the newspaper building that life was not a liturgy. He always encouraged us to confront the obvious and create stories by natural reason.

Odysseus told me to create native scenes in six books inspired by the memories of my uncle, by his eternal tease, by his stories, and, of course, by his great sense of integrity and irony. The trader convinced me that great stories were best recounted in sixteen scenes. He meant, of course, the twenty-four books or sections of *The Odyssey*. Augustus traveled with me in memories and in many stories, and he must have favored me with a native tease to survive the First World War.

>>> <<<

William Hole in the Day was the first native of the White Earth Reservation to become a sailor and then later a soldier in the military. He enlisted in two distinct branches of the armed forces, in two countries, and waged his name in three separate wars. He served as an honorable warrior on land and at sea, and with a great sense of adventure, humor, and bravery.

William was our distant cousin, and much older by experience, blood, and stories. He participated in the annual celebrations on the reservation, and we remembered him as a fancy dresser in a dark suit coat, wing collar, necktie, and fedora.

Private Hole in the Day first served in the United States Navy in the Spanish American War. He had paddled on Lake Itasca and Bad Medicine Lake but had never seen the sea. He returned to the reservation in uniform and with incredible stories of other cultures and countries that we would read about in the *Tomahawk*.

Augustus and others were surprised to learn that Hole in the Day had enlisted in the North Dakota National Guard and served on the border with Mexico. Minnesota and North Dakota guard units had been activated during the Mexican Revolution. The *Tomahawk* reported at the time that General John Pershing commanded the Eighth Cavalry Regiment in search of the revolutionary Pancho Villa who had boldly crossed the border and raided citizens of Columbus, New Mexico.

Hole in the Day never explained why he crossed the state border and enlisted in the North Dakota National Guard. Augustus was convinced that our cousin would never march with the Minnesota National Guard because the unit had joined forces with federal soldiers to attack his relatives and other natives at Sugar Point near Bear Island on the Leech Lake Reservation in 1898.

The Minnesota National Guard sent one company of mostly young farm boys and recent immigrants to fight against the liberty of natives. The Third Infantry Regiment of the regular army and National Guard soldiers raided the vegetable garden and cabin of Bugonaygeshig, or Hole in the Day, an eminent warrior and spiritual healer, and stole sacred medicine bundles and eagle feathers as war booty. William, our cousin, was the nephew of the great Bugonaygeshig.

President Woodrow Wilson at first ventured to preserve the peace and neutrality of the United States in the First World War. He posed as a moralist, and seesawed between the politics of militarism and the denunciation of war. Augustus had mocked the slogans of the war pacifists, and examined statements by the socialist Eugene Debs, "I have no country to fight for; my country is the earth; I am a citizen of the world." Our uncle consented to the earth as a country, and to natives as world citizens, but he shouted that only a vagrant would not fight for his country, and natives have fought for centuries to be citizens of the earth, the reservation, and of the country. Augustus declared that the president was a milksop and could not understand the forces of evil in the world. Some readers were surprised that his actual editorial comments published in the newspaper were more reasoned and particular.

The *Tomahawk* published an editorial, for instance, on the front page, April 12, 1917, about the declaration of war. "The Democratic campaign early last year was 'He kept us out of war,' but since the election President Wilson has had such a strong pressure brought to bear upon him that he finally used his influence to secure a declaration of war by Congress."

President Wilson finally moralized the cause of the war and condemned the evil Germans. Later, on April 6, 1917, Congress declared war with Germany. General John Pershing was named the commander of the American Expeditionary Forces in France.

Hole in the Day was eager to serve two countries. He was a warrior at heart and could not wait for the United States to enter the war. So, by political omission our cousin enlisted at once in the Canadian Expeditionary Forces and served as a private in the Ontario Regiment in France.

Private Hole in the Day was a distinguished native warrior in Canada and the United States. Sadly he was wounded, poisoned by mustard gas near Passchendaele in West Flanders, Belgium. He was a fancy dresser and world adventurer, and he died at the Canadian General Hospital in Montreal, Canada, on June 4, 1919.

Ellanora Beaulieu, our cousin, enlisted as a nurse and served in the American Army of Occupation in Germany. Theodore Hudon Beaulieu, her father, was the spirited editor of the *Progress*, the first newspaper published on the White Earth Reservation. Ellanora served as a nurse for only about five months and then she died in the influenza epidemic. She was buried on the reservation in the Episcopal Calvary Cemetery.

Aloysius had carved a blue raven medal for our cousin, but at the end of the war we were in Paris, France. We placed the pendant on her gravestone when we returned to the reservation. Ellanora was four years older, a loyal cousin who respected our secrets, ambitions, and always appreciated my native stories and the original blue raven art of my brother.

Private Charles Beaupré was killed in action at Saint-Quentin, France, on October 8, 1918, on the very same day that our closest cousin, Ignatius Vizenor, died nearby in Montbréhain. Charles was trained in the American Tank Corps and served with the British Expeditionary Forces.

Private Ignatius Vizenor was the son of Michael Vizenor and Angeline Cogger. Ignatius was trained at Camp Dodge, Iowa, and Camp Sevier, South Carolina, before he boarded a troop ship on May 16, 1918, for duty in France. Hole in the Day and Ignatius were always dressed to the nines on the reservation. They wore suit coats, smart shirts, ties, and fedoras. Aloysius honored them with blue raven medals.

Private Fred Casebeer, son of Joseph Casebeer, was drafted on March 30, 1918, and trained at Camp Dodge, Iowa, and at Camp Mills, New York. He was wounded in combat and died the same day on September 30, 1918, in France.

Becker County selected more than twelve hundred soldiers out of some four thousand who were registered for the draft under the Selective Service Act of 1917. Sixty native soldiers were drafted from the eastern part of White Earth Reservation. The soldiers were sent to more than thirty camps around the country, and most of the soldiers were trained with units of the National Guard from various states, and those units became the first divisions of the American Expeditionary Forces.

Becker County lost more than fifty soldiers in the First World War, and five of the war dead, four soldiers, Charles Beaupré, Ignatius Vizenor, William Hole in the Day, Fred Casebeer, and one nurse, Ellanora Beaulieu, were natives from the same community on the White Earth Reservation.

Father William Doyle, the Trench Priest, died in the Battle of Ypres on the very same day as our uncle Augustus. The priest was the chaplain for the Eighth Royal Irish Fusiliers and served soldiers in the trenches. He was killed ten years after his ordination while he brought spiritual comfort to the wounded. The saints in the trenches were anointed by chance in military uniforms.

Odysseus arrived that early summer with Calypso and Bayard on the Soo Line Railroad at the Ogema Station. The trader and his loyal horses were old and weary of the noise and risks of the trade routes. Some of the old trails were fenced, or had become highways crowded with motor cars and machines, and crossed by railroad tracks.

Calypso followed the wagon road from the train station to the livery stable at the Hotel Leecy. We heard the hearty voice of the trader at a distance as he rounded the mission pond. The tone of his voice was heartfelt, and melancholy, as he sang the chorus of "Over There" by George Cohan. The music was appropriate for the serious mood of the reservation, the war, and selective service.

Over there, over there,
Send the word, send the word over there
That the Yanks are coming, the Yanks are coming. . . .
We'll be over, we're coming over,
And we won't come back till it's over, over there.

Aloysius had carved thirty blue raven medals for the trader, and we carried ten medals into combat in France. Odysseus secured his wares in the stable, and then surprised us both with two perfect presents. The trader gave me a Hammer Brand Elephant Toe pocketknife with a red pick bone handle. Aloysius was given the same knife with an amber pick bone handle. Naturally, my brother would carve blue raven medals with his knife, but the trader stressed that we should use the knives as weapons in close combat. Our conversations that summer were dominated by the war.

The Sears Roebuck Military Equipment Catalogue was distributed early that year in time for the war. We ordered two olive drab wool sweaters with no sleeves for $13.50 each, and a chamois money belt for 65 cents. The catalogue was for officers, but no one checked our rank before the order was shipped to the Ogema Train Station. The prices were rather expensive even though we earned a good wage at the Hotel Leecy. Hats, uniforms, collar ornaments, canvas and leather puttees, holsters, waterproof match-boxes, and hundreds of military wares were illustrated on twenty pages of the catalogue. We were amazed that anyone with the money could easily order a Colt Machine Gun for $865.00, and for $16.50 a Colt Automatic Pistol. Naturally, that machine gun came to mind many times in combat with the Germans.

John Clement Beaulieu and his younger brother Paul Hudon Beaulieu, our cousins, were among the first to register for the draft early in the year. We registered at the same time with our cousins and many friends, Lawrence Vizenor, Ignatius Vizenor, George Jackson, Everett Fairbanks, John Roy, John Razor, Louis Swan, Patch Zhimaaganish, and others. Ignatius and his brother Lawrence were activated on February 25, 1918, and sent to Camp Dodge, Iowa, and then for more infantry training at Camp Sevier, South Carolina. They were in fierce combat a few months later in France.

Reservation natives were listed on the Registration Card as "natural born" at White Earth, Minnesota. Height, marital status, color of eyes and hair, and occupation were noted on the card, and most natives were listed as "laborers." There was no designation for reservation or natives. The government decided there was no reason to record race, but the class category of laborers was necessary. So, we may not have been considered citizens of the country because we lived on a federal reservation, but our distinct culture was apparently not relevant on the Registration Card for the Selective Service Act in Becker County.

The *Tomahawk* published a letter about native citizens and the draft by

Lieutenant Colonel Hugh Johnson of the War Department on August 30, 1917, a few weeks after the death of our uncle Augustus. "Tribal Indians, that is Indians living as members of a tribe, are not citizens, and are not covered by the provisions" of the Selective Service Act. "The Indians should be advised of this, and that they can present the claim of exemption prepared for aliens, as they are to be considered such for the purpose of this act."

No native "aliens" prepared an exemption, or at least no native boasted the claim of exemption from the draft on the White Earth Reservation. Younger natives were ready for the adventure of combat, not for a passive alien exemption of service in the Great War in France.

The federal government decided, after a wrangle between the War Department, eager wardens, unbearable protectors, guardians, federal agents, and progressives, that natives should serve as regular soldiers and not in segregated military units. Augustus would have railed at the post office, at the bank, over dinner with friends at the Hotel Leecy, and in the *Tomahawk* against the very idea that natives would be separated from other soldiers.

Black soldiers were segregated in special military units and were mostly deployed behind the battle lines in support units. In spite of the obvious prejudice and segregation black soldiers demonstrated their loyalty and proved their bravery in every combat situation. No soldier who had ever fought in the same combat areas as the Harlem Hellfighters, otherwise named the Fifteenth New York National Guard Regiment, would ever doubt that the soldiers were spirited, strong, and brave warriors. The regiment was awarded the Legion of Merit by the War Department. The French presented the Croix de Guerre to the Harlem Hellfighters.

Aloysius could not convince the draft board that he was a native artist not a laborer. We were both designated as laborers, mere stable boys. My brother painted a blue raven and in the talons the word "artist" was boldly printed on a Registration Card.

10

GAS ATTACK

—————— 1918 ——————

Augustus arrived at the livery stable one early morning last spring, a few months before his death, to talk about the war. He was aware that we had registered for the draft, and several cousins had already been mustered for service. Our uncle was worried that so many young native men, and mostly our relatives in one generation, would be at risk of death and serious wounds in the war.

Augustus might not have appreciated the adventures of war that we two imagined at the time. Our uncle was eighteen years old at the end of the American Civil War and had never forgotten how the nation was ravaged by savagery and lasting misery. The war ended just three years before the federal treaty that established the White Earth Reservation in 1868.

Sadly, our favorite uncle died before we went to war, and before the creation of my first stories. That quiet morning in the stable he promised to publish in the *Tomahawk* the stories of my experiences as a soldier, and to designate a weekly section in the newspaper for my war stories. Augustus had already created a new series headline, *French Returns* by Basile Hudon Beaulieu. A heady moment, of course, but my uncle insisted at the time that my stories must be written with a first and second person voice, and contain some historical information and descriptive scenes of soldiers and combat, and with the horror, humor, and irony of war.

That glorious promise by my uncle was the start of a native literary presence and lingered in the moist air that spring morning, and stayed with me, and the saddles, straw bales, and cobwebs on the windows. The horses were silent, and seemed to wait for my response. My brother turned and answered for me, "Basile will create war stories." I came to my senses and told my uncle that my stories would never be written with an omniscient point of view.

Augustus considered monotheistic creation an ironic story, at best, and argued that critical view many times with Father Aloysius. The two were good friends, and the discussions between a priest and an editor with strong ideas were always lively, especially over a bottle of sacramental wine. I was present several times when the subject of monotheism was "resurrected," as my uncle exclaimed, only to provoke the necessary examination of polytheism, churchy liturgy, and original native stories and literature. Augustus declared that monotheism spawned the farcical notion of omniscient points of view by authors, and without any sense of irony. Tricky shamans, my uncle told the priest, were more clever healers than disciples, scripture, and omniscient authors because shamans devised the practice of irony to overturn separatism and singular stories of creation. Even a dunce could imagine stories with more chance and wriggle than an omniscient author with no sense of irony.

Clement Hudon Beaulieu had not been told about the promise his brother had made to publish my stories in the *Tomahawk*, and he worried as the new editor about the financial success of the weekly newspaper. A few months later, just before we were activated for military service, he revised that golden promise and agreed only to publish my stories about the war as a separate newsprint pamphlet, but not in the *Tomahawk*. The change of the promise bothered me, of course, but the decision was practical and actually a protection. My stories would be complicated to compose on the patent pages, and should the newspaper be discontinued after more than twenty years of publication on the reservation, my stories would continue to be published as a pamphlet. My stories would be set in type, printed and folded on a single sheet of newsprint, and circulated on the reservation as a series. So, the newsprint pamphlets of my original stories were published, and my family continued to print the series for many years after the war and the termination of the *Tomahawk*. The *French Returns* stories were always free on the reservation and remained in my name.

I started my series of stories the minute the train departed from the Ogema Station. The war for every soldier starts at a train station, and our war started one balmy morning that summer. Aloysius painted a scene of several soldiers with the wings of blue ravens, and later he gave a blue raven medal to Patch Zhimaaganish. John Razor, Robert, Allan, and Romain Fairbanks, Louis Swan, and Johnson King had been mustered and were on the train to war. The mighty engine surged and steam shrouded the platform.

Patch Zhimaaganish, our good friend, saluted the station agent and was the last person to board the train. Patch, the soldier, who had been hired as a real assistant station clerk a few months before he was drafted, wore a smart new uniform ordered from the Sears Roebuck Military Equipment Catalogue. Patch waved to his mother, and we waved to our family and friends on the platform, adieu, au revoir, goodbye. Aloysius turned away with a wistful smile. We were native brothers by heart and honor on our way to war.

The Soo Line Railroad made the usual stops at Callaway, Detroit Lakes, Alexandria, and soldiers boarded at every station on the line. We had boarded the very same train nine years earlier, our first adventure outside the reservation. Aloysius remembered similar scenes on our first journey to Minneapolis.

Augustus had encouraged us to discover the world, and he paid our train fare, and had reserved a hotel in the city. We visited the great public library, the West Hotel, the Nicollet Hotel, and the Orpheum Theatre. Aloysius was inspired by the *Woman in the Garden*, a painting by Yamada Baske. The Japanese artist was an instructor at the Minneapolis School of Fine Arts.

Late that afternoon the train arrived at the Milwaukee Road Depot in Minneapolis. We walked two blocks to the Great Northern Depot on the Mississippi River with hundreds of other soldiers and boarded the Oriental Limited for Chicago. The exotic train crossed the Stone Arch Bridge, roared through the countryside, and my melancholy face was reflected on the window that night between the stations.

Soldiers boarded at every town on the route, and the train arrived the next day in Chicago. The houses in the city had been built with white pine from the White Earth Reservation. Our reservation was never the same, and most of the houses were in need of paint. We waited for more than six hours at the crowded station and then boarded the Norfolk Southern Railroad for Spartanburg, South Carolina.

Camp Wadsworth, a new divisional cantonment, one of many recent military training sites in the country, was located about three miles from Spartanburg. The city was overrun with soldiers on their way to war. The camp was in the foothills of the mountains south of Asheville, and west of Charlotte, North Carolina. We arrived late at night, tired, hungry, and forlorn. Hundreds of other soldiers had just completed their training and were departing for war from the station at the same time. More than thirty thousand soldiers were at the camp in various stages of combat training.

The First Pioneer Infantry was constituted that early summer at Camp Wadsworth. Soldiers who were hunters and had experience in nature and woodcraft were selected to serve in advanced combat infantry units to clear and construct roads. Most reservation natives were hunters and lived closer to nature than soldiers from the city.

Aloysius was associated with art, the abstract images of art, but he was not a heavy hunter or timber cutter. I was considered a writer, and that was true, but never by the separation of nature. So, the officers encouraged me to teach illiterate soldiers how to read and write. Some soldiers thought that was a racial contradiction, that a backward reservation native would teach others how to write. My brother worried at the time about the absolute selection of soldiers for road construction in combat.

Later, however, we were nominated for even more dangerous duty as scouts in several combat battalions and regiments. The native artist and writer were chosen to infiltrate enemy positions at night and gather strategic information. Patch was selected to play the bugle and sing with the Regimental Band. Robert Fairbanks and Louis Swan were selected and trained for combat construction in the First Pioneer Infantry.

Aloysius was elated the next morning when he saw the Blue Ridge Mountains. The trees had created a blue haze, and the scene was an inspiration of natural art. He carried a small notebook and drew blue ravens over the haze of mighty trees. Catawba natives, we learned later, had hunted in the nearby mountains, but the only natives we met at the training camp were soldiers from Minnesota, Wisconsin, and New York.

The soldiers were inoculated, examined by a doctor, and the next day ordered to complete an army intelligence test. No one had ever heard of a brain or mental test. The scores were not revealed to the soldiers, so we created smart scores as a tease. My practice of reading the *Tomahawk* and memorizing a few paragraphs to hawk the newspaper at the train station must have increased the score of my intelligence. There was nothing on the test about natural reason, the seasons, horses, plovers, peyote, mongrels that detected diseases, or ironic stories. Surely native artists and descendants of the crane totem and the fur trade were smarter than federal agents and the reservation police.

Reveille was at six in the morning, and after our first assembly, mess, and fatigue detail we reported to the quartermaster for new uniforms, wool shirts, trousers, brogans, canvas leggings, and other equipment. The shirts, shoes, and trousers of hundreds of soldiers were sized by eye. The sergeant who sized us was a tailor from New York. He never made a mistake. We were truly restyled as soldiers in campaign hats with blue cords. Naturally, the color of the hat cord was notable. By seven in the morning some soldiers reported to the stables, others to fatigue duty. We had experience with horses but that would not matter in the schedule of fatigue duty, company drills, and combat training. We were there to be trained as infantry trench soldiers, not to ride horses. Once we were issued our equipment, canteens, mess kits, canvas backpacks, first aid packet, wool blankets, ponchos, identity tags, and practiced to march in a military manner, it was time for dinner.

Ten soldiers lived in a pyramid tent with a wooden floor and partial sidewalls. There were thousands of tents pitched in perfect rows, a city of canvas pyramids. Aloysius was assigned a bunk directly across from mine. John Razor was near the entrance, and the other natives from the reservation were in nearby tents. The bunks were metal and covered with a thin mattress. We lived and trained for weeks with strangers from other states.

Springfield bolt-action rifles were issued to every new trench soldier, and rigorous combat training started on the third day. First we were instructed to fight with bayonets, throw hand grenades, and fire mortars. The start of our training was not much of a challenge, but later it became more intense. The officers had ordered extended exercises for a few days in preparation for a twenty-six mile march to the rifle range at Glassy Peak Mountain.

Aloysius fired ten times and every round hit the center of the target. John Razor and Robert Fairbanks were singled out along with my brother as marksmen in the first round of shooters on the rifle range. There were about sixty targets at fifty yards, and the shooting lasted most of the day. My ears were ringing. We camped overnight in the area, and then continued training for three more days in the elaborate trenches.

Senior officers had studied the strategies of trench combat in France and returned to construct a series of similar trenches at the camp. There were eight miles of trenches, eight to ten feet deep, and several grand bunkers that were more than thirty feet deep. We simulated combat with the enemy in the front line trenches, and then moved back to the reserve trenches. Grimly, we were ordered to practice "over the top" assaults through tangled barbed wire. Every soldier realized at the time that "over the top" of the trench in the face of the enemy was certain death, an absurd military suicide. The simulated maneuvers were executed at night, and with sudden feigned mustard gas attacks. The officers calculated that a real gas attack would have lingered over the trenches. Our sergeant shouted that mustard gas stinks just like the name, mustard and horseradish. The training with gas masks that night was terrifying but very effective. Several soldiers in various sections of the trenches were assigned to sound the alarm, beat a bell, or rattle a chain of cans at the first trace of poison gas.

The French officers who were appointed to train us in trench combat denied that their country ever used gas, and condemned the evil Hun, Boche, or Germans. Gas warfare was worldwide, even the warhorses and dogs wore gas masks. The French officers were courteous, but with a firm hand instructed the soldiers how to survive in trench combat. The British officers were haughty, rather detached, and not effective combat instructors. The British were mocked every night when we returned to the reserve trenches. The arrogant poses and manners were so easy to imitate.

A thunderstorm and heavy waves of rain flooded the trenches on the second night, and there was no escape. The water washed out ammunition niches and huge rocks on the trench walls. We waded for hours in the muck and carried out our military duties of map and compass reading. We were trained to direct artillery fire against the enemy. There in the rain, stuck in the mud, we read out loud from a wet War Department manual on how to use a compass. Suddenly, between bolts of lightning the officers ordered another feigned gas attack, a perfect time to test the readiness of soldiers. We adjusted our wet masks and continued the compass course.

The lightning and thunder were spontaneous simulations of war. Place and direction in a war were more than a native gesture or sense of presence in a story. Yet, the azimuth of a compass and the map contours of the earth would never surpass the subtle turns of hand, head, eye, or lip in native stories.

The Vanderbilt Road was under construction, and the train service was unreliable, so we walked the three miles with hundreds of other soldiers along the railroad track to Spartanburg. The streets were lined with soldiers, and every store was crowded with buyers no matter the merchandise. The hotels were overrun, of course, and the social center could not accommodate the number of soldiers in town over the weekend.

Aloysius, Robert Fairbanks, John Razor, Louis Swan, and Patch Zhimaaganish, a native contingent from the reservation, joined me in a grocery store to buy food for an improvised picnic. The shelves were almost bare, but we managed to buy cheese, apples, hardboiled eggs, crackers, Ginger Ale, and Hershey's Kisses.

Rock Creek Park was crowded with soldiers, but we found a grassy area to eat our lunch. Naturally our stories started with the recent trench experiences, and then easily turned to relatives on the reservation.

Aloysius drew blue ravens at the picnic, and with claws of Hershey's Kisses. Louis Swan was fast asleep on the grass. John Razor told a story about a distant relative who had lost a leg in the American Civil War. Patch talked about his grandfather who lost a leg in the same war, and recounted his many duties as the assistant agent at the Ogema Station. He was nostalgic about the days we hawked papers at the station, and was forever grateful to my brother for the gift of blue ravens. Robert Fairbanks was quiet, lonesome, and mused on memories of his lover on the reservation. We teased him back to humor with erotic stories about our very distant lusty relatives, the women of France.

Odysseus came to mind because the grocery store had sold every box of Post Toasties. The trader never traveled without several sealed boxes of his favorite cereal, an emergency gourmet meal with Eagle Brand Sweetened Condensed milk. He laughed and told the same story over every bowl of Post Toasties about the pious pastors who had objected to the original name of the cereal, Elijah's Manna. The first time we ate cereal with him was during his recuperation at the White Earth Hospital. Later we shared his cereal at the livery stable. John Leecy made sure the hotel dining room served Post Toasties, and with fresh cream, when Odysseus arrived for the summer. Aloysius was convinced that the trader fed his horses Elijah's Manna and later Post Toasties.

Patch remembered the songs and humor of the trader, but he was never around for the stories in the livery stable because he worked every day at the Ogema Station. Patch leaned back against a sycamore tree and with the cicadas sang the "The Last Rose of Summer" in memory of the trader.

The soldiers and citizens in the park were moved by the baritone voice and melancholy music.

> *When true hearts lie withered,*
> *And fond ones are flown,*
> *Oh! Who would inhabit,*
> *This bleak world alone?*

The DuPre Book Store advertised in *Gas Attack*, the camp magazine, that the store was the largest in South Carolina. Yes, it was large and one of the few sanctuaries that summer weekend in Spartanburg. We were the only soldiers in the store, and it was the only place we actually met ordinary citizens. The owner was courteous, of course, but he studied our features, and some of the customers seemed to be wary of soldiers from Camp Wadsworth. Really, how would the owner and customers know that we were natives from the White Earth Reservation? Most of the natives in the area had been murdered or driven west to Indian Territory. Our skin was not dark enough to be segregated, and color was always a cruel measure of civilization. The bookstore, no doubt, was the southern heart of the townie civilization.

>>> <<<

I found a copy of *The Odyssey* by Homer, a translation by the novelist Samuel Butler in 1888. Odysseus gave a leather-bound copy to me with a special dedication that was too special and precious to take to war. I had decided to read at least one or two chapters, or books, each week in training and service in France.

My literature of native memories and endurance in the war became *The Odyssey*, and the first chapter of my visionary journey started that very night before taps in the camp. *Tell me, O muse, of that ingenious hero who travelled far and wide after he had sacked the famous town of Troy. Many cities did he visit, and many were the nations with whose manners and customs he was acquainted; moreover he suffered much by seas while trying to save his own life and bring his men safely home; but do what he might he could not save his men, for they perished through their own sheer folly.*

Samuel Butler surmised that a woman created *The Odyssey*, and that the scenes were situated near the coast of Sicily. I was not aware of this at the time, and later the controversial theory made the adventure stories much more captivating. Odysseus would have been astounded that *The Odyssey* might have been the adventure stories of a woman.

〉〉〉 〈〈〈

The Liberty Theater at the camp scheduled regular vaudeville shows, and other entertainment. We heard many versions of the stories about the woman who danced nude one night on stage. The theater was packed for several weeks, but there never was a repeat performance. Mostly the vaudeville shows, the dancers and singers, were not very talented.

The YMCA, Jewish Welfare Board, and the Knights of Columbus provided activities and programs for the soldiers, such as letter writing, singing, and games. Patch was a great baritone singer and joined a choir of soldiers.

Frank Moran, the prominent boxer and movie actor, was at the camp that summer to teach soldiers how to box. His "Mary Ann," a powerful right-hand punch, was famous, but he lost a fight with Jack Johnson for the Heavyweight Championship of the World. Frank took an interest in my brother and me and taught us how to fight in the ring. He was a huge man, but he respected our size and energy, and he was fond of natives. He admired our courage that we were soldiers and not yet citizens. Aloysius was a natural, a great dancer in the boxing ring. Frank was certain that my brother could shadow dance his way to a prize.

The Camp Wadsworth mascot pageant and parade was an incredible military spectacle. Soldiers presented and paraded their pets down the main street of the camp. The mascots were not trained for exhibitions, of course, so the parade was mostly devoted to a tug of war with donkeys, dogs, cats, raccoons, snakes, and many fancy chickens. Only a parrot seemed to have experience in parades. The first prize was for the homeliest or most unattractive mascot in the camp, the second prize was for the cleverest, the third for the most attractive, and the last prize for the most handsome mascot. An old donkey won the first prize, a six-toed cat the second, a Blue Hen third, and with irony the last prize went to a blotchy mongrel. The soldiers told fantastic animal stories about every creature in the parade. We actually felt at home that afternoon.

Everyone in the camp had heard the steady story about the gullible soldier from New York City who had purchased a shiny opossum as a mascot. Naturally he placed his expensive gold watch in the pouch of the marsupial for safekeeping, and, as the story goes, the opossum ran away with a valuable timepiece. Aloysius laughed the first time he heard the story, and then he continued with the anecdote that the soldier had to buy his precious watch back from a pawnshop in Spartanburg.

The *Gas Attack* was a weekly magazine published by soldiers at Camp Wadsworth. Former news reporters, artists, cartoonists, and fiction writers contributed to the magazine. "Dere Mable" was a series of fictional letters by the dimwit Private Bill to his dopey girlfriend Mable. And another regular series was "Private Ethelburt Jackbelly," an absurd aristocrat who complained about every event and experience at the camp. Aloysius was asked to contribute art to the magazine, but he declined because he would never create caricatures or cartoons of soldiers.

Private Charles Divine, the associate editor, invited me to write one of the letters for "Dere Mable," but the stereotypes and steady stupidity of the letters were never my style of stories. The editor accused me of arrogance, no sense of esprit de corps, and would not consider any of my proposed stories for the magazine. My stories would have created a sense of presence not an absence, not mere caricature or mimicry. A few weeks at the camp was hardly enough time to worry about an invitation to write a fictional letter in the name of the simpleton Private Bill.

At the time, the most recent issue of *Gas Attack* published "A Soldier's Letter to His Sweetheart," by Private Bill. "Dere Mable," the letter started, "It takes a woman, Mable, to get things all balled up. I aint agoin to say much about this though cause the joke was mostly on you. I forgive you and I wont hold nothing against you. You can tell your father and mother right away sos they wont worry any more. I hope they wont blame you too much for makin all this trouble. An that it kasnt thrown off your fathers liver. Hes bad enough already.

"So now when the wars over we can get married again just like we was goin to. Ill have more time then. I guess thats all I will have but we don't need much money cause I dont care much for luxuries anyways. Simple, thats me all over, Mable. . . .

"Theyve put me on the special detail. The special detail, Mable, is a bunch of fellos what knows more than any one else in the camp. I sit on a hill all day with a little telephone in a lunch box and take messages. They got an awful system of sending messages in the artillery. . . .

"Its awful dangerous work cause where I sit aint more than half a mile from the shells. If they ever put a curve on one of them its good night Willie. I aint scared of course. I just mentioned it sos you wouldnt worry. Ill tell you more about the telephone next time. I may know more about it then myself.

"Yours till they curve one, Bill."

11

SAÂCY-SUR-MARNE
1918

The *Mount Vernon* cut through the haze and slight crests of waves that early morning, a camouflaged troopship on course near the west coast of Brittany. The gray decks were wet and cold, and the sunrise was muted in thin clouds. My heart beat faster when noisy sea gulls circled the four giant stacks and landed on the bow of the ship.

I could not sleep that night and was out early to catch the first sight of the country of our distant ancestors, the fur traders. The war provided the curious notion of a magical return and at the same time a discovery. Actually the native romance of the fur trade and agonies of war was a revelation of the heart not the irony of discovery.

Nearby four sailors were at close watch on the bow for any sign of submarines. Soldiers were enticed by a cash reward to watch for submarines. One soldier mistook a huge log for a periscope and was teased with a single dollar purse. The bands and curves of white and black camouflage were not enough to disguise the ship, not even in the sea haze.

The Germans had attacked hundreds of tankers and troopships, and some with elaborate camouflage. Enemy torpedoes sank the *Lusitania*, *Gulflight*, *President Lincoln*, *Covington*, *Nebraskan*, *Aztec*, and many, many others. The ship named *Tippecanoe* was torpedoed and sank a month earlier near the port of Brest in Brittany. A sailor boasted that since the war the *Mount Vernon* had safely sailed twelve times to Brest, France.

Aloysius teased that my early morning watch had more to do with the fear of submarines than the sunrise. The tease may have been accurate, the open deck was more secure than the hold, and there was no better place to read the second book of *The Odyssey* than on deck at dawn as the massive steamship silently cruised closer to the war and the mystique of France. *Now when the child of morning, rosy-fingered Dawn, appeared, Telemachus rose and dressed himself. He bound his sandals on to his comely feet, girded*

his sword about his shoulder, and left his room looking like an immortal god.
He at once sent the criers round to call the people to assemble. . . . As the sail
bellied out with the wind, the ship flew through the deep blue water, and the
foam hissed against her bows as she sped onward. . . . Thus, then, the ship
sped on her way through the watches of the night from dark till dawn.

Later the sun burst out of the clouds, and then turned faint, again and
again, bright and muted, as the *Mount Vernon* approached the rocky granite coastline of Brittany. Hundreds of soldiers rushed to the deck for the first
sight of land. The pale seasick soldiers raised their arms and threw kisses
ashore. One soldier shouted on deck that he would rather walk the frozen
Bering Strait than cross the Atlantic Ocean. The captain steered the great
ship slowly into the huge bay of Rade de Brest.

Aloysius painted a huge blue raven on the navy dock as the ship was
guided to the Penfeld River and Le Port Militaire. A trace of red stained
one feather of the raven. Moored wooden boats with red sails moved with
the waves. Fishermen waved, sailors waved, soldiers waved, and war was a
faraway scene.

The soldiers shouldered their packs and rifles and marched down the
gangway to France. More than three thousand soldiers had disembarked
that morning and assembled in separate military units on the dock.

Brest was once a seventeenth-century walled city. Le Château, an ancient castle, overlooked the bay. The navy dock was bordered with railroad
tracks and massive warehouses. Four French soldiers, dressed in distinctive
blue uniforms, had arrived to guard the ship. As our unit turned in columns
and prepared to march toward the center of the city, ambulances and other
military vehicles drove slowly down the dock and parked near the gangway
of the ship.

The *Mount Vernon* and other troopships delivered newly trained soldiers
and then immediately returned with the casualties, the badly wounded in
the war. Suddenly the wave of red sails and excitement of our arrival had
ended, and every soldier on the dock stared in silence at the wounded. The
medical vehicles were loaded with wounded soldiers, hundreds of desolate
soldiers with heads, hands, and faces bound in bloody bandages. Many of
the soldiers had lost arms and legs. Aloysius was moved to tears and turned
away to draw blue ravens in waves of torment.

This was not the war that we had imagined that summer in the livery stable with our uncle Augustus. This was a war provoked by an empire demon, more sinister than an ice monster, and the enemy of natural reason, and not by native visionaries, our sturdy ancestors, fur traders, or by the French. I could hear in the distance the great baritone voice of Patch Zhimaaganish. He sang the chorus of "When This Lousy War Is Over," a song he had learned in the choir of privates at Camp Wadsworth, South Carolina.

> *When this lousy war is over,*
> *No more soldiering for me,*
> *When I get my civvy clothes on*
> *Oh how happy I shall be.*

A wounded soldier on the gangway turned and raised his last arm and shouted out the last line, "Oh how happy I shall be." The new soldiers on the dock saluted the wounded and cheered, and later on the soldiers on the long march toward the city sang a popular song about home, honor, and camaraderie.

> *Goodbye Broadway, Hello France,*
> *We're ten million strong,*
> *Goodbye sweethearts wives and mothers,*
> *It won't be long.*

A German submarine torpedoed the *Mount Vernon* early in the morning a week later on September 5, 1918, at sea, west of Brest. The troopship carried only wounded soldiers on the return voyage. The periscope of a submarine was sighted and sailors dropped depth charges, but the torpedo exploded amidships killing more than thirty members of the crew. The *Mount Vernon* and three destroyers returned slowly to the port at Brest. The wounded soldiers boarded the *Agamemnon* and returned safely to the United States.

Brest was a remote hilly city overcrowded by soldiers, but the people, mostly women, children, and old men, were cordial and grateful for the presence of the American Expeditionary Forces. The children waited for coins, any coins, the young women smiled and wore bright flowers, the old women wore black, and the tired old men gestured with a hand or eyebrow and leaned on stone walls.

The soldiers marched smartly past Le Théâtre, Gare de Brest, and

over the Pont de Recouvrance. Brest was located on the right bank of the
Penfeld River. The soldiers continued a performance march with military
cadence on narrow curved streets for four miles past Saint-Sauveur in Recouvrance, the oldest parish church, and the Maison de la Fontaine, the
oldest house in Brest. I learned about the names and places from a French
language booklet issued at Camp Wadsworth.

Finally in a light rain we arrived at the Pontanezen Barracks, a camp the
military had built for soldiers to rest for a few days before combat assignments. No one dared to mention the wounded soldiers on the dock. The
food was good, and the stories of women and wine were overstated and
celebrated by the hour, and with every name and place mispronounced in
French.

> *Mademoiselle from Armentières,*
> *She hasn't been kissed for forty years.*
> *Hinky dinky parlez-vous.*

Four days later we boarded open boxcars and toured for two long days
the beautiful late summer countryside. The boxcars were noisy, unsteady,
and designated for forty soldiers and eight horses. For the comfort of the
soldiers the number was reduced and we traveled without horses. The
drafty wooden floors were covered with straw. The boxcars were open and
the slow train meandered near small farms and through quaint villages and
circled the city of Paris. The Eiffel Tower was visible in the distance.

The train arrived late that night near La Ferté-sous-Jouarre, a commune
on the Marne River between the cities of Meaux and Château-Thierry.
Paris was only about thirty miles to the west near the Marne River. We
could have floated in peace by the light of the stars almost to the great city.
The Germans had destroyed the train stations and bridges, so the soldiers
marched to nearby Gare Nanteuil-Saâcy and Saâcy-sur-Marne.

The night sky was decorated with the explosion of rockets, and the thunder of enemy artillery beat in my chest. The war was close at hand, an unnatural and spectacular scene, and the soldiers were hushed and hesitant
that night near the river.

The Marne River flowed in silence, an ancient course and motion
through the cruel memories of many wars. The shoreline was bruised with
battens and memories of the dead. The glance of rockets shivered on the

dark water, and revealed the steady flow of leaves, broken trees, and human debris from the nearby war upriver near the city of Château-Thierry.

The soldiers were shadows near the shore of the river, only the slight glow of cigarettes lingered after the blaze and distant thunder of artillery. That night the war was a curious spectacle of sound and distant light. Not yet a real war, not yet the silent ruins of merciless rage. The rubble of the nearby train station was only a tease of the war disease that decimated so many ancestral cities, communes, and family farms in France.

The night sky was a constant mystery, solace on a strange road, the star traces of memories and stories, and that one night on the way to war was an exceptional consolation of a poetic canopy.

The Germans waited with a vengeance for the new maneuvers of unseasoned soldiers, the rush and break down, and yet the enemy worried more about native warriors. They were unnerved by stories of native stealth, capture, torture, and about being scalped at night in the trenches.

The war was close, a long walk away. Just a walk away, the same distance as Bad Boy Lake from the Hotel Leecy on the White Earth Reservation. My uniform was clean, my heart steady, but the river revealed by scent and shadow the scraps and detritus of war. The Marne River reflected that night the actual horror of combat.

I leaned back on the riverbank, but could not sleep. I could not even close my eyes for more than a minute. Every sight was new, an exotic and treacherous tableau, and every visionary scene was heightened by sounds, by the constant motion of insects, by artillery, the moist reach of the earth, and by my recent visual memories.

The wounded were on ships at sea, and the dead soldiers, pieces of young bodies, shattered bones, were buried in the earth, some by tillage of mince and morsel, and others by name and poignant commissions at military ceremonies. The larger human remains were tagged by religious order, covered and stacked on trucks. The earth would return once more to mustard and sugar beets, and rivers would carry forever the bloody scent of these ancient scenes of war out to the sea.

Aloysius was beside me on the riverbank, but we never spoke a word that night. He told me later the next day that he had created by visual scenes of memory and imagination the many stories told by our friend Odysseus about the American Civil War.

12

CHÂTEAU-THIERRY
1918

Aloysius told the sergeant that early morning that he was a native artist in a union of three armies, the sum of three times his military service. The sergeant heard only the precious word "artist" and ordered my brother to latrine duty, to carve a crapper pit in the thicket near the river. Later we learned to be more incidental and never to linger for any reason over a hole in the earth. No soldier was ever at ease once he heard the stories about enemy snipers and strategic bowel movements.

The American Expeditionary Forces was actually a union of three armies in combat with the enemy in France. The Germans probably never made that same distinction, other than the forces of the British, French, and Americans.

The United States Regular Army, National Guard units from various states, and the National Army of volunteer and conscript soldiers were the union of three armies. The Regular Army was already in service and National Guard soldiers were activated as soon as war was declared with Germany. Drafted soldiers of the National Army were assigned to both the Regular Army and to train with various divisions of the activated National Guard for service in France.

Private Ignatius Vizenor, our cousin, was drafted and assigned to train with the Thirtieth Division of the activated National Guard in North Carolina, South Carolina, and Tennessee. The division was trained for infantry combat that summer at Camp Sevier, South Carolina, a few weeks before we arrived at the nearby Camp Wadsworth in the National Army. Corporal Lawrence Vizenor was drafted at the same time as his brother and assigned to train with the Thirty-Third Division of the Illinois National Guard.

The designation of military units mustered for service in the war was complicated, and we never fully understood why brothers, and our cousins, were drafted at the very same time and assigned to separate units. I was lucky to be assigned to the same military unit with my brother. We trained and served together in combat, and we experienced the same miseries and stories of the war.

Ignatius Vizenor completed training and was assigned to serve with the British Expeditionary Forces in combat near Saint-Quentin and Mont-bréhain, France. Lawrence Vizenor was decorated for his service in the Battle of the Argonne Forest. Patch Zhimaaganish, John Razor, Louis Swan, Robert Fairbanks, and many of our relatives were never more than fifty miles away from each other during the war, but the distance was as great as life and death. The only thing we each had in common as soldiers was our combat heartache and hatred of the Germans.

More than fifty natives were drafted from Becker County and the White Earth Reservation. Most natives served in combat infantry units. Only a few natives were assigned to serve in the same training and combat units, and others were selected for special military duty. William Heisler, for instance, was assigned to the Medical Corps. Romain Fairbanks was assigned to a Gas Regiment. Frederick Broker served as Blacksmith First Class. Several natives were drafted to serve in the Spruce Production Division in Oregon, Washington, and in France. Natives, of course, had real experiences in forests on reservations, and that was mostly watching the forests disappear in two generations. More than ten thousand soldiers cut and processed spruce trees for the war. Sitka spruce was light, strong, and durable to build military airplanes.

During the civil war with natives thousands of white pine trees were cut on the White Earth Reservation and used to build houses in Chicago, not airplanes or boxcars for the First World War. Federal agents and timber companies were eager to cut down ancient trees for new houses in cities but not to build houses for native families on reservations. Natives and reservations were the means to an end in timber and in war.

The First Pioneer Infantry was ordered to wait another few days on the banks of the Marne River. French *camions*, or trucks, were not available to transport the new soldiers to combat positions near the trenches at the front. The rumor spread that every truck was loaded with rations for the hungry horses. Actually the narrow roads were impassable, rutted, muddy, and crowded with horses, wagons, ambulances, artillery, and military equipment. Only two mess trucks arrived that afternoon with food for three companies of soldiers.

The army chaplain took advantage of the delay to baptize scared soldiers on their way to war. Seventeen infantry soldiers were converted overnight and baptized the next afternoon in the Marne River. The military congregation of saintly soldiers on the riverbank shouted out new christened nicknames, Angel Eye, Porky, Banjo, Stinky, Glance, Chief, Trigger, and nine more ironic names. Chief was a native from a southern dirt farm who found religion and a family in the army. *Bless us in body and in soul, and make us a blessing to our comrades*, the new converts chanted as they stood in the steady stream of the war-stained Marne River.

Aloysius painted four blue ravens that afternoon on the shore of the river, reclined, wings expanded with a touch of rouge on the flight feathers, and blue heads of seventeen soldiers afloat. We heard the artillery of the war, but the truth of a military stance and bloody sacrifice was far away. I leaned against a tree and read book three of *The Odyssey. But as the sun was rising from the fair sea into the firmament of heaven to shed light on mortals and immortals, they reached Pylos the city of Neleus. Now the people of Pylos were gathered on the sea shore to offer sacrifice of black bulls to Neptune lord of the Earthquake. There were nine guilds with five hundred men in each, and there were nine bulls to each guild. As they were eating the inward meats and burning the thigh bones in the name of Neptune, Telemachus and his crew arrived, furled their sails, brought their ship to anchor, and went ashore.*

The Germans had been slowly driven back, day by day, across the river, and the casualties were enormous. The Marne salient was a major allied military operation. More soldiers died in one hour of combat than the total number of natives who ever lived on the White Earth Reservation.

French cities and communes were decimated by heavy enemy artillery. We only heard the thunder and military rumors, nothing secure, and even the most reliable information that summer was promptly overstated, and some rumors were wholly outrageous. Mata Hari, for instance, was never executed as a spy and carried on as an exotic dancer for the generals. The Christmas truce was not a few carols with the enemy but a trench disease. French soldiers were in mutiny over the cooties in their blue uniforms.

Yet, rumors to a soldier were necessary, the very sources of comedy and ingenuity. Rumors were communal, shareable, ironic, and otherwise caretaker conversations in the extreme situations of war and peace. The most obvious contradictions and distortions of fact were hardly significant or even remembered by soldiers who waited for the creative solace of new rumors.

Rumors on reservations were strategies.

The First Pioneer Infantry moved in waves of regiments by train and truck to the war. The first wave of infantry soldiers were trucked to the Marne Valley, and then the regiments marched to Cierges, Ronchères, and Goussancourt between Château-Thierry and Reims. Construction soldiers mined quarry rocks and packed and repaired the ruined roads in the area.

The Germans had bombed Saint-Quentin in the Somme Valley with huge high explosive artillery shells at an incredible distance, some seventy miles. The enemy early in the war then advanced on the British and French soldiers on farms and forests near the Aisne River.

Major General John Pershing was the commander of the American Expeditionary Forces in France. He gave the very first order to enter the war and defend Château-Thierry. The French and American soldiers routed the enemy from the city and from nearby Bois-de-Belleau and the Marne River Valley. The allied casualties were severe and weighty. Gruesome shrapnel wounds, shattered and mashed faces, severed legs, and seared flesh. The war continued without mercy or mushy memory. We were in the last wave of the First Pioneer Infantry and arrived a month later to carry out the assault against the fortified positions of the Germans.

Marshal Ferdinand Foch was the Supreme Commander of the Allied Armies, the British, French, and Americans. He was a fancy officer, a stipulator, a mystery to most soldiers, and we heard rumors about the willful word wars between Pershing and Foch. General Pershing honored military traditions and the integrity of distinctive regiments and divisions, and he was determined to protect every American soldier from arbitrary assignments and the sacrifice strategy of fill in soldiers with units commanded by the French.

The First Pioneer Infantry was fully engaged in the last major offensives of the war, the Second Battle of the Marne, the Battle of Soissons, and the great battles in the Argonne Forest and the Meuse River. The German army three months later, and after four years of destruction, was driven out of France. The Kaiser, the ice monster of war, was defeated, disgraced, and to survive the wrath of citizens the German emperor ran away to another country. I created original stories about the ice monster, an obvious relative of the ice woman in the native stories of the Anishinaabe.

Wars changed familiar native stories.

The French Berliet trucks arrived at the encampment on the Marne River, and, much to the surprise of the soldiers, most of the drivers were Annamese and Chinese from colonial France. This was a war for hire, and a cynical turn of domestic fortunes in the colonies. American soldiers were the passengers at risk with colonial drivers, and we were paid in francs not dollars. I was never sure if the poor peasants and the displaced citizens of war that we met on the road would rather earn dollars or francs for their eggs, cheese, bread, wine, and favors.

The Berliet trucks parked in a perfect row on the road near the river that morning, and soldiers were assigned by platoons to specific trucks. The canvas covers had been removed, and the ride in light rain on hard rubber tires was hardly more comfortable than the boxcars on the train from Brest.

The Chinese drivers started the trucks one by one, a deceptive clank and jangle of a mighty army, and slowly drove across the bridge near Saâcy-sur-Marne. The Germans had bombed the bridge over the Marne River at Château-Thierry. The ruins of churches, farms, and entire communes became a common sight as the trucks moved in a column on the narrow roads west to Villiers-Saint-Denis and Château-Thierry.

The soldiers leaned in silence as the trucks bounced through the communes in the Marne River Valley. The train station was damaged but still standing in Château-Thierry. German artillery had exploded the roofs, collapsed the walls of houses and apartments, and cracked louvers exposed the private scenes of the heart, bedrooms, closets, kitchens, furniture, and abandoned laundry on a rack. A carved interior door was cocked on a single hinge, a stiff gray towel covered a wooden chair, broken crockery, and the legacy of lace curtains set sail for liberty. Familiar shadows were disfigured at a primary school, and children searched for the seams of memory. The scent of ancient dust lingered forever in the favors of the country.

Aloysius painted blue ravens perched on apartment buildings with wide wings spread over the collapsed walls. The gaze of the ravens was fierce. The points of the blue flight feathers were touched with rouge. Remarkably, my brother used black for the first time in his paintings, a thin vein of black on the mane of the ravens. He bounced in the back of a truck and painted mighty blue ravens in the eternal heart of Château-Thierry.

Churches, hotels, storefronts, and warehouses were in ruins, but the narrow streets of the city had been cleared of dead horses, bloated bodies, and war debris for the passage of weary soldiers, horses, cannon wagons, water carts, commanders in motor cars, trucks of food and ammunition. There were more American Ford ambulances on the road than motor cars on the entire White Earth Reservation and northern Minnesota.

The few citizens who had remained in the city waved to the soldiers and some shouted *Vive l'Amérique*. The soldiers cheered and shouted back *Vive la France* to the citizens. The soldiers were heartened by the salutes and the courage of the survivors, and enraged at the same time by the sinister motives of a grabby empire, the demons and ice monsters of destruction.

The Boche burned libraries and museums, wrecked cathedrals, universities, and hospitals, a degenerate act of soldiery entertainment with no military strategy. Notre-Dame de Reims was bombarded and burned overnight. The angels wounded, saints disfigured, and molten lead oozed out of the stone gargoyles.

That slow journey on the back of trucks through the wreck of many communes in the river valley transformed the new soldiers of conscription and adventure into fierce warriors, or at least some of the soldiers were visionary warriors.

The convoy of trucks turned north and later that day delivered several hundred soldiers to the final destination at Fère-en-Tardenois, a commune located between Château-Thierry and Fismes in Picardy. The Rainbow Division and other allied soldiers had driven the enemy across the Vesle River only a few days earlier, and inherited by wary conquest the havoc, wounded soldiers stacked on ambulances and trucks, shattered trees, the reek of dead humans and horses, and the pockmarked earth. The dead had been collected, piece by bloody piece from the ruins, a grotesque heap of body parts, the last ghastly gesture of a military muster. The First Pioneer Infantry soldiers camped in the light rain at Forêt de Nesles near the fortified positions of the Germans.

Aloysius was haunted by the nearby death of more than six thousand soldiers of the Rainbow Division only a few days before we had arrived by truck. The Rainbow Division was a union of soldiers from more than twenty

state National Guard units, Iowa, Wisconsin, Illinois, and many more, truly
a rainbow of volunteer soldiers. Later we learned that one of the casualties
was the romantic poet Joyce Kilmer, a sergeant in the Rainbow Division.
He was a poet of the war and a scout assigned to risky reconnaissance missions. Kilmer had turned down a commission as an officer and remained an
enlisted volunteer in the war.

> *I think that I shall never see*
> *A poem lovely as a tree.*

Joyce Kilmer was shot in the head by a sniper on the Meurcy Farm near
the commune of Seringes-et-Nesles. The French honored him in death
with the Croix de Guerre. Kilmer probably wrote about a white oak near
his home in New Brunswick, New Jersey, but my brother decided that a
blue raven medal carved from any of the trees in the nearby forest would
rightly honor the poet.

Sergeant Kilmer was buried in Oise-Aisne American Cemetery near
Fère-en-Tardenois. "Rouge Bouquet," the poem that Kilmer wrote to
honor the death of some twenty other brave soldiers in the Rainbow Division, was read at his own memorial service.

> *For Death came flying through the air*
> *And stopped his flight at the dugout stair,*
> *Touched his prey and left them there,*
> *Clay to clay. . . .*
> *There is on earth no worthier grave*
> *To hold the bodies of the brave*
> *Than this place of pain and pride*
> *Where they nobly fought and nobly died.*

The Rainbow Division pursued the withered enemy with courage, resolute vengeance, and the sorrow of a terrible sacrifice. The Germans turned
the forests and countryside into a wasteland, and killed hundreds of thousands of civilians and allied soldiers. Private Phillip Plaster from Oskaloosa,
Iowa, died at age seventeen in a bombardment near the Marne River in
Champagne. He was the youngest soldier in the infantry regiment. Private Arnold Wright carried a French officer to a first aid station and was
wounded by an artillery explosion and died in hospital near Châlons-sur-

Marne. Private Victor Frist from Villisca, Iowa, died from severe facial wounds at Croix Rouge Farm near Château-Thierry. Private Elmer Bruce from Joplin, Missouri, survived combat in Château-Thierry and the River Marne in Champagne and then drowned in a swimming accident in the Marne River near Saint Aulde.

First Lieutenant Merle McCunn from Shenandoah, Iowa, was badly wounded in Forêt-de-Fère and died in a field hospital. He had served eleven years in the Iowa National Guard, including service on the Mexican Border. Private Charles Hudson, who was born in Waterloo, Iowa, was the first soldier in his infantry company to die in Château-Thierry. Corporal Pierce Flowers from Coin, Iowa, was on patrol and died in machine gun fire near Sergy. Private Howard Elliot, from Wilmette, Illinois, was killed by machine gun fire in Château-Thierry. Private Eddie Conrad Momb from Rorchert, Minnesota, died from mustard gas at Château-Thierry. Private Charles Bordeau from Frazee, Minnesota, near the White Earth Reservation, died in action at Château-Thierry.

Sergeant Oliver Wendell Holmes from Council Bluffs, Iowa, died in a bombardment near the Ourcq River. The sergeant was the namesake of Oliver Wendell Holmes, the medical doctor and author of the famous poem "Old Ironsides." The poem was written when the navy announced a scheme to scrap the *Constitution*, a celebrated warship, but the wooden frigate was saved by a poem.

> *Oh, better that her shattered hulk*
> *Should sink beneath the wave;*
> *Her thunders shook the mighty deep,*
> *And there should be her grave;*
> *Nail to the mast her holy flag,*
> *Set every threadbare sail,*
> *And give her to the God of storms,*
> *The lightning and the gale!*

Corporal Thomas Evens from Glenwood, Iowa, was wounded and died near Château-Thierry. An explosion severed his leg as he connected telephone wires near the front lines. Sergeant Harry Hart from Oskaloosa, Iowa, died at twenty years old, the youngest sergeant in his regiment, in combat near the Ourcq River. Corporal Paul Dixon from Mystic, Iowa, died in combat at Château-Thierry. Private Frank Keech from Otsego, Michigan, died in combat at Château-Thierry. Private Charles Cunningham from Dyersville, Iowa, a litter bearer, was wounded in an artillery explosion and died in an evacuation hospital near several soldiers he had rescued earlier in the day.

Second Lieutenant Christopher Timothy, from Chattanooga, Tennessee, was wounded by machine gun fire and died near the Ourcq River. Enemy bullets punctured his lung, and when he was evacuated by ambulance he told the driver, "Tell Tommy to tell the folks goodbye, tell them I died an honorable death. I died fighting."

German soldiers were heavily entrenched on the other side of the Forêt-de-Nesles. They waited with machine guns, mortars, bayonets, mustard gas, deathly fear, and the fury of revenge. Allied and enemy artillery flashed and thundered through the night, a heavy bombardment on both sides of the forest and the front.

>>> <<<

Aloysius carved blue raven medals that night from chunks of wood shattered by artillery explosions. The Elephant Toe knife he used was a present from Odysseus a few months earlier, just before we were mustered into the infantry. The trader told us to attack the enemy at night with our knives, but naturally my brother would rather carve totemic blue ravens for the soldiers than search for the enemy with a pocketknife. The blue raven pendants created a sense of peace, and that touch of rouge on the ravens reminded me of the red crown of the totemic sandhill crane.

The sandhill crane was our native visionary totem.

We had pitched our tent on a secure slope of the forest very close to other soldiers. No lights were allowed, not even cigarettes under a poncho that dreary night of rain, thunder, lightning, and the roar of artillery. The steady rain spattered on the tents, and ticked on metal materiel. The tick, tick, tick sound was an annoyance, and a menace. A soldier nearby had left a mess kit outside his tent to be washed by the rain.

Raindrops shivered with artillery explosions.

My brother carved in the dark by touch and memory, and we told hushed stories about our friend Odysseus. The trader was always with us in memories and stories.

Suddenly Sergeant Sorek pushed his wet helmet and head into our tent and ordered us to report immediately to the command post for our first mission as native scouts.

The reverie of our stories ended on a rainy night.

There was no courtly initiation of scouts, and certainly not for native scouts. Our first night of stealth and surveillance in the rain was solemn but only conceivable in a shaman story. No other scouts were ordered that night to penetrate enemy lines on the east side of Forêt-de-Nesles and to gather critical information on machine gun emplacements, fortifications, or capture one or more enemy soldiers for interrogation.

That night was a decisive moment, and not the only one, when we could have raised questions about the order, but any expression of doubt would have demonstrated unacceptable fear and cowardice for a soldier, and especially a native soldier. We were selected only as natives, and not because of any special training.

Sergeant Sorek was not romantic but he was convinced that stealth was in our blood, a native trait and natural sense of direction even on a dark and rainy night in a strange place, otherwise we would have been breaking quarry rocks for road construction. The choice of risky missions over breaking rocks for roads could not be reversed for any reason.

The only real doubt we might have expressed that night was about the absurdity of a late night capture and protect strategy in the rain, but instead we saluted and accepted our first mission. Natives were selected as scouts more than other soldiers because of romantic sentiments, and, of course, because the missions very were risky. Later the sergeant talked fast in the dark and dank command post, and he provided only minimal information about possible enemy positions on the other side of the forest.

So, we sauntered into the forest with only the security of an absolute cover of darkness and roar of artillery. At first not even the leaves near my nose were visible. The sense of sight, though, was not only by light. Misaabe told stories about a hunter who could sense the presence of animals by the faint puff and waft of breath, and by the glint and spirit of blood, bone, and the distinctive scent and stink of bodies.

The Boche soldiers were wild, demonic, but not animals with a natural sense of presence. No shine or cast of spirit was sensible that night in the forest of the enemy. Actually, we could smell the enemy even in the steady rain.

Aloysius crouched and moved slowly ahead of me through the forest with his rifle close to his chest, and in only a few minutes of concentration we could sense the presence of the trees, but not yet the brush and branches. We wore soft hats to avoid the sound of rain on helmets. Remarkably, we could sense the spirit of trees, but not by the ordinary light of sight. Misaabe once described what we see as more than the perception of the light. The eyes sensed the blue spirit and glint of life. I should have asked the old healer then if he could sense a dead body or the enemy.

Aloysius moved with wariness in the forest. He paused every few minutes to listen and to change the pattern of his hesitant pace. We tried to imitate the natural motion of the rain, and there was a great silence in the forest between artillery explosions.

I could hear the beat of my heart. Our presence in the hilly forest was not noticed for several hours. Past midnight the rain and bombardment ended, and we were distracted by an inscrutable silence in the forest. Creatures moved, or we imagined motion, and the only other sound was the turn of heavy leaves and late dash of rain on the earth.

I sensed the presence of someone by the hush of insects, and hunched my shoulders like a praying mantis to listen and imagine the faint sounds. I opened my Elephant Toe pocketknife and prepared to attack and wound the enemy. We were aware that only a frightened and untrained soldier would shoot into the night. The flash and sound of his weapon would only reveal his position, and bring about certain death. The more we moved in the forest the more we were determined to capture an enemy soldier that night, and that act alone would confirm our courage and instinct as native scouts.

Aloysius groaned and whispered my name. His body leaned to the right and collapsed in the brush. I turned, raised my rifle and was directly disarmed by a soldier with his bayonet at my throat. The enemy spoke softly in an unfamiliar language, but not German. Later, we were surprised when the enemy soldiers talked to each other in perfect English.

The soldiers who had captured us were on a similar mission to capture the enemy for interrogation. The gestures and whispers of the soldiers were familiar, but we could not distinguish faces or features in the dark. The soldier who had disarmed my brother was angular and strong. The other soldier who easily grounded me was smaller, a wrestler who pushed my face into the musty earth.

The soldiers we thought were the enemy had muzzled and bound my brother and me. The soldiers were convinced that we were disguised enemy agents, and marched us back toward the allied military encampment. A short time later in the faint morning light we discovered that the captors and captives were natives. By some incredible coincidence the two teams of native scouts that night were in the same section of Forêt-de-Nesles.

Naturally, we were shied and humiliated as captives, but we were not amazed to realize that we had been outmaneuvered by two of the best native scouts in the infantry. Natives must be naturals at stealth, who else would have the instinct to imagine the scent of blood and capture other native scouts?

Aloysius was right, we could not return to our companies without at least one enemy soldier. So, as a team of four native scouts we turned around and moved quickly through the forest to the enemy positions.

The Rainbow Division scouts were more experienced so we learned stealthy strategies from the native shamans of the decimated forests. The new strategy was to capture as many enemy soldiers as we could that night, but at least one for each team of scouts. We were obliged to impress our sergeant.

Strut, the huge angular native scout, was Oneida from Green Bay, Wisconsin. Hunch, the wrestler, was Oneida from New York, one of the first five nations of the Iroquois Confederacy. Oneida was the first language we heard whispered that night, and then English. Hunch had served in a National Guard regiment that became part of the great Rainbow Division in the American Expeditionary Forces.

Hunch suggested that we choose a likely natural pathway in the forest close to the enemy and camouflage ourselves nearby in the brush. Most of the trees had been shattered by artillery explosions and provided a strategic cover and unnatural concealment. The strategy was similar to the way natives once hunted animals, to enter the forest early in the morning and then fall asleep. The tension of the hunter was released, and when the hunter awakened he became part of a natural scene, not a breathy invasion of the surroundings.

Four native scouts waited about an hour that early morning for the enemy. I thought about the trader Odysseus, Misaabe, and the mongrel healers, and could not fall asleep. Luckily the enemy was not as perceptive as animals in the forest.

Three German soldiers entered the forest and followed the natural pathway. Two soldiers set their rifles aside, and lowered their trousers to defecate. The third soldier, the youngest, stood guard nearby but looked away.

Strut cracked a stick as the signal and we pounced on the soldiers. Two were already disarmed, and were easily subdued with their trousers around their ankles. The third soldier panicked and fired one shot in the air. Strut reached from behind the young soldier and cut his throat. The soldier gurgled on blood, stared at me with fear, and died in the wet broken brush. Quickly we covered the body, and marched the other two soldiers double time through the forest back to our military units.

Naturally, our sergeant was pleased that we had captured one enemy soldier, but the interrogation revealed nothing of value to our regiment. The soldier was a replacement without much knowledge of the defensive positions of the Germans.

Hunch was a storier and he would not hesitate to include in his repertoire of native stories the capture of two scouts from the White Earth Reservation. So, we anticipated his stories and recounted the reverse, that we had almost, yes, almost, captured two Oneida scouts from the Rainbow Division.

The Germans had been driven across the Vesle River and two months later out of France. So, our risky missions as native scouts were decreased and then hardly necessary. German soldiers were captured in the thousands, and many thousands more surrendered near the end of the war to the British, French, and Americans.

Strut and Hunch were at a reserve encampment when we met them for the last time at the end of the war. We were united by chance that afternoon at a Cootie Machine created by the Rainbow Division. The marvelous machine killed enemy body lice on our uniforms. We had survived the war, captured the cooties, and after a warm shower, the first in several weeks, we were restored, clean, and ready for the tease of stories that night at the mess tent.

Hunch told the story about Private Arthur Elm, an Oneida from Wisconsin, who served with a machine gun company in the mighty Red Arrow Division. Elm was wounded and survived the battle at Ronchères and Bois-de-Cierges east of Reims near Verdun. Elm and his machine gun team advanced to Juvigny in the deadly Oise-Aisne Offensive. Elm encountered three enemy soldiers with Red Cross armbands who were about to throw grenades, so he killed them with his bayonet.

The Red Arrow Division was bombarded and under direct enemy fire for two days and without food. Elm and another soldier volunteered to return to the supply depot and secure food for the company. They traveled under fire with a compass and map through the brush, craters, barbed wire, and bodies to a mobile supply depot behind the line of combat.

Elm secured a wagonload of beans and tomatoes and was about to leave for the front when he heard the sound of an artillery shell. He ducked in a trench for cover. The shell exploded on the wagon and killed the mule and two soldiers. Hunch gestured with his hands and shouted there were beans and tomatoes everywhere, in the trees, on helmets, and beans covered the supply trucks.

Hunch recounted the native story about the explosion, the shower of beans and tomatoes, as a comedy first and then the casualties as a tragedy. Chance was a distinct native story, the irony and comedy over the misery and tragedy. Not everyone, however, appreciated the manner and tease of native stories.

Private Elm and the other soldier observed boxes of food at the back of a supply truck. The Military Police guarded the truck, so he told the story about hungry soldiers at the front and the explosion, and asked for a couple of boxes of prunes. The request was refused, and at that very minute there was the sound of another round of artillery shells. The Military Police took cover in a bunker.

Elm and the other soldier stole two boxes of prunes and ran toward the trees. They retraced the route but could not locate their company, so they shared the food with another hungry unit near the front. The captain recommended the two soldiers for a medal, but the Military Police had their names and reported them as thieves. The recommendation of bravery was enough evidence to withdraw the criminal report, but the soldiers were ordered to pay for the cost of the prunes. Elm lamented that he had almost won but for the stolen prunes a Distinguished Service Cross.

13

VESLE RIVER

—————— 1918 ——————

Aloysius painted one, three, four, and seven blue ravens, never more in one scene, and with a trace of black and rouge. He painted in the back of trucks on the rough roads to war, at meals, and even in the beam and roar of enemy bombardments. My brother carried the paste of three colors in a compact, and moistened the brush with his tongue. His tongue was blue most of the time. Blueblood became his new nickname as an infantry scout.

The blue ravens were marvelous creations that late summer, the visionary images of peace, sway, irony, and, of course, a native sense of presence in the pitch and atrocities of war. The totemic ravens were forever our solace and protection. Ravens were blue in creation stories, and remained blue in the name of storiers. Black ravens turned blue by visions and ingenuity. The new woad blues of the ravens were subtle hues, and the scenes created a sense of motion and ceremony. The woad blues were elusive, never the flamboyant blues of royalty or the Virgin Mary.

Aloysius traded a blue raven pendant for a wad of woad, the blue paste made from the crushed and cured leaves of a plant that grew in the area. Harry Greene, an ambulance driver, located the woad in a nearby commune and arranged the trade for my brother. Harry was a novelist from Asheville, North Carolina, and a volunteer driver who lived most of the time in Paris. He had never met natives, and was impressed with the totemic blue ravens. Harry became a good friend, and later he introduced us to the City of Light.

Odysseus came to mind, of course, when my brother used the traded woad to paint with, and we actually considered the life of traders in France. Aloysius could easily trade his art, but words and stories were my only objects of commerce. Stories and original art by natives would not be a fair trade for food or favors at the desperate end of the war. Odysseus might have declared that peyote, white lace, and absinthe were hardly necessary to trade in France.

I read book four of *The Odyssey* that night in the corner of a trench and traveled with the spirits in the ancient stories. *At times I cry aloud for sorrow, but presently I leave off again, for crying is cold comfort and one soon tires of it. Yet grieve for these as I may, I do so for one man more than for them all. . . . . He took nothing by it, and has left a legacy of sorrow to myself, for he has been gone a long time, and we know not whether he is alive or dead.*

Aloysius carved blue raven medals for the native scouts Strut and Hunch. My brother had collected broken wood to carve the pendants. Some of the local trees were similar to those on the reservation, *arbre de chêne*, oak tree, *charme*, hornbeam or ironwood, *cendre*, ash, and *hêtre* or beech. The hornbeam was hard with a close grain, and the polished image of a raven absorbed the blue in muted hues. The peace pendants were slowly carved under constant enemy bombardment and the bloody rage of war.

My brother presented the pendants at a timely second cootie and shower ceremony. The stories told by scouts are not the same as other combat stories. Scouts were secretive, moved by stealth, and there were very few observers to comment on the risky missions at night to capture enemy soldiers.

We were worried about two of our close cousins who were in separate divisions. Ignatius Vizenor was an infantry soldier in the Thirtieth Infantry Division near Saint-Quentin under the command of the British Expeditionary Forces. Strut and Huntch said they would ask about our cousin Lawrence Vizenor in the nearby Thirty-Third Infantry Division. The Rainbow Division was deployed a few days later to the south near the Meuse River for the decisive and bloody Battle of the Argonne Forest.

The Third Army Corps, engineers, and other companies of the First Pioneer Infantry gathered at Bois Meunière between Cierges and Goussancourt. From there the soldiers marched east in rain and thunder near Dead Man's Curve to Fismes. The Boche soldiers were on high ground, a strategic enemy position over the river valley.

The First Pioneer Infantry was ordered by French commanders to rush the enemy at Fismes on the Vesle River between Soissons and Reims. The soldiers had driven the enemy out of Fère-en-Tardenois and then advanced toward the Vesle River.

Fismes was in ruins and the central road was covered with the smoldering debris of buildings, wagons, bodies, and the wreckage of military equipment from several days of enemy bombardments. The explosions dismembered the soldiers, and armies of rats ate the faces, eyes, ears, cheeks, and hands. My face shivered as the rats devoured the exposed bodies. Two soldiers shot at the rats, but the sergeant shouted not to waste ammunition.

The soldiers marched quickly through the town of ghosts and shadows, and then were ordered to pursue the enemy across the river to Fismette. There, the infantry encountered heavy fire from machine guns and were caught within hours in a massive barrage of enemy artillery. The soldiers were under direct enemy fire and there was no immediate military support or escape.

The French had ordered two companies of infantry soldiers to carry out a frontal attack against an entrenched enemy. The strategy was borrowed from some ancient manual of ritual war. The French and British courtly commanders had lost many, many battles and had endured hundreds of thousands of casualties over the centuries by a direct charge of soldiers with no strategy of stealth or recovery. The French officers were unready and should have learned elusive maneuvers and how to outwit the enemy some century earlier from native warriors in North America.

Fismes and nearby forests were bombarded the entire night by the Germans. Two infantry regiments were under constant machine gun fire and besieged by the entrenched enemy across the Vesle River in Fismette. The French officers who ordered the offensive should have been the first to face the enemy, and the last to leave the field of battle. The opposite was more obvious that stormy night as hundreds of soldiers were blown to pieces in the bombardment. The officers had gathered in secure tents to dine, study maps, and pose war strategies.

Sergeant Sorek ordered his two native scouts on another risky overnight mission. I protested that my rifle was too bulky and, as a scout, demanded a pistol. His stare was mean and steady, the tiny black eyes of a predator, then he turned away in silence and prepared a military requisition for two Colt pistols and regulation holsters. The order might have taken several weeks, even months, and the great ironic war might have ended by then. So, the taciturn sergeant borrowed two pistols from other soldiers, a driver and a telephone engineer.

Sergeant Sorek acted at once and only because we had already captured five enemy soldiers on seven missions, and the most recent captives provided important information about enemy artillery and machine gun positions. The Germans had been routed to the east in the past few days and the gun positions changed nightly.

Aloysius painted his face late that afternoon, wide bands of blue with black and rouge circles, in preparation for our overnight mission to locate the current enemy machine gun emplacements. My brother had never painted his body as a warrior. The pattern of his face colors was original, more aesthetic than menace, a comic mask, but not the war paint of a traditional native ceremony.

I blackened my face and hands, and with no trace of blue or rouge. Camouflage was more important than war paint, but my brother was persuasive. Seven infantry soldiers in the regiment wanted their faces painted for combat. Aloysius painted the blue wing feathers of abstract ravens on the cheeks of the soldiers. The spread of primaries created the illusion of a face in flight. Yes, every painted soldier returned safely from combat that night. Blue was a secure color of peace, courage, and liberty. The soldiers saved the paint on their faces, and later my brother retouched the feathers.

Later that night we floated a short distance on a pontoon boat through the debris of war on the black Vesle River. The river was about thirty feet wide and seven feet deep in the middle. The boats were towed back by the engineers. We waited in silence near the shore, and then moved into the fractured forest. We were armed with Colt pistols, four magazines of ammunition, and our Elephant Toe pocketknives.

Aloysius wore a floppy hat to protect the distinct paint on his face. He was determined to scare at least one enemy soldier before the paint washed away overnight in the rain. I wore a soft hat too, but the rain actually improved my face paint, the ordinary disguise of a withered tree trunk.

The gusts of wind and rain, flashes of lightning, and thunder were head to head that night with mighty explosions, the roar and shudder of allied and enemy artillery bombardments. Once again we took advantage of the rainy weather, the crash of artillery shells, and thunder that pitchy night to cover the slight sounds of our moves in the forest.

Aloysius led the way through the forest muck in leaps and bounds with each burst of lightning and explosion to a secure natural mound in the center of huge cracked trees. Our strategy was to fall asleep there despite the weather and artillery, to become a native presence in the folly and deadly chaos of the war. My brother was a warrior beam with a mutable comic face in the rain and in every flash of lightning.

The artillery bombardment ended early in the morning. The trees around the mound emerged in the faint traces of light as black and splintered skeletons. We were native scouts in a nightmare, a curse of war duty to capture the enemy.

The war was surreal, faces, forests, and enemies.

The Boche reeked of trench culture, and we could easily sense by nose the very presence of the enemy. An actual presence detected by the cranks and throaty sounds, and by the very scent of porridge, cordite, moist earth, biscuits, and overrun latrines at a great distance. Some odors were much more prominent, urine, cigarettes, and cigars, that moist morning. Officers smoked cigars, so we knew we were close to a command bunker. The most obvious scent of the enemy was the discarded tins of Wurst and Schinkin, sausage and ham, and the particular rations of Heer und Flotte Zigaretten and Zigarren.

The Great War could be described by the distinctive scent of machine oil, mustard gas, chlorine, the malodor of urine, putrefied bodies, cheesy feet, and by cigarettes, Heer und Flotte, Gauloises Caporal, and Lucky Strike.

The artillery bombardments were suspended time and again before dawn, an unspoken truce so the soldiers could eat breakfast in peace, crap at ease, and then restart the war. We took advantage of that truce absurdity and moved slowly to outflank the enemy.

Seven common cranes soared over the desecrated forest to the south. The animals, rabbit, deer, wild boar, and fox, had escaped the ravages of the enemy, but few birds survived the war. The poison gas and constant bombardments were devastating to natural flight and the ordinary songs of the seasons. Later we saw more cocky northern ravens, the *grands corbeaux*, than any other bird, and only one magnificent *aigle botté*, a booted eagle with great white shanks.

Aloysius lowered his head and moved in the smart spirit of an animal, sudden leaps, lurches, and slithers on his belly. I followed in the same manner, and our moves were precise, only at the instance of other sounds in the forest. I was close to my brother, at his side, and could hardly hear his moves over the wind, or over the distant sound of trucks, airplanes, and the noisy light tanks, mainly the French Renault.

Once the artillery barrage started again we could move with greater speed, but with increased caution, of course, not to create a silhouette, or show of face or shoulder on the move. Snipers were certainly positioned to cover the entire area, communes, forests, rivers, and patiently waited for a single rise of eye, turn of cheek, or slight exposure, a face above a ravine, trench, or bomb crater. Scouts are trained by stories and by experience to anticipate the secret shot of a sniper. Every scout must envision the sniper with even the slightest moves. Native hunters moved in the same way to avoid the sight and scent of the animal. The sniper waits to shoot, and the wise animal converts familiar silhouettes and escapes the scene.

Aloysius gestured with his finger in the direction of a machine gun place-ment. We had detected the scent of moist earth, cold metal, machine oil, and slithered in the muck a few feet at a time to the right and behind the enemy position, and waited for the roar of artillery.

We could not yet see the enemy but we sensed the presence of two or three soldiers in a new trench with a machine gun. Minutes after the first rounds of artillery that early morning we raised our heads, crouched in the muck, and then rushed toward the enemy soldiers. I shot the first soldier who had raised his rifle, and my brother leaped into the trench and stabbed the second soldier in the stomach and chest with his Elephant Toe knife, and then with a swift back swing of his hand cut the throat of the enemy. The third soldier raised his hands to surrender, and pleaded not be scalped as my brother raised his bloody Elephant Toe. The soldier pointed to other machine gun emplacements nearby, and one by one we attacked the enemy positions.

Aloysius shouted, a wild curse, and rushed the enemy. The Boche soldiers were stunned by the face paint and surrendered for fear of being scalped by a fierce native warrior. We assaulted three machine gun em-placements that morning and captured seven young soldiers who were grateful not to be scalped and eager to end the desperation, fear of death, and the war.

I shot and killed only two soldiers and my brother scared the others with his bloody knife to surrender. As we marched the seven enemy soldiers through the forest back to the river ten other soldiers surrendered without

a fight. We forced the seventeen enemy soldiers to wade and swim across
the Vesle River to Fismes. Early the next day several infantry regiments and
other military units had advanced beyond the machine gun emplacements
that we had seized and put out of action. The two-day battle was fierce and
the infantry soldiers captured Fismette.

The Boche were routed from the Vesle River.

Sergeant Sorek counted the captives twice, and ordered me to write
their names. Later he told me not to worry about the borrowed pistols. We
could return them at the end of the war. The sergeant promised to recom-
mend my brother and me for the Distinguished Service Cross. The blue
face paint, a woad dye, was smeared and lasted for more than two weeks.
The black charcoal on my face easily washed away in the morning rain.

>>> <<<

Aloysius carved three wooden boats from pieces of shattered *arbre de
charme*, or hornbeam trees. The boats were about the length of hand grenades with blunt bows and wide sterns for stability. He had collected chunks
of various broken trees, oak, hazel, wild cherry, and beech with smooth
bark similar to maple. The best grain for boats and pendants was *charme*,
hornbeam, or otherwise named ironwood on the White Earth Reservation.

My brother painted each boat blue with a rouge bridge and carved the
name of Odysseus on one boat, Misaabe on the second, and Augustus on
the third. The three boats of tribute were christened and launched one
sunny morning on the Vesle River. We recounted stories of the trader, the
healer, and our uncle on the reservation and walked with the boats down
the river. Someone, a lonesome child or an old man, might discover the
boats ashore in England, Portugal, Spain, or on an island in the Caribbean.

The *Odysseus, Misaabe,* and *Augustus* sailed with the flow of the
Vesle River from Fismes to the Aisne River, joined the Oise River, and
then sailed down the River Seine near Paris to the port of Le Havre and
the English Channel. We were scouts on risky missions at the end of the
war, and the boats carried our stories and memories out to sea. Later my
brother painted blue ravens and boat scenes on the River Seine in Paris. We
searched for the *Odysseus, Misaabe,* and *Augustus* on rivers, docks, lakes,
ocean beaches, and in many ports.

I leaned against a tree near the river that afternoon and read book five of *The Odyssey. In the end he deemed it best to take to the woods, and he found one upon some high ground not far from the water. There he crept beneath two shoots of olive that grew from a single stock—the one an ungrafted sucker, while the other had been grafted. No wind, however squally, could break through the cover they afforded, nor could the sun's rays pierce them, nor the rain get through them, so closely did they grow into one another.*

14

MONTBRÉHAIN
—————— 1918 ——————

Margaret, our mother, wrote that she had read newspaper stories in the *Tomahawk* about the major offensives against the Germans at the Vesle River and Fismes in France. She mentioned several divisions and places of combat but she never expressed her worries directly. My stories were published several weeks later on the reservation, and even then she did not comment on our risky missions as scouts.

My mother always wrote separate personal letters to me and to my brother. She understood our individual sentiments and selected just the right words of intimacy, and special memories. In a recent letter she mentioned our cousins in the war, major military offensives, the proud bandage brigade, gold star mothers, and the purchase of war bonds on the reservation. Luckily very few native soldiers from the reservation died in the war. Specific names were censored, of course, but general references and some regional place names were acceptable, such as Château-Thierry, Fismes, the Vesle River, and Picardy.

Ignatius Vizenor wrote to his mother, for instance, but could not reveal by name that his division was under the command of the British Expeditionary Forces. Angeline was not aware that her son Lawrence Vizenor had been deployed in the Battle of the Argonne Forest. Naturally, we were eager to have more recent information about our cousin and the advance of the Thirty-Third Division in combat near the valley of the Meuse River.

Strut and Hunch, our scout comrades, had agreed to meet at the Y Hut or canteen in a military reserve area. Soldiers in reserve units were on a slight pause and prepared to relieve other units and divisions in combat. The canteens were common in training areas, but scarce near the front lines. The canteen was a combat café and sold groceries, cigarettes, and other items.

Frances Gulick was our mother, sister, reverie lover, and saint on the manly way to combat. No doubt thousands of soldiers were charmed by her warm smile. I remember the dimple on her chin, the dark gray uniform with a blue collar, and she wore black stockings and laced shoes. Frances was the first canteen worker we had met in France. She was astonished that we had hawked the *Tomahawk*, and that my articles on the war were published on the reservation. She was rather sentimental about the absence of natives in history, and had no idea that there were so many native soldiers in the war. We drove with her once as she delivered newspapers, the *Paris Herald*, *Chicago Tribune*, *Daily Mail*, and *Stars and Stripes* to soldiers near the front lines. My brother painted the blue wings of a raven over a canteen, a gift that brought tears to her eyes. Naturally we expected to meet her at another canteen. Frances, we learned later, had been permanently attached to the First Engineers.

The Young Men's Christian Association sponsored the canteens and many other activities for soldiers. The Salvation Army, Jewish Welfare Board, and the Knights of Columbus were active in services to soldiers. I would proudly serve the native Knights of Augustus, or my uncle, the Knights of Aloysius, my brother, Margaret, my mother, Odysseus, the trader, or Misaabe, the healer, but not as a token in a chess game or in the name of Christopher Columbus.

The canteen was a tent, nothing more, with a few tables and chairs. We ordered hot chocolate and waited for our comrades. The roads were badly rutted and crowded with supply trucks, artillery wagons, and equipment moving in both directions. We could hear in the distance the lurch and clatter of light tanks, always the disabled and noisy French Renault.

I leaned back in the chair and imagined that the war was over and we had returned to the livery stable at the Hotel Leecy. The maple leaves had turned magical and radiant in the bright morning light that brisk autumn on the reservation. The sandhill cranes were on the wing, ravens bounced on the leafy roads, and the elusive cedar waxwings hovered in the bright red sumac.

The forests around the canteen tent were creased by savagery, and shattered from constant artillery explosions. The hornbeam, oak, and beech were broken, turned awry and slanted in grotesque war scenes, but the few tattered leaves that remained on the trees were brilliant, the glorious banners of nature not nations.

The French Fourth Army and fifteen divisions of American Expeditionary Forces had advanced against the enemy on the front line more than twenty miles wide near the Meuse River. September, the first phase of the offensive, was cold and rainy, and the narrow muddy roads to the hilly combat areas were blocked with command motor cars, ammunition trucks, and artillery wagons.

The Meuse offensives and the Battle of the Argonne were so massive that the logistics to move equipment and supplies to the soldiers were unworkable. Many soldiers in fierce combat, for instance, had not eaten for four days. The soldiers carried out the strategies of the generals on empty stomachs. The allied command decisions to deploy and supply so many divisions were only mighty mappery.

The Hindenburg Line of enemy trenches, bunkers, and other defenses ran more than a hundred miles from Lens, a commune northeast of Arras, near Saint-Quentin, and Reims, and then to the south past Verdun. The Germans used prisoners of war to build concrete bunkers, emplacements for machine guns, and secure command posts to direct artillery.

The military objectives of the first two phases of the offensive were to penetrate the lines of the enemy and capture the commune of Sedan, a major railroad center near the Meuse River and the border with Belgium. The American Expeditionary Forces crossed the Aire River near Verdun and advanced through the Argonne forest and the valley of the Meuse River.

The French forces crossed the Aisne River and advanced at the same time on the left of the American infantry toward Mézières on the Meuse River north of Sedan. The casualties, dead and wounded, were very high at every commune, farm, forest, and turn in the road, and extremely high in the Battle of Montfaucon. The Germans directed artillery fire from concrete bunkers on a hill near a church. The intense resistance slowed the surprise advance of allied soldiers in the first phase of the offensive.

The American Expeditionary Forces in six weeks suffered some twenty-six thousand dead in combat and more than ninety-six thousand wounded in the Meuse River and Battle of the Argonne.

The American Expeditionary Forces that served in the two offensives that defeated the enemy and ended the war included former National Guard divisions, the Red Arrow, Rainbow, Blue and Grey, Keystone, Santa Fe, and the Buckeye Division. The Regular Army divisions included the

Statue of Liberty, Pine Tree, Trailblazers, Buffalo Soldiers, and Ivy, or the nicknamed Poison Ivy Division.

Corporal Lawrence Vizenor, our close cousin, was drafted and mustered early to train at Camp Logan, Texas. He was transferred to Camp Merritt, New York, and then boarded the *Mount Vernon* at Hoboken, New Jersey. The ship docked at Brest, France. We sailed on the very same troop ship and arrived at the same port, but about a month later. Lawrence was a soldier in the Thirty-Third Infantry Division. He survived the bloody battle of Château-Thierry only a few weeks before we drove through the ruins, the Second Battle of the Marne, the Battle of Saint-Mihiel, and he was an infantry soldier in the Battle of the Argonne, the second phase of the offensive in early October 1918.

Hunch arrived with a heavy bandage on his right hand. A few days earlier he had disarmed an enemy soldier and was cut by a bayonet. Aloysius teased him that the protection of the blue raven pendant would not cover the ordinary cuts and bruises of a scout. Hunch returned the tease with a reference to our fur trade surname and native rights to the nearby Forêt-de-Beaulieu. We pretended that our relatives once owned that forest in France.

Strut ordered hot chocolate, a favorite at every canteen, and then he turned, smiled, and declared how natural that four native scouts drank chocolate because the actual drink was first prepared by the native Aztec and Maya.

Strut had talked to several scouts in the Thirty-Third Division and was told that Corporal Lawrence Vizenor had been awarded the Distinguished Service Cross a few weeks earlier on October 8, 1918, for extraordinary heroism at Bois-de-Fays in Forêt d'Argonne, the Forest of Argonne. Bois-de-Fays was a hilly wooded area more than twenty miles wide between Cunel and Brieulles-sur-Meuse.

Lawrence was on patrol with several other infantry soldiers, a reconnaissance mission to gather strategic information on enemy positions and fortifications. The patrol encountered intense fire from an enemy machine gun emplacement in the forest. Three soldiers turned back and found cover in a trench. Lawrence and the officer in charge of the patrol, and one other soldier, continued to advance on the enemy positions. The officer was mortally wounded in the chest by gunfire from a machine gun. Lawrence and the other soldier circled the enemy machine gunner and shot him in the head and chest. Lawrence disabled the machine gun and then carried the wounded officer to a medical aid station.

Private Ignatius Vizenor died in combat at Montbréhain on Tuesday, October 8, 1918. He was a close cousin and one of the most elegantly dressed natives on the reservation. Ignatius died on the very same day that his younger brother Lawrence was decorated for heroism some hundred miles away at Bois-de-Fays.

The brothers wore blue raven pendants.

Montbréhain was a commune east of Saint-Quentin, near Ramicourt and Brancourt-le-Grand, and a critical military position close to the Hindenburg Line during the Hundred Days Offensive. The artillery bombardments had weakened the enemy, but in turns the military strategies were savage and catastrophic to the ordinary way of life in the countryside. The pastoral cultures of sugar beets, Charolais white cattle, bygone chapels, and houses with fancy brick patterns, concrete lintels, and heavy lace window curtains were in ruins. The allied casualties sustained to recover these common country scenes have forever wounded the relatives of the dead soldiers, haunted the memories and stories of war veterans on the reservation, and the strategies of the military commanders have been recounted around the world. The war started with empires, horse parades, and manly military traditions and ended with havoc, constraint, enormous tanks and cannons, and new commune cultures of women without men.

Private Ignatius Vizenor and other soldiers of the Thirtieth Infantry Division were assigned to the British Second Army in northeastern France. Later, several infantry regiments were ordered to advance against the enemy at Bellicourt and Bony. Ignatius and the Hundred Eighteenth Infantry Regiment advanced under machine gun fire on Sentinel Hill near Bellicourt. The Australian infantry moved on both flanks to enclose the enemy. Ignatius survived the fierce combat and served bravely with the British and Australian Corps.

The Hindenburg Line was breached in late September 1918, and thousands of allied soldiers defeated the enemy in bloody battles at Montbréhain. The Thirtieth Division was ordered to the front lines a few days later to continue the advance against the enemy in early October 1918.

Ignatius rested overnight in the ruins of a farmhouse. Early the next morning the infantry regiment secured positions in the muddy trenches east of Montbréhain. Private Vizenor and other soldiers in the Hundred Eighteenth Infantry Regiment were ordered to lead the perilous offensive. The military objective was Prémont to the east of Montbréhain. The infantry regiment advanced with artillery and heavy tank support early that rainy morning, Tuesday, October 8, 1918, sixty-two days into the Hundred Days Offense. Ignatius was shot in the chest by an enemy machine gun. He collapsed and died slowly on a cold and muddy verge near a new series of trenches east of Montbréhain.

Private Ignatius Vizenor entered service on February 25, 1918, and trained at Camp Dodge, Iowa, and then was sent to Camp Sevier, South Carolina, a new military training cantonment. Ignatius and the other soldiers were then transported to Camp Merritt, New Jersey. A few days later the division embarked from Hoboken, New Jersey, on the *Haverford* for a twelve-day voyage to Liverpool, England.

The soldiers were transported by train to Dover and by channel steamer to Calais, France. The Thirtieth Division continued training at Reques, France. Ignatius and other infantry soldiers were ordered to exchange their standard Springfield Rifles issued by the American Expeditionary Forces for British Lee-Enfield bolt-action rifles, belts, bayonets, and other equipment. The Thirtieth Division was assigned to the British Expeditionary Forces in France.

Tuesday, October 8, 1918, was no ordinary day in the course of war or peace. That day became an epoch of native memories. Private Charles Beaupré, for instance, served in the American Tank Corps and died in action at Saint-Quentin, France. He was born on the White Earth Reservation and died in combat on the same day as Ignatius Vizenor, and the same day that Corporal Lawrence Vizenor was awarded the Distinguished Service Cross.

Sergeant Thomas Lee Hall received the United States Medal of Honor for valor on October 8, 1918, at Montbréhain. Sergeant Hall, who served in the same infantry regiment as Ignatius Vizenor, advanced on an enemy machine gun position and killed five enemy soldiers. Ignatius and Thomas Hall died on the same day in combat.

Corporal Alvin York received the United States Medal of Honor and the

French Croix de Guerre for valor on October 8, 1918, at Chatel-Chéhéry in the Argonne Forest. He had served with the Eighty-Second Infantry Division. York was the leader of an attack on enemy machine gun positions and in the course of the maneuvers he captured more than a hundred soldiers.

I read more of book five of *The Odyssey* that night. *Then, as one who lives alone in the country, far from any neighbor, hides a brand as fire-seed in the ashes to save himself from having to get a light elsewhere, even so did Ulysses cover himself up with leaves; and Minerva shed a sweet sleep upon his eyes, closed his eyelids, and made him lose all memories of his sorrows.*

Ellanora Beaulieu lost her memories and her sorrow as a military nurse in the Army of Occupation. She was buried at the Episcopal Calvary Cemetery on the White Earth Reservation. Ellanora and Ignatius Vizenor were the only direct native relatives who died in the First World War.

John Clement Beaulieu, Paul Hudon Beaulieu, Paul Vizenor, Lawrence Vizenor, Robert Fairbanks, Allan Fairbanks, Romain Fairbanks, Everett Fairbanks, Truman Fairbanks, George Fairbanks, Arthur Fairbanks, Herman Trotterchaud, Allen Trotterchaud, and other relatives served with honor in the American Expeditionary Forces in France and returned to the White Earth Reservation.

Patch Zhimaaganish returned a corporal and was honored as a hero at the government school. Even the federal agent celebrated his service in the war. Patch was hired by the Soo Line Railroad as a conductor on passenger trains and sang his way around the country for more than twenty years.

The First World War continues forever on the White Earth Reservations in the stories of veterans and survivors of combat. We were the native descendants of the fur trade who returned with new stories from France.

15

PONT DES ARTS
———— 1919 ————

The German government had consented to end the war on November 11, 1918. Yes, a mere promise between generals, an agreement to cease the brutality, but never an actual declaration of surrender. The armistice was formally signed in a railway carriage in Forêt de Compiègne, the Compiègne Forest, between Saint-Quentin and Paris.

The birds of misery cautiously returned that afternoon of the armistice to the decimated forests. Tawny owls and marsh harriers had evaded the battlefields. Bohemian waxwings migrated around the poisoned forests. A wing of cranes circled the river, an uncertain flight of peace, and then flew south to a bird sanctuary. The weary citizens of the war emerged from the ruins and waved the tattered national colors of liberty, and saluted the future of the French Third Republic.

Three common ravens cawed at a great distance, a tease of presence, and then a haunting silence. Nature was hushed, and the shadows of the entire countryside were uncertain scenes of wicked rage, bloody, muddy and mutilated bodies stacked for collection at the side of the roads. Later the elation of the armistice was rightly overcome by the undeniable memories of slaughter, separation, and the inevitable sense of suspicion and vengeance.

The commune survivors craved an ordinary mention of mean suns and easy weather, evasive sounds of white storks, common scoters, the cluck of hens and crow of roosters in the morning, and wine with dinner, and the shy turns and smiles of children. More men were dead than women and the culture of *église de village*, church, families, and farms would never be the same.

The eternal rats tracked down the last dead soldiers and civilians on the armistice to scratch out an eye and chew a tender ear or cold hairy jowl. The native forests and fields would bear forever the blood, brain, and cracked bones in every season of the fruit trees and cultivated sugar beets.

The soldiers were honored, ceremonial graves were marked, and the glorious national monuments were envisioned with godly stained glass and heroic stone sculptures. That poignant sound of military taps at the graves of honorable soldiers would be heard for more than a hundred years.

12 November 1918

Soldiers of the Allied Armies:
After having resolutely stopped the enemy you have for months
attacked him without respite, with an untiring faith and energy.
You have won the greatest battle of history and saved the most sacred
of causes: the liberty of the world.
Be proud.
You have covered your colors with immortal glory.
Posterity will hold you in grateful remembrance.

The Marshal of France
Commander in Chief of the Allied Armies
Ferdinand Foch

The First Pioneer Infantry and other military units marched into Luxembourg two weeks after the armistice, and a few weeks later entered Germany as the Army of Occupation. Allied soldiers had defeated the enemy, but the armistice was not an admission of defeat, or surrender, and not a peace agreement. The end of the war was actually a negotiated armistice, and we learned later that the French were prepared to continue the war if the Germans had not accepted the peace specified in the Treaty of Versailles.

The First Pioneer Infantry soldiers were quartered at the ancient Ehrenbreitstein Fortress on the eastern shore of the Rhine River overlooking the city of Koblenz. Finally, and for a few months, the division, scouts and trench survivors, were stationed in positions of comfort, cold custom, and royalty.

The kitchen trucks served regular meals at the fortress, but many soldiers could not resolve the obvious contradictions of peace, occupation, and moral conscience of the war because starvation was common in Germany. Mighty artillery, machine guns, and scouts were essential to defeat the enemy, but the routine provisions of food determined the actual outcome of the war, and civilians were starved to serve the soldiers.

Christmas Eve was a natural touch of remembrance, family, reservation, and country, the first lonesome celebration and tease of peace since we had been mustered for active military service. The tease was native, not monotheistic, and the music was a communal sentiment. Centuries of monotheism had been weakened by the demons of nationalism and empires. There were no godly reasons to justify the horror of that war. The desperation of the war lingered in every ordinary word, peace, love, angel, virtuous, forgive, miracle, genuflect, and signs of the cross. The Regimental Band played familiar carols that evening in an ancient fortress of the enemy, an ironic conclusion of the war.

Patch Zhimaaganish played military taps on a trumpet at the end of the carols. The emotive sound carried across the river and could be heard on the main streets of Koblenz. Naturally, we were moved by the concert and trumpet recital, and then our friend sang *La Marseillaise*, the national anthem of France. His baritone voice carried the most suitable, inspired, and memorable music of war and peace that night.

> *Allons enfants de la Patrie*
> Arise, children of the Fatherland
> *Le jour de gloire est arrivé*
> The day of glory has arrived
> *Contre nous, de la tyrannie*
> Against us stand tyranny
> *L'étendard sanglant est levé*
> The bloody flag is raised

Aloysius painted several enormous blue ravens over the dark fortress and over the bridges on the Rhine River. He had obtained a larger book of fine art paper with deckled edges, and the new raven scenes were magnificent. My brother once again painted with a sense of native presence, imagination, and visionary power. The military occupation billets in the royal fortress must have roused his new raven images of liberty.

Aloysius was inspired to paint as we traveled several times by steamboat down the Rhine River. His portrayals of blue ravens on the river, blue wake and shadows on the water, traces of rouge on the bridges, castles, and ancient houses were the most dramatic and abstract that he had ever painted. Yes, we had survived the war as scouts and brothers, a painter and a writer, but were unnerved by the wounds and agonies of peace. My literary scenes were more fierce and poetic, and the images my brother created were more intense and visionary. No one would wisely endorse the experiences of war and peace as the just sources of artistic inspiration, and yet we would never resist the tease of chance, turn of trickster stories, or the natural outcome of native irony.

Soldiers were allowed a furlough for one week after four months of active service. We had served for six months, and, since scouts have no actual combat duty in a military occupation, we requested a leave for two weeks in Paris. The military encouraged furloughs when the war ended so our leave was approved for ten days in early January.

Sergeant Sorek advised us not to travel to major cities because there were no hotel rooms available, especially not in Paris. Aloysius assured the good sergeant that we would stay with a friend, the ambulance driver Harry Greene.

The Paris Peace Conference convened on January 18, 1919, a few days after we had returned from furlough. The onerous peace negotiations continued for five months. The Treaty of Versailles became a tortured tongue of grievous reparations and vengeance, and was finally endorsed on June 28, 1919, by representatives of the new government of Germany.

Aloysius was prepared to present his most recent blue ravens to the owner of the Galerie Crémieux in Paris. He carried two small art books of his war paintings in a backpack, and the recent book of fine art paper under his arm. I reminisced about our first train journey ten years earlier to Minneapolis, the hotels and theaters, the gracious librarian who served cookies, the friendly streetcar conductor, the nasty curator at the art gallery, and the great artist and teacher Yamada Baske, who had encouraged my brother to paint a trace of rouge in the blue raven portrayals.

Paris meant more to us than a luminous tourist destination of culture and liberation. The city had become our vision of art and literature, and a chance of recognition as native artists. We departed before dawn by truck to the train station in Koblenz. More than a hundred soldiers were on furlough that morning, but only a few were on their way to Paris.

The Central Station was new, massive, a spectacular ornate sandstone structure. Hungry civilians were huddled in every corner and cover of the station. The carriages were crowded with soldiers and downcast civilians who were leaving the city with huge bundles. We changed trains four times. Luxembourg was the first transfer, and then at Metz, Nancy, and Vitry-le-François in France. The noisy train moved slowly through the mountains, and then into the bleak abandoned farms and shattered forest areas. The stations at Thionville and Épernay had been badly damaged in the war.

I read book six of *The Odyssey* as the train traveled through forests and farmland closer to Paris. *Thus did he pray, and Minerva heard his prayer, but she would not show herself to him openly, for she was afraid of her uncle Neptune, who was still furious in his endeavors to prevent Ulysses from getting home.*

The train lurched and wobbled from one track to another through the steely industrial areas and arrived late the following morning in the smoky cavern of the Gare de l'Est in Paris. The Orient Express had departed from that very station, but not since the start of the war.

The city was cold and gray, but we hardly noticed the weather in the noise and crush of people, horses, wagons, and the noisy rush of new motor cars. Parisian taxicabs circled the station and lined the streets in every direction. The same clunky Renault taxicabs, more than a thousand, that had delivered infantry soldiers to the First Battle of the Marne to save Paris.

Aloysius sat on the steps of a hotel across the street from the station and painted several great blue ravens perched at the entrance to the Gare de l'Est. Three scruffy boys pointed at the portrayal and praised the blue ravens, and then held out their hands for food or money. We were dressed in combat uniforms, so there was no way to evade the hungry children near the station. American soldiers were the most generous, and the most popular, visitors to Paris.

We walked directly down the busy Boulevard de Strasbourg and Boulevard de Sébastopol toward the River Seine. Boulangeries, cafés, A. Simon corsets, and hundreds of other stores with window displays of clothes, shoes, and books, lined both sides of the street. The corset displays were similar to the regular advertisements in the *Tomahawk*. Les Halles, the incredible central marketplace, was on the right side of the boulevard, and on the left the Jewish community of Le Marais.

The Seine River was slow and solemn that morning as we crossed the Pont au Change and walked past the Paris Hall of Justice over the Pont Saint-Michel to the Place Saint-Michel in the Latin Quarter. The monuments and statues were shrouded in the gray coat of the city. The cafés were more seductive, with bright red and blue canopies, than the gray and green metal generals mounted on fierce horses. We walked directly to a red canopy, the Café du Départ, on the corner and sat outside with a view of the River Seine and the Cathédrale Notre-Dame de Paris.

I was hungry and ordered a double omelet with herbs and a café au lait. Aloysius ordered a baguette with *jambon* and a café with chocolate. Then he moistened the woad and painted a blue raven with enormous wings extended over the Pont Saint-Michel, and a second blue raven with traces of rouge on the faint blue gargoyles of the Cathédrale Notre-Dame. The waiter was fascinated by the raven paintings and explained that the gargoyle waterspouts had once been painted in bright colors. How would my brother know about the color of the waterspouts? Aloysius had envisioned the gargoyles, and never knew that they had once been painted in bright colors.

The waiter did not recognize the name Harry Greene, the novelist and ambulance driver for the American Field Service, but he gave us directions to his residence at L'Hôtel, 13 Rue des Beaux-Arts. We walked slowly along the River Seine past the *bouquinistes*, book dealers and artists, to the Pont des Arts. Aloysius leaned over the rail and watched the barges cruise on the dark river. Many artists have been roused and inspired to paint scenes of the River Seine. Henri Matisse, Claude Monet, Camille Pissaro, and Eugène Isabey, mostly impressionist painters, might have created their river scenes on the Pont des Arts.

Aloysius painted an uneven row of three bright blue ravens on the Quai' des Grands-Augustins near the Pont Neuf. The stone quay or wharf was crowded near the bridge with mattress makers, tinkers, and other discrete trades, crafts, and veterans of the war. An older woman was working over a framed mattress. She raised her head toward the bastion on the bridge, folded her arms, smiled, and then returned to the mattress. We walked down the stairs to the quay, and my brother showed the portrait to the woman. She laughed and turned away, surprised that the blue ravens were not humans.

Mattresses were precious possessions, and ancestral, and the workers repaired and cleaned the covers and horsehair cushions on the quay near the River Seine. Most of the people who worked on the quay were friends and compatriots, and they looked after each other. When it rained everyone took cover under the bridge.

〉〉〉 〈〈〈

Two veterans sat on narrow benches near the riverbank. They wore military coats, smoked cigarettes, and fished for perch and white suckers. Three small perch, enough for dinner, writhed in a bucket. The eager expectation, we learned later, was to catch a stray salmon from the Atlantic.

The veterans wore black fedoras, and their faces were obscured in clouds of cigarette smoke. They jiggled fish lines, mumbled words with an unusual accent, *amorce*, *presque*, *oui*, *dîner de poissons*, and gestured with their elbows, hands, and fishing poles, but the veterans never once turned away from the River Seine.

Aloysius sat next to the two veterans on the riverbank and painted an enormous blue raven perched on a barge. The wings of the raven raised the barge above the waves. The veterans turned to see the portrait of abstract flight, and revealed the masks they wore to cover ghastly facial wounds.

The metal masks were painted to simulate the precious tones of distinctive skin, and the contour of cheeks and noses with no bruises or pockmarks. The masks covered monstrous shrapnel scars, the wounds of war. The painted faces were clear and precise, and yet peculiar, even grotesque with no expression. The smiles, frowns and ordinary gestures were resolved by style, the aesthetic disguises of war wounds. The masks were blank stares without motion, the meticulous contours, satiny hues, and decorative camouflage of war wounds and broken faces.

Aloysius painted two blue ravens with abstract masks, a cubist ravenesque masquerade on the River Seine. The eyes, claws, crowns, and great beaks of the ravens were slanted, curved, and distorted by fractures. The curious breaks in contour feathers were touched with heavy blue hues, and the perceived faces of the ravens were restored with faint traces of rouge.

Henri and André, the *noms de guerre*, or war names of the two masked veterans, had served as infantry soldiers in separate units of the Rainbow Division in the American Expeditionary Forces. They were maimed on the very same day by enemy artillery. Henri lost his nose, nasal bone, and right cheekbone, slashed and crushed by shrapnel. André lost his jaw, lower lip and teeth, and his shattered right leg was amputated above the knee.

André turned directly toward my brother, and his bright blue eyes lighted the metal mask. Henri looked away, down the river, and told us they had met on an ambulance, heavily bandaged, and were transported and treated at the American Expeditionary Forces Base Hospital at Bazoilles-sur-Meuse, a commune near Neufchâteau, southeast of Paris.

Lieutenant Lucien Brun, the dental surgeon at the hospital, was interested in facial fractures, and restored by surgery sections of bone and skin on the faces of the soldiers. They were hospitalized for several months, and were denied access to mirrors. André related that he caught sight of his broken face for the first time reflected in a water trough for horses. He shivered and cursed the war, and then smashed the surface of the water with his fist. Some time later he looked in a mirror for the second time to see a marvelous mask that covered the grisly wounds on his broken face.

Henri and André were mutilated soldiers, *mutilés de guerre*, and became friends in the Base Hospital at Bazoilles-sur-Meuse. The hospital had been an estate, and the countryside was beautiful, a natural sanctuary. André told me that most of the wounded soldiers had returned home, but he and Henri refused to leave France. The reasons were personal, and the politics of aversion and rehabilitation in a military hospital at home would have been unbearable.

André told me that hundreds of wounded soldiers, many with mutilated faces, were paid with other soldiers to perform as a ghostly horde, the actual *mutilés de guerre* in the film *J'accuse* directed by Abel Gance. Some of the war scenes were real, filmed on the actual battlefields of Saint-Mihiel at the end of the war. André was a scary figure in a fantastic scene of the return of dead soldiers.

Henri caught another perch, and as he slowly removed the fishhook he told stories, almost recitations, about Liberty Limbs and the thousands of wounded soldiers on a wait list for facial surgery. Military doctors were restricted to minimal restorative surgery, and the government would not provide prosthetic masks.

André raised his fishing pole, changed the lure, turned, and stared at me in silence. I was caught in his uncanny gaze. The slant and mirror of light on the metal mask was marvelous, mannered, and spooky at the same time. He cracked his right wooden leg twice with a hook remover and explained that the military had provided only cheaply manufactured Liberty Limbs.

The government limb was fabricated of compressed wood fiber with a flexible knee and strapped at the waist, but the modular prosthesis was awkward and not reliable.

André refused to wear the composite military limb, and was wrongly reproached as a shirker who would not accept the new government policies of rehabilitation. He was a mutilated soldier and resisted in his own way the cultural aversions to disability.

The French and the American Red Cross provided basic peg legs, fastened with a shoulder and waist strap. He wore a peg leg for a few months and then carved an elegant resemblance of his right leg from selected *charme*, or hornbeam, a durable hardwood.

André handed me the fishing pole, reached down, lifted the pant leg, and presented a beautifully curved and polished prosthesis with simulated muscles and a bony ankle. The hornbeam leg was a work of art, hinged with precision at the foot and knee, and not a mere composite. The tree had been downed by enemy artillery.

Aloysius painted four abstract blue ravens on huge masks that were mounted on the bastions of the Pont Neuf. My brother wanted to paint a tiny blue raven on the metal masks, a mask with a natural image of motion, but the two wounded veterans refused and turned away. No, they would never change the masks, and revealed later that the very idea of a face mark, blue raven or beast, was a cheeky tease.

I insisted that we meet the sculptor who created the *mutilés de guerre* masks. Henri cleaned, filleted, and wrapped the four perch in paper for dinner. First we walked to their shabby hotel, and then continued a few blocks more to the Red Cross Studio for Portrait Masks for Mutilated Soldiers on Rue Notre-Dame-des-Champs between the Jardin du Luxembourg and Boulevard du Montparnasse. The studio was on the fourth floor, and the scent of plaster and paint was stronger with each flight of stairs.

Anna Coleman Ladd, the sculptor who had established the studio, and created the masks, was dressed in the distinct formal uniform, jacket, wide black belt, and the insignias of a Red Cross Nurse. I was enchanted by her affection and generous smile. She served chocolate and white wine.

Aloysius was interested in how the masks were made and painted with such precision. Anna presented the various stages of the meticulous creation of a distinctive mask, a plaster cast and thin galvanized copper. The prosthetic masks were painted with enamel to avoid cracks and shines, and the hues of each mask matched the skin color of the soldier, even the bluish tint to simulate a shaved beard.

Each mask was original, an artistic creation, and not a mere disguise or camouflage. Dozens of plaster casts were mounted on the back wall of the studio, the chalky and poignant resemblance of the *mutilés de guerre* sentinels of the war. The avant-garde masks were the new aesthetics of war and mutilated soldiers.

Anna had created distinctive masks for André and Henri and three other Americans. She created more than ninety masks for other soldiers since the studio was established a year earlier. Anna was exact, and with the concentration of a humane artist she fashioned eyebrows with real hair.

Aloysius was inspired by the distinctive portrayal of the masks, the stature and guise of an aesthetic pose, and yet he worried about the ironic resemblance of the mutilated soldier as camouflage. My brother was determined to restyle the meticulous resemblance of the lost faces on the masks with abstract blue ravens. The masks would become an abstract work of art, not an aesthetic disguise.

16

GALERIE CRÉMIEUX
1919

Aloysius Hudon Beaulieu became one of those great artists inspired by the ancient vitality of the River Seine. My brother created a surge of blue waves on the river, and he painted a blue raven with enormous translucent wing feathers spread across the entire entrance to the Pont des Arts.

The Institut de France was on the south side of the pedestrian bridge and on the north side, the Musée du Louvre. At that moment on the Pont des Arts, in the middle of two national monuments, and the end of a savage war, we created a scene of native art, the presence of visionary ravens and the River Seine by expressionistic waves of color, poetic images, and the traces of totemic motion in words and paint. On that very first day in the city we revealed a native presence in our names, blue paint, and in my stories.

Naturally, we celebrated our notable surname and fur trade ancestors from France. The surnames and streets were ancient, and other artists and writers must have walked the same route through an alley to Rue de Seine. We turned right to L'Hôtel on Rue des Beaux-Arts. The street was messy, and the entrance to the hotel was shabby. No one was at the reception desk.

Oscar Wilde had died in L'Hôtel about nineteen years earlier. His name was posted near the entrance. We had expected at least an ordinary greeting at the hotel. The lobby stank of cigarette smoke, out-of-date newspapers were scattered on the floor, and the leather chairs were stained and cracked. We decided not to wait for anyone in that lobby. I left a note for Harry Greene that we had arrived and would be waiting in a nearby park on the corner of Rue de Seine and Rue Mazarine behind the Institut de France.

Aloysius painted several scenes of blue ravens at the Musée du Louvre and perched on statues in the park. We waited for several hours and then returned to L'Hôtel. No one was there and the note had not been read. The guest register was behind the desk, so we searched the pages and found the name of Harry Greene, and the note, *une erreur dans la note*, an error in the bill. His room was located on the second floor. We knocked, and then entered the cold, dark, tiny room that faced another building at the back of the hotel. There were several empty notebooks on a table near the window.

Harry Greene appeared after dark, surprised, and with many apologies. Later, after some conversation about the war, he conceded that he had actually forgotten the date of our arrival in Paris. Never mind, you are here on leave at last, he said, and we rushed out of the hotel to the nearby Métro at Saint-Germain-des-Prés. He took us to dinner at the Café du Dôme in Montparnasse.

Harry was a familiar customer at the restaurant, so the waiters directed us immediately to a side table near the windows with a view of the terrace and the entrance. The novelist declared that we were new Dômiers, the artists and authors who gathered almost every day, in the late morning for café and late at night for wine and dinner.

Harry ordered a pitcher of white wine, declined the menu, and suggested that we try the *Saucisse de Toulouse*, salty, heavy pork sausage with mashed potatoes. We were hungry, the sausage was delicious, and later we learned that the signature sausage was the least expensive meal on the menu.

The Dômiers were seated at every table, but we could not recognize anyone. We were familiar with the names of some artists and writers but not with faces. Harry gestured with his eyebrows to one table and then to another as he pronounced the names of Pablo Picasso, Amedeo Modigliani, Georges Braque, Fernand Léger, André Breton, Blaise Cendrars, Jean Cocteau, Guillaume Apollinaire, and even the newsy revolutionaries Leon Trotsky and Vladimir Lenin. Naturally, we looked in every direction of his eyebrow gestures as he mentioned each great name.

Where is Pablo Picasso?

Not here yet, maybe later.

Where is Modigliani?

Painting at his studio in Montmartre.

How about André Breton?

Yes, at the entrance, he likes to meet everyone.

Guillaume Apollinaire?

No, he died last year of influenza.

So, how about Vladimir Lenin?

No, not tonight, Lenin is at the Kremlin.

Aloysius heard the names of artists and painted blue ravens perched at window tables in the Café du Dôme. The ravens by gesture and wave hinted and teased the presence of the artists by the turn of a beak, talons on the back of a chair, or fierce eyes, and with slight traces of black and rouge on wing and shank feathers. Picasso was blue, a natural presence with a distinctive cubist beak. Apollinaire was a blue raven with a slight bandage and the obscure words *reconnais-toi*, perceive or recognize yourself, painted in cubist traces of rouge. Lenin was perceived with an intense gaze reflected in the eye of a raven. The waiter recognized at once the blue ravens as Dômiers. The easiest trace of artistic presence was a cubist tease.

Harry drank a large pitcher of wine that night, and he laughed louder with each glass. He sang popular music and stumbled on the way back to L'Hôtel. Once in the room he smiled, waved, and was asleep in minutes. Aloysius slept on the floor near the door.

I read book seven of *The Odyssey* in the faint light near the window. *The walls on either side were of bronze from end to end, and the cornice was of blue enamel. The doors were gold, and hung on pillars of silver that rose from a floor of bronze, while the lintel was silver and the hook of the door was of gold.*

Aloysius awakened very early so we decided to write a note of appreciation for the dinner and stories and leave the hotel in silence. Wispy clouds caught the rosy sunrise on that cold morning in Paris. Only a few people were on the streets, mostly workmen and taxicab drivers. We walked down Rue Bonaparte turned right at Les Deux Magots on Boulevard Saint-Germain to the Café de Flore.

André Breton and Guillaume Apollinaire once gathered with other writers and artists at the Café du Dôme and at Café de Flore. No doubt Apollinaire made the rounds of several master cafés to pose with poets, artists, and musicians.

There were only three other customers that early morning at the Café de Flore. One patron was a policeman who wore a natty cape. Paris apparently was not a sunrise culture. The waiter was silent, surly, and avoided eye contact. We ordered the same fare as the policeman, the standard *petit déjeuner*, a basket of croissants, baguette, butter, and café. That morning we were content, even in our military uniforms, and we actually talked about how a native painter and a writer could survive in Paris. The Café de Flore was a delightful place to watch the city come alive in the morning. We sat at a small table near the window for about three hours, and by then most of the chairs were occupied. I listened to the customers and quickly learned how to speak with respect to the waiter. So we ordered more café, *s'il vous plaît*, and talked about our future in Paris.

Aloysius decided not to paint that morning, so we browsed in a nearby bookstore, Maison des Amis des Livres, at 7 Rue de l'Odéon, near Boulevard Saint-Germain. Mostly, we looked at the plain covers of new books and tried to translate the more obvious titles. Adrienne Monnier, the owner of the bookstore, rescued our most awkward translations and directed me to poetry, and my brother to books on art history. Adrienne was generous, slightly anxious, and her blue eyes were totemic, ready to touch the obscure. I was enchanted with her lovely round face, sturdy motion, the gentle movement of her hands, and the way she touched each book. The authors must have sensed her marvelous presence, and every book in the store waited to be touched by a reader.

I bought a copy of *Alcools*, cubist poetry, and *Calligrammes*, a selection of poetry and stories by the soldier and poet Guillaume Apollinaire. Adrienne pointed to a chair near the entrance, and said the author sat there many times. Naturally, my brother teased me about my attraction to the bookstore owner, and about my literary ambition to learn how to read poetry in French.

Calligrammes was published at the end of the war, a cubist irony of literature. The poetic words were visual scenes, the natural motion of images, direct in translation, and more memorable than the tiresome lessons of time, tense, and grammar. I tried to translate the first few descriptive lines of "A La Santé" from *Alcools*.

> *Avant d'entrer dans ma cellule*
> Ahead of entering my cell
> *Il a fallu me mettre nu*
> It was necessary for me to be naked
> *Et quelle voix sinistre ulule*
> And the shouts of sinister voices

Guillaume qu'es-tu devenu
Guillaume what have you become

Café du Départ was close to the Galerie Crémieux, but we had no sense of direction at the time. We walked down the sunny side of Boulevard Saint-Germain to Rue Dante and then to the art gallery at 4 Rue de la Bûcherie, a block from the River Seine and the Cathédrale Notre-Dame.

Nathan Crémieux, the owner of the gallery, was away for lunch so we waited in the tiny park across the street. Native ledger art, red and blue horses, bold feathers, painted pottery, curious objects from various native cultures, and from several pueblos in the American Southwest, were displayed in the gallery windows.

Harry Greene told us that Rue de la Bûcherie was one of the oldest streets in Paris. A perfect location for a gallery devoted to native creative and ceremonial arts. There were stately antique dealers on the street, several conventional and modernist galleries, and restaurants nearby.

Nathan Crémieux saw us in the park as he returned from lunch. He opened the door, turned on the threshold, smiled, waved, and invited us into the gallery. His fedora and natty tailored clothes reminded me of William Hole in the Day and our dressy cousin Ignatius Vizenor.

The walls of the gallery were covered with native ledger art and other paintings, and rows of wooden cabinets contained pueblo pottery, clay figures, mantas, kilts, sashes, and blankets. We learned later that he refused to negotiate the trade of kachinas, or medicine swathes and bundles, a decision we obviously respected.

Nathan was moved by the memories of our friend Odysseus who had worked for many years with his father and uncle as a trader in the Southwest. He fondly remembered many stories that his father Henri told about the traders, especially Jefferson Young and his son who were the most honorable traders with natives. He pointed to the art and objects in the gallery to show what his father and uncle had collected over more than twenty years as traders.

Aloysius studied the ledger art in the gallery and told Nathan that Odysseus had given him original paintings of blue horses by two Cheyenne artists, Bear's Heart and Squint Eyes. Nathan described himself as a modern trader of native art, a natural continuation of the just trade that his father started with natives. The names of ledger artists were familiar, of course, and then the trader turned to open a cabinet drawer to show us similar visionary paintings by other native artists who had been political prisoners at Fort Marion, Florida. Nathan was emotional, deeply troubled by the visionary scenes, that so great and natural an artistic perception was both stimulated and contained in a military prison.

Only a few of the native artists continued to paint once they were released from prison. I told the trader that most native art was a natural vision of liberty. The trader seemed to be heartened by my comments. We assured the trader that most native stories were distinctively ironic, a necessity to evade the romance of the primitive and sentiments of victimry.

Nathan seemed very concerned that we had not eaten lunch. He awkwardly embraced me by the shoulders as we walked out of the gallery, and promised that we could examine the entire collection later. Nearby in a café he told more stories about his father and the experiences of his family as Jews in France. A distant relative had changed the family surname, but only to overcome the initial bias and political exclusion of certain names in France. Crémieux became an honorable name in politics, native trade, and as the name of an art gallery. Nathan and his father were active in religious practices and duties of the synagogue.

Aloysius told the trader about our surname and the union of fur traders and natives on the White Earth Reservation. Hudon dit Beaulieu was conveyed by the *voyageurs* in the fur trade, and many natives returned with the same family name as soldiers in the defense of France.

Nathan was familiar with the names of Jewish traders that Odysseus mentioned in his stories. Julius Meyer, for instance, was one of the most active traders in Omaha, Nebraska, and the Northern Plains, and had boldly escorted natives to the Paris *Exposition Universelle* in 1889. Nathan had actually met Julius and natives on a tour of the Eiffel Tower. He invited the travelers that afternoon to visit his new gallery. Nathan was only twenty years old at the time, and he was impressed that Julius had paid the entire cost of travel for the natives. The natives on tour and the address of the Galerie Crémieux, a street of butchery, were mentioned in stories told by Odysseus.

I was awkward, at first, and could not easily talk with Nathan about the fur trade and our ancestors, not because of his manner or anything he actually said, but probably because of insecurity. I was overawed by his generosity, education, and experiences. My tendency was to tease the trader, but that seemed inappropriate at the time.

Nathan invited us to stay in a guest room at the back of the gallery, and later that day he escorted us to the Eiffel Tower and then to Montparnasse. The sun fluttered between streams of clouds, and lighted our faces on the stairs of the tower. The trader was a great storier, and a tentative teaser, a creative practice that he had learned from his father. Nathan was not hesitant, and his stories were rich in details but not in contradictions. The tease of the obvious, and ironic stories were natural to most natives.

Nathan introduced us to Rosalie Tobia, the feisty cook and owner of the Chez Rosalie restaurant at 3 Rue Campagne Première in Montparnasse. Mère Rosalie was Italian, a former nude model for Amedeo Modigliani, and she prepared outstanding meals in a tiny kitchen. The restaurant was narrow, smoky, and crowded with four marble tables. The daily menu was printed on a chalkboard.

Mère Rosalie bought fresh fruit and vegetables every day at the markets in Les Halles. Nathan translated the menu, and we ordered *Tranche de Melon*, *Soupe aux Legumes*, *Spaghetti*, *Aubergine à la Turque*, and *Pont l'Évêque*, a special *fromage*, or cheese. For dessert we had café and *Gateau de Semoule*, a semolina pudding. I was very hungry, the food was great, a truly family meal, and we were teased with every bite by Mère Rosalie.

The cost of the meals was very inexpensive, only two francs for *Aubergine à la Turque*, and less for the melon and cheese. Two francs was less than ten cents in dollars, and the entire cost of the dinner for three was about a dollar. The wine was separate but not expensive. Nothing was expensive at the time.

Nathan then invited us to have a drink at the Café du Dôme a few blocks from Chez Rosalie. He was truly surprised that night when the waiter recognized my brother. Nathan was amused by our stories of Harry Greene and the blue ravens my brother had painted the night before at dinner. Aloysius had left his art books of recent blue ravens at the gallery.

The Café du Dôme and La Rotonde were located on the Boulevard du Montparnasse near Boulevard Raspail, two sovereign cafés that sustained the grace and rivalry of art and politics, and the manners of each café must have thrived on favors and waned on the slights of intense artists and authors.

Nathan ordered a carafe of wine and later insisted that we stop by Le Chemin du Montparnasse at 21 Avenue du Maine, a famous alley of raggedy ateliers of great artists, writers, composers, and sculptors, Pablo Picasso, Henri Matisse, Georges Braque, Jean Cocteau, Amedeo Modigliani, Guillaume Apollinaire, Juan Gris, Erik Satie, and many others. I recited the first two lines of images in "*Les Fenêtres*" from *Calligrammes* by Apollinaire, and so revealed my passion for his poetry.

> *Du rouge au vert tout le jaune se meurt*
> Red with green and all the yellow dies
> *Quand chantent les aras dans les forêts natales*
> When the macaws sing in the native forests

Le Chemin du Montparnasse, the alley of ateliers, was only a few blocks from the Café du Dôme. Nathan directed us to the entrance of the narrow alley and told marvelous stories about a special dinner held two years earlier to honor Georges Braque, one of the most inspired cubist painters at the time. Nathan pointed to the atelier where the actual banquet was held. Braque had been wounded in the war and had returned from service. Blaise Cendrars, or Frédéric Louis Sauser, the poet and novelist, as Nathan related, was at the banquet for Braque. Cendrars had served with the French Foreign Legion and lost his right arm in the First World War.

Mariya Ivanovna Vassiliéva, or Marie Vassilieff, the cubist painter, and Max Jacob, the poet and painter, had arranged the dinner at Le Chemin du Montparnasse. We walked slowly into the dark alley, the ateliers were faintly lighted but no one was there at the time. Nathan had attended many artistic events, dinners, musical performances, exhibitions, literary parties, and lectures in the atelier of Marie Vassilieff. She had founded the Académie Vassilieff.

Nathan imagined the alley of ateliers that night at the dinner table to celebrate Georges Braque. He named and then pointed to each person seated at the conjured table in the alley. Marie Vassilieff was at one end of the banquet table with Henri Matisse who held a platter of roast turkey. Seated on the same side of the table in the alley were Blaise Cendrars, Pablo Picasso,

Marcelle Braque, in that order, Walther Halvorsen, Fernand Léger, and at the very end Max Jacob.

Nathan moved to the other side of the table in the alley and pointed to Erik Satie, the pianist and composer with a trimmed beard, then Juan Gris, the painter, Georges Braque, with a laurel wreath crown, Alfredo Pina, who was standing with a raised pistol, and then the seductive Béatrice Hastings.

The trader told stories about each of the dinner guests and at the same time he moved to the theatrical positions of the artists in the banquet scenes in the alley. Pina, a sculptor, aimed his pistol at Modigliani who had not been invited to the banquet because of his drunken rages, and because of his jealousy. Marie pushed her boozy friend Modigliani down the stairs and outside into the alley. Picasso and Manuel Ortiz de Zárate, the painter, locked the door to the atelier.

Nathan assured us that no shots were fired and no artistic bonds were ever broken or lost that evening. The politics of painters was similar to native conduct on the reservation. Béatrice, a poet, and former model and lover of Modigliani, was at the banquet with her new lover Alfredo Pina. Nathan moved closer to the imagined table in the alley, paused near Pina, and mentioned the portraits that Modigliani had painted of Béatrice. The erotic elongated neck, narrow face, and distinctive eye squint in the portraits might have driven the poet into the arms of the serious, handsome sculptor Pina.

Aloysius moved closer to the trader as he described the scenes of the banquet in the alley. My brother created an outline scene of the table on a newspaper. Most of the painters and poets were about ten years older than we were at the time. I imagined the singular artists and the original portrayals, the tease and touch of the poets, and yet we hardly knew anything about the artists and the great wave of cubist paintings.

We learned later that cubism and other avant-garde styles were censured as subversive and Germanic. The police had seized cubist art at the gallery of Daniel-Henry Kahnweiler, and the art was sold at auction after the war. Picasso, who had been discovered by the art dealer, was so concerned as a foreign artist that he turned to ordinary portraiture to avoid any suspicion of ironic or decadent enemy art.

Everything was so new, original, immediate, enlivened at the end of the war, and even more fantastic because of the stories the trader told that night at Le Chemin du Montparnasse.

Aloysius painted several blue raven scenes at the banquet in honor of Georges Braque. That night we pretended to be included in the marvelous occasions of artists, poets, sculptors, and novelists. The sounds and memories of the war were almost out of mind after only two days in Paris.

Marie Vassilieff walked around the corner at a convenient moment that night and concluded the last scene of the banquet in the alley. Her arrival was a miraculous coincidence, or a strategy of the story. That she walked into the actual story about the banquet was fantastic, by chance or maneuver, and persuasive either way.

Marie was short, nimble, and wore a black gaucho hat with a wide brim. She smiled, turned with a slight bow, a coy gesture in the presence of Nathan. We were introduced as native artists who had survived the war. Marie reached for my hand, and the warm caress touched my heart. I was enchanted with her manner and motion, the serene turn of her thin lips, and beautiful dreamy blue eyes.

Marie invited us into her atelier and home on the alley for wine, baguette, and cheese. I had first imagined the banquet of artists in the alley, and then pictured the actual scene at the table in her home. The last scene continued that night over wine and stories. Magnificent paintings by Marc Chagall, Modigliani, Matisse, Léger, and several drawings by Picasso covered the walls of the atelier. Marie was nude in one painting by Modigliani. I pretended not to stare at the seductive portrayal. The pose and colors of her body were magical in the faint light.

Marie presented several of her own innovative paintings, *Femme Assise*, a nude with two masks and a red heart, a child with a doll, a woman with a red bird on her head, abstract scenes, dancers, and cubist figures. Aloysius commented on the red bird and told stories about his blue ravens, and the trace of rouge he learned from Yamada Baske. At first my brother was troubled that he could not show the ravens that night, but later he was grateful for a reason to return to the atelier and show his blue ravens to Marie.

Nathan was not familiar with the watercolors of Baske, but he mentioned Léonard Tsuguharu Foujita, an eccentric Japanese artist who once shared an atelier with Modigliani. Foujita ate and drank at La Rotonde and the Café du Dôme. He wore earrings, a tunic, tattooed a watch on his wrist, and painted women, children, and many, many cats.

Marie told us she was born in Smolensk, Russia. She moved to Paris in 1905 and studied with Henri Matisse. Her atelier became a regular salon for Picasso, Modigliani, Juan Gris, the cubist painter, Ossip Zadkine, the sculptor, Chaim Soutine, the expressionist painter, Erik Satie, Jean Cocteau, Apollinaire, and Nina Hamnett, the wild bisexual artist, and many other artists and writers.

Aloysius politely interrupted her stories and revealed that the only artist he had ever meet was Yamada Baske in Minneapolis. My brother, however, was not an apologist for his limited experience. He continued with stories about our uncle Augustus Beaulieu who had published the *Tomahawk*, the first newspaper on the White Earth Reservation.

Marie was astounded to learn that natives actually published newspapers. The French romance of natives and nature excluded the possibility of any cosmopolitan experiences in the world. She could not believe that we had actually read international news stories on the reservation and sold papers at a train station.

Marie seemed to be impressed that my stories about the war were published in a series and distributed free on the White Earth Reservation. Natives read the stories and could better understand the experiences of the war. Nathan mentioned several other native newspapers, and specifically named the *Cherokee Phoenix*, the first native newspaper published in both English and Cherokee in Oklahoma Territory in 1828.

La Cantine des Artistes served cheap meals and wine to hungry artists and writers during the First World War. Marie was concerned that foreign and expatriate artists were desperate during the war so she started a soup kitchen, or canteen, at her atelier. She served meals to many artists, Picasso, Marc Chagall, André Salmon, Matisse, Jean Cocteau, Marie Blanchard, the cubist painter, Soutine, Braque, Léger, Cendrars, Modigliani, Jacob, Apollinaire, Zadkine, Béatrice Hastings, Pina, and others. Russian artists, dancers, creative writers, and revolutionaries were even more miserable at the time. Leon Trotsky and Vladimir Lenin dined at the canteen.

The atelier and canteen became a regular gathering place for artists after the cheap dinners were served. The Café du Dôme, restaurants, and other cafés were closed at night because of a war curfew, but the canteen was a private atelier and salon, so the artists congregated in the alley for music, dancing, and the politics of art late into the night. The canteen closed at the end of the war, a few months before we had arrived in Paris.

Paris homes and apartments were seldom heated, and partly because of a serious shortage of coal. The Germans destroyed the coalmines at the end of the war, a demonic vengeance. Hotels provided hot water for baths only on the weekends. Cafés were heated and a natural place for artists and writers to gather on a cold day, or any day.

Aloysius presented that morning at the gallery his most recent portrayals of blue ravens. My brother had painted eighteen war and river scenes in a new book of art paper. Nathan touched only the deckle edges, raised each blue raven scene to the light and studied the hues and details, and then he placed the paintings on a rack against the wall. He was silent, and sometimes caught his breath as he compared the ravens one by one. Several times during his close and deliberate review of the paintings he looked out the window, turned back, and then smiled. His concentration was a complement to any artist.

Nathan never commented as he studied the blue ravens, not a single word, until he had placed the entire collection of paintings on the rack. Only then he raised his hands and declared that the blue ravens were the creation of an intuitive painter, a genius and visionary of original native totemic art. Nathan was truly inspired by the scenes, the traces of rouge, and considered the abstract images a natural course of innovative native art that would be reviewed as avant-garde. He considered most native art as visionary, scenes in natural motion, innovative in color and composition, but never primitive. The blue and green buoyant horses, for instance, in native ledger art were mistaken as naïve and primitive art. Nathan worried that the suave salons and museum curators would only convey the mundane romance of primitive art and disregard the most obvious creative wisdom of visionary native expressionism. Native artists were inspired by the seasons, natural reason, motion, chance, and a sense of presence, not by perspective, harmony, monotheism, pious customs, or the hocus pocus of theatrical modernism.

Naturally, my brother was pleased, and relieved, because the close review was by a respected art trader and collector. Nathan announced that he would frame the blue ravens and display several at a time in the Galerie Crémieux. When two sold he would present three more paintings, and in that way indicate the precious nature of the portrayals, and the natural totemic tease of *les corbeaux bleus*, the blue ravens.

Aloysius later that morning created a throng of blue ravens at the entrance of Le Chemin du Montparnasse. The great abstract wings embraced the cubist beaks of seven ravens, and the tiers of baroque talons were traced with rouge. That evening we were invited to dinner at the atelier and my brother presented his most recent blue painting as a gift to Marie Vassilieff.

Marie studied the blue scene of the enormous raven wings and talons at the entrance of the ateliers, and named three cubist beaks as the raven simulations of Apollinaire, Picasso, and Marie Vassilieff. Picasso was a raven with a blue beak. Apollinaire was a raven with traces of black, a funeral scene. Marie the raven was painted with bright blue eyes, and with traces of black on the mane. She was touched by the gift of original native art, and told my brother to pose, then and there at the end of the huge banquet and canteen table, for a silhouette portrait. At the same time she created a silhouette of me. Marie had prepared a roast turkey dinner in our honor, and then she told more stories about the great banquet several months earlier for Georges Braque.

Modigliani, she declared, could not remember that he had been pushed out down the stairs and into the alley. She promised to invite us to parties at Le Chemin du Montparnasse.

Marie was beautiful, an elegant portrait in the muted light at the end of the table. Her voice was clear, and her words were mellow and meditative. The precise motion of her hands enhanced the stories. I was captivated by her blue eyes, and encouraged more stories about the banquet, and about the hungry artists and writers who were served meals during the war. I never wanted to leave the atelier.

Marie agreed to read poems by Guillaume Apollinaire. The sound of her poetic voice and the words of my favorite poet changed me that night. The images of poetry created visual scenes that lasted forever in my memory. I heard her voice in every poem. Marie read several poems from *Le Bestiaire ou Cortège d'Orphée*, *Alcools*, and *Calligrammes* in French.

I raised my glass of wine to honor the memory of our cousin Ignatius

Vizenor who died in combat three months earlier near the commune of Montbréhain. The spirit of our cousin returned to the earth of his fur trade ancestors.

Aloysius raised his glass and proposed a toast to honor the *voyageurs,* our ancestors of the fur trade, and the great traders Jefferson Young, Odysseus Young, Julius Meyer, and Henri Crémieux. My brother told several stories about Misaabe, Animosh, and the mongrel healers on the White Earth Reservation.

The stories that night turned to native totems and animals, and the presence of animals and birds in art and literature. Marie was perceptive about animals, but had not thought about the visionary presence of animals and birds in art. She looked around the atelier at her collection of paintings and wondered how animals and birds could be imagined in the scenes. Léonard Tsuguharu Foujita painted many domestic cats, but no other animals.

The *Manabozho Curiosa* came to mind late that night as the stories turned to native totems and animals. The ancient monastic manuscript described the sexual practices and pleasures with various animals, mostly furry. The carnal curiosities of wayward monks were transcribed in the fifteenth century. The monks lived near natives at the headwaters of the *gichi-ziibi,* the Mississippi River.

Aloysius was worried about the response to my native stories about the sensuous monks. He smiled and then turned toward the window. Nathan cocked his head, and seemed to wonder if my stories were actually about sex with animals. Marie encouraged me to continue with the fantastic animal stories. She surmised that the Japanese painter Tsuguharu Foujita must have had *érotique* thoughts about his many cats.

I made it clear that the monks would never mount domestic animals, and were stimulated only by wild creatures, a union of monastic habits and animal curiosities. Nathan was a great listener and celebrated the irony of the curiosa stories. He insisted on the story of an actual sexual encounter with an animal.

I recounted the ancient stories of the erotic scenes of monks and rabbits, and especially that night because of the culinary preference for *civet de lapin,* rabbit or hare stew in France.

Marie poured more wine, served cheese, and leaned closer to hear the *érotique* stories of monks, masturbation, and animals. I was excited that night by her blue eyes, and by the portrait of her graceful nude body. I could imagine her erotic eyes in the portrait, and her nude presence at the banquet table. Naturally, my descriptive stories of sensuous animals were more passionate in her presence, and in that sense more ironic.

The monks were aroused by the erotic reach of the snowshoe hare and masturbated on the soft, white, silky coat, a natural pleasure of the season. Everything about the snowshoe hare was erotic. The monks transcribed the sensual pleasures of huge soft paws, and the warm underbelly as the hare browsed on bark. The monks wrote other erotic stories about bears, beaver, otter, and white-tailed deer. Sensuous encounters with a porcupine were the most favored and ironic of native storiers.

Marie was amused by the *érotique* hare stories. She watched me closely and seemed to anticipate in the tone of my voice traces of irony. I decided not to continue with the actual descriptions in the manuscript of masturbation with totemic bears, beaver, and sacred river otter.

I paused and then turned the stories to a parody. The monks were teased by natives, and mocked in stories and mimicked in seasonal dances. A native shaman created the *debwe*, a heart dance that mocked the eroticism of the pious monastic monks. The reach of the snowshoe hare was one of the most sensual poses of the ironic heart dancers.

That night at the atelier never ended in my memory. Marie was forever a presence in my stories, and came to mind in every reference or trace of art and literature in France. I heard the gentle tone of her voice forever in the poetry of Apollinaire.

Nathan had never traveled across the ocean, but he accepted our invitation to visit the White Earth Reservation. The next day the trader introduced us to several art galleries, including the gallery at 28 Rue Vignon owned by Daniel-Henry Kahnweiler. He decided not to go with us to the Musée du Louvre. Yet, he urged us to return soon and set aside a week or two to view some of the great treasures of art in the vast collection.

Nathan insisted that he escort and introduce us to the Musée d'Ethnographie du Trocadéro, the national ethnographic museum of African, South American, and North American Indian art and cultural objects. Most of the cultural objects had been stolen, seized as colonial possessions, and some obtained by trade. Many French explorers had returned with cultural booty, the sovereign rights of godly conquests and a covetous civilization. The Canadian National Railway gave the museum huge native totem poles. The ancestral poles were from British Columbia. What right does a railroad have to give away native cultural property?

The building was cold, damp, and smelled moldy. Scientists and ethnographers hoarded tens of thousands of cultural objects and art in the museum. The collections had been misused, neglected, poorly displayed, and in disarray. I understood why the trader was determined to show us through the museum. He actually resented the way native objects were treated, and wanted natives to object in the name of cultural property.

Aloysius was furious that the museum had abandoned native arts. Ethnologists, he shouted in the corridors, were no better than the thieves of the native property. Pablo Picasso, he learned later, had visited the museum about ten years earlier and was depressed by the musty building and disregard of the objects. African masks had partly inspired his cubist portrayals of the women in *Les Demoiselles d'Avignon.*

France was rightly shamed by the musty museum, and the cost of the war was no excuse to abandon the collection. Native cultures and sovereign nations were peculiar unions and at times enemies. Civilization in the name of national museums never conveyed a real prominence in the humane protection of native art. The notion of civilization represented as much shame in the world as headway and betterment.

The first scandal of enlightenment was the theft of cultural and sacred objects. The second scandal was the abuse of precious cultural memories. Yet, the actual native spirit of the art was never shamed or abused by possession. Native art was collected in a national ethnographic museum for the first time with art from other cultures around the world, and the voices of the spirited artists have been heard forever in museums.

Picasso and other artists heard the voices of native artists in exhibitions and musty galleries, and created original portrayals that honor a union of cultures not ethnographers. The voices of visionary artists were never derivative, and the voices of native artists were heard in the hues of blue horses afloat, in hide paintings, masks, crowns, ceremonial feathers, water drums, medicine bundles, wing bones, bears, sandhill cranes, ravens, great waves of blue, and traces of rouge. Curators and custodians of native art never mentioned these cosmototemic voices in museums.

The train swayed that night through the gritty industrial areas outside the great circles of art, galleries, ateliers, and memories of Paris. My brother was asleep, his head rested against the frame of the carriage window. I watched the slight reflection of my face in motion through the dark countryside and was reminded once more of the war.

The Paris Peace Conference was about to start. Our furlough was over and we would soon return home. I read book eight of *The Odyssey* that night and then waited for the first tease of morning light. *The company then laid their hands upon the good things that were before them, but as soon as they had had enough to eat and drink, the muse inspired Demodocus to sing the feats of heroes, and more especially a matter that was then in the mouths of all men, to wit, the quarrel between Ulysses and Achilles, and the fierce words that they heaped on one another as they eat together at a banquet.*

17

DECEIT OF PEACE
1919

The First Pioneer Infantry marched down the dock at Le Port Militaire in Brest and one by one the regiments boarded the shabby steamship *Ancon*. The departure was solemn that early summer, no salutes or martial music to honor the soldiers who had defended the French Third Republic.

Slowly the bright colors of the sailboats and steady beams of the solitary harbor vanished in the distance. The Atlantic Ocean was stormy, heavy waves, and the constant heave, mount, and shudder of the ship was the last reminder of the war, but the return voyage was more secure with no chance of enemy submarines. The ship docked two weeks later without notice, fanfare, or even a biscuit to honor the soldiers at Newport News, Virginia, on July 7, 1919.

The American Expeditionary Forces had entered the war late and yet became a critical episode, and a mighty sway in the modern history of France. We were the crucial native soldiers of defense, the worthy descendants of the fur trade, a painter and resolute writer, and we had survived with pluck and backbone as combat scouts. Then, at the end of the war, we carried out with other soldiers the dreary winter mission of a military occupation in Germany.

The Paris Peace Conference started on January 18, 1919, in Paris. The agents of a new German government endorsed the Treaty of Versailles five months later on June 28, 1919. The First Pioneer Infantry had occupied Koblenz during the final political maneuvers of peace. We might have been home earlier if the treaty had not been concocted with such vengeance.

Once a soldier, once a war, once an armistice, our honorable discharge from military service was processed in a few days time and then we returned with other soldiers and our mail order olive drab wool sweaters and chamois money belt to the Ogema Station on the White Earth Reservation.

The train stopped at the same godly towns that we had counted on our way to war last summer. A year later nothing seemed to have changed, nothing but the memory of many soldiers who would not return from the First World War.

Ogema Station was almost at the end of the railroad line, so we observed the exaltation at every station for the soldiers who had survived, and at the same time the great sorrow for the wounded and the many soldiers who had died in combat and were buried in France. More than a hundred thousand American soldiers had died in the war, and twice as many soldiers were wounded in service with the American Expeditionary Forces.

The railroad stations were decorated with patriotic banners, and as the train arrived parents and teachers coached the children to salute with one hand and with the other hand wave miniature Stars and Stripes. The soldiers who returned that summer were hardly prepared to become the precious resurrection of patriotism and cheap labor in wearisome small towns.

Patch was seated at the window with his trumpet and at the ready to play military taps at every railroad stop between Chicago and the Ogema Station on the White Earth Reservation. Naturally, we were moved by the sound of ceremonial taps, and yet we were constantly reminded of the political misuse of the rituals of honor and the extravagance of patriotism at every station.

Aloysius painted nothing on our return to the reservation. He could not paint the reversal of war. In that sense our return was an absence of creative motion and energy. We were both inspired by the mystery, anxiety, and irony of the passage to war, to the country of our ancestors of the fur trade, but the actual return was futile, and the sense of vain nostalgia only increased with the patriotic hurrah and celebrations at each station.

My brother turned away from the romantic praise of uniforms, heroic war rumors, and courage promoted by military decorations. He honored only the actual soldiers, and could not imagine any scene of our reversal that was worth painting. The blue ravens refused to return to the reservation that summer at the end of the war. The homey overtones of peace, the war to end wars, were deceptions and scarcely worth comment, paint, or conversation.

The fury of the war continued in our memories, and there were no easy reversals of our experiences as scouts. The wistful notion of peace was more of a hoax, a theatrical and political revision, than a turnaround of hatred and remorse. Count more than fifteen million bloody bodies, twenty million wounded soldiers, and then consider the use of the word *peace* over wine, banquet conversations, and war memories.

The French count more than a million dead soldiers, or about four percent of the national population. The survivors must honor the dead at the end of war, but not by the political return to the deceit of national and cultural peace.

Naturally, we embraced the presence of the seasons, chance, native stories, and memories, but the horror of the war, and our experiences as combat scouts became a burden of nasty shadows and a revulsion of the political postures of patriotism. Yes, we were once soldiers, but never the patriots of a nostalgic culture of peace. Most soldiers returned to small towns and cities. We returned to a federal occupation on the reservation. Our return to the reservation was neither peace nor the end of the war. The native sense of chance and presence on the reservation had always been a casualty of the civil war on native liberty.

My spirit had been wounded by the war, but the notion of a bruised war memory was much too conceited an emotion to share with others in conversations. The soldiers with actual bloody wounds of combat, shattered, burned, blistered, disfigured faces, and severed limbs deserved the greatest honors, quiet honors, cautious humor, and the humane native tease of remembrance.

I was aware of my wounds when we hawked newspapers and first visited the library in Minneapolis. The comparisons of federal and church politics on the reservation, the repressive government schools, and the generous cosmopolitan world of art and literature revealed the wounds of my spirit.

Even more of a burden, my spirit was weakened by the sudden death of Augustus. He demanded that we learn about other worlds, and he was not sentimental or romantic. My uncle always lived by the native courage of resistance, and at the same time he celebrated chance and the ironies of liberty. He was direct, difficult, tricky, a steady teacher, and never wavered in his loyalty.

There were great native stories but no inspired literature or art on the reservation, and it was not easy on our return from the war to imagine otherwise. My mother would understand, of course, but she would be over burdened because of her perception and empathy of my moody ideas about an indefinable and wounded spirit.

I know my mother had read the published stories about the war, and since the end of the war my stories have obviously avoided the gratuitous and conceited notions of my abstract wounds and miseries. Surely she understood that there were more war scenes that were not published in my stories.

I watched the reflection of my face on the train window, the ethereal motion of my eyes in the trees and meadows, and was reminded of that moment outside the art gallery ten years earlier when the setters and our faces in the window moved with other faces on the streetcar. I considered the creation of my stories in motion, a great literature of motion, but not on the reservation.

Paris easily came to mind, and especially in motion on the train. My memories turned easily to the stories of the banquet and to that marvelous dinner party with Marie Vassilieff and Nathan Crémieux at Le Chemin du Montparnasse.

I read book nine of *The Odyssey* as the train departed from the Milwaukee Road Depot in Minneapolis. *There is nothing better or more delightful than when a whole people make merry together, with the guests sitting orderly to listen, while the table is loaded with bread and meats, and the cup bearer draws wine and fills his cup for every man. This is indeed as fair a sight as a man can see. Now, however, since you are inclined to ask the story of my sorrows, and rekindle my own sad memories in respect of them, I do not know how to begin, nor yet how to continue and conclude my tale, for the hand of heaven has been laid heavily upon me.*

18

BANQUET FRANÇAIS
—————— 1919 ——————

The Soo Line Railroad engineer sounded the screechy whistle four times as the train approached the decorated platform of the Ogema Station. The soldiers on the train were mostly our relatives, fur trade boys from the White Earth Reservation.

William Hole in the Day, Ignatius Vizenor, Charles Beaupré, and Fred Casebeer were honored by five traditional native elders at the train station, and our cousin Ellanora Beaulieu, who had served as a nurse and died of influenza at the end of the war, was honored with the soldiers.

Corporal Lawrence Vizenor, our cousin, who had received the Distinguished Service Cross, was revered that late afternoon for his extraordinary bravery in combat with the enemy.

Then seventeen other soldiers who had served in the war were honored at the station. The beat of the drums was strong and steady, and the native soldiers were ordered to stand at attention on the platform. The traditional singers and elders wore native ceremonial vests, beaded sashes, and carried medicine bundles. The spirited voices of the elders reached to the thunderclouds, and the sound rose above the steady steam of the train engine.

We honor the flag
We honor your bravery
And we sing to honor
Your return as warriors.

Patch Zhimagaanish played ceremonial taps on his trumpet. We saluted the elders, and then at the verge of rage shouted out the names of the dead, Hole in the Day, Vizenor, Beaupré, Casebeer, Beaulieu, to honor the memory of their spirits and native presence as warriors. Public tributes to the warriors and the native dead were never the end of stories, or a truce of remembrance, and likewise peace was never a reversal of war memories.

Father Aloysius gestured with the sign of the cross, and then he bowed his head to honor the singers and the soldiers. I was moved by the songs, by the honors, and then looked to the thunderclouds over the station.

The railroad engineer waited for the ceremonies to conclude. He had delivered soldiers to many towns since the end of the war, but had never delayed the schedule of the train until our arrival at the Ogema Station. The engineer admired natives and he was especially impressed by the dedication of Patch Zhimagaanish. The entire memorial scene would have been shrouded in steam, and the sound of native singers, drumbeats, and trumpet obscured had the engineer started the great engine on schedule.

Odysseus stood near the railroad engineer, and at the end of the honors and native ceremonies he moved slowly through the crowd on the platform, and sang loudly the patriotic anthem, "My Country, 'Tis of Thee."

We were not surprised that he had heightened the anthem with the addition of new verses. As the trader walked and sang others joined in the music, and the crowd on the platform became a great patriotic choir. Men and women removed their hats, touched their hearts, and sang to the thunderclouds.

> My country, 'tis of thee,
> Sweet land of liberty,
> Of thee I sing;
> Land where my fathers died
>
> . . .
>
> From ev'ry mountainside
> Let freedom ring!
>
> . . .
>
> My native country, thee,
> Where all men are born free, if white's their skin;
> I love thy hills and dales,
> Thy mounts and pleasant vales;
> But hate thy negro sales, as foulest sin.

Odysseus had omitted a single line from the original patriotic song, *Land of the Pilgrim's Pride*, and then included a selection from the sardonic verses written by an abolitionist. The trader was never reluctant to tease anyone with an ironic reference to the pride of pilgrims and native land. The station choir hesitated over the absent verse, and then most natives sang along with the revised section of the anthem.

Odysseus inspired most of the natives at the station, but never the federal agent who frowned at the words "negro sales" and was clearly pained by the irony of music. Foamy had never been at ease with natives or at public events. I smiled and waved to the agent, but he knew my gestures were not sincere. He turned to leave and never honored the soldiers.

Naturally, our parents were there at the train station. They had waited in the shade near the ticket office with the station agent, and then when the ceremonies ended they pushed through the crowd and beamed with excitement.

Margaret reached out and embraced Aloysius. Honoré hobbled down the platform and clutched my shoulders with his huge hands, a memorable moment because my father was seldom affectionate. He had injured his right leg in a logging accident last winter and could no longer work in the woods as a lumberjack. My father continued to hold my right shoulder for support as we talked about the troop ships, enemy submarines, rough seas, military food, and the trains crowded with soldiers.

My father rightly praised Patch for his dedication and good nature, and for playing military taps to honor the soldiers at every station. I decided not to reveal that afternoon my critical thoughts about the rage of patriotism and the deceit of peace.

Honoré asked me about the portrayal of painted faces in my stories as a scout. He wondered who had taught us how to paint our faces as warriors, and seemed rather concerned over my simple explanation that the decorations were invented, and nothing more. We painted our faces only to menace the enemy.

Margaret worried when she read my stories about the enemy machine guns, and the destruction of so many towns. She was ready to care for the children of the war. Aloysius mentioned the hungry children on the streets of Paris.

Honoré was rather talkative at the station, which was unusual, and vexed that we had served in the occupation, the enemy camp of the Germans. He expressed the native sense of the enemy way, and declared that native warriors should never carry out an occupation of the enemy. Capture, liberate, or terminate, but never occupy.

I moved closer to hear my father, and touched his face as the engine roared out of the station. He stared at me, and then smiled, but did not move away. I tried but could not remember the image of his rugged face that year in France. Honoré was moved and actually embraced me, a heartfelt but awkward motion. He was protective, distant, never severe, and hardly listened to me as a child. No doubt the scenes in my published stories, his worries about the war, the stature of two sons in uniform, and our return without wounds brought tears to his eyes.

John Leecy provided the transportation from the station to an informal reception for the veterans at the hotel. The Ford truck was new and had been converted with seats in the back, similar to the ambulances in the war. The familiar horse-drawn wagon was no longer necessary. He explained that in the past year there were fewer travelers, more motor cars on the reservation, and the hotel no longer had a reason to provide a livery stable.

John was discreet and diplomatic at the reception, and handed out personal and formal printed invitations to Odysseus, Doctor Mendor, Misaabe, Catherine Heady, Shona Goldman, a cultural anthropologist who studied totems and music of the fur trade, Basile Beaulieu, Aloysius Beaulieu, Patch Zhimagaanish, and Lawrence Vizenor, who had returned a few months earlier, to a special Banquet Français at the Hotel Leecy. The banquet was scheduled a week later. Lawrence and Patch had never been invited to the high table. Patch pressed his uniform, and polished his bugle.

The soldiers were feted for two weeks, dinners, celebrations, services, salutes, and then the dreadful memories of the war returned with the solitude of the lakes and forests. The native soldiers who were once the military occupiers had returned to the ironic situation of the occupied on a federal reservation.

Margaret prepared a delightful family dinner for everyone that night at our home near Mission Lake. Father Aloysius saluted each and every soldier at the train station, and later that night he arrived with two bottles of sacramental wine from the namesake Beaulieu Vineyards of Napa Valley, California.

Prohibition of alcohol would soon be the new national law, but alcohol was already banned on reservations so the only real worry was the federal agent. My mother thought it was shrewd to invite the agent to dinner. Maybe so, the agent always came by without an invitation. Foamy, of course, declined the invitation with regrets, but we knew he would appear in time for dessert. Father Aloysius, in the spirit of the moment, insisted that we toast the peace, honor the dead, and finish the bottles of wine with dinner and before the dessert visitation of the nosey agent.

Margaret and Honoré prepared fresh walleye pike, roasted chicken, wild rice with bacon, corn, carrots, potatoes, and blueberry pie. I was home with friends and family and my wounds of the spirit were easily disguised that night at dinner.

Patch deserved the greatest recognition, and his service as the regimental bugler was rightly celebrated. Everyone was moved by the story that he had played taps at every station on the route of the Soo Line Railroad. I told the story about the power of his magnificent baritone voice, and the incredible moment last Christmas Eve when he sang the French National Anthem, *La Marseillaise*, from a fortress overlooking the Rhine River and Koblenz, Germany.

John Clement Beaulieu, our cousin, learned several love songs when he was in France, and he wanted Patch to sing *La Marseillaise* that night at dinner. We were the descendants of the fur trade, and the anthem of *fraternité*, *égalité*, and *liberté* was necessary on the White Earth Reservation.

Father Aloysius praised the service of the soldiers, and twice repeated that so many were from the White Earth Reservation. He raised his glass to toast the memory of those who returned only in spirit. Michael Vizenor and Angeline Cogger pointed to a picture of their son, and our cousin, Ignatius Vizenor. My mother had thoughtfully placed two framed pictures on the sideboard to honor the memory of Ignatius and Ellanora Beaulieu. Angeline recounted a tender version of the familiar story that Ignatius was coddled at night in a cigar box because he was so tiny as a baby.

Father Aloysius surprised me with an exaggerated and ironic story about the holy baptism of Ignatius at Saint Benedict's Catholic Mission. The priest related that the mission sisters worried that the tiny baby might be doused, so a sacramental finger thimble from the school sewing class was used to measure the holy water.

Margaret naturally collected my seven published stories in the series

French Returns. She bound the newsprint with a ribbon, and placed the stack of stories on the sideboard next to the photographs. On the wall above the sideboard were two framed paintings, scenes of blue ravens at the train station and at the White Earth Hospital.

Reverend Clement Hudon Beaulieu, our uncle, praised my stories and promised as the new editor of the *Tomahawk* to continue the publication of the newsprint series once or twice a month, but with a new title, *French Returns: The New Fur Trade*. Yes, and my uncle agreed that the theme of my new stories would obviously be on native veterans.

Foamy arrived with the precision of a master dessert spy, and at the same time he tried to detect the trace of alcohol. He nosed the laughter and easy conversations, but we had already consumed the sacramental wine with multiple toasts two hours earlier, and the bottles had been buried out back with fish guts, bones, and chicken feathers.

The *Tomahawk* had reported that the Eighteenth Amendment to the Constitution of the United States had been ratified and would become the prohibition of alcohol law on January 17, 1920. Actually we read that the Wartime Prohibition Act banned alcohol to conserve grain during the war, but the war had already ended when the law was passed.

The federal government had banned the use and sale of alcohol on the reservation. Foamy was the enforcer, and he took pleasure in the capture of native drinkers and traders who provided the alcohol. The agent was born nasty, sober, reactionary, authoritarian, and his conceit was hardened with the arrogance of an outsider. The greyback might have been more likable as a drinker. He demonstrated the absolute absence of any sense of humor, irony or compassion for natives.

Foamy anticipated the national ban on alcohol and decided to enforce prohibition with a vengeance, a triple prosecution of the ratified and future law, the federal law to conserve grain, and the common prohibition of alcohol of any kind on reservations. So, our toasts that night were mighty violations of prohibition. The ceremonial use of sacramental wine was exempt from the prohibition laws, and so we designated the dinner reception a sacred ceremonial service.

Foamy asked me about my duties in the war, and moved closer to nose my breath for alcohol. I overstated my experiences, breathed heavily, and embellished my combat stories because the agent was not really interested in natives, and was so easily distracted that he never appreciated my stories or the irony.

At first my father and uncles were amused by the mockery of my elaborate agent stories, and everyone at the dinner table waited for some response from the federal agent. I invited the agent to speak about his service in the military, but he changed the subject and tried to dominate the dessert conversation with tedious comments about native moonshine and stolen sacramental wine from the reservation missions. Foamy smiled smugly over the blueberry pie and refused to name the vintage of stolen sacramental wine.

Aloysius shunned the agent more that night than at any other time in the past. My brother could not bear to listen to the southern yammer of the agent. Yes, as soldiers we were obliged to respond to military morons in positions of authority, but not at home on the reservation. We were strained but mannered that night only because of the invitation by our generous mother, but we loathed the agent for ordinary political reasons, and because he reminded us of the dopey dangerous officers in the military.

Honoré shouted that the agent was a cadger and bloodsucker with no soul or spirit. My father was angry about the sale of war bonds on the reservation. Poor and patriotic natives sent their sons to war and then the families were shamed to buy bonds to support the war. My father was right that a greater percentage of natives died in the war than other soldiers, and natives were frequently given more dangerous missions.

I had never heard my father speak with such intensity. He had always tried to avoid the agent and the government when he was a lumberjack near Bad Medicine Lake. The logging accident changed his manner and native dodge, and he declared a verbal war on the deceit and treachery of the agent.

John Leecy regretted that he could not reinstate our jobs in the livery stable. He was worried that so many veterans returned from the war and could not find work. The government provided most of the jobs on the reservation, but the agent made the final decision on every person hired, and he would never hire two veterans who were related to the founder of the *Tomahawk*. For that reason we had actually hoped to return to the stable for at least a few months, and yet we understood the obvious decrease in travelers on horseback, and the increase in motor cars. So, we suggested that John Leecy establish the first gas station on the reservation and hire us to service cars not horses. He was impressed with our proposal, but not for another few years. Meanwhile the only jobs he could offer were as waiters in the dining room. We declined the offer so he invited us to live at no cost in one of his tourist cabins near Bad Boy Lake.

Aloysius needed solitude to resume his painting, and the cabin was remote, a perfect location on the shore of the lake, and very close to Misaabe, the mongrels, and Animosh. We decided to return to a basic native sense of survival, to hunt, fish, and in the autumn gather maple syrup and wild rice. The plan was simple, secluded, and a peaceful transition from the military, and we could save most of our money. We had saved almost our entire pay for one year in military service. The government paid us forty-four dollars a month and we each saved about five hundred dollars.

》》》 《《《

Messy Fairbanks, the famous native *chef de cuisine*, chopped, stirred, stewed, seasoned, baked, and prepared with incredible concentration the Banquet Français at the Hotel Leecy. The actual menu for the special dinner was selected from a country cookbook published in Paris. Messy converted the weights and measures and Catherine Heady, the government schoolteacher, translated the recipes into English.

The Banquet Français reminded me of Nathan Crémieux and the marvelous stories about the atelier banquet in the alley at Le Chemin du Montparnasse. John Leecy told me that he had conceived of the banquet when he read my recent stories about the Café du Dôme and the cubist painter Marie Vassilieff in Paris. So, he decided to arrange a memorable banquet at the Hotel Leecy to celebrate our return, to respect the native casualties of the war, to praise our ancestors of the fur trade, and to honor the courage of Corporal Lawrence Vizenor who had received the Distinguished Service Cross.

John Leecy was inspired by ceremonies, and he suggested that the honored veterans wear uniforms to dinner, one last time to celebrate the end of the war. Aloysius decided at the last minute to paint two blue vertical bands on his cheeks. The blue decorations of a warrior were sensational at the banquet, and the curiosity about the face paint cued the stories about our missions as scouts, but the face paint that night was not a menace. I wore my campaign hat, web belt, and carried a canteen of water.

We entered the hotel as usual through the side door to the kitchen. Messy was beating egg whites in preparation of a wispy dessert. She turned, slapped her thighs, burst into laughter, and then wanted to know why my brother had painted his cheeks blue, and pretended he was a warrior. Aloysius smiled, the blue bands curved, and he provided no explanation.

Messy swayed toward my brother, a wild, erotic motion, and reached out with her strong arms for an embrace. Messy wore a smock and apron that disguised her huge belly. My brother tried to dodge the belly but he was caught in the corner. Messy was a heavy breather and determined to press against his blue cheeks and body. She always wanted to press on our bodies.

Messy seldom read the *Tomahawk*, or any newspaper, and she had not read my published stories, so, as a distraction, we recounted the night that we painted our faces as scouts to scare and capture the enemy. She was captivated by our war stories, but not sidetracked from the preparation of the banquet that night. Suddenly she waved her arms and pushed us out of the kitchen.

The Banquet Français menu was printed on deckle-edge paper in fancy calligraphy. The title, *Soldiers of the Fur Trade*, and four names, *Lawrence Vizenor, Basile Hudon Beaulieu, Aloysius Hudon Beaulieu, Patch Zhimagaanish* were printed on the cover, and inside with the actual menu were the names of the invited guests and banquet storiers. That invitation became a historical document of the reservation and the end of the war.

I could pronounce most of the descriptive names of the four courses printed on the menu. The French banquet was our first country dinner, the sublime irony of a fur trade legacy and a federal reservation. Mostly we had ordered omelets and sausage at the Café du Départ, Café de Flore, and Café du Dôme. Nothing we ate was ever fancy or even the daily fare of peasantry. Marie Vassilieff had served roast turkey and potatoes at her atelier in Paris.

Leecy organized the elaborate banquet celebration because he honored veterans, of course, and because he was very close to our uncle Augustus Beaulieu. The Hotel Leecy was always advertised on the front page of the *Tomahawk*. Augustus and John had shared some business interests, commercial trade, and land development on the reservation, but that remained a mystery.

Messy prepared and two native waiters served four courses at the Banquet Français. She had served a similar dinner four years earlier in the hotel when we were mere stable boys. We were twenty years old at the time and drank the Green Fairy, the banned absinthe, for the first time that night. I remembered the stories about traders and the federal agent that were told by Augustus and Odysseus.

Odysseus was rather mystical as he told the stories of tricky commerce to secure four bottles of wine from France. Messy stored the bottles on crushed ice, and on cue with the first course she rounded the table and poured *Château La Tourelle*, a white wine from Bordeaux. John Leecy raised his glass to honor the three veterans at the table, and then he read out loud my story about the death of Ignatius Vizenor.

Private Ignatius Vizenor and the Hundred Eighteenth Infantry Regiment advanced with artillery and heavy tank support early that rainy morning, Tuesday, October 8, 1918, sixty-two days into the Hundred Days Offensive. Ignatius was shot in the chest by an enemy machine gun. He collapsed and died slowly on a cold and muddy verge near a series of trenches east of Montbréhain, France.

Silence, and then the trader teased me about the words "muddy verge." The tease was perfectly timed to relieve that solemn moment, and the memories of our dapper cousin. The wine was delicate, exceptional, and the taste reminded me of Paris. Aloysius saluted the trader, and as a gesture of gratitude he promised to carve more blue raven pendants. My brother had not painted or mentioned the blue ravens since we boarded the ship at Brest, France.

John Leecy, the *vin blanc*, and later the moonshine were praised many times that summer night, and the quirky scenes of ironic stories transformed the mundane cast of the reservation. Aloysius declared that Sergeant Sorek, the man who had ordered us on risky missions as scouts, was more humane than the federal agent. Doctor Mendor was more inspired in his tribute to the soldiers and recited a few lines of poetry from *Leaves of Grass* by Walt Whitman.

The moon gives you light,
And the bugles and the drums give you music,
And my heart, O my soldiers, my veterans,
My heart gives you love.

Messy changed the solemn mood as she sounded a chime and marched into the dining room with the first course of the Banquet Français. She wore a thin black gown, black apron, a blue cape, and bound her black hair with a thick white turban, a very exotic pose in any great restaurant.

The first course was *Soupe de Poissons*, or puréed fish soup with sunfish, perch, and crappies, and stewed with fennel, tomatoes, garlic, orange peel, and black pepper. The soup was served with fresh butter and warm baguettes. Animosh caught the fish that very day at Bad Boy Lake.

Messy told the first story that night about the federal agent as she poured more wine, and as the waiters removed the soup bowls. Foamy had tracked the scent of prohibited alcohol that morning to the kitchen of the Hotel Leecy. The agent had an acute nose for the wine in the *Coq au Beaulieu*, the main course of the banquet. The red wine, sliced onions, celery, carrots, garlic, smoked thick bacon, and peppercorns were simmered with two chickens. Later the chickens were garnished with baby onions, mushrooms, and parsley.

Messy raised a cleaver and shouted at the agent that she would chop his skinny *niinag* right down to the short hairs and throw it to the dogs if he ever came sniffing around the kitchen again. Foamy protected his crotch with both hands, turned and hurried back to the government house. Misaabe announced with a tricky sense of native stories that only a rabid dog would eat a federal pecker.

Messy and the waiters served *Coq au Beaulieu*, the main course, or *plat principal*, and with salads and fresh vegetables on the side. The *Truffade*, a potato cake with cheese and bacon, *Poireaux Vinaigrette*, leeks with shallots, chopped boiled eggs, cider vinegar, mustard, and parsley, *Petits Pois à la Française*, sweet, fresh green peas with butter and sugar, and *Fèves à la Tourangelle*, baby lima beans, bacon, butter, baby onions, chives, and parsley, were so distinctive and delicious that each vegetable on the menu could have been the third, fourth, fifth, and other courses at the Banquet Français. Lima beans were a substitute for the *fèves*, fava or broad beans, because no one on the reservation had ever heard of fava beans or the country recipe. Messy smiled as she circled the table and related that fava beans were colonial not fur trade stories.

John Leecy poured out Wiser's rye whiskey, his favorite from Ontario,

Canada, in thick glasses with the third course of cheese, a special selection as usual from the Marin French Cheese Company in California.

Odysseus, Catherine Heady, and Doctor Mendor were heavy whiskey drinkers. John Leecy was a connoisseur of singular white lightning, and later the moonshine drinkers were extremely pleased to savor Cape Breton Silver, a special raw moonshine distilled from potato skins in Nova Scotia, Canada. The moonshine was served from a mason jar and with no label. My tongue hurt, and my eyes smarted over a torture taste with no name that could have been distilled in a rain bucket on the reservation.

Wine was my choice, a palatable drink with a culture and a savored memory. Whiskey and moonshine were too strong for me, and the outcome was risky in the best of company. My choice of wine was a serious deviation on the reservation. The big boasters of white lightning were scored as more manly, an ancient pretense, and wine drinkers were teased as pompous outsiders. I was only an outsider among the hard drinkers. Yes, the fur trade created a new culture of outsiders with traces of a wine culture. France and the war only increased my deviation from the reservation of white lightning drinkers.

Augustus was an outsider, and yet he was a heavy drinker. The distinction of his influence and cultural acceptance was based more on his ambition, courage, and generosity. He drank with a sense of the future, a new native culture of art, literature, education and commerce, and those who named him an outsider were drunk and twitchy with nostalgia and lazy traditions.

I drank wine with a sense of chance and the future, and especially since my risky missions as a scout in the war. I was a writer, my brother was an artist, and with the memory of our uncle we were the best of the outsiders on the reservation.

Odysseus cut thick wedges of Camembert and slowly savored the Cape Breton Silver. French cheese, white lightning, and ironic stories were worthy courses of the trader, or the marvelous dance moves of respected outsiders. Odysseus, as usual, told a perfect story about a moonshiner with crazy hair that night between the banquet courses of cheese and dessert.

Carolina moonshiners were the first revolutionaries to resist every tax and government edict by the sovereign right of white lightning production and commerce. The age of the moonshine was measured in hours and days, not in years. The distillation of alcohol was backwater and more dicey than the culture and fermentation of grapes for wine.

Handsome Bird was a famous moonshiner and resolute drinker of his own concoctions. Handsome distilled white lightning on a wagon in the Blue Ridge Mountains of South Carolina. Government agents, tax inspectors, and the moon detectives might have noticed the scent of the sweet moonshine but they never tracked down the actual mobile distillery. The wagon was always on the move, and the scent was only a teaser. Only the dedicated drinkers could locate his wagon at night. He sold distinctive white lightning in clay jugs, tin cans, and mason jars. The jars were never marked but drinkers could easily recognize by the smack of mountain air the potent Handsome Bird Sweet Midnight Moon.

Odysseus paused to swig more of the Cape Breton Silver, and then he roamed around the dining room table and continued with the story and a song about moonshine, "Carolina on My Mind."

> *In my mind I'm gone to Carolina.*
> *Can't you see the sunshine,*
> *And can't you just feel the moonshine,*
> *And ain't it just like a friend of mine*
> *To hit me from behind,*
> *And I'm gone to Carolina in my mind.*

Handsome Bird was a serious drinker of his own moonshine, and sometimes drank the alcohol by tasty drops directly from the still in the early morning. He was lanky and rawboned, more secure in moonlight than as a planter in the sun. After a decade of nightly white lightning coarse hair sprouted out on unusual parts of his body. The steady moon customers noticed dark, curly, crazy hairs on his ear lobes, elbows, forehead, and fingers. The crazy hair grew several inches out of his nostrils. Some drinkers wondered why hair grew on certain parts of the body and not others, but crazy hair grew even on the palms of his hands wild and wolfishly. Crazy hair heightened the demand for the white lightning, and some drinkers were convinced that the chance to become a wolf with hairy palms was much better than blindness or the risk of a ginger jake walk.

Handsome Bird sweetened the backcountry weather with white lightning and at the same time he became a shaggy legend in the Blue Ridge Mountains. The crazy black nostril hair, and the hair on his elbows, ears, forehead, and nose grew at least an inch a month with moonshine. Doctor Mendor touched his thick beard and toasted the white lightning wolves of the mountains.

>>> <<<

Catherine Heady was roused by the crazy hair stories and then she wobbled around the table to toast each soldier at the banquet. There were more toasts with white lightning than with wine, and the stories seemed to be more obscure and disconnected. Catherine commented that most of the soldiers from the reservation were her students, and she taught them literature. She had promised that literature would be the salvation and liberation of native students on the reservation. Yes, the stories and literature of war, as it turned out, were more memorable than the politics of peace.

Toast the peace and fall asleep, toast the war and strut the colors, and she strutted the colors with several toasts and tributes to the soldiers that night at the banquet table.

Catherine turned to an empty chair and with school stories created the presence of Ignatius Vizenor. She proclaimed that he was one of the worst students of literature, but she raised her arms and swooned with the recollection that he was natty, naughty, witty, and never worried about grammar or the agreement of verbs and subjects. She turned teary and announced her true love for our cousin, and at that crucial moment we launched a tease of bad grammar to rescue the woozy revelations of the romantic teacher and storier.

Misaabe mentioned the nativity cigar box.

Aloysius shouted out that his grammar was much worse than any other student, and grammar don't make no difference in war, and maybe don't not make no difference in peace.

Catherine rushed to the other side of the table and kissed my brother on the forehead, smudged the blue warrior bands on his cheeks, and ruffled his hair. She was grateful for the gentle tease. Doctor Mendor toasted the necessary play and parody. Odysseus and John Leecy celebrated the absolute worst of grammar, the structure of poetry. I shouted out that my grammar don't make no difference either, and in the spirit of the native tease and gentle rescue our tender teacher kissed the forehead of every man at the banquet table.

Misaabe was shied by the touch of the teacher.

Patch had only been kissed by his mother.

Shona Goldman, the cultural anthropologist, surely mocked the double negatives of reservation grammar and waited to be teased for her great love of native soldiers. One by one we teased the fur trade anthropologist, and she happily made the rounds to touch and buss the banquet men.

I declared that the war goes on in memory.

Misaabe smiled and was silent.

John Leecy saluted Messy.

Aloysius honored our uncle Augustus.

Odysseus praised his father and the old traders.

Lawrence celebrated his parents.

Patch honored his mother.

Shona promised a lusty song of the fur trade.

Messy announced the dessert course.

Doctor Mendor invited Lawrence Vizenor to recount the story of his combat bravery and the presentation of the Distinguished Service Cross. No one on the reservation had ever been awarded the decoration. Lawrence was a storier, one of the best when we were students at the government school, but he could not easily convey the details of what happened on October 8, 1918, at Bois-de-Fays in the Argonne Forest. He was not actually nervous that night, but rather hesitant because of the expectations of any account or description of his bravery.

Lawrence could not separate the actual action of combat with words or even remember the descriptive details. He told me later there were no reliable words to represent his own experiences in the rush of war. He was in combat, not a natural motion, and was not the observer. There was no natural story or course of irony. So, he calmly recited the basic facts that had been provided by commanders to describe his courage and the award of the Distinguished Service Cross.

My cousin stood at attention at the end of the table and stared above the listeners. His response was rather concise and military. Messy turned and swayed closer, concerned that he had gone rigid with fear. Then he lowered his gaze and seemed to be more at ease. He described the pitch and crash of artillery, and the aftermath of the attack on the enemy machine gunners as blood, blood, blood, bloody hands, bloody fingernails, cheeks, nose, boots, and a blood-soaked thick shirt. There were no mirrors or time to consider his appearance, but other soldiers stared at his bloody face and clothes. A few days later the regiment was relieved, and the bloody scenes returned in memories, and as brown swirls in the field shower. He shouted that no one could ever know by sight if the bloody stains were traces of a private, an officer, or the enemy.

Lawrence paused, smiled at each person around the table, and then closed the description of his decoration with an ironic story about the only clean new uniform available from the quartermaster. The replacement was much too large, long sleeves, bulky shirt, and huge baggy trousers. He was promoted to corporal in an oversize uniform and teased by other soldiers that he would never be big enough to fill his own trousers.

John Leecy and the others stood to salute the decorated veteran and honorable storier. Naturally, there were many ironic toasts that night to the courses of the banquet, the fur trade, the *niinag* of the federal agent, crazy hair, and oversized trousers to be sure the white lightning was consumed properly and fully.

Shona was roused by the moonshine and declared that the banquet table was a great birch bark canoe and the diners were the *voyageurs*, the sailors of the fur trade, and the federal agent was a *coureur de bois*, an outlaw trader on the reservation. She paddled around the table and chanted an obscure song in the woodsy patois of French Canadians.

> *Mon canot est fait d'écorces fines*
> *Qu'on pleume sur les bouleaux blancs*
> My canoe is made of fine bark
> That is stripped from white birch

Messy served two desserts for the last course of the banquet. The *Oeufs à la Neige*, or snow eggs, a fluffy meringue, custard, and caramel, the same dessert she served at a memorable dinner four years earlier. The second dessert was *Clafoutis Limousin*, a delicious pudding with black cherries. The pits were cooked with the *clafoutis* for a slightly bitter taste.

Odysseus imitated the sound of a bugle as he presented two bottles of

Anis de Mono, a special anise liqueur imported from a distillery in Catalonia, Spain. The green label was dry and the red label was sweet. The trader prepared heavy glasses and poured the liqueur over spears of clear ice.

Messy moved a chair next to Misaabe at the end of the table and was ready to toast the desserts, the soldiers, the summer, and the last stories of the banquet. The scent of anise was natural, and the taste aroused the murmur of secrets, resistance, and serenity.

I read three short sections of *The Odyssey* and told the last banquet story that night at the Hotel Leecy. My story was a strategic tease of our friend the generous trader Odysseus. I stood behind the trader and declared that Homer, the author of *The Odyssey*, was a woman, as many scenes were a womanly sway of obvious virtues and dominance. Circe, the lovely enchanter, and other female deities in the adventure were created by a woman storier, and not by a man with the mere nostalgia of sexual fantasies. Circe could turn her enemies into animals. The literary style was spirited and womanly, and the mythic sentiments of transformation were curvy, or at least not patently manly.

Samuel Butler, one of the many literary translators, surmised that a woman wrote *The Odyssey*. The character virtues and style indicated the distinction, and demonstrated the controversial theory. The ancient adventure stories were actually more ironic than womanly.

Odysseus had given me the precious leather-bound edition of *The Odyssey* that was translated by the poet William Cullen Bryant. I bought a war travel edition from a bookstore in Spartanburg, South Carolina, near Camp Wadsworth. I presented, in the best tradition of the trader, a creative version that night at the banquet of sections from book ten of the translation by Samuel Butler.

Circe, how can you expect me to be friendly with you when you have just been turning all my men into pigs, mongrels and federal agents? And now that you have got me here myself, you mean me mischief when you ask me to go to bed with you, and will unman me and make me fit for nothing. I shall certainly not consent to go to bed with you unless you will first take your solemn oath to plot no further harm against me.

When Circe saw me sitting there without eating, and in great grief, she came to me and said, Ulysses, why do you sit like that as though you were dumb, gnawing at your own heart, and refusing both meat and drink? Is it that you are still suspicious? You ought not to be, for I have already sworn solemnly that I will not hurt you.

Circe, no man with any sense of what is right can think of either eating or drinking in your house until you have set his friends free. . . . If you want me to eat and drink, you must free my men and bring them to me that I may see them with my own eyes.

Odysseus raised his empty glass and shouted out his praise of the storier Lady Homer. Catherine was astounded that the banquet had ended with a critical reference to learned literature. Naturally she claimed me as her best student, and continued to wobble around the banquet table. Doctor Mendor reminded the federal teacher that native stories were natural literary irony and the stories never end on a reservation.

Messy had not read *The Odyssey*, but she could not conceive of a good story that was not inspired by a woman. Misaabe whispered the names of the mighty healers, Mona Lisa, Ghost Moth, Nosey, and Shimmer. The mongrels rushed into the dining room and nosed the banquet storiers.

19

WAR MAGGOTS
1919

Bad Boy Lake reflected the bright colors of maple, birch, and sumac that autumn. The crowns of red sumac and golden birch shimmered on the water, and the hue and sway of leaves became abstract scenes with the slightest breeze. The course of bright waves and the natural motion of color were beached at night with a tease, wince, titter, and pout.

Aloysius was moved by the wild colors, the aesthetic waver of the leaves. He painted the blue wings of ravens on the surge, and the abstract watery curves were brightened with traces of rouge. My brother painted in silence that morning, and raised a brush only after hours of meditation on the shoreline. The natural motion and sleeves of color touched his native memories.

Misaabe watched at a distance, and later the healer invited us to supper at his cabin. The last rays of light shimmered in the reach of red pine and glorious maple leaves, a magical radiance that could have been either a native creation story or the sardonic end of the world.

Animosh caught seven sunfish in the shallows earlier in the day, and then roasted the whole fish with potatoes and onions on an oak stake near an open fire. The mosquitos were defeated by the first waves of cold weather and the turn of the leaves, so we ate out under a natural stand of red pine. The healer had built a high plank table connected to the trees.

The mongrels held the black bears at bay.

Misaabe was silent as he ate, and then at the end of the meal when the mongrels circled the healer, he told a story about the fur trade, and the war against animals. So, he wanted to know how the birds and animals had survived the war in France.

Naturally, the healer was very perceptive to mention the war by way of nature and the fur trade, because he must have known that we had avoided any thoughts about the war that autumn. I tried to lose the memories of the war, but could barely restrain the memory of the scent and sounds of

the war. The just visions of an autumn day near the lake turned to dreadful
scenes of the war at night.

Misaabe wanted to hear more irony in the native stories that had turned
bloody with the war, and he wanted to see the portrayal and great reach of
blue ravens. The healer coaxed me to create new stories, to tease the burden of my memories.

I was miserable almost every night, and could not escape the conjured
stench of bodies and the ruins of war. Every sound in the dark cabin, the
crack of beams, tease of lonesome insects at the lantern, and the shadows,
the menace of shadows, became the cues and traces of my war memories.

I heard artillery explosions every night, and the memory of the sounds of
war was louder than the beat of my heart. The explosions were concocted
with fear and frightful thoughts, and sleep was scary in the shadows. I never
told my brother about the nightly sounds or my fears, and he never revealed
his obsessions of the war. Only the early morning light and the gentle pitch
and whisper of the leaves created a sense of certainty and liberty.

Natives have forever danced with shadows and created stories in the
early morning light. I was enlightened by the tease of shadows and the visionary stories of creation, but memories of the sounds and shadows of war
generated fear and weakened my stories.

Misaabe sat on a bench near the kerosene lantern, and the flutter of light
created veins of shadows on his face. The light could have turned a frown to
a smile that night. The healer had invited me to create new stories about my
miseries, and then he leaned back with the mongrels at his side and waited
to hear the stories of the fight over my memories of the war.

Horses were wounded, abandoned, and the dead were stacked at the
side of the roads. The horses strained to haul the artillery wagons and supplies over the rutted and muddy roads. The trucks were mired, and only
tanks and great farm horses moved around the obstructions. The horses
were starved, abused, and had no place to rest. The supply trucks were
loaded for the soldiers not the horses.

I told the healer about two horses that exploded and scraps of flesh, slivers of broken bones, and bloody coarse hair were scattered everywhere, in
the trees, over the tents, and on the nearby soldiers. Later hordes of flies
swarmed the chunks of bloody flesh. The gory remains of the horses and
the ruins of war attracted an immediate swarm of flies, first the scouts and

then the entire corps of flies and rats. The war maggots thrived on putrid flesh, the brain and bone of horses and soldiers, but not only the bodies of the dead.

Some soldiers actually survived because of the swarms of flies and nasty maggots. The dead flesh of war wounds was a banquet for the maggots, and the natural treatment of the maggots healed the wounds better than surgery and caustic treatments. I understood the ironies, the writhe of curious healers, but the maggots were never a source of visions, and instead the bloody wriggle of the maggots devoured my memories.

Mona Lisa was my mongrel healer. She moved closer, leaned against my thigh, and sighed with her wet chin on my knee. Nosey pushed against my back and nosed my nervous, noisy belly. Ghost Moth licked my hand and sat at my side. Meals were never a good time to recount stories of the war, but my heart beat faster that night, and caused me to shiver with the stories. My words were descriptive scenes of the war, and directly connected to my visual memories, and in that way my stories became more intense and anxious.

I was forever tormented by the visual scenes of those gruesome swarms of maggots, and by the beastly sound and chase of the flies. Maggots were never an inspiration of native songs, totems, or visionary stories. Maybe maggots were native shamans in disguise, the incredible goad of healers, and a sense of an ironic nasty presence at the very heart of every native story.

I revealed to the healer that the visual memories of natural motion and nasty maggots waited for me alone in the dark. The maggots slithered with the shadows in my head at night, and then vanished with the early morning light.

Misaabe told a short story about a blue fly that lived through the winter in his cabin. Carmen the fat fly would rest near the warm lantern, and she survived by not landing on food or tormenting the mongrels. She learned to land on a shoulder not a nose, on a box but not a face. Carmen, one of the oldest flies of the season, cleaned her wings near the lantern, and survived the severe cold. She flew away on the first warm day of spring.

So, the healer listened at a distance, and as the mongrel healers gathered around the faint light of the lantern he told me to picture and then name a stout fly as a friend for the winter. Yes, by name, the name and presence of a fly. The healer smiled and encouraged me to imagine saving that fly from a spider web. That was the heart of the story, nothing more than simply a hint and promise to imagine the ordinary gestures of a fly in the war sounds and shadows of the cabin at night.

José flew that very night with Carmen. I created an opera of two friendly flies that landed near the lantern in the cabin, walked together on the table, circled a box of crackers, and danced down an ax handle. José was an acrobatic flyer, and later that night he got caught in an intricate spider web. The huge spider, a fierce warrior, bounced on the threads and was ready to devour the fly. José was a healer and yet he could not buzz his way out of the web. I created a perfect lure of war, a writhing juicy maggot that distracted the spider, and my friend the fly broke free from the web.

Three nights later the hideous scenes of maggots in my mind never returned or tormented me again. José and Carmen were my opera stories of liberty. Misaabe was a great healer by stories. Yet, he insisted that the only serious healers were listeners. The stories that heal were the creation of listeners. The stories that heal must have an origin, a mark or notice, and a native sense of natural motion and presence. A story must create a new sense of presence with every new version of the story.

⟩⟩⟩ ⟨⟨⟨

I read book eleven of *The Odyssey* that night. *He looked black as night with his bare bow in his hands and his arrow on the string, glaring around as though ever on the point of taking aim. About his breast there was a wondrous golden belt adorned in the most marvellous fashion with bears, wild boars, and lions with gleaming eyes; there was also war, battle, and death. The man who made that belt, do what he might, would never be able to make another like it.*

Bad Boy Lake was covered with a thin shiny layer of ice the next morning. The sun and waves melted the ice near the shoreline and the center of the lake by afternoon. Seventeen Canada Geese circled and then landed with incredible grace on the last shimmer of cold water. The geese stretched their great black necks, cackled over the state of rest and the weather, and then continued the migration. That show of neck, wing, and travel cackle must have been created for me to describe in a story.

I cut several downed birch trees and split the logs for use in the fireplace. The scent of ancient trees was in the air that morning. The cabin was built only for the summer, always drafty, damp, and cold, so we covered sections of the floor with newspapers and slept near the stone fireplace. Mona Lisa and Nosey came by every morning at dawn and nosed me awake.

Aloysius hunted for game, but when he aimed the shotgun at the geese or mallard ducks he could not shoot. He tried again, and again, but the thought of dead birds and animals only reminded him of the wars against animals. He decided instead to paint blue ravens in flight with the geese rather than shoot the birds for our dinner. The choice was easy, and we were always hungry.

Several weeks later the lake was frozen thick and cracked at night, and the first heavy snow had covered the ice and bright leaves. We cut holes in the ice and caught enough fish to survive. My brother had hunted and trapped animals with me many times in the past, and we honored the animals but never hesitated to shoot game for food. That winter, however, was not the same. We set out one cold morning to hunt for deer, squirrel, and rabbits.

Aloysius banked the snow into a natural blind, and we waited in silence for the animals. Several rabbits pranced at a great distance. The squirrels sensed our presence and were very cautious on the back of trees, out of sight. Finally a whitetail deer moved slowly across a nearby creek bed. The morning air was cold and crisp, and my breath frosted the breech of the rifle. I aimed at the heart of the deer, an easy shot with no windage, but raised the barrel at the last second and fired high over the head of the animal. The sound of the gunshot shattered the winter scene and the natural peace of the forest. The sound of the gunshot never seemed to end that morning, and the sound of war had never ended in my memory.

The animals had vanished, and the birds had ducked into secure places. The trees cracked and shivered, and the war against animals had almost started once more on the reservation. The sound echoed in the cold shadows, bounced on the boughs of snow, and the deviant sound of the explosion tormented my brother that night in the cabin. That single sound of a gunshot reminded us of the war, and we decided we could never again live as hunters. We could never declare war on animals. The fur trade wars had decimated animals and weakened native totems. We could never overcome by stories the miserable memories of war, and endure the tormented visions of bloody animals.

Aloysius started to paint and carve blue ravens. I wrote stories about the fur trade war against totems and animals, but we could not survive on native art and stories. The obvious choice that winter was to either hunt or perish, but we decided to resist the actual traditions of the hunter.

Misaabe invited us to supper many times, and he was worried about our torment, but not our resistance. We learned that even the most original and ironic stories alone could not overcome the bloody scenes of hunters. Naturally, we could not continue to depend on his generosity. So, one early morning we ran with the mongrels near the lake, packed our bundles in the afternoon, and returned to live with our parents for a few weeks.

20

ORPHEUM THEATRE
—————— 1920 ——————

Patch Zhimaaganish had been invited to audition as a singer and trumpet player for the vaudeville orchestra at the Orpheum Theatre in Minneapolis. Baron Davidson, a friend and fellow bugle player from the First Pioneer Infantry, had arranged the audition. Baron worked on the stage crew at the theater.

Aloysius was ready to paint again, but he was determined to live in a city. He wanted to meet with other artists, and encounter a new world of chance. I continued to write about our tricky memories of the war, and mostly about our experiences as veterans. Wary of native traditions, the vengeance of nature, and politics of federal dominion, we decided that first cold week of January to leave the reservation and search for work in Minneapolis.

Patch had waited five months for the Soo Line Railroad to consider his application for a position as an assistant conductor. So, our decision to leave the reservation encouraged our friend to accept the invitation to try out as a singer and trumpet player. Patch was admired as a soldier and good citizen, and the station agent was bothered that the company had not yet hired our friend.

Aloysius wondered how difficult it would be to play a musical instrument. He was moved by the sound of the saxophone, but we quickly dismissed his speculation, and with the reminder that he was recognized as a brilliant painter not a musician. The generous station agent gave us, three veterans of the war, free tickets on the train to Minneapolis. Naturally, he was worried that we would never return to the reservation.

The train pulled into the Ogema Station on time that morning. We quickly boarded, turned, and saluted the station agent. Twelve years earlier we had hawked the *Tomahawk* to the passengers on the very same train.

I had written ahead to reserve a large room with three beds at the Waverly Hotel near the Minneapolis Public Library. Augustus had been a close friend of the manager, and we stayed at the same residence hotel ten years earlier when we visited the city for the first time.

No one was surprised, not even our parents, when we decided to leave because veterans could not find work on the reservation or in nearby small towns. Many native families bought war bonds, but the money was never used for native veterans. The Liberty Bonds were issued in several series that earned three to four percent, but bonds were not redeemable for at least ten years.

The reservation had changed since the war, of course, and the arguments were more about machines than any sense of native presence. Native veterans and others were moving almost every day to find work in cities. Since the war the reservation had been taken over by motor cars. The new politicians had no sense of tradition, and no sense of chance, memorable stories, or irony. Yes, we had returned to the mere echo of native traditions, and, for my brother and me, the reservation would never be enough to cope with the world or to envision the new and wild cosmopolitan world of exotic art, literature, music, and vaudeville at the Orpheum Theatre.

Augustus had been sharply critical of the pretenders, native and otherwise, and exposed the scoundrels in the *Tomahawk*, but since the death of our uncle the federal bunko boys have dominated the politics of the reservation. We honored the traditional elders, the healers, and the natives who celebrated totems, and told stories of presence, but the reservation was overrun with invaders, pretenders, patchwork shamans, and timber grifters.

Patch had never visited Minneapolis. His only experience was between trains to and from the war. We arrived early on a cold and sunny afternoon, and walked directly to the Waverly Hotel. Pickel, the manager, that was his last name, remembered us from ten years earlier. He commented on our brave service in the infantry, and then he talked about the war, the struggle of veterans, especially native veterans, and after two years continued to mourn the sudden death of our uncle and his good friend, Augustus. Pickel, my uncle told me, had been abandoned as a child, and then adopted, but he had no connections or memory of his blood relatives on the White Earth Reservation.

Aloysius steered us directly to the nearby Minneapolis Public Library. Gratia Alta Countryman, the head librarian, invited us to her office with the curved windows, and we teased her about the first time we visited and she served cookies to the children. Gratia was delighted to meet us again, and praised our courage as soldiers.

Patch carried his trumpet and naturally that became a cue to discuss our combat service in France and the occupation of Koblenz, Germany. Gratia was deeply moved by the number of soldiers who had been killed in the war, and those who had returned wounded and disabled. She had organized special programs for veterans at several libraries in the city. Patch, she insisted, must play military taps in the main reading room of the library. Many veterans who could not find work gathered for the day in the library.

Patch stood at attention and played taps that afternoon, and each new note on his trumpet was more poignant than the last. I was moved by the emotive sound, and the music delivered me back to the pride and courage of my military service. When taps ended, the librarian was in tears, and many veterans stood at attention near the reading tables and saluted our good friend. That was a memorable moment, and the best way to start our search for work in the city.

Aloysius was told that the Minneapolis School of Arts had moved five years earlier from the Minneapolis Public Library to the new Julia Morrison Memorial Building on Stevens Avenue South. My brother was determined to meet once more the artist Yamada Baske, or Fukawa Jin Basuke, who had praised his blue ravens and suggested a trace of rouge in each portrayal.

Patch had an audition scheduled late that afternoon with the manager of the Orpheum Theatre. The holiday decorations, strings of colored lights, giant imitation bells, and bright stars over the streetcar tracks had not been removed on Hennepin Avenue. We walked three blocks, turned right and there, across the street from the Hotel Majestic, was the Orpheum Theatre. The enormous marquee covered the entire sidewalk at the entrance on Seventh Street.

Baron Davidson met us at the door, and we followed him into the theater. The huge auditorium was marvelous, and my brother once again heard murmurs and the hushed voices of actors on stage. We sat in the balcony and imagined the whispers, sighs, titters, and cackles of the audience.

Baron introduced us to G. E. Raymond, the resident manager of the Orpheum Theatre, a stern, stout man with a vest and watch chain, in his office above the marquee. Patch was not prepared for a sudden audition, but he was directed to play both classical and popular music then and there. He did so, and after the third trumpet recital the manager declared that he was hired to play in the orchestra, and would be paid for twenty hours a week. The manager explained that the orchestra provided the music for circuit vaudeville shows, two performances a day and every day of the week. That would have been about thirty hours a week, but the manager contended that musicians never play every hour of the performances.

We learned later that the unions had protested the policy but were not able to change the pay or hours for temporary musicians and stagehands. We were introduced that afternoon to the rough politics of the theater. A new Orpheum Theatre was under construction at the time on Hennepin Avenue near the Minneapolis Public Library.

Baron was a veteran and lucky to have a good but temporary job with the stage crew. Naturally, we inquired about work at the theater, and he promised to let us know if there were any vacant positions there. Aloysius had started to paint again, but he was eager to become a stagehand with me. We could not wait, of course, and had to find work immediately.

Patch was curious about the initials A O U W on the three-story stone building next to the Orpheum Theatre. The Ancient Order of United Workman, we learned later, was the name of an organization that supported the interests of labor, employers, and owners. That seemed to be the perfect place to find work.

The Taylor and Watson wallpaper store on the ground floor displayed original patterns in the window, but the sales clerk was not familiar with either the owner of the building or the Ancient Order.

The F. J. Willimann Art Store next door to the theater exhibited formal styles of landscape scenes, but the manager was not interested in our questions about employment. He sold art but would never consider an amateur artist or veterans as employees.

Hennepin Avenue was lively late that afternoon. The sun had almost set and the decorative street lamps, five globes on a single post, were lighted along the street. Dryers Bowling and Billiards was smoky, busy, and noisy. The players shouted over the crash of pins in the alleys, and teased each other over the steady crack of billiard balls. The Winter Garden ballroom next door was ready for an evening of dancers.

Patch marveled at the Masonic Temple, and then he reached out with both hands and touched the massive sandstone blocks of the eight-story building. Aloysius studied the windows, and the curved reflections of the streetcars in motion. Black motor cars were parked on both sides of the street, a radical change of transportation from our first visit to the city. I remembered the familiar sound of horse-drawn wagons on the cobblestones, and the police used horses and wagons at the time. Ten years later the same city streets were crowded with new Liberty Taxi Cabs.

The West Hotel on Hennepin and Fifth Street was grand, classy, and luxurious. My brother pointed out the gabled roof and bay windows. The lobby had not changed since our first visit ten years earlier. We sat in the same blue cushy settees. I talked about famous visitors at the hotel, and the blue ravens my brother had painted that summer. The doorman was impressed at the time that our uncle was the editor and publisher of a newspaper. Patch had read stories by Mark Twain, but he had never heard of Winston Churchill, who stayed at the hotel and lectured on "The Boer War" almost twenty years earlier at the Lyceum Theater. The *Tomahawk* had published a story about Winston Churchill when he was First Lord of the Admiralty.

We crossed the busy streetcar tracks and walked back on the other side of the street. The wind was cold, and we could see the breath of every person on the busy street. Aloysius walked into the Busy Bee, a tailor shop, to have a button sewn on his winter coat. We decided to eat an early supper at the nearby New Grand Lunch. John Leecy had given me twenty dollars to buy our meals for a few days in Minneapolis.

Patch could hardly sleep that night, and he was out early the next morning to meet with Albert Rudd the music director of the Orpheum Theatre Orchestra. Patch told us later at supper that he was hired to play dramatic movie music and concert programs scheduled twice a day, early in the afternoon, and in the evening.

Patch was seated at the back of the orchestra pit at the ready to play his trumpet but the music that night was only background with strings and the piano. We bought cheap twenty-five cent tickets in the balcony and attended the program that evening. The Kinogram newsreels were very interesting, travel and politics, scenes of the United States Capitol in Washington, but the short stage plays were mannered, and the vaudeville impersonators were rather tedious, and not memorable.

Aloysius told the employment director at Dayton's Dry Goods Company, the giant department store on Nicollet Avenue near the Orpheum Theatre, that he had worked on a farm as a laborer, and as a painter. He did not specify artistic painter, and would have named houses, or at least the *Tomahawk* newspaper building, but there were no jobs open for veterans or anyone. We were natives from a reservation, needless to say, and much too old to be considered as stock boys.

We visited dozens of companies and inquired about work, any kind of work, but by late that afternoon we were convinced there were no jobs open in the entire city. Actually, there were jobs but we did not understand at the time that no one was hired without some personal connection, association, and recommendation. We learned later that most companies were wary of new employees because of union sympathizers. We had no direct experiences with any unions, but the more we tried to find work the more convinced we became of the need for union representation.

The Allen Motor Car Company on Hennepin Avenue had no job openings. The production and sale of motor cars had declined since the end of the war. Wyman and Partridge, a wholesale dry goods company on Fourth Street and First Avenue North, would consider occasional laborers, but only with local references.

The owner of Pioneer Printers on South Sixth Street supported veterans and was impressed that we had worked for the *Tomahawk*, but he needed experienced typesetters.

The Wonderland Theatre was a serious and ironic introduction to the struggles of unions and the political power of employers in the city. The theater was a narrow building at 27 South Washington Avenue, near the train stations and Gateway Park. The employment director at Dayton's Dry Goods Company suggested that we might find work at the theater. The director was being deceptive because the only work there was on the union picket line, an ironic reversal, but we were ready to consider anything.

The Wonderland Theatre had been picketed by the Motion Picture Machine Operators Union for more than three years. We could not understand at the time why anyone would protest for so many years against a small theater. The banners carried by the picketers declared in giant words, "This Theatre Unfair to Organized Labor." We decided not to enter the theater, of course, and instead walked with the picketers and listened to the union stories. The wind was cold so we warmed our hands over a fire in a barrel and talked about the war. Some of the picketers were veterans. They were paid by the union and had never been employed at the theater.

John Campbell, the owner of the Wonderland Theatre, decided to run the movies himself and laid off two motion picture operators to save money. The theater actually lost money because of the daily picketers. I learned later that the owner of the theater had been paid to stay in business by the Minneapolis Citizen's Alliance, a group of business owners and employers who strongly opposed the unions.

Aloysius carried a union banner for an hour in front of the theater that cold afternoon. No doubt there were private spies there to report on the picketers. We ate lunch at a local cafeteria with several picketers, and then returned to the hotel to search the classified sections of the *Minneapolis Journal* and the *Minneapolis Times*. That was a total waste of time because the only jobs listed were for technicians and union trades.

Jews, natives, newcomers, veterans, and socialists were hardly ever hired without connections in the city. We needed the union to find a job, but the economy had weakened, and there was a recession at the end of the war. Production, wages, and work hours were down, too many veterans were looking for work, and labor unions had lost their power. The end of the war was not a good time to look for work.

I read three books of *The Odyssey* that night at the hotel, and a selection from book fourteen was a particularly relevant metaphor. *These men hatched a plot against me that would have reduced me to the very extreme of misery, for when the ship had got some way out from land they resolved on selling me as a slave.*

The next day we tried to find work as temporary laborers in produce, dry goods, and other companies near Washington Avenue and Hennepin. Jews owned most of the business in the area, and the merchandise was customary. We talked to the managers and owners of warehouses, and businesses that sold clothing, leather goods, and supplies for lumberjacks. We were immediately hired for two hours to unload bundles of leather, and later the owner of a scrap metal company near the river paid us a flat rate to move and stack used pipes. That was hard work, and very cold. My hands were frozen. The owner invited us to the company shack, and we warmed our hands over the kerosene stove.

Jacob Schwartz was curious about our family and how natives lived on the reservation. We told him about our father who was a lumberjack, about the federal agent, and the newspaper published by our uncle. He was interested in our experiences, and compared our family to his own before the war in the German Empire. The Jews under the emperor encountered a double burden of discrimination during the First World War. Germany was an enemy name only six months earlier, but hardly relevant because the Schwartz family had escaped the empire wars and emigrated first to New York City, and then to Minneapolis.

The Schwartz family had lived in the city for more than twenty years. Jacob could not find a job after high school, so he continued his studies and graduated from the university but still could not find a job. He continued in the scrap metal business that his father had established as an immigrant. He paid us for our time and told us to return in a few days for two or three more hours of work.

Later that week we were hired as temporary stagehands at the Orpheum Theatre. Patch had impressed the music director and the resident manager with his great baritone voice, and we were hired for the season. Patch sang *La Marseillaise* at every performance and the audience cheered and applauded wildly. Aloysius was so excited that he painted an enormous blue raven at the entrance to the theater. I was reassured to see my brother paint again, and we were both delighted to work in the sentimental murmurs and traditions of the theater.

Patch played and sang only during vaudeville performances. Our work schedule was the same except we worked a few more hours when a new show arrived at the theater. We carried huge trunks for actors, unloaded stage property, assisted in the construction of stage sets, and two or three times a week we raised and lowered the curtain. We never complained, but the pay as stagehands was only a dollar and sixty cents for each performance, and a small bonus for moving the trunks.

Only a few of the stagehands were members of a union, but we were never asked to attend or join anything. The union had decided to picket the Wonderland Theatre but for some obscure reason not the Orpheum Theatre. I was told the union was more active in the new movie theaters, and that most movie projectionists were members of the Motion Picture Machine Operators Union. The movies had become more popular than some stage productions, and this was worrisome to the producers of expensive vaudeville circuit shows. The Orpheum Theatre reacted to the new interests and started each stage performance with short movies to satisfy the new audiences. The Kinograms were newsreels and very popular.

Aloysius opened the curtain for several productions that winter. We worked the same hours, but as stagehands we were not always together. A recent program included visual news of the world, a freakish minstrel comedy show, dancers, impersonators, blue or sexy women, and short theatrical scenes such as Jennings and Mack in "The Camouflage Taxi." The circuit stage production of "Who Is She" was about a lawyer and his wife in New York City. Buster Santos and Jacque Hays acted in "The Girl with the Funny Figure." Buster was an unusual name for a woman. Bert Ford and Pauline Price presented "Birds of a Feather," a pantomimic fantasy of the forest. Kennedy and Rooney, Bailey and Cowan, and Harry Jolson, an operatic blackface comedian, were very popular vaudeville circuit performers.

Jacob Schwartz continued to hire us two or three hours a week to move, sort, and stack scrap metal that had been delivered to the yard. We moved scrap metal in the morning, and were stagehands at the theater in the afternoon and evening. Jacob became a loyal friend, and sometimes his wife arrived with a prepared lunch. Sara treated us like members of the family.

Jacob was always scrupulous, ethical, and he paid for our time to the penny. We told him many stories about our uncle, the trader, our experiences as scouts in the war, and about the federal agent on the reservation. He told us stories about his family in Berlin before the First World War, and about the cruelty and folly of the German Empire. Aloysius gave him one of his recent blue ravens painted at the library.

The Minneapolis School of Arts had moved about a mile south of the city. We headed out one cold morning and walked to the new school. Aloysius wondered why the word "fine" in the original name of the school had been deleted in the move. We decided that the arts were not necessarily fine.

Yamada Baske was in his studio talking with two art students about watercolor landscapes, the visual sense of artistic touch and experience, and the impressions of color, light, and style. Aloysius was captivated by the discussion that morning at the Minneapolis School of Arts. Yamada turned, smiled, and then he recognized my brother.

The spacious studio was a marvelous sanctuary in gentle light, and the sweet scent of watercolor paint was soothing. I might have become a painter encircled in that lovely aesthetic space, inspired by natural motion, and devoted to the impressions of landscapes.

I might have become a painter instead of a creative writer, the conversion of an image or a visual scene, an original impression conveyed with color and brush, rather than the tease and trace of memories in the chance of words. My words and tease of presence were created with a sense of color, tone, touch, style, and a choice of literary brushes. Yet, words and stories must be imagined without colonies of studios, curators, or museums.

Yamada Baske had invited my brother to visit the studio once a week in the early morning to talk about his blue raven watercolors. Aloysius was encouraged by the invitation, and after each discussion with the artist he returned to the hotel with a new energy to paint, and in a few weeks time the blue ravens were more impressionistic, and with hues and traces of other colors.

Aloysius painted the contours of blue ravens in the scrap yard, and the heavy metal objects became abstract impressions in various muted hues. The wings of the blue ravens were spread widely over the outline of material artifacts, and with a faint speck and shimmer of color. The soft curves of abstract scrap metal would not consent to a name or representation. My brother was inspired once again to portray blue ravens in a new style. The abstract outlines were comparable to the hints and hues of natural motion, and the brush cruises of *sumi-e* and artistic calligraphy by the Japanese.

Aloysius painted blue ravens at the theater, on the streets, and at the hotel. His new and original style was spirited, as usual, and his portrayals were feisty and impressionistic. Every day he painted magnificent blue ravens with a natural aesthetic sway. Three months later my brother had painted scenes in more than a dozen new books of art paper. The arrival of spring, the slight turn of colors, and early blooms, inspired a new sense of presence and solace.

Patch was summoned by the resident theater director and told that his mother had died at home. He received the terrible news at the end of the afternoon programs. That night at the conclusion of the evening performance he sang *La Marseillaise* to the spirit of his mother with incredible emotive power. The audience was moved to tears by the tone and temper of his voice. The natural grace of spring had turned cold and desolate with the death of his mother.

Aloysius notified the director and the stagehands that we would attend a funeral and be absent for a few days. We bought tickets and prepared to leave by train the next morning. Patch was distant that night, and he softly sang, almost in whispers, the old dream songs we remembered from our time together that summer at the Ogema Station.

The light snow was wispy that morning as the train moved slowly out of the city and stopped at the same familiar small towns. The gray and white houses were shrouded in a late spring storm, and stories of the heart were renounced with a cold shudder. The snow was wet and heavy to the north, and every platform on the route became a white lonesome memory. The bright sturdy tulips and daffodils stood above the snow. Patch sat at the front of the passenger car and stared out the window. The slant of heavy snow moved with the train.

Harriet had slowly died in an accident at the family cabin near the hospital. We learned later that she was splitting wood for the fire that cold morning, and the double-bit ax glanced on a log and struck her ankle. The sharp blade cut a critical artery. She bound the injured leg to stop the bleeding, and then started to walk toward the White Earth Hospital.

The mongrels ran ahead and barked to alert the nurses. Harriet fainted in sight of the hospital, and died from a loss of blood. She left bloody footprints in the snow. Several hours later a hunter heard the hoarse barks of the loyal mongrels and discovered the frozen body.

Patch had played military taps on the platform at each station only eight months earlier. Harriet was on the platform when we returned at the end of the war and she rushed toward the train to touch her only son. She squeezed his cheeks, both arms, and pulled his ears to be sure he was the whole boy that she had sent away to war in France. She learned only that afternoon that her son had become a celebrated military bugler and singer. Motherly pride that afternoon was an understatement, and the ordinary words of praise, care, and affection could never describe her mighty love.

Patch was teased by students at the government school for the love and devotion of his mother. She made his clothes, cut his thick black hair, and had fashioned a smart uniform with bright buttons for his volunteer service as an assistant station agent. So much love and absolute affection could never be held back at a train station.

The Ogema Station was a miserable place that afternoon as the train arrived in the heavy snow. John Leecy drove down to meet us and provided transportation. He had scheduled a native wake in a private room at the hotel because the small family cabin was buried in heavy snow. Messy had prepared food for a reception in the dining room after the funeral.

Father Aloysius, Margaret, our mother, the mission sisters, and the station agent and his wife arranged for a special funeral service at Saint Benedict's Mission. Patch was silent at the wake, and at the burial he sang native dreams songs, and later he played mournful taps for his mother. The heavy snow covered the coffin, the priest, the sisters, and others at the burial site. Only the trumpet shined that day at the cemetery.

Patch avoided the reception and retreated to grieve for his mother at the cabin. He was the family woodcutter, and blamed himself for the accident because he had not split enough wood for the winter, but his mother had encouraged him to audition at the Orpheum Theatre. Coincidence seldom rode in the shadow of misery, but that was exactly the situation three days later as we prepared to return to work in Minneapolis.

The Soo Line Railroad instructed the Ogema Station agent to announce that Patch Zhimaaganish was hired as an assistant conductor on the passenger train route between Minneapolis and Winnipeg, Canada. Patch was grateful, of course, but he broke down in tears because his mother was not alive at the moment he became an actual conductor in uniform. Our friend started work on the very train that we boarded to return to Minneapolis.

Aloysius painted three blue ravens at a gravesite in heavy snow. The portrayals were intricate impressionistic crystals of snow and blue wings, and the trumpet was a trace of rouge. He painted the abstract outline of blue wings around the snowflakes.

The train arrived late but we had time to report to the afternoon performance at the theater. We were summoned to the office of the resident manager and told that we must pay the salaries of the substitute stagehands that had worked in our absence. We protested, of course, but the rules had been established for many years. Not only were we required to pay our salaries for substitutes, but we also paid the three days of cover salary for Patch.

The management was cruel to dock our money over the sudden departure to attend a funeral. The theater, in a sense, docked salaries for the dead
and buried. We were instantly converted to support union representation
that would protect the ordinary rights of workers. Naturally, we were prepared to strike or to quit, but we could not have found another job as interesting as the theater. So, we worked more than three days each to cover the
actual salaries of the substitute stagehands.

Patch learned about the cover salaries and paid us the same amount. He
could not have been happier as an assistant conductor, but we only saw him
once or twice a month when he stayed over in Minneapolis.

Several months later our mother wrote and included a letter from Nathan Crémieux. Aloysius read the letter once, turned and smiled, and then
read the letter a second time out loud. Most of the original blue ravens that
he had painted during the war were sold at the Galerie Crémieux in Paris.
The raven money, a total equivalent of more than three hundred dollars,
had been deposited for my brother in a separate account at the gallery.

Aloysius was inspired by the sale of his watercolors, and that spring he
painted magical blue ravens with traces of other colors, impressionistic hues
with the usual faint touch and curve of rouge, and the outline of scenes in
nature and the city. The reverse images of snowflakes, leaves, and wild daffodils were original and created a sense of natural motion.

May was warm, the willow and maple leaves were almost mature, and
the blue lilacs were radiant in the parks and churchyards of the city. The
theater productions changed with the weather and by the week. The dancers were similar, the impersonators were mundane, but the vaudeville comedians were great performers.

June was warmer and rainy, and my brother painted blue ravens reflected
in black pools of rainwater, and perched on the wet sidewalks with the trace
shimmers of plum and apple blossoms. His blue raven portrayals were impressionistic points, curves, contours, and soft traces of color.

My brother was awakened late that summer with a vision and hurried at
dawn to the Stone Arch Bridge. He was silent that early morning, carried a
large book of new art paper, and with an incredible passion painted brilliant
scenes of the river, the granite arches of the bridge, and lightened with blue
the murky warehouses. He created a storm of water, hues of mighty waves,
and the solemn spectacle of sturdy blue ravens in the mist near Saint An-

thony Falls. The Great Northern Railroad had built the Stone Arch Bridge over the Mississippi River.

The blue ravens were in the arch of stones, windows, haze, and shapes of buildings, and the wings of warehouses on the river. The abstract blue ravens were present in the granite of the bridge, and in the natural motion of curves, contours, blue roman beaks, claws, and mighty eyes, an artistic grace of totemic stature. My brother had awakened with a great vision that would forever change the world of native art.

Aloysius had created a new series of blue ravens that were transformations of the material world. The abstract images of the blue ravens emerged from the stone, the rush of water, and were possessed in the currents and waves on the Mississippi River.

The blue ravens were enormous in his earlier portrayals, the blue wings contained the entire scene, but the new abstract and impressionistic blue ravens emerged, were revealed, and came out of material and nature. The blue ravens were the transformations of stone, water, and machines, an incredible totemic animism.

I wrote, my brother painted, and it rained that warm summer morning. We took cover under a canopy at Gateway Park, and my brother continued painting, painting, painting. He was moved by a vision and completed more than twenty original and magnificent blue raven scenes in the next few days.

Every slant of rain that morning, and the tick and turn of leaves ran down the canopy and gathered in the river. I convened there and wrote to the river, to the mighty river, and recounted native scenes and stories of the river from the source at Lake Itasca to the storm and earthy rush over Saint Anthony Falls. The *gichiziibi*, the Great River, had run forever in native memories and stories, a natural sense of presence.

I reminded my brother that we had to leave for the afternoon performance at the Orpheum Theatre. The stage crew was expected to arrive in the early afternoon to move trunks, and once or twice a week to construct new stage sets.

Aloysius declared that he was at a funeral forever and would not return to work as a stagehand. Naturally, he would rather paint than talk or carry trunks for arrogant actors. My brother convinced me that we no longer needed to work at the theater. So, he suggested that we telephone the resident manager and explain that we would be away for several years because of a substitute family funeral on the reservation. We would attend a funeral forever to avoid another day as stagehands.

We actually returned to the theater that late summer afternoon, but three months later in the autumn we delivered our rehearsed and ironic declaration that we were leaving to attend the funeral of a native mongrel healer. Ghost Moth had died and we decided to return and honor one of the great healers and detectors of disease at the hospital on the White Earth Reservation.

21

Mona Lisa

1921

John Leecy was concerned, of course, but not surprised that we had quit our jobs as theater stagehands, and then decided to become expatriate native artists, a painter and a writer, in Paris. He respected our ambitions, and he actually assumed that we would have returned much earlier to France. My published stories about our experiences were persuasive, and even more inviting was the exhibition and sale of blue ravens at the Galerie Crémieux.

Most natives were not recognized as citizens, not even veterans, so we decided to apply for passports. We avoided the federal agent, of course, and traveled by train to the Federal Office Building and Custom House in Minneapolis. Father Aloysius prepared copies of our birth and baptismal records. We used as our home address the Waverly Hotel. The postal service was not reliable, and we worried that the federal agent might open our package from the Division of Passport Control. Pickel delivered the passports to Patch at the train station in Minneapolis.

Aloysius bought several books of fine art paper in preparation for our departure. The cost of an ocean liner ticket was about three weeks of our salary at the Orpheum Theatre. We had expected the cost to be much more expensive. The meals and wine were included in the price of the tickets.

The *France* departed from New York that late December and docked about seven days later in the port of Le Havre, France. The majestic, spacious, and luxurious four-funnel ocean liner had been commissioned nine years earlier, and during the war transported soldiers to France, and then at the end of the war returned the wounded to New York.

John Clement Beaulieu, our cousin, served with an army engineer company and was transported to war on the *France*. The refurbished liner accommodated some two thousand passengers, more than the entire population of the White Earth Reservation.

Aloysius painted in the Salon Ravel in the morning and on the enclosed and warmer starboard deck in the afternoon, and at night we dined with hundreds of other tourist-class passengers. Stories of actual and imagined adventures were practiced and interrelated, and many tourist recitations were restyled overnight.

I sauntered on the decks in the morning, watched the mighty surge of waves creased by the bow, and in the afternoon marked the seethe of the ocean at the stern of the ship. The steady hum of the steam engines moved through my body night and day. The pages of my notebook were heavy from the ocean spray. My visual notes, scenes, descriptions of characters, and outlines of stories were mostly about the crew and passengers. I imagined and merged the unique characteristics of more than thirty tourists, and created conversations between the characters.

I met several passengers who intended to visit war memorial cemeteries, and to honor the remains of immediate relatives, but most of the passengers seemed to be on holiday, and boasted about their rich associations and accomplishments in business and various professions, but not the arts. The tourists were consummate by steady boasts and admissions, but most of the stories seemed to be uncertain poses of some fantastic proficiency. I never heard even one tourist mention melancholy, doubt, fear, or a natural totem in their stories. Such exclusions were sensible, no doubt, because no ordinary worries, moods, or totems would survive the great voyage of revision and conceit. We were afloat with many cocky braggers, a tourist liner of wags, grousers, and jesters.

I listened to the steady boasters and then decided to counter with my own elaborate stories. My actual recounts of experiences were not ornate enough to hold the attention of the tourist posers and gloaters. So, we participated in the liner dinner game to conceive the uncommon and then overstate the obvious. My start that night was to imagine the presence of the trader Odysseus, and to create a tricky story in his memory.

Guillaume Apollinaire became my brother in one elaborate story. The French poet was famous, of course, and died in the First World War. I did not mention influenza as the tragic cause of his death. My brother stole the *Mona Lisa* was the first overstatement that captured the attention of the audience at dinner. Aloysius, my actual brother, burst into laughter, and contributed an ironic gesture, a finger wag caution not to reveal too much about the theft of the *Mona Lisa* from the Musée du Louvre. The gesture enhanced the intrigue of the story. I remembered the vaudeville comedians and actors and practiced some of the stage gestures that we had observed at the Orpheum Theatre.

Apollinaire was a poet and a fur trader, and a surreal suspect because he was born in Russia, became a citizen of Italy, enlisted as a soldier in the French Army, and lived in Paris. Pablo Picasso was also a suspect because he was a cubist painter and born in Spain. The precious *Mona Lisa* was rescued by the police and returned unhurt, unsullied, and with a steady, sly smile to the Musée du Louvre.

Apollinaire was a poet and soldier of fortune, and he was actually arrested and jailed for the possession of stolen art and statues from the museum. He wrote poems in the war and in prison, and was wounded as he read *Mercure de France*, a new literary magazine. Surely the first wound in military history associated with an erudite journal. His presence and wounds were literary events.

I slightly stained a linen napkin with red wine and wrapped it around my head to simulate the wounded poet, and then continued with a recitation of selected crude and erotic scenes of war and prison by Apollinaire. *I am naked in my cell, a tomb, with the girls, clowns, and jailers.* ... I paused over the actual descriptive position of sex with clowns and jailers, smiled, and declared that the poems were an understatement of his fleshy experiences, and the erotic scenes were not exactly by my brother Apollinaire.

Guillaume Apollinaire was my imagined brother, of course, a poetic totem, and always a presence in my stories. I wanted to meet him more than emperors, presidents, or popes. My story that night was the first ironic and public introduction of my brother the poet of war wounds and four days in prison.

The tourist-class meals were served in the Salle à Manger Versailles, and dinners were distinctive courses of chicken, duck, rabbit, quail, turkey, pigeon, veal, kidney, and beef tongue with potatoes, carrots, turnips, leeks, and other vegetables. The Saint Tropez was the name of the other tourist-class salon, and the café was named the Rive Gauche. The service was courteous and indulgent, the complete opposite of our troop ship experiences as infantry soldiers on the *Mount Vernon* to Brest, France.

〉〉〉 〈〈〈

Sinclair Lewis was thirty-five years old when *Main Street: The Story of Carol Kennicott* was published in October 1920. We were ten years younger than the author, and on our way to live in Paris. The book was very popular, and the author was from Sauk Centre, Minnesota. My brother bought me a copy of the novel in New York as we waited two days to board the *France*.

Sauk Centre was Gopher Prairie in the novel, and the main street was similar to every other small town we counted on the Soo Line Railroad between Ogema Station and Minneapolis. Gopher Prairie was probably built with white pine from the White Earth Reservation. Every board and brick of the main street was created with an absence of irony, and the tedious humdrum of manners, hypocrisy, and patriotism was reported as the grand and proper rise of civilization.

Natives had been persecuted in the name of civilization, as everyone knows, and distinct cultures were either terminated or removed to treaty reservations. The prairie, lakes, and woodland were considered vacant and available, and the original native place names were changed to accommodate the eager migrants of a new nation. The primary objective of civilization was to rename the land and cultivate a surplus of handsome corn and wheat.

Sinclair Lewis created a mundane main street of taint and remorse. The Anishinaabe, or Chippewas, were mentioned on the first page, as the minimal mirage of an ancient history. "On a hill by the Mississippi where Chippewas camped two generations ago, a girl stood in relief against the cornflower blue of Northern sky. She saw no Indians now; she saw flourmills and the blinking windows of skyscrapers in Minneapolis."

Gopher Prairie was a "frontier camp," declared the omniscient author. "It was not a place to live in, not possibly, not conceivably." *Main Street* would have been easy to close after the first few chapters, but several passengers talked constantly about the book at dinner and in the salons. So, the readable, but privileged and wearisome adventures of Carol Kennicott were worth the literary comments and conversations.

The dinner readers were mostly critical of the mores of main streets, and praised the author of the novel, but had no sense of the irony. The novel delivered the hypocrisy of the small town through light ironic dialogue and descriptions. I had talked many times about literature with my brother, mother, and uncle, of course, but never talked with anyone about a specific novel. So, that was a new literary experience with captive tourists on an ocean liner.

Sinclair Lewis was a brilliant writer, and he created a sense of main street realism in omniscient conversations, rather a tease of realism in a main street town. Native totemic realism and ironic stories were the opposite, but that was hardly appreciated by most readers. Even the mockery of smug national realism competed with native shadows, stories, and a sense of presence. I asserted at dinner that the author was much more than a mere clever critic or gadfly. He was a master ironist of main streets everywhere. Lewis wrote, "Main Street is the climax of civilization."

Lewis described a country lake as "enameled with sunset." The tourists at dinner thought the word "enameled" was industrial and not a clear or appropriate metaphor. The sheen of that sunset was material, not natural or romantic. The enameled lake was a material glaze rather than a reflection of nature or a totem. Lewis, the omniscient narrator, created several natural and ironic perceptions of the seasons and weather in Gopher Prairie. Carol Kennicott, once a city librarian, mused that the "snow, stretching without break from streets to devouring prairie beyond, wiped out the town's pretense of being a shelter. The houses were black specks on a white sheet."

Aloysius thought about the "black specks on a white sheet," and in the morning he painted two singular abstract portrayals of blue ravens on the deck of an ocean liner, and blue ravens afloat on huge waves. The horizon lines in both portrayals were muted, the puffy clouds were blue, an abstract scene in reverse, and with an almost imperceptible trace of rouge.

Some sixty blue ravens in the second portrayal were buoyant on the rise and curve of waves, and touched with minimal traces of rouge, brown, and black. The ravens were abstract shapes, various and uneven contours, and with only the slightest lines, curves, or specks of color to suggest the likeness of a beak, claw, a raven eye, or wing. My brother created two magnificent and subtle paintings on our return voyage to France. His new abstract style was original and experimental with abstract shapes and muted colors.

I read five books of *The Odyssey* that night in the cabin as the ship gently swayed onward to France. One section of book nineteen lingered in my thoughts. *Ulysses would have been here long ago, had he not thought better to go from land to land gathering wealth; for there is no man living who is so wily as he is; there is no one can compare with him.*

>>> <<<

The *France* cruised through La Manche, otherwise named the English Channel, and late that morning entered the dreary industrial harbor of Le Havre. A pilot came aboard and directed the steamship through the Bassin de la Manche. The city and enormous international port, once the world market center for coffee, cotton, and many other commodities, had become a gloomy tableau of warehouses, mountains of imported coal, rickety ships, and the ruins of the war industry.

The gray, gloomy harbor was at the mouth of the great River Seine. The same river two years earlier that carried three carved wooden boats, the *Odysseus, Misaabe,* and *Augustus,* down four rivers, the Vesle, Aisne, Oise, and Seine, out to La Manche and the Atlantic Ocean. My brother carved the boats and we christened them in combat on the Vesle. Our three boats were at sea, surely on a steady course to Portugal, Spain, or the Caribbean.

Le Havre was covered overnight with light snow, damp and cold. We boarded the passenger boat train with hundreds of other tourists, and about three hours later the train moved slowly through untold shantytowns, past makeshift covered wagons, marooned railroad cars, the shacks of *zoniers,* displaced workers, veterans and their families, and arrived at the Gare Saint-Lazare in Paris. The station was dreary, and crowded with pushy travelers. Scruffy children roamed with pluck and determination, cut and weaved between the tourists, and with a sleight of hand, the blink of an eye, begged for a few coins, and then retreated to wait for the next train.

The persistent children at the station reminded me of hawking the *Tomahawk* ten years earlier at the new Ogema Station. We cut and cornered every passenger on the train and sold a few papers, but we were not so desperate or hungry, and had no reason to beg to eat for the day.

Our family was removed to the reservation, an empire civil war, and natives were abandoned by most democratic politicians, but never set adrift as vagrants or refugees near cities. So many young mothers and their children had lost husbands and fathers in this war and thousands of towns, churches, homes, and farms had been totally destroyed by the Germans.

I was moved by the courage of the children at the train station, and compared our experiences on the reservation to the aftermath of the war in France. Honoré, our father, worked as a trapper, hunter, and logger, and our family was poor, partly because natives had been renounced by the federal government, but we were never desolate, abandoned, or starving.

The White Earth Reservation was a familiar landscape, and became a political treaty homeland, and at the same time a place of totemic traces, native traditions, and memories of the fur trade that transcended the contempt of outsiders and federal agents. Yet, most natives on the continent had been removed from familiar landscapes and cultural places, and detained as political prisoners by the federal government in a civil war.

The *zoniers* could have been our native brothers, descendants of the fur trade, and veterans of the war, but we were distracted with a personal mission to discover and create art and literature in Paris. We had traversed the main streets of chance and poverty in seven distinct worlds apart in thirteen days. Native totems were the stories of the first world on our journey, the second, remains of the fur trade, and the third world was the reservation. We walked for a day down the crowded main streets of the fourth world of destitute immigrants in miserable tenements in New York City. We had arrived two days early and waited near the harbor to board the *France*. The tourist-class passengers were the fifth world, and the shantytown *zoniers* the sixth world apart. The cafés, art galleries, and museums were the seventh world in thirteen days.

Lastly, we were haunted by the misery of another world apart, and grieved for the procession of wounded veterans. Young soldiers with shattered, disfigured faces, severed arms, legs, ears, and cast in silent anguish in the waiting room at the train station. Some of the soldiers wore metal masks to disguise hideous facial wounds. We entered the waiting room, saluted the soldiers, and gave our money, only a few hundred francs, to the masked veterans. My heart ached for the wounded veterans. The war was not over in the station, but what else could we do for them that afternoon? We walked in silence to the Paris Métro.

Aloysius could hardly wait to present his new paintings at the Galerie Crémieux. The Métro train was slow, noisy, and crowded with workers, and yet we felt at home. Paris had become our new course of *égalité* and our natural means and sway of *liberté*, and more secure because of our reservation experiences. Yes, we were embraced, teased, and honored by our native relatives, by the trader, healer, chef, hotelier, doctor, and others as original artists, but the power and curse of federal agents would never en-able art, literature, or native liberty on reservations. The triple prohibition of wine, whiskey, and absinthe on the reservation would be reason enough to avoid the creepy dominion of federal agents.

Aloysius pointed to our reflections in the train window, and declared that we were at last natives of liberty. That was a great moment, and a natural presence, of course, but not without a sense of native chance and trace of irony. The horrors of war had delivered us as eager soldiers to an art gallery in France.

Nathan wrote several months earlier and invited us to stay at the Galerie Crémieux. We arrived before dark and he was waiting at the gallery door. He waved his arms and shouted out his welcome and delight to see us again, *entrez, bonjour, je suis très content de vous revoir.*

The decision to leave the theater and reservation, the blues of our actual departure, the chance and excitement of the journey, the boasters and stories on the ocean liner came to a memorable close that evening. Only the wounded soldiers and the children at the station remained in my visual memory. Otherwise there was a sense of peace in the great warmth of the gallery. The native objects were a reassurance, and there were two blue ravens framed on the gallery wall. Nathan had decided not to sell the last two paintings, not until my brother painted more. He always wanted at least two blue ravens on display in the gallery. Nathan was a generous and trusted friend, and his care and humor were the very reason that we had dared to imagine our presence as native artists in Paris.

22

ÉCOLE INDIENNE

– – – – – – – – 1922 – – – – – – – –

The River Seine shimmered and curved with an eternal smile, and the natural traces of that disguise were underway on the waves of winter lights. The reflections never slighted tinkers on the stone, wounded veterans, wanderers, and trusty fishermen who steadied the stream that morning.

The waves of plane leaves, swollen beams, and barges of coal creased the slow water under every bridge of honor and tribute. The ancient sources and new catch of the river, and stories of moue and memory ran away overnight to the channel and the sea.

Aloysius had started a new series of portrayals, *Blue Ravens and Bridges on the River Seine*, on our first weekend in Paris. We walked the entire day on each side of the river from the Cathédrale Notre-Dame de Paris to the Pont de l'Archevêché and Pont Mirabeau. The River Seine curved to the west under the Pont Royal, Pont de la Concorde, Pont de l'Alma, and past the Eiffel Tower.

Guillaume Apollinaire had published "Le Pont Mirabeau" in *Alcools* seven years earlier. Nathan Crémieux read the poem out loud at dinner and encouraged me to translate the first stanza.

> *Sous le pont Mirabeau coule la Seine*
> The Seine runs under the Pont Mirabeau
> *Et nos amours*
> And our love
> *Faut-il qu'il m'en souvienne*
> The river must remember me
> *La joie venait toujours après la peine*
> Joy always came after sorrow

Aloysius made several outline drawings of each bridge in a notebook. He usually painted at the scenes, the actual portrayals of inspiration, but the blue ravens and the bridges were imagined and painted later. The notes were impressions, creative configurations, and pictures of the architecture and the many moods of the river. My brother traced and set the bridges afloat several times but could not decide how to create the scenes of ravens and the river.

Later that week he imagined the blue bridges afloat with mighty ravens on the curve of waves. The bridges were unmoored, and moved with the river and ravens. The memorial bridges were portrayed in natural motion, a tribute to the actual traces, totemic reflections, and impressions overnight in the River Seine.

Nathan was delighted, of course, with the description of the new abstract bridge paintings, and he was eager to schedule an exhibition of the new series. The earlier blue ravens were the first contemporary native art to be presented with traditional, ceremonial and native ledger art at the Galerie Crémieux.

Marie Vassilieff invited us to dinner a few days later at Le Chemin du Montparnasse. Since our first visit three years earlier she had created fantastic terracotta figurines, rough dolls dressed with motley, untidy material, an artistic counteraction of classical images and sculpture. The faces of the figures were handsome, some with huge eyes, more spirited than models of the ordinary. The figurines might have been the ancestors of every culture. Marie was moved when my brother told the story that our grandmother had made similar rough figures decorated with feathers and leather for the children on the White Earth Reservation.

Aloysius was eager to start the stories over dinner with an episode about the nasty federal agent with a nose for the scent of wine, the prohibition of alcohol, and politics of white pine on the reservation. I continued with stories about labor unions and our work as stagehands at the Orpheum Theatre in Minneapolis.

Marie was a revolutionary and honored labor unions over the bourgeoisie, of course, and raised her voice to salute the mere mention of unions, and yet she was hesitant to favor the obscure communiqués of the communists, and would never stand with the fanatics or extremists of the Parti Communiste Français.

Marie assumed that we had been active in communist labor movements and the Industrial Workers of the World, and anticipated our stories of the obvious proletarian maneuvers of natives on federal reservations. Naturally she was enthusiastic about native traditions and liberty, but not as *au courant* with the colonies and reservations as she was with political revolutions, visionary literature, and the great innovative artists of Paris.

I described the situation of labor and radical movements on federal treaty reservations. Native politics and parties emerged from cultural bloodlines, not from the abstract ideologies of nationalism, and the sources of resistance were natural, personal, and complete. The seasons, a severe winter, could have been more serious than the revenge of an enemy.

Honoré, our father, was a lumberjack, and we hawked the *Tomahawk* at the train station in the summer, but labor unions were never established on reservations. Augustus, our uncle, was an entrepreneur and publisher, Odysseus was a trader, Misaabe was a healer, and John Leecy was a hotel proprietor, neither laborers nor the bourgeoisie. Marie realized at once that natives and others were excluded because of culture and politics from many jobs and labor unions. She was agitated by the general discussions of natives and trade unions and denounced discrimination, bigotry, and the hatred of Jews in the country and in the Communist Party.

Aloysius mentioned that he had once carried a banner and marched with the union outside of a movie theater in Minneapolis. He paused, smiled, and then revealed the ironic exaggeration that his protest against the unfair theater owner lasted only about an hour on a cold and windy day. I carried on the union stories that night and asked why communist men, dressed in dark bourgeois suits, ties, and fedoras, touted tiny bouquets of wild flowers at the entrances to the Paris Métro.

Marie laughed and explained that the flowers were picked near Chaville, a commune southwest of Paris. Nathan had never thought much about the politics of flower vendors. So, the fierce communists and critics of the bourgeoisie were steady hawkers of primroses and violets, an irony of labor history.

Nathan was hesitant to discuss political movements, and we had never heard him criticize a person or organization, but that night he denounced the fascist sentiments that promoted the primacy of the primitive, and the myths of peasants and savages. He respected our sense of native traditions and native aesthetics, and would never designate our creative work as primitive.

Nathan was particularly critical of the political philosopher Georges

Sorel for his pronouncement that science was a fiction, and for his crusade of the primitive, the proletariat, and the virtues of political violence. Sorel denounced the war and *l'union sacrée*, the sacred union, the necessary political truce and patriotic support of the French government in the course of the First World War.

I entered the discussion and declared that traditional native stories, creative literature, aesthetics, natural reason, and artistic portrayals have always been reduced by romantic arguments and political assessments of savagism. Explorers and priests concocted the savage and primitivism as cultural entertainment. Nathan was convinced that natives had always been modernists, and the only savages were those who created the fascist models and categories of the primitive.

Nathan had always demonstrated his critical and aesthetic appreciation of the native ledger artists, the sense of blue horses in natural motion, and he never consigned any native traditional or creative art or story to the romance of the primitive. We trusted his vision of native art at the very start, even before we met, because his father was a respected trader, and known by our friend Odysseus.

Marie was an innovative painter and active in radical politics, and she was troubled by the *chemins détrempés* of fascism. Yes, she used the words mushy paths, in translation, for the first time that night to describe the ruses of racists, and the swampy machinations of the new fascists since the end of the war.

Marie was easily provoked by the critics and nationalists who exploited the distinction of *École de Paris*, the brilliant and worldly cubist, abstract, and expressionist artists in Paris, with the new fascist notion of the *École Française* artists, a nasty political and racist cut and separation of creative artists and communities. The fascists censured avant-garde and abstract visual art and tried to elevate the secure pastoral scenes in portrayals.

Marie delivered that passionate critique on art and politics as she served roasted chickens with vegetables. Naturally she had engaged in many serious and intense political discussions during the war at La Cantine des Artistes. The cheap meals attracted many hungry abstract artists, French, Spanish, Italian, Russian, and Vladimir Lenin and Leon Trotsky.

The Pernod anise apéritif reminded me of the banquets at the Hotel Leecy. Nathan remembered my story about the precious and prohibited absinthe on the reservation and raised his glass to honor the trader Odysseus. We had already consumed two bottles of white wine with the entrée of pâté, sliced sausage, ham, and tiny pieces of toast, during the hearty discussions of art and politics. Marie served with the roasted chickens a special reserve of Pavillon Blanc, Château Margaux, from Bordeaux.

I waited for the suitable moment and then related a traditional practice of native storiers. My story was a preamble to the necessary revision of the memorable Banquet Français at the Hotel Leecy. The warriors and traders on the trail once named a native in the morning to be the storier that night around the fire. In that way the nominated native could imagine and rehearse the best stories in silence on the trail, and the stories that night would be enhanced to amuse and astonish the other natives, and with an adept sense of irony. That, in fact, was my practice that night at dinner with Marie and Nathan.

Aloysius presented ironic variations of the stories about the Banquet Français. We decided not to reveal the marvelous menu in celebration of native veterans that night at the Hotel Leecy. Instead we created stories of a traditional native menu because any abstract description of the actual French cuisine that Messy prepared would have been unbelievable on a reservation and a discourteous story in the company of our new friends. Our native stories that night about the dinner were double ironies.

My reservation banquet stories mimicked the fantastic stories that Nathan had created in the alley three years earlier at Le Chemin du Montparnasse. John Leecy could have been Erik Satie, and Foamy the dopey agent could have been the pesky Amedeo Modigliani, but only in the artsy banquet game stories. Odysseus could have been Pablo Picasso, Misaabe could have been Fernand Léger, Doctor Mendor could have been Blaise Cendrars, Catherine Heady could have been Béatrice Hastings, and Messy could have been Marie Vassilieff at the banquet table in my stories that night.

I related actual and imagined scenes. Messy raised a cleaver and chased the federal agent out of the hotel kitchen. Foamy had tracked down the scent of wine, and he was obsessed with another scent, the rose and linen aroma of the coy schoolteacher Catherine Heady. I pointed at chairs around the table and named the diners that night at the Hotel Leecy. Messy was indeed a famous chef and the dinner was underway in my imagination.

Foamy rushed back to the hotel with his pistol drawn, shouted out his love for the schoolteacher, and then aimed at Doctor Mendor. Catherine ducked under the table, and took cover between the legs of the doctor. Odysseus disarmed the covetous lecher, and hogtied him in the corner of the room. Messy poured sweet birch bark moonshine on the agent, and then continued the dinner service.

Messy prepared a traditional native feast of game, fish, and commodity fare, fatty and salty, to celebrate the native veterans who had returned from the war. We praised the heroic combat service of Lawrence Vizenor and honored the memory of our cousin Ignatius Vizenor. My creative and equivocal description of the cuisine that night was an unusual concoction of wild game and *ashandiwin*, or commodity rations, delivered by the federal government.

The first course of the traditional meal was *giigoonhwaabo*, a hearty fish soup with heads, eyes, and bones of sunfish, crappies, and northern pike. Messy prepared blue chicken, *miinan baaka aakwenh*, or chicken baked with blueberries, a signature main course, mashed pumpkin, rose hip wine, and pinch bean coffee. Baked potatoes were served with mounds of commodity peanut butter, and fatty salt pork was delivered in a wooden barrel. Salt pork was a manly meal, and some natives were convinced the grease healed wounds. Traditional healers once used bear fat, but hardly salty pork grease.

I quickly turned from the meal stories to the intrigue of politics and lovers because the overstated commodity fare was not healthy or edible enough to hold an audience. Messy had her eye on Misaabe, and Catherine Heady, the schoolteacher, gulped white lightning and swooned over Doctor Mendor. Foamy the aloof federal agent was smitten with the schoolteacher.

Father Aloysius turned down the invitation to the raucous banquet because he had declared in a recent sermon that commodity food was an extermination cuisine. More natives had vanished on a commodity diet of federal fat, salt, and sugar than by love, politics, war, weather, or any other cause. Fry bread was the most pernicious eradication fare on the reservation, a nasty concoction of bleached white flour, processed white animal fat, white salt, and white sugar, and the greasy doughnut of death was promoted as a native tradition at ceremonies.

Marie was moved and pained by the perception of native death by federal doughnuts, and the commodity warrant encouraged me to continue the double ironies of a rations revolution. I raised my voice and declared that the first radical act of a native revolutionary on the reservation was to change diets, and then to capture and serve fry bread to the romantics and federal agents, the same extermination fare that had endangered the health of natives. The second act was total sedition, a just and ironic reversal of the reservation. Close the borders of the reservation and establish a new frontier minstrel, a vaudeville show of federal agents and elected politicians with rouge face paint. Yes, the Funny Federal Minstrel of the Wild West.

My dinner stories were a union of sentiments, characters and cuisine, and the stories brought together the contradictions and ironies of radical politics and aesthetics between the White Earth Reservation and Le Chemin du Montparnasse in Paris.

Aloysius rescued my satirical scenes of doughnut death with descriptive stories about his outlines of blue ravens and bridges over the River Seine. Nathan was certain the paintings would be viewed as a new native school of art, *École Indienne*, and once again he promised to arrange a major exhibition of the series at the Galerie Crémieux.

Marie was ecstatic about the new series of blue ravens, and loaned my brother an extraordinary book of original art from her library, *Les Trente-Six Vues de la Tour Eiffel*, or *Thirty-Six Views of the Eiffel Tower*, by the painter Henri Rivière. The handcrafted book was printed in a limited edition of five hundred copies, and signed by the artist in 1902. The color lithographs were thirty-six marvelous views of the Eiffel Tower, and the obvious inspiration was *Thirty-Six Views of Mount Fuji* by Katsushika Hokusai.

Aloysius studied each of the thirty-six images of the Eiffel Tower, and counted sixteen scenes near the River Seine. The colors were muted, tan, gray, and white. The puffy clouds were abstract outlines, and the autumn leaves were enormous. The tower was set in the clouds, pictured with an umbrella in the snow, and in another scene the tower was next to vents on a rooftop.

The Eiffel Tower was painted near a man and his dog on a beach, by a railroad track, in view on a river ferry, and in some scenes the great tower was barely a gray silhouette on the horizon. The Eiffel Tower was ironic in one scene, a slight dark spire obscured behind the silhouette of the Cathédrale Notre-Dame de Paris.

Japonisme, the tradition, manner, and practice of woodblock prints and the *sumi-e*, or ink painting, was once a distinctive art movement in France. The aesthetic pleasure of natural motion, an image of bright plum blossoms on a black stone, or the scene of blue ravens on a winter bough, stimulated many impressionist painters, Claude Monet, Camille Pissarro, Édouard Manet, and Pierre-Auguste Renoir. Paul Gauguin and Vincent van Gogh were similarly aroused by the art of the Japanese.

Aloysius decided then and there that he would paint thirty-six views of blue ravens and bridges over the River Seine. He told Marie about the Japanese artist and teacher Yamada Baske who encouraged him to use traces of rouge in his portrayals. Nathan only imagined the proposed paintings and yet he hailed the new series of blue ravens and bridges as masterful impressionistic scenes, and with an original composition of familiar views.

The *Thirty-Six Views of Mount Fuji* by Hokusai had inspired many painters and artists in France. Hokusai, an *ukiyo-e* master of woodblock art prints, created ordinary evanescent and transient scenes of geishas, kabuki actors, samurai, and mountains in bright colors, an *ukiyo*, or aesthetic "floating world." Rivière created the same number of aesthetic scenes of the Eiffel Tower. Aloysius would continue the artistic practice and perception of scenes in a "floating world," a double homage to Hokusai and Rivière.

Nathan located an apartment for us to rent at 12 Rue Pecquay in Le Marais, about a mile from the gallery on the Rive Droite, or Right Bank of the River Seine. The rooms were bright, and the furniture was old, worn, but tidy. The apartment was cold and fuel was rationed, but the front windows faced the sun and provided some heat by day. Aloysius painted near the large front windows over the street, and sometimes in the parks and cafés. He was dedicated to the creation of thirty-six views of the bridges in time for an exhibition that early summer at the gallery.

I wrote my stories and drank wine at the nearby cafés on Rue Rambuteau, Rue des Francs-Bourgeois, and Rue des Archives. The cafés were heated, and naturally crowded. We bought used clothes for the winter and most of our food at the bustling markets at Les Halles. Our French vocabulary was greatly increased with the names of bread, cheese, fruit, and vegetables. Some food was rationed, but we bought as much food as we could eat, an absolute visual delight. My brother was even tempted to paint blue ravens over the colorful baskets of fruit and vegetables. Messy would have praised the daily markets as a paradise.

The Goldenberg Delicatessen on Rue des Rosiers became our favorite place to dine, and mostly we ordered goulash, or herring and latkes. The busy restaurant and kosher butcher shop nearby were new and established by Jo Goldenberg and his brothers, Jews from Eastern Europe. The more we ate there the more we were teased by the owner, an ironic gesture of native acceptance, and the restaurant became our reservation without a federal agent.

I read three books of *The Odyssey* one morning at a café on Rue du Temple, and was moved by a scene in book twenty-two. *Then Ulysses searched the whole court carefully over, to see if anyone had managed to hide himself and was still living, but he found them all lying in the dust and weltering in their blood. They were like fishes which fishermen have netted out of the sea, and thrown upon the beach to lie gasping for water till the heat of the sun makes an end of them. Even so were the suitors lying all huddled up one against the other.*

The Métro at Place de la Concorde became the touchstone of my new imagistic prose and poetry. Ezra Pound conceived of his perfect poem, "In a Station of the Metro," at that very station near the Jardin des Tuileries and the Musée de l'Orangerie. The scene of faces and spirits in the crowd was a trace of native motion and reason. The fourteen words of the poem, and without a verb, created a sense of presence, and at the same time, a perception of impermanence in the precise metaphor of petals on a wet black bough.

The apparition of these faces in the crowd;
Petals on a wet, black bough.

I would have composed "blue petals on a wet, black bough," a necessary imagistic motion of color in the poem. Pound created an image of a black bough. Why not blue petals? The natural motion of the concise images was an inspiration, and that poem carried on in my memory and imagination. Ezra Pound published "In a Station of the Metro" in *Lustra*, a collection of poems, in 1916. I walked slowly down the stairs of every entrance to the Place de la Concorde station and recited the poem with each access. Later, the images of that poem came to mind in every crowded station in Paris.

I borrowed copies of *Ripostes* and *Lustra*, recent collections of imagistic poems by Ezra Pound, from Shakespeare and Company, an English language bookstore and lending library. The new bookstore moved from 8 Rue Dupuytren to 12 Rue de l'Odéon, a more spacious storefront near the Boulevard Saint-Germain. Yes, the famous French language bookstore, La Maison des Amis des Livres, established by the lovely Adrienne Monnier, was across the street.

Shakespeare and Company was near the Place de l'Odéon. A music store, nose spray maker, corset maker, orthopedic shoemaker, and book appraiser were located on the same street. Nearby were the great Théâtre de l'Odéon and Café Voltaire, and the Jardin du Luxembourg. I had walked with my brother many times on the same streets, and compared the Orpheum Theatre in Minneapolis to the Théâtre de l'Odéon in Paris. Not a respectable comparison of theaters, of course, but we practiced the stories and similarities of two personal experiences.

Sylvia Beach smiled and told me that the great Ezra Pound had built the bookshelves in her bookstore. The poet as the builder of bookcases was not common, but at the time the practice seemed rather natural. Pound was a precise imagist poet, but not a precious poser. I learned later than he built furniture, and doubly associated with the poet as an imagist and builder. Ezra Pound created poetic images with a natural sense of presence.

Sylvia always read the books she sold and lent, and she was pleased to mention the names of many famous authors, André Gide, the novelist, Valéry Larbaud, the poet and translator, George Antheil, the pianist and music composer, James Joyce, the poet and novelist, and many other authors and musicians who bought and borrowed books at Shakespeare and Company.

Sylvia was surprised, as most people were, that natives had established newspapers on reservations, and she ordered copies of *French Returns: The New Fur Trade*, published by the *Tomahawk*. She was certain that many readers would be interested in my stories of the war and the White Earth Reservation. She had accepted me as an author, a new experience for me in a bookstore, and my only fear at the time was that she might have expected me to comment on the poetry of John Milton, or the plays of William Shakespeare.

I could have told stories about Mark Twain, Jack London, *Main Street* by Sinclair Lewis, *Moby-Dick* by Herman Melville, and Oscar Wilde in America, but instead related my appreciation for the poetic innovations and the cubist originality of Guillaume Apollinaire and the images of Ezra Pound. My declared passion for certain poets was partly to disguise my ignorance about most literature. She was truly moved by my intuitive story about the apparition and spirits at the station entrance, the "blue petals on a wet, black bough" at the Métro Place de la Concorde.

Sylvia was eager to talk about the chance situations, symbolic scenes, and magical adventures of Ishmael in *Moby-Dick.* She had recently suggested the novel to Adrienne Monnier. Augustus came to mind that afternoon in the bookstore, of course, because he had teased me many times to become a writer, and had introduced me to the books of many authors, including *The Call of the Wild* by Jack London, and *Moby-Dick* by Herman Melville.

The conversations turned to scenes in literature, and the poetic spirit of language, and were enlivened by her gentle and affectionate personal stories about the many authors who had borrowed books, and authors who had read their work at the bookstore. She sang the praises of modernist poets over the steady metronome lectures of heroic or romantic poetry. Sylvia was natural, graceful, independent, and humane, and with a perfect touch of sympathetic gestures and stories. I was enchanted by her spirit, sense of humor, and personal manner. There were many, many good reasons never to leave the bookstore that afternoon in the cold rain.

Sylvia invited me to celebrate the publication of *Ulysses*, an extraordinary, ingenious, and epic novel by James Joyce, and the fortieth birthday of the author, later that Thursday, February 2, 1922, at Shakespeare and Company. Sylvia had paid the entire production cost for a thousand copies of the novel. She told me the novel, more than seven hundred pages, was printed by Maurice Darantière in Dijon, France. Selected chapters had been published earlier in *The Little Review*, so the production of the entire novel was a very significant literary event, and more than a hundred copies had been sold in advance to subscribers and customers of the bookstore.

The Dijon printer sent the first two copies of the novel by train to the Gare de Lyon in Paris. Sylvia met the train that early morning, she told me later, and collected the first two copies of the novel. She delivered copies of *Ulysses* to James Joyce at 9 Rue de l'Université on his birthday. The author was mystical about finances, numbers, and memorial dates. The creative order of his wordy world was restored on his birthday with the delivery of the first edition of *Ulysses*.

Sylvia was very generous and appreciated the significance of that sacred union of publications and birthdays. I was moved by the gesture and became a wholehearted subscriber and active member of the lending library of Shakespeare and Company.

The coterie that gathered a few days later at the bookstore to celebrate the publication of *Ulysses* included the grand authors and painters of Paris. I was shied at first by the presence of so many great authors, André Gide, the novelist, Paul Valéry, the poet, Ernest Hemingway, the flamboyant journalist and short story writer, Gertrude Stein, the art collector and littérateur, André Breton, the poet and mastermind of surrealism and inspiration of the review journal *Littérature*, and many curators, painters, and musicians. We mingled with the artists and collectors but never encountered Gide, Breton, or Hemingway.

James Joyce was seated at the back of the store, almost hidden in the shelves of books. He was surrounded by admirers, mostly women, and by other eager subscribers to the publication of *Ulysses*. He crossed his long spider legs, right to left, and his white hands drooped over the arm of the wooden chair, the secure manner of a domestic animal.

Aloysius moved closer with the crowd and tried to greet the author. Joyce was distracted by the constant murmur of voices, the smack and smiles, and the wave of lights, and turned away. The author seemed to be in creative flight. He was not prompted or stage ready to acknowledge anyone in the crowd that night. Not me, and not the shirttail relations of modern literature.

I wanted to chat with the author about *The Odyssey*, and about our good friend the trader Odysseus. Joyce would surely have appreciated the story of the name, at least, but my comments apparently were lost in the literary rush and murmurs at the back of the bookstore. I move closer to the author, and leaned to his right ear, a native maneuver in the presence of hesitance and timidity, and whispered two lines of his new novel. *Pain, that was not yet the pain of love, fretted his heart.* I paused but the author was not moved by my gesture of respect. *Paris rawly waking, crude sunlight on her lemon houses.* Finally he turned with caution, and caught me in a distant gaze. His eyes were far away, only the slightest dance of communion under the thick spectacles. I leaned close once more and recounted my visual memory of selected images and scenes in the first few chapters of the novel. *Ulysses* was displayed in the window of Shakespeare and Company.

James Joyce carried the scent of wax, raw soap, the sweat of blue funk, creases of weary muscles, and marrow in the lung. His bones were decorous, reedy, weak, and obvious, almost transparent, and a glorious blush moved over his cheeks, the sunrise of his ancestors in a lazy smile. Joyce and his bones were cautious, and the ordinary slant and reach of a hand revealed a blue rise of heartbeats, the tender return of precious blood to his heart. My gratitude for the literary was unsteady that night, but the sound of rock doves and tinkers on the river stones evoked a sense of natural presence and native liberty.

Nathan introduced me to Daniel-Henry Kahnweiler, the prominent art collector and owner of the Galerie Simon at Rue d'Astorg. He was formal, serious, and precise. He paused near the entrance to the bookstore, and with only slight gestures explained that his first art gallery was established thirteen years earlier at Rue de Vignon on the Right Bank. Parisians observed street names, the *quartier*, or distinct area, the *arrondissement* or districts of the city, and *Rive Droite* or *Rive Gauche*, to denote social status on the Right Bank or Left Bank of the River Seine. The most successful art galleries were on the Rive Droite. The Galerie Crémieux on Rue de la Bûcherie was historic and an exception to the riverbank class and culture.

Kahnweiler told me in a casual conversation about his first gallery and the cubist paintings the French police had seized at the end of the First World War. The police sold the entire collection of art, more than a thousand cubist paintings by Pablo Picasso, Georges Braque, Juan Gris, and Maurice de Vlaminck, at public auctions over several years.

The Galerie Kahnweiler was a German name, and that was enough cause for the police to declare war reparations. I was amazed that he was not embittered by the outright political thievery. He seemed to be more concerned that the value of the cubist art would be diminished at public auctions.

Moïse Kisling, the painter, was intense, straightforward, and resolute about his art and stories. Naturally, we talked about our evocative dreams and memories of the First World War. He was a wounded veteran of the

French Foreign Legion. Nathan translated parts of our conversation, and a few days later we visited his studio and viewed some of his paintings. Aloysius was drawn to the blues, of course, and slowly moved his hands in a natural flow over the sensuous shapes of the nudes in the portraits.

Moïse had lived at Le Bateau-Lavoir, a commune with many other artists and authors in Montmartre, and later he moved to Montparnasse. The stories he told about the famous "boat laundry" residence of artists were similar to the ironic spirit of stories told by natives on the White Earth Reservation.

Moïse was born in Kraków, Poland. Nathan mentioned that he had studied art and was inspired by impressionism. An art teacher encouraged him to study in Paris. The style of his painting was original, of course, but the erotic shapes of nudes were similar to the portraits by Amedeo Modigliani, and the character and colors were similar to the scenes of Marc Chagall. The landscapes were natural scenes in motion, waves of color, bright and spirited. The faces of nudes and other portraits were oval, calm, and weary.

My comments about art and literature in the presence of the artist or author were descriptive but never comparative. I learned to study and respect individuality, and at the same time conceded that the best stories told on the reservation were inspired and improved by many other stories. Published stories were similar to the mutable native oral stories. No author or storier could have invented the entire structure and use of language, but only the original, elusive images, and ironic scenes of characters. Painters likewise created innovative scenes and portraits with curious motions, semblance, and color, but not the actual composition of the paint.

Moïse became a citizen for his military service and wounds, and he was proud to be French. He aimed his pipe at several artists around the store, those who had not served to defend the liberty of France. Nathan translated the stories we told about our experiences of the war, and later he urged me to write the very same stories for publication. That was the first time that he had ever mentioned the translation and publication of my stories into French. The enticement was revealed at the very heart of my chat with the Moïse Kisling.

Moïse had never encountered natives, but he understood that the enemy was haunted by the fear of being scalped. The Polish, he declared without hesitation, would have been native compatriots, not the enemy, and never scared away by the *Indien*. He pointed in the direction of his stories and seemed to know everyone in the world of art, including the impressionists, cubists, fauvists, and surreal artists, and many art gallery owners, Daniel-Henry Kahnweiler and Nathan Crémieux. Moïse remembered with tears of pleasure the great heart and generosity of Marie Vassilieff and La Cantine des Artistes.

Nathan reminded me later that he certainly had decided to translate and publish a selection of my new stories and some stories published in *French Returns* by the *Tomahawk*. Nathan had never published an author, but he was impressed with the publication of *Ulysses* by James Joyce. Sylvia Beach and Shakespeare and Company had published several books in the past, and the most significant was *Ulysses*. Galerie Crémieux would be my publisher. Nathan paused and decided then and there the title of my stories, *École Indienne* by Basile Hudon Beaulieu.

Nathan surprised me that night. I was excited, naturally, that he would translate and publish my descriptive and ironic stories. Aloysius had already thought about the cover art. To celebrate the event we invited Nathan to dinner at the Goldenberg Delicatessen in Le Marais. We had no idea, at the time, that he knew the owner and was a regular customer at the restaurant. Jo Goldenberg greeted Nathan at the door, and teased him about crazy art and artists. Our association with the famous gallery owner was always remembered at the restaurant.

Nathan ordered gefilte fish with carrots and horseradish, his favorite, and told stories about several artists and gallery owners before the First World War. Pablo Picasso had envisioned cubism and painted *Les Demoiselles d'Avignon* fifteen years earlier at Le Bateau-Lavoir in Montmartre. That radical cubist portrayal of nudes, two with masks, in a brothel, was a decadent torment to some, and a mockery of the fascination with constitution, manner, representation, and poise of brush and color.

Nathan continued the stories about Le Bateau-Lavoir, the commune of artists located near the Basilique du Sacré-Coeur. Max Jacob, the painter, created the nickname Le Bateau-Lavoir, an ironic description of a rickety laundry boat. The commune was nothing more than a ramshackle building divided into tiny inexpensive art studios. Most of the artists who lived and painted there were poor, migrant, innovative, and influenced the new movements in cubist and surrealist art.

Le Bateau-Lavoir was in ruins, without heat or electricity, and yet the artists created radical visions and conversions of portraiture and landscape that became a signature of modern art. Picasso, Jacob, Juan Gris, Amedeo Modigliani, André Salmon, Georges Braque, Henri Matissse, and the great poet Guillaume Apollinaire lived and worked at times at the laundry boat.

Daniel-Henry Kahnweiler had established his first art gallery at 28 Rue Vignon in 1907, the very same year that Picasso painted the sensational *Les Demoiselles d'Avignon.* Kahnweiler was a regular visitor at the shabby Bateau-Lavoir in Montmartre.

Nathan pushed his chair back, posed at the side of the tiny table with one hand on his chin, and waved his other hand as he continued the stories. The dramatic gestures were persuasive as he mocked the manner of Kahnweiler. Tease and gentle mockery were common practices in the new world of art dealers and gallery owners, and in that sense the galleries could have been located on the White Earth Reservation.

Picasso was slouched in a corner chair. The studio was dark, and stank of wine, sex, tobacco, and kerosene. Kahnweiler studied the five angular images of women in a brothel. Nathan touched his cheek and ear with one finger, cocked his head and moved closer to the table, pointed at the imagined easel in the story, and proclaimed with a slight accent that *Les Demoiselles d'Avignon* was extraordinary, admirable, and indefinable. The word "crazy" might have been heard later in a sotto voce comment. The primitive gaze, shards of angular bodies, and the ironic bunch of fruit, were not native visions or creative scenes. Cubism was in a mighty transition on the right side of the huge canvas of *Les Demoiselles d'Avignon.* There, two figures wore ceremonial masks, and the women in the painting were much taller on the canvas than Picasso, Nathan, or Kahnweiler.

Jo Goldenberg was delighted to hear another version of the famous painter and art dealer stories, and then he teased us that native ceremonial art had never been a movement of prostitutes or brothels in brick, blocks, and cubes. Yes, but inspired native artists had created many colored horses and visionary memories on ledger paper.

Guillaume Apollinaire, Amedeo Modigliani, and many other artists moved from Le Bateau-Lavoir in Montmartre to La Ruche at Passage de Dantzig, west of the Cimetière du Montparnasse and the graves of Charles Baudelaire, the poet, and the statesman Adolphe Crémieux.

Marc Chagall had already lived and worked for several years at La Ruche, the octagonal beehive studios, with other migrant artists from Belarus and Russia. Chagall and many other artists spoke more Yiddish and Russian than French. He had returned recently from the Vitebsk Arts College in Soviet Belarus. The artists in the hive forever groused about the stink of the nearby slaughterhouses.

The Pont Royal, one of the oldest bridges over the River Seine, connects with the Jardin des Tuileries and Pavillon de Flore on the Rive Droite, and on the Rive Gauche, with Rue du Bac and the fantastic Beaux-Arts Gare d'Orsay. The electric train station was completed for the Paris *Exposition Universelle*, or World Fair, in 1900.

Aloysius sketched outlines of the Pont Royal and the flow of the River Seine. We walked across the bridge several times that afternoon and studied the curves and weathered stone, down one side of the bridge and returned on the other. We walked along the Quai des Tuileries, the Quai Voltaire, and Quai Anatole France near the Gare d'Orsay.

Aloysius created several rough outlines of ravens perched over the tiers of four stone buttresses between the five elegantly curved arches of the bridge. Then my brother decided to paint blue ravens at the train station. There, near the Hôtel de la Gare d'Orsay, we encountered the mighty James Joyce. He lived a few blocks away and walked along the river once a day, in the late afternoon. Aloysius reminded him of our presence at the book event at Shakespeare and Company.

Joyce smiled and leaned to the side on his cane, but we doubted at the time that he recognized our faces from the bookstore. He was a spirited roamer in the literary world, and steadied the sentiments of love and death with his cane. Sylvia Beach once told me a story about the time she first met the author, and that became my approach near the hotel. My inquiry was the same, *Is this the great James Joyce? Yes, James Joyce,* the author said firmly and then reached out to shake my hand that afternoon, as he had done with Sylvia Beach. She told me his hand was limp, a boneless hand, and he wore a heavy ring on his left middle finger. Yes, his right hand moved with casual grace, but an ordinary gesture was miscarried in the hesitant reach of manners.

Joyce recognized my voice, however, and my poetic recitation of two sentences from his novel *Ulysses*. He was gracious, and much more pleasant on the Quai Anatole France than he was seated in a crowd of literary admirers at Shakespeare and Company.

Aloysius declared that James Augustine Aloysius Joyce shared his given name. The White Earth Reservation was envisioned in the names of three saints, Saint Aloysius Gonzaga an Italian Jesuit, Saint Ignatius of Loyola, and Saint Augustine the Blessed. Augustus Hudon Beaulieu was our uncle and publisher of the *Tomahawk*, Ignatius Vizenor was our cousin, and Father Aloysius was the name of the priest at Saint Benedict's Mission.

Joyce raised a single white finger to his cheek and explained that the name Auguste was French, Augustin was Irish, and he was named in the spirit of two saints, Aloysius and Augustine. The Irish endured in the names of saints, and in poetry. Pray there are more saints in my names by heart and history, and so he counted out the most obvious given names, James the Just, James the Less, James the Deacon, and Saint-James, a commune in Manche, France. The Epistle of James, and the surname Joyce, or Josse and Goce, in Ireland, were joyous compositions of deceit and irony in literature. James of Irony, a saint to honor, and he turned to continue his walk across the Pont de la Concorde.

23

APRÈS GUERRE

1923

Paris was a sanctuary that year for posers and at least seven expatriate native veterans of the First World War. The City of Light was our solace and bright promise, and, at the same time, an easy retreat for the many pretenders, native and otherwise.

Pierre Chaisson, one of these seven native veterans, was born in the bayou, a marvelous river storier. The other natives were from woodland reservations, motivated and unworried as we were by the chance of liberty in Paris.

The poser natives were crafty, but never wicked or treacherous, more domestic than shamanic, and more ironic than despotic. The pretenders had concocted native traditions in the stately guise of warriors, and other eccentric traits that befit the romance of native postures and spectacles in museums, theaters, and cafés.

Olivier Black Elk, for instance, was a poser with great charm and he never missed the regular gathering of natives once a week at the Café du Dôme. He was always the first to arrive at the native commune and meticulously selected a chair and table that was the most conspicuous on the terrace or near the entrance.

Olivier wore a Boss of the Plains black hat with a single bald eagle feather tied to the beaded hatband. His mere presence announced our weekly native commune at the café, and he actually provided tourists with a signature in the name of his contrived ancestors. His vanity was only comparable to the stories of native tricksters.

Black Elk the pretender never conceded that he had fabricated a native surname and descent. He was sturdy, moody, and his face and hands were darkened with cosmetics, but his country accent and strained gestures were not native and he was much too young to be the son of Black Elk, the Oglala Lakota visionary from the Pine Ridge Reservation in South Dakota.

Olivier recounted many times and with unnatural precision that his father was a ceremonial dancer and warrior and that he was conceived at a hospital by a young nurse and a shaman in Paris. The inception stories of his ancestors were nifty but the conception and other circumstances were not feasible.

Nathan told me that Black Elk had indeed traveled one season with William Frederick Cody, more than thirty years earlier, and the catchy exhibitions of Buffalo Bill's Wild West. Black Elk had toured England, France, and other countries, and performed for the mighty Queen Victoria.

This Black Elk was actually bedridden in Paris, near death with a serious disease, but slowly recovered and returned home to the Pine Ridge Reservation. Nathan had never heard stories or even rumors about a devoted nurse or progeny.

Buffalo Bill's Wild West performed for several months at the Paris *Exposition Universelle* in 1889. Nathan had attended the fair and met the trader Julius Meyer with a group of natives on a tour of exhibitions, the Gallery of Machines, and the Eiffel Tower. Nathan was downcast over the memory of the *Village Nègre*, Negro Village, at the exhibition, but he reminisced with pleasure about the native rodeo riders, ceremonial dancers, and the spectacular performances of the sharpshooter Annie Oakley.

Coyote Standing Bear was another prominent pretender who attended our weekly native commune at the Café du Dôme. He declared with no shame or hesitation that his father was Luther Standing Bear of the Oglala Lakota on the Pine Ridge Reservation. Coyote either denied or was not aware that several natives had the very same translated nickname that became the surname of Standing Bear. Chief Standing Bear, the Ponca from Nebraska, the Lakota Standing Bear, cousin of Black Elk, who traveled with Buffalo Bill's Wild West in France, Germany, and Austria three years before the Wounded Knee Massacre in 1890, and Luther Standing Bear who graduated from the Carlisle Indian Industrial School and traveled later as a translator with Buffalo Bill's Wild West.

Nathan was certain that one season of Buffalo Bill's Wild West shows opened in April 1905 in Paris, and closed in Marseilles six months later in October. That was the critical exhibition season that complicated the paternity stories of Coyote Standing Bear.

Coyote was a generous romancer and related that he was the true son of Luther Standing Bear. He was pleased to declare that his mother was Louise Rieneck, an Austrian from Vienna, and the family returned to live near the Pine Ridge Reservation and later moved to Chicago.

Coyote had confused the names and stories of his counterfeit native ancestors the three Standing Bears. Luther had not arrived in Paris until 1905, and his wife was Nellie de Cory. Chief Standing Bear was Ponca and married to Susette Primeau. She was not a nurse, and they never lived on or near the Pine Ridge Reservation. The Oglala Lakota were the enemy of the Ponca.

The Lakota Standing Bear traveled with Buffalo Bill's Wild West to the Austrian Empire. He was seriously injured in an accident and hospitalized in Vienna. He recovered and married a young nurse named Louise Rieneck. Standing Bear and Louise raised three daughters, Hattie, Lillian, and Christiana, at White Horse Creek near Manderson, South Dakota.

The Café du Dôme was our native commune. We were Dômiers, cordially bound by the convention of native stories and the ironies of character and liberty in Paris. Aloysius teased Coyote and Olivier about their great ancestors, and at the same time praised their curious tribute and promotion of the names Black Elk and Standing Bear. We actually celebrated the pretenders because they were always out front to enchant and distract the romancers of native cultures.

Coyote and Olivier were eager to recount the ironic stories of native traditions, and generously provided the promise of cultural prominence to the curators, tourists, and romancers at the Café du Dôme. Our tease of the posers was an ironic tribute to their escape from the burdens and boredom of the customary.

The Enlightenment and heyday of civilization had ended in the bloody trenches of the *zone rouge*, the deadly destruction of reason, manners, piety, ordinary humor, and empire traditions, and at the same time native soldiers created a sense of presence with ironic and visionary stories, and restored the pleasure of imitation and mockery. So, we named the pretenders the *gardians*, our cowboys, and teased that they were conceived slowly in the back of a circus wagon on the Camargue south of Arles, France. Later the teases were graced with the ironic paternity of monks in the Order of Saint Benedict.

The pretenders were overeager to be recognized as natives, and grateful to be asked by admirers about native traditions and cultural practices, so the rightful native veterans at our weekly commune were seldom summoned by curious strangers or obligated for any reason to relate or counteract a cultural anecdote, misconception, or the secrets of shamans.

Pierre Chaisson was the mastermind of the weekly commune of native Dômiers. He had served in the infantry, and was wounded by shrapnel at Château-Thierry. The long gash down his right forehead to eyebrow and jawbone was slow to heal because of an infection, so he was hospitalized for more than three months in the Base Hospital at Bazoilles-sur-Meuse near Paris.

Pierre was Houma, an ancient native culture from the many bayous at the great mouth of the Mississippi River near New Orleans, Louisiana. He returned home to Terrebonne Parish, scarred forever by the war, and was altogether discouraged by the policies of the state and federal governments. Houma children were forsaken, he told the native Dômiers, and not allowed to attend public schools, and the reason was racial savagery.

French Acadian relatives had provided a home and a chance for him to be educated in New Brunswick, Canada. Pierre lived there for several years and graduated from public school. He returned to the bayous and then enlisted to serve as an infantry soldier and scout in the American Expeditionary Forces in France. Private Lawrence Chaisson, his cousin, enlisted and served nearby in the Twenty-Sixth Infantry Battalion of the Canadian Expeditionary Forces.

The native situation was similar at both ends of the river, the federal fraud and grift at the source and mouth of the *gichiziibi*, the Mississippi River. Our ancestors might have met as continental traders and storiers on the river routes, hundreds of years before the *voyageurs* of the fur trade, and clever sway of the French. The Café du Dôme became our new commune of native storiers that had started many centuries earlier on the Mississippi River.

Pierre decided three years after the war to leave the bayous, and returned to study philosophy, ethnology, and literature at Sorbonne University in Paris. He was a fluent speaker of Houma, English, and Louisiana French. The French waiters at the Café du Dôme tried to imitate his bayou accent and dialect.

The stories that afternoon were more memorable than at any other native commune. Pierre leaned forward over the three round tables, turned his head to the side and steadily chanted *mille huit cent quatre-vingt-douze*, the ordinary numbers of the year eighteen ninety-two, in the tone and style of a plainsong. Then he turned in the other directions and clearly chanted *mille huit cent quatre-vingt-treize*, the year eighteen ninety-three, in a deep and tremulous voice. He paused, turned toward me, raised the tone of his voice and sang *mille neuf cent seize*, nineteen sixteen, several times. The waiters and customers in the café turned toward our tables. The chant of dates ended with a lingering tone and then silence.

Pierre glanced at the waiters, smiled, and then turned away. The Gregorian chant or plainsong was intense and heartfelt, but the significance of the dates was not obvious. We waited for some idea or explanation of the chanted numbers and dates.

Pierre ordered three carafes of white wine and then told the incredible story about the woman named *Mère de la Zone Rouge* who chanted early in the morning at least twice a week for seven years the very same numbers and dates at the *épicerie* and street markets on Rue Mouffetard near the Panthéon.

Aloysius was moved by the passion of the chant and stories, and painted a scene of blue ravens with the dates daubed on the bridges and huge numbers adrift on the river. The other natives at the commune that afternoon were hesitant to intrude or inquire about the meaning of the dates that were chanted to honor the woman.

I had never heard a chant or plainsong of ordinary numbers with such emotion, vocal power, concentration, and certainty. The chanted dates created a sense of native presence, but with no direct reference or obvious meaning. Names and dates in songs, recitations, canticles, and shouts could be ironic, but the apparent calendar years chanted at the market were surreal by intonation and character.

The grocers and street merchants never learned the actual name of the woman who chanted, but they interpreted the distinct numbers as the birth dates of her two sons, and *mille neuf cent seize*, nineteen sixteen, as the year her two sons died on the very same day in the Battle of Verdun on the Meuse River.

That lonesome woman earned the nickname *Mère de la Zone Rouge*, Mother of the Red Zone. The *zone rouge* was a designation of the area of total devastation in the war zones of France. Nothing more than scraps of bones, slivers of femurs, shards of foreheads, cheek and nose bones, traces of broken molars, tendons, tufts of hair, buttons, buckles, helmets, and unexploded enemy artillery shells remained in the deadly muck of the *zone rouge*, a wasteland of forsaken memories.

Mother of the Red Zone chanted at the street markets on the Rue Mouffetard to honor the birth, memory, and death date of her sons, *mille neuf cent seize*, and by her dedicated chant honored the memory of more than three hundred thousand other sons who had died in the same crazed Battle of Verdun.

Pierre recounted a marvelous and spirited chant one morning last spring at the street markets. Mother of the Red Zone was always greeted by the *chiens bâtards*, the mongrel dogs, on the street, and the *chiens* howled in harmony when she chanted *mille neuf cent seize*, nineteen sixteen. That spring morning the *chiens bâtards* howled with great favor, more harmonic than in the past, and the people on the street and at the markets turned and chanted *mille neuf cent seize* for the first time. The chants were gentle, hesitant, almost whispers, but slowly the tone and volume increased, and a few minutes later every person on the street chanted to honor the memory of the soldiers who died at the Battle of Verdun.

Most of the chanters were moved to tears, and the very last and most hesitant of the street chanters, the market owners, became the most emotional, and actually conducted other chanters on the street. The market owners had heard Mother of the Red Zone chant on the street for many years, and the rhythmic phrases of that plainsong, *mille neuf cent seize*, were chanted with the spirit and rhapsody of memory. Several hundred people chanted the date several times in variations of harmony.

〉〉〉 〈〈〈

Aloysius was out early every morning to sketch scenes of the bridges over the River Seine. The sway and turns of the weather that late spring, hazy, gray, and rainy, presented a ghostly character of the moody river. He painted several direct abstract scenes of the bridges, instant portrayals for the gallery exhibition, but mostly my brother walked slowly around the bridges, lingered on the stone quays and riverbanks, and noted ideas, concise images, and themes. He painted the final crucial scenes of blue ravens and the river bridges in the afternoon light at the window of our apartment.

I walked with my brother two or three times a week along the River Seine. We gestured to each other but hardly spoke on those brisk mornings. The fishermen and others on the riverbank in the early morning conserved a sense of presence and privacy with only minimal gestures. The river ran high that late spring, another threat of floods in the city.

The River Seine was a great course of memory, and the natural motion created a sense of personal and communal presence for hundreds of people. Quai des Grands-Augustins near the Pont Neuf and other quays and riverbanks nurtured a humane sanctuary, and many people were loyal to certain bridges.

The Pont Saint-Louis, Pont des Arts, and Pont Mirabeau were my favorites of the more than thirty bridges over the River Seine. The Pont Saint-Louis was modest, almost stone bare, and yet the bridge had a heroic history, a truly unpretentious beauty. The bridge was destroyed by many floods and was always built anew. The Pont Saint-Louis could have been a native bridge over the headwaters at the source of the Mississippi River in Lake Itasca.

The Pont des Arts was a forthright gesture, gangly, always a good friend at any time of day, and the first iron bridge over the River Seine in Paris. The Pont Mirabeau was a muse of poetry, and my artistic inspiration in the natural motion of the river. The serene naked statues at the prominent bow and fantail of the arches sailed forever in both directions of the river, and one symbolic bronze figure raised a trumpet to celebrate the great memories of natural motion and native adventures.

I pointed at times to obvious scenes, the motion of waves, the slant and shimmer of sunlight, plane leaves in the eddies, and the curious shadows on the river, but never said a word to my brother. The River Seine was forever a natural state of sovereign gestures in the gentle hues of the morning.

Camille Pissaro painted winter scenes of the Pont Neuf and Musée du Louvre. The river was creased by shadows of steamers, and light was cursory, tousled with blue waves. The union of artistic perception and color was a spectacular turn of impressionism. Some twenty years later my brother created visionary scenes and portrayals of the bridges afloat with blue ravens on the River Seine.

Aloysius concentrated on the shadows, creases, and waves on the river, and imagined the shadows and natural motion of the stone arches, and the marvelous flight of the bridges. My observations and notes were about the many communes on the quays and riverbanks. I gestured, of course, and then lingered with respect to talk with the fishermen, children, and with the veterans of the war.

The river anglers were the masters of forbearance and silence. The soldiers gestured with minimal glances, the turn of an eye, and with the slight motion of a hand or shoulder. Yes, the gestures were familiar, a common duty of battle memories, and the fugitive nature of war. The silent heralds of the anglers and veterans were the same from day to day, a certain cue of presence and natural dominion on the River Seine.

I read book twenty-three of *The Odyssey* on a park bench under the chestnut trees at the Square du Vert-Galant near the Pont Neuf. *When Ulysses and Penelope had had their fill of love they fell talking with one another. She told him how much she had had to bear in seeing the house filled with a crowd of wicked suitors who had killed so many sheep and oxen on her account, and had drunk so many casks of wine. Ulysses in his turn told her what he had suffered, and how much trouble he had himself given to other people. He told her everything, and she was so delighted to listen that she never went to sleep till he had ended his whole story.*

〉〉〉 〈〈〈

Odysseus, our friend the trader, came to mind that afternoon on the River Seine. Paris might have become the sanctuary of the traders. I raised my hand to salute his presence, and reminisced about his grand gestures and ironic stories. Odysseus would have recited a few lines of a poem and then teased me about the womanly scenes of adventure by Homer.

The Square du Vert-Galant was a prominent point downstream of Île de la Cité, and with a spectacular view of the Pont des Arts and Musée du Louvre. The sun was radiant between the thin curtains of clouds, and the reflections bounced with the wake of steamers and tugboats on the river. The chain steamers and barges carried loads of timber, manure, wine, stone, bricks, and coal. The veterans told me that wounded soldiers of the British Expeditionary Forces were once transported down the river by steamers to hospital ships in the port of Le Havre.

André and Henri, the *mutilés de guerre*, and other veterans who wore metal masks to camouflage broken faces, were always in my thoughts near the River Seine. I searched for the masked veterans at every quay and bridge on the river, saluted every fisherman who wore a fedora, or caught a perch, but never heard from them again. The last time we saw them was about four years ago with Anna Ladd at the Red Cross Studio for Portrait Masks for Mutilated Soldiers.

Pierre Chaisson delivered lunch to the wounded veterans once a week at the Square du Vert-Galant. He served white wine, fresh baguettes, sausage, ham, and cheese. Most of the veterans were French, only one was American. They recounted the stories of the war, and disguised the memories of their families. The war stories were never the same, of course, and the obvious wounds were never mentioned over the late lunch.

I was heartened by the courage and humor of the veterans, and moved by the spirit and generosity of the stories. Most of the stories were ironic, the chance encounters with the enemy. The stories of the wounded veterans at the square would have inspired an audience of natives on the reservation. The sounds of the war, the rumble, crash, and shatter of explosions were hard to describe, and every veteran created original metaphors of sound. One veteran used the specific sounds of the river, the screech of steam whistles, the bump and shudder of heavy barges on the wooden docks.

The sounds of the Great War were over, and should have been forgotten, but the visual scenes and necessary metaphors continued in ordinary peaceful places and the River Seine. I had imagined the sound of enemy machine guns in the dry leaves that scraped across the river stones.

Pierre was one of the best storiers, and he declared that our stories as veterans were the only trustworthy memories and histories of the war. Our stories were reliable histories, he repeated at every lunch, because our stories were inspired by visual memories. The stories were original, and not mere recitations, so the storier never told exactly the same version of the story. Liturgy was a religious and political recipe of authority, and not creative or reliable as the visual memories of stories.

Pierre was a native teaser, and a clever storier, but the wounds of war were never the secure sources of taunts or ironic decoys. The veterans practiced the tease of manners, gestures, and clothes, service chance and regrets, the wave of a middle finger, threadbare trousers, saintly socks, a pink shirt, mismatched colors, but never scars or war wounds. No one ever commented on scars, burns, broken faces, or severed limbs.

The commune of river veterans became our native sanctuary, and we were the only native veterans of the Great War. Granger Gross was the only other river veteran from America. Naturally, my reservation accent was mocked, and the veterans teased me about my notebook, and my brother about blue ravens. I never directly wrote in the presence of anyone. My notes were discreet, and yet the mere practice of private records was a separation, a pose of authority. So, on the third river meal with the veterans my private notes were translated into French and read out loud by a wounded veteran from a farm near Château-Thierry.

Granger translated and then my notebook was passed around several times over lunch. My imagistic entries, notes, and selected descriptive comments were read openly with constant teases, shouts, critical overstatements, and astonishment in a particular tone of voice. Three weeks later the notebook scenes were no longer a source of ironic humiliation, or even communal mockery. The native tease on the reservation was mostly a trial by chagrin, and the mockery by wounded veterans was the same. The ordeal ended and the veterans actually started to dictate notes and heartfelt stories to me, and those notes became another source of my stories about wounded veterans of the First World War.

Aloysius painted every day and completed thirty-six original paintings in the series *Thirty-Six Scenes of Blue Ravens and Bridges on the River Seine* for the special exhibition that early summer at the Galerie Crémieux.

Nathan had widely advertised the exhibition, and he posted notices at museums, bookstores, and in public places. The notices described the series as visionary native portraits of the River Seine. The portrayals were creative scenes of more than twenty individual bridges, and some were painted several times. My brother painted the Pont Neuf and Pont Mirabeau several times, and each portrait in the series was an original abstract perception of the bridges.

ÉCOLE INDIENNE DES CORBEAUX BLEUS
Aloysius Hudon Beaulieu
White Earth Reservation
State of Minnesota
Trente-Six Scènes des Corbeaux Bleus

Thirty-Six Native Scenes of Blue Ravens
Bridges over the River Seine
Saturday, June 14, 1924
GALERIE CRÉMIEUX

Nathan framed the entire series, thirty-six scenes of the river, and displayed the paintings on three walls of the gallery. He placed four scenes of the Pont Neuf on separate easels near the entrance to the gallery. The crowd of artists, art collectors, students, and some veterans from the café and river commune were naturally drawn to the four easels and portraits of blue ravens and the glorious bastions and stone arches of the Pont Neuf.

The Pont Neuf was built with twelve bastions over the river on one side of the Square du Vert-Galant, and eight more bastions on the other side of Île de la Cité. Aloysius painted twenty stone bastions afloat with great blue ravens on enormous crests of white and blue waves on the River Seine. The bastions floated with uneven cants in the faint rouge shadows, the broken shadows of the Pont Neuf. The waves in the portrait of the bridge were traced by inspiration to *The Great Wave*, a woodblock print by Katsushika Hokusai.

The second abstract portrait of the bridge was a fractured scene, cracked and crooked in the hues of a muted sunrise on the River Seine. Great blue ravens were perched at the seams to steady the bridge. The third portrait thrust the sections of the bridge out of the dark blue river in the claws of blue ravens. The waves reached to the sky with the sections. The fourth abstract portrait of the bridge was in natural flight over the huge muted blue leaves on eddies in the river, and the billows of clouds were the wings of the blue ravens.

Aloysius painted the faint rise of the sun, only a trace of rouge on the horizon, and created the slight rouge reflections of the sun in wavy tiers on the River Seine. The reflections of the bridges in the series were broken by waves, and the fractured, erratic, breach of the watery reflection became the portrait of the bridge and blue ravens.

Native visionary artists created a sense of presence with the perceptions of motion, a native presence in the waves of memory, and in the transience of shadows. Birds and animals perceive motion in water, rain, the waves on lakes and rivers, the shimmer of light and fugitive reflections on the water, as an artist might with contour and colors, and breach the image and custom of the seasons and the perceptions of the ordinary.

Misaabe, the native healer, taught me to create stories with the perception of motion and the belted kingfisher, and with vigilance breach the surface of reflections to catch a fish. My brother painted to fracture the obvious reflections of the bridge with images of great blue ravens. Native perception and imagination can easily reverse the course of waves, and the familiar images and reflections of faces and monuments. The Pont Neuf and other bridges were always more beautiful in the natural motion of waves and in the fractured reflection of a sunrise.

The Pont Neuf abstract portraits were compared to river scenes painted by Camille Pissaro and Claude Monet. Pissaro painted the original impressions of ephemeral winter lights on the River Seine. Monet painted *Soleil Levant*, an inspired bloody sunrise with muted water blues and greens, and the incredible reflection of the sun on the harbor at Le Havre. Pissaro, Monet, and other serious and original visionary painters were not comparable to my brother. Yet the casual resemblance to the water scenes created by Pissaro, Monet, and Aloysius Hudon Beaulieu revealed a natural obligation to create motion with hues of color and an abstract sense of presence with fractured or cubist reflections.

The art collectors crowded in silence around the four portraits of the Pont Neuf. Nathan stood nearby and listened to the comments about the blue raven portrayals. I observed that most visitors to the gallery expected a native artist to represent some traditional scene, or at least depict a trace of native culture or inheritance in the portrayal of the river scenes.

The Great War fractured the ordinary stay, wily scenes, native reflections, ethnographic warrants, and empire cultures, and nothing has ever been the same on the White Earth Reservation, Montbréhain, Rue Mouffetard, or the River Seine.

I moved closer to the four portraits on the easels, introduced myself as a native veteran and writer, and explained to the visitors that blue ravens were native visions, and the historical name of the Pont Neuf was not always a representation of the real bridge. The name was figurative, and the meaning of the bridge was discovered or perceived in the traces of natural motion in stories, but not in the cultural liturgies or structural expositions.

I pointed at each of the four scenes and told the visitors that the presence of the bridge was imagined, and not the mere copy of an image or reflection. The abstract scenes of the bridge were visionary, and that was a common native practice in stories and art, similar to native visionary scenes of blue horses painted in magical flight on ledger paper.

Franz Marc came to mind in the conversation at the gallery because he had painted great blue horses, and was plainly inspired by native artists and by Marc Chagall. Natives had painted abstract horses in bold colors long before the portrayals of blue horses and red cows by other painters. Only the mere mention of a German, Franz Marc, a member of *Der Blaue Reiter*, was a serious detraction to some of the visitors at the gallery, but that awkward reaction was allayed when the visitors learned that the artist had died in the First World War.

Seven years later the hatred of the enemy had become an obsession. The sentiments of vengeance had reached into the very heart and authenticity of avant-garde art, and the marrow of popular culture. Cubism was once denounced as a German perversion, and the censure was so persuasive that some cubist and avant-garde painters changed styles during the war. Pablo Picasso, who did not serve in the military, shunned cubism and turned back during the war to classical themes and portraiture.

Aloysius painted the Pont de Passy as a blue skeleton under the gauzy waves of the River Seine. The scene was horizontal, just below the reflection on the water, and revealed enormous concrete piers and ominous spiny creatures. Three blue ravens floated on the mirage of the river with wings spread widely between the cutwaters and elegant metal arches.

Four great blue ravens were perched on the stone pillars at the entrances to the ornate Pont Alexandre III. The bridge was built for the Paris *Exposition Universelle*, World Fair in 1900. The blue ravens had unseated four elaborate golden statues on the pillars, the statues that represented the symbolic history of France. Aloysius had painted traces of rouge on the claws of the ravens. Some artists at the gallery were rather amused by the tease of aesthetics and ironic conversions of national narratives, but other visitors were sidetracked by the creative arrogance. The French were rightly protective of state art and monuments.

The Pont au Change was curved under water, and envisioned in a current of blue raven feathers. Sections of the bridge emerged, and the shadowy buildings were afloat on the river. The Palais de Justice and La Conciergerie at the Île de la Cité were portrayed as reflections in the water, and marbled blue.

The hazy images of the buildings were buoyant, the towers wavered, the windows were wispy hues of blue on the river, and the stone statues were daubed with traces of rouge and faint black. The medallions of Emperor Napoleon were bent and creased as pendants in the huge claws of two blue ravens. Gauzy shadows of the blue ravens were spread over the broken surface images of the Palais de Justice.

Aloysius painted with a trace of rouge the abstract silhouettes of a guillotine on the windows of La Conciergerie. Only the most perceptive viewers of the Pont au Change might have noticed the slight silhouettes of guillotines. Marie Antoinette was imprisoned there, and later executed by guillotine.

I told the visitors at the exhibition that native painters were visionary artists and had always created scenes of visual memories, and native visual scenes were never based on the liturgy of names or institutions. The visitors easily recognized the recent innovations of impressionistic, fauvist, and cubist art, the original abstract scenes and elusive hues of form and structure. The bright colors conveyed the heart, passion, and creative perceptions of instinct and natural motion.

Some visitors at the gallery that night compared the blue ravens and bridges painted by my brother to the particular abstract, fauvist, and cubist styles of paintings by Georges Braque, Pablo Picasso, Juan Gris, André Derain, and Marc Chagall.

Aloysius was inspired by other original painters, of course, but never directly influenced by impressionism, fauvism, or cubism. He honored the great avant-garde painters, but not the mere ideologies of artistic styles. My brother painted ravens with natural wild blues, but never painted political ideas or competed with any other artists in the world. He created visionary native scenes in natural motion, a style that was original, untutored, and conceived on the White Earth Reservation.

The Pont Mirabeau was the most sensational blue ravenesque portrait in the series of the thirty-six blue bridges at the exhibition. The scene was mounted separately on the back wall of the gallery. Aloysius had painted an unsteady and awkward totemic tower of four bronze statues, and with the same number of blue ravens. The actual green statues on the two piers of the bridge were painted hues of blue on the totemic tower.

The abstract totemic statues only slightly resembled the four majestic bronze figures on the arches of the glorious Pont Mirabeau. Two actual statues, allegories of navigation and commerce on the prow and stern of a symbolic boat, were mounted in downstream positions. The statue at the prow carried a *francisque*, a hatchet or tomahawk, and the other statue at the stern carried the gear for the symbolic boat. The two bronze statues on the second symbolic boat, a nude woman with a golden horn at the prow, and a figure with a torch at the stern, were mounted on the bridge pier in the upstream positions on the River Seine.

Aloysius created the abstract totems of four blue ravenesque figures with tomahawks, torches, boat gear, and temple trumpets. Several blue ravens were intertwined over the tower. The cones of the blue temple trumpets were touched with rouge.

Sections of the metal bridge were curved and stacked at the bottom of the totemic tower. The abstract images of blue feathers, temple horns, and torches were afloat on the River Seine.

The Pont Mirabeau portrait was more than a reflection, but rather an intrinsic perception of the abstract reflection of the bridge on the water. The ravenesque portraits in the entire series were the mythic presence of color and motion in the reflection of the River Seine.

Nathan Crémieux stood near the sensational portrait of the Pont Mirabeau and read out loud the poem "Le Pont Mirabeau" by Guillaume Apollinaire. More than forty visitors gathered around to hear my favorite poem read in French. "Le Pont Mirabeau" was published in *Alcools*, a selection of his recent poetry. Nathan read slowly, and with a resonant voice. The audience was moved by the visual images of each word of the poem.

> *Sous le pont Mirabeau coule la Seine*
> *Et nos amours*
> *Faut-il qu'il m'en souvienne*
> *La joie venait toujours après la peine*

Olivier Black Elk, Coyote Standing Bear, and other natives in our commune at the Café du Dôme arrived later at the exhibition. No one was surprised that the two prominent pretenders were more interested in the ethnographic representations of native traditions and cultures. Predictably the most uncertain and anxious pretenders were the negotiators of native conventions and authenticity.

The abstract visionary scenes of blue ravens and the broken images of bridges on the river were not easily poached or earmarked as customary. The pretense of native ancestry withered with abstract images and native irony. Olivier and Coyote were never critical of natives, and wisely used elusive praise, grand, bright, brilliant, to comment on the blue ravenesque portraits.

The wounded veterans of the commune at the Square du Vert-Galant on the River Seine were truly transformed by the totemic presence of blue ravens and the fractures of the obvious. The veterans had discovered in the abstract portraits of the bridges the creative rage and passion of blue ravens, and the cracks and marbled scenes of mirrors. Once the natural scenes were changed by the creative turns of reflections and breaks of the ordinary, the wounds of the body, the *mutilés de guerre*, became only ephemeral reflections on the surface, and easily transmuted by imagination and the natural tease of aesthetics and disability.

Pierre Chaisson was inspired by the portraits of the blue ravens and declared at the exhibition that the wounds of the veterans were the very first cubist perceptions. Wounded veterans were the artists of their body images and reflections, and the natural motion of the river forever created a new aesthetic face in the water.

The common and familiar body was only a cultural reflection, he announced, and the amputations, scars, creases, burns, patchwork pare and skin, cracked features, and cockeyed ears, arms, and more, were abstract creations of wounds and original scenes and reflections in the new aesthetics of humane cubist portraiture.

Daniel-Henry Kahnweiler closely studied each of the blue raven portraits. He returned to peruse the Pont Mirabeau and Pont Alexandre III several times, but never gestured or commented on the composition or style. Silence, and no obvious gestures, discussions or descriptive observation of paintings was his signature manner as a gallery owner.

Kahnweiler remembered our conversation several months earlier, rather the translation of our conversation, at Shakespeare and Company. I presumed he was impressed with at least one portrait, but he was resolute and avoided even the invitation of a general comment.

I mentioned *Ulysses* by James Joyce, but the art collector evaded any comments about literature in the same manner as art. We talked awkwardly about the *mutilés de guerre* and forsaken wounded veterans in France and Germany. I was moved by the lonesome gestures of his eyes, the ordinary consequence of a wise and perceptive outsider. Kahnweiler was a German more at home in the liberty of France.

Kahnweiler and Georges Braque were engaged in a serious conversation later about the portraits of the Pont au Change and Pont Mirabeau. I only heard the words *guillotine* and *poteau de totem*, but the gestures of the cubist artist and the art collector were animated and favorable. Naturally, the hierarchy of the blue ravens was much higher on the totemic towers than the bronze statues on the Pont Mirabeau. Kahnweiler was the first gallery owner to exhibit the cubist paintings of Braque.

Marie Vassilieff was prepared to purchase the portrait of the Pont des Arts, but we refused to accept the money. The Pont Neuf portraits were priced at twelve hundred francs, or about sixty dollars at the time, and each of the other portraits were one thousand francs, or about fifty dollars. Aloysius was actually amazed that anyone would pay a thousand francs or fifty dollars for one of his blue raven portraits. My brother was an extraordinary painter, but he worried that the sale of only one portrait was the total average salary for two weeks of labor in Minneapolis, and even more hours of labor in Paris. Aloysius reminisced that night that we had started out hawking the *Tomahawk* for a few pennies a copy some sixteen years earlier at the Ogema Station on the White Earth Reservation.

Nathan invited the visitors at the gallery to gather around and honor the cubist painter Marie Vassilieff for her artistic integrity and generosity during the war to a generation of hungry artists in Paris. Aloysius removed the framed portrait from the wall, and most of the visitors signed the back of the Pont des Arts.

Georges Braque hailed the memorable dinner that Marie had prepared when he returned from the war as a wounded soldier. The artists and others at the gallery saluted the exceptional devotion of Marie Vassilieff who had established La Cantine des Artistes at Le Chemin du Montparnasse.

Sylvia Beach, the proprietor of Shakespeare and Company, Adrienne Monnier, proprietor of La Maison des Amis des Livres, and Gertrude Stein, an avant-garde art collector, attended the exhibition at the Galerie

Crémieux. Sylvia told me that she was impressed with the similarities of innovative authors and avant-garde painters, and that words and images had
been transformed by the experiences of the war.

Gertrude Stein studied the scenes of blue ravens in the new École Indienne in France. Naturally, she had cornered the apparent native artist.
Olivier Black Elk wore his Boss of the Plains black hat, so she assumed that
he was the actual artist. The pretender was pleased, of course, to describe
the new school of visionary native artists, and then wisely directed her attention to Aloysius.

Gertrude was curious about native avant-garde artists and writers, and
she was aware of my newspaper stories about the wounded veterans. I
instantly resisted her direct, severe, and rather possessive manner, and
changed the subject with equivocal comments. My stories were evasive
representations, an abstract native practice that was suitable for arrogant
inquisitors, and hardly descriptive, punctual, or dramatic. At the time my
responses were effective evasions. Gertrude was distracted and looked
away, but a few minutes later, as she was leaving the gallery, she asked me
if I knew the young writer Ernest Hemingway. No, but she insisted that we
should meet.

Nathan sold nine portrayals that night at the gallery, including the four
scenes of the Pont Neuf. He was certain the other portraits would be sold
that summer. Nathan earned thirty percent of the sale price of the portraits.
Aloysius was ecstatic that so many portrayals had sold at the first formal
gallery exhibition. Nathan was in high spirits and invited Marie, Aloysius,
Pierre, and me to celebrate the outcome of the exhibition over a late dinner
at the Café du Dôme.

Nathan was acquainted with many poets and writers but he had never
actually met Ernest Hemingway. Several waiters explained that the writer
had caroused at the café many times with other writers and artists. The
waiters looked around the café and confirmed that the writer was not there
that night.

Marie was at my side at the table. We drank white wine and talked
about the gallery and the heartfelt reaction of the wounded veterans to the
blue raven portraits. She was intrigued by my new stories of the veterans.
Georges Braque and Guillaume Apollinaire, she reminded me, were both
wounded in the war.

I was enticed, as usual, by her passion, generous spirit, and sympathetic gestures, and aroused by the motion of hands, the turn of her eyes, and especially the touch of her thigh under the table. My thoughts turned to the image of her reclined and nude in the portrait by Amedeo Modigliani.

Marie reached out to hold my hand at the end of the dinner, and we walked to her atelier at Chemin du Montparnasse. I was silent, and almost breathless with excitement that night. Marie was radiant in the faint light, and the touch and scent of her lovely body lingered forever in my memory.

Nathan sold eleven more ravenesque portraits that month, and for that reason and the revolution he was eager to celebrate Bastille Day. Naturally, he was our escort that Saturday, July 14, 1923. First we were present for a traditional military parade in the morning on the Avenue des Champs-Élysées. The French soldiers wore smart uniforms, tricolor sashes, white plumes, and shiny helmets, and the enthusiasm of the citizens on the streets was marvelous.

We had not been exposed to military formations or ceremonies since our honorable discharge five years earlier, but that morning the martial music and rhythmic sound of the precision march of soldiers inspired strong emotions and memories. The banners, trumpets, horns, and national music were everywhere. We were excited and ready to become citizens of France.

Nathan had reserved a table for lunch at a café near the Place de la Bastille, the location of the former prison, and the very site of the start of the revolution. The children wore hats, starched cotton, high white stockings, middy blouses, and danced in the streets. We were inspired and humane natives at the very heart and memory of a great liberty, the commemoration of a brutal war with the aristocratic *ancien régime* that began on July 14, 1789.

The French fur trade and the *coureurs des bois*, tricky outlaw traders, and later the *voyageurs*, fur traders in canoes, had already declared by stories and songs a premier union with our ancestors the native Anishinaabe near the *gichigami*, Lake Superior, and at the legendary headwaters of the *gichiziibi*, the Mississippi River.

The *Colonne de Juillet*, July Column, a monument dead center of the square, was created to commemorate the stories of the prison, the visual Storming of the Bastille, and the inevitable war with *l'ancien régime*. The *Génie de la Liberté*, the Spirit of Freedom, was a golden statue, a winged

spirit, mounted on the crown of the great column at the Place de la Bastille. Together we saluted the golden spirit of the *Révolution française* and
the esprit de corps of *liberté* in France. Then, of course, we ordered our
lunch to avoid the crowds. More than eight thousand citizens were there
that morning of the French Revolution in 1789.

Singular names of the dead, golden statues, and marvelous state monuments were much easier to remember than the abstract cause, excuse, and
fury of revolutions. Everyone was prepared for the grand celebration of the
insurgence, revolution, and liberty, but no one was ready to remove the par-
tisan shrouds of slaughter, and recount the actual cadavers of sovereignty
abandoned in mortuaries and morgues.

Aloysius outlined an enormous blue raven on the column, and native visionary wings replaced the golden wings of the *Génie de la Liberté*. No one
is prepared for revolution or war, or for the revisions of peace, but only for
the celebration of victories and surrender treaties. We were not prepared for
war, and we were never prepared to live on federal reservations. We learned
to evade dominance with ironic and visionary stories. We became creative
artists, a writer and a painter, and conceived of our sense of *liberté* in Paris.
The world of creative art and literature was our revolution, our sense of native presence and sanctuary.

I was a native literary expatriate, not an exile. My brother was a visionary expatriate painter, not an exile. We created our native sense of presence
with imagination and a sense of chance, and not with the sorrow of lost traditions. Yes, we were exiles on a federal reservation but not as soldiers, and
we were never exiles in Paris. So, we were expatriates in the City of Light,
in the city of avant-garde art and literature. Paris was our sense of presence
and liberty.

Nathan told stories about the revolution over lunch, and then continued
that afternoon as we walked along the River Seine. Most of his stories were
connected to sites on the river, the actual scenes of the *Révolution française*. The stories were elusive and ironic, but not obscure, and celebrated
the anxious citizens who had endured the curse of power.

Bastille Day continued into the night, and we were ready and grateful
to be part of the excitement and celebrations. Nathan had invited Marie
and Pierre to a special dinner celebration at the Café du Dôme. The waiter
secured one round table and five wicker chairs on the terrace, and we sat

close to each other, drank wine, and shouted to be heard over the rush and roar of the celebrants.

The Boulevard du Montparnasse was packed with several hundred carousers, and the human waves surged from one celebrity café that night directly across the boulevard to the next, from the Café du Dôme to La Rotonde, and to the new Le Jockey. Chinese lanterns decorated the trees on the boulevard, and the busy intersection with Boulevard Raspail. Music, poetry, and song were heard in every direction that night.

Bastille Day was more than a celebration of the *Révolution française*, the day was a national rave of the spectacular, not only liberty, but the erotic and cultural excitement of the crowds, the rush of promises, art, literature, music, and sensational adventures of stories, memory, and cultural liberty.

Nathan ordered seven carafes of wine, and we toasted every memorable poet and novelist we could name. Apollinaire, Pound, James Joyce, of course, and Blaise Cendrars. Herman Melville, Jack London, and Sinclair Lewis were my only advantage in the author name game. Everyone at the table named at least a dozen authors, and then we turned to toast artists.

Nathan raised his glass to honor the marvelous conception of blue ravens by Aloysius. I raised my glass to Marie, of course, and then Georges Braque, Henri Matisse, and Marc Chagall. Many artists were named and then we toasted the *Révolution française*. I was tipsy, excited, delighted by the frenzy, and the natural sense of liberty, and yet cautious enough never to abuse the gentle affection of Marie.

We drank more than we ate, and then we decided to walk on the boulevard with the lively celebrants. Nathan pointed to the other side of the boulevard, so we entered the great waves of carousers, and docked together near La Rotonde. Nathan asked and the waiter reported with a wave of his hand that Gertrude Stein and Ernest Hemingway had been seen at the café that night.

Gertrude was hardly worth the rush and shoulder of sweaty bodies through the throng of the café, only to tolerate the praise of native pretenders, but the search for the endorsed author became an ironic diversion. There were many authors, poets, and painters gathered around tables at La Rotonde, but we never found Ernest Hemingway. He was not there, and we learned later that the author was at the bullfights in Spain.

Malcolm Cowley, however, was there that night, and inspired sensational stories about the sudden and unprovoked assault on the proprietor of La Rotonde. Nathan and Marie had heard the name of the young man, and remembered that he was interested in Dada, an ironic and absurd art movement, and the new theories of surrealism by André Breton, but he became famous for his gesture of realism that night.

Cowley had been drinking, of course, and probably made too many toasts to authors, when a spirited discussion turned to accusations that the proprietor was a *mouchard*, an informer. More than five hundred celebrants were there, and most of them heard about the encounter that night at La Rotonde. Cowley actually shouted *petit mouchard*, an insult that the proprietor was small and had informed on the café patrons for the police.

Cowley rushed forward and struck the proprietor on the jaw, a glancing blow that became a memorable literary story. Cowley was seized by two policemen and marched to a nearby police station. He told the actual story of the assault to André Salmon, the poet and art critic, who must have recounted the occurrence as a cubist portrayal of a revolution against the *petit mouchard* on Bastille Day.

24

MUTILÉS DE GUERRE
1924

Aloysius Hudon Beaulieu was a visionary painter inspired by natural motion and waves of color, by abstract contours, shadows, and that marvelous brush of flight in the original portrayals by native stone, hide, bark, and ledger artists, and by the ethereal succession of blues in scenes by Marc Chagall.

Painters of this blue arc created evocative curves, muted hues of presence, green rabbis, the ghostly heart of blue ravens, red nudes, magical flight, tender guises, the reverie of native motion on the White Earth Reservation, and trusty portrayals at Vitebsk on the Pale of Settlement. These marvelous scenes were more memorable than the churchy, cultural, and mundane ethnographic duty of naturalism and authenticity.

Aloysius and Chagall were enlivened by the artistry of natural motion, and they created visionary traces of state exclaves, military outposts, traders, soldiers, shtetls, violinists, green faces, blue statues, bridges, synagogues, passenger trains, hotels, and hospitals, the mighty Dvina River, and headwaters of the Mississippi River. These creative scenes were natural unions of visionary art and community.

Chagall once lived and painted great visionary scenes in a shabby studio at La Ruche, the legendary colony of expatriate artists at Montparnasse. Aloysius first painted at the actual scenes of his portrayals on the reservation, in the livery stable, at the train station, near the rivers, and then at the front window of our apartment on Rue Pecquay in Le Marais.

Chagall had endured poverty, bigotry, and the persecution of governments, and yet he was encouraged by the great promises of the Communist Party and the Russian Revolution. Jews would be respected as citizens and granted liberty. He was surely discouraged by the trivial politics and factions of the revolutionary bureaucracy, and returned to the casual wiles and cultural teases of expatriate artists at La Ruche.

Paris was the magical sleeve of visual memories at the time, painterly scenes of exotic feigns, avian adventure, intrigues, ruses, tribute, and states of melancholy. Chagall was never secure in any country as an artist and a Jew. The colors and contours of faces in his magical paintings were sacred waves of light, the crucial motion of liberty, and the mysterious traces and cues of evolution and family.

Chagall created brilliant scenes that lingered in my dreams and memory, and these three especially: *The Violinist*, with a fantastic green face, *I and the Village*, a magical mutation and elaboration of sentiments and gestures, and later the elegant, sensual, and lasting affection in *The Birthday*.

Nathan was mainly moved by three other portrayals by Chagall, *Adam and Eve*, *The Soldier Drinks*, *To Russia, with Asses and Others*, and *The Cattle Dealer*. Blaise Cendrars, the hasty poet and novelist who lost an arm in the war, provided the title, *To Russia, with Asses and Others*, a portrayal of a rouge cow, a blue church, a perforated figure with a bucket in the dark, and a detached head afloat. Nathan first saw these paintings before the war at La Ruche. He had visited several artists at the colony, and told stories about Blaise Cendrars and Marc Chagall.

Cendrars was one of the first artists to visit Chagall in the early years at La Ruche. The poet roared with laughter, and teased his new friend about prostitutes and piety. They gathered at cafés and bars with hundreds of other expatriate artists. La Ruche was indeed the hive of wild, inspired, and visionary painters, poets, and sculptors. Le Bateau-Lavoir was another painterly lair in Montmartre. These two shabby unheated structures actually housed many of the great expatriate painters of the century and stimulated an incredible movement of visionary art and avant-garde art in Paris.

Amedeo Modigliani created portraits of lovers and more than a dozen poets and painters, such as Moïse Kisling, Pablo Picasso, and the singular oval face, elongated nose, cocked eyes, and narrow jaw of Blaise Cendrars. The poet in turn created a fantastic imagistic poem about Marc Chagall.

> *He's asleep*
> *He wakes up*
> *Suddenly, he paints*
> *He takes a church and paints with a church*
> *He takes a cow and paints with a cow*

Chagall moved back to paint in Russia, and at the end of the war taught art in his hometown of Vitebsk, and then exhibited his recent paintings in Berlin. He returned to La Ruche nine years later and discovered that hundreds of stored paintings had vanished in his absence. Cendrars, one of his closest friends, was accused of betrayal and blamed for the disappearance of the paintings. Cendrars denied the accusation, but the lingering doubts ended the friendship.

Nathan told me as many stories about poets and novelists as he recounted about expatriate painters. Blaise Cendrars and Guillaume Apollinaire were the first creative writers to promote the avant-garde artists and styles of cubism, that artistic resistance to romantic scenes and perspectives, and created only outline dimensions similar to the abstract pictures by native artists.

Nathan related with conviction the prominent resistance to despotic empire politics, colonialism, the savagery of war, and the artistic resistance to the fakery of nationalism and notions of enlightenment. The obvious artistic and literary connections were the radical aspects of cubism, avant-garde, and geometric portrayals. Even so, many expatriate artists served in the military to defend the liberty of the French Third Republic.

Cendrars, for instance, was born bourgeois in Switzerland, and served in the French Foreign Legion. He lost his right arm early in the First World War at the First Battle of Champagne. He became a citizen of France.

Apollinaire celebrated the abstract dimensions and mutations of representation in cubist art and poetry. Painters fragmented the forms of perspective, and he changed the stance and stay of words in poetry. He was born Wilhelm Apolinary Kostrowicki in Russia, and changed his Polish name and moved to France. The poet survived shrapnel wounds to his head, and died of influenza shortly before the end of the war. He was honored at death by painters and poets and buried at Père Lachaise cemetery in Paris.

Apollinaire and Cendrars and many other soldiers were the actual *mutilés de guerre* in the war movie *J'accuse* directed by Abel Gance. The narrator in the movie hallucinated dead soldiers revived in the grave, and in motion on the road. André and Henri, the masked *mutilés de guerre* veterans and shy fishermen at the Quai des Grands-Augustins, were in the very same movie but had not met the two writers during the production of the cemetery scenes. Cendrars was pictured in a ghostly procession with bandages unfurled on the stump of his right arm. Apollinaire was cast in scenes with bandages over the actual wounds on his head.

The French military commanders had allowed some soldiers to participate in the silent scenes of horror, the return of the dead in the movie, and later many of those soldiers were themselves killed in action by the enemy. They had survived the cinema of war and then died in the actual war, an ironic legacy.

My brother was excited, of course, about the innovative scenes painted by other artists, the impressionists, fauvists, and cubists, but he alone had conceived of color and contour as natural motion, and abstract blue ravens were avant-garde creations on the White Earth Reservation.

Native artists envisioned a semblance of the avant-garde in the perceptions of natural motion, and in the ordinary experiences of visual memory, the creases and fragments of reflections, impressions, stories, and visionary portrayals.

Natives were hardly considered as original and innovative artists by gallery owners and museum curators. The burdens of tribal traditions that were once denatured by missionaries and then reconstructed by romancers, federal agents, and ethnographers, and then understated in dominant theories of race, primitive cultures, and genetics. The crude discoveries and ethnographic concoctions of native stories and art precluded any inspired or sensible presentation of original native portrayals with other artists of the avant-garde at established galleries.

Daniel-Henry Kahnweiler, Paul Rosenberg, Berthe Weill, and Ambroise Vollard established galleries and promoted avant-garde painters in Paris. Paul Cézanne, Henri Matisse, Marc Chagall, Pablo Picasso, Juan Gris, Georges Braque, Amedeo Modigliani, Fernand Léger, Robert Delaunay, and many other innovative artists were presented in singular and group exhibitions at galleries.

The Galerie Paul Rosenberg was located at Rue de la Boétie north of the Grand Palais. The Galerie B. Weill was first established at Rue Taibout and later moved to 46 Rue Laffitte near Rue la Fayette. The Galerie Vollard was established at 6 Rue Laffitte and then during the First World War the gallery was moved to the apartment of the owner at Rue de Martignac in Faubourg Saint-Germain.

The inaugural Galerie Kahnweiler was first located in a narrow space at

28 Rue Vignon, but the police seized the entire collection of avant-garde art as reparations because the owner was German. Kahnweiler returned after the war and established with a colleague the Galerie Simon on Rue d'Astorg. These and several other galleries advanced the great revolution of avant-garde and visionary art in Paris. The Galerie Crémieux was the only gallery that presented original native visionary arts.

Nathan Crémieux had attended most of the exhibitions at the other galleries. He was acquainted with the owners and understood that visionary native portrayals were not considered suitable with the exhibitions of other avant-garde artists. The general conception of native visionary art had not been widely promoted in Paris. Nathan envisioned that native art would be exhibited with other avant-garde art as a course of nature at galleries in Paris.

Nathan introduced us to the gallery owners at exhibitions, and we met most of the avant-garde artists. Aloysius was reserved and only rarely talked about blue ravens at exhibitions. We were both evasive about native culture and the politics of federal reservations. My brother was courteous to other artists, of course, but mostly he only wanted to meet Marc Chagall.

Nathan in fact solicited an invitation for us to visit Chagall in his new studio at 110 Avenue d'Orléans near the Métro at Porte d'Orléans. The entrance to the six-story building was under arched windows. We walked through huge double doors into a private courtyard. Nathan told me later that the very same address had once been used by Vladimir Lenin and the Russian Board of the Central Committee of the Democratic Labor Party in Paris.

Chagall would be anxious and cautious, we were told, but he was rather genial and compassionate, and embraced us as artists, not as curious natives. His eyes were bright and playful, almost gestures of innocence. Marc spoke mostly in Russian, and at times in hesitant French, and yet we seemed to be united with the artist in our own uncertain French.

Chagall was almost as shy as my brother was reserved, but the two painters immediately engaged in mutual ideas about visionary art, the natural motion of color, and the notions of ethereal and evasive representations. Nathan translated the lively discussion with the assistance of Bella Chagall.

Aloysius considered each painting that was mounted in the studio, and turned with the rhythm of the marvelous visionary scenes, a natural sway and stay of contours. He was moved by the stately colors and motion of the figures. Then my brother turned once more and told several stories about his early inspiration to create blue ravens of liberty. He rarely talked to anyone about his portrayals, but he was captivated by the vitality of the art in the studio and by the generous spirit of Chagall.

Bella Chagall was precise, spirited, and warmhearted, and she closely watched my brother as he moved around the studio from one picture to the next. He paused, moved closer, turned, and then raised his hands to celebrate the genius of *The Birthday*. I praised the very same painting, and was excited to see the original with the painter in his own studio. *The Blue Horses*, *The Poet Reclining*, *Praying Jew*, *I and the Village*, and other paintings were mounted and stacked against the back wall of the studio. Ida Chagall, the only child of Marc and Bella, was eight years old that summer, and she pretended to smoke a white candy cigarette.

I changed the painterly tone of the moment with celebratory and ironic stories about the trader Odysseus Young, the healer Misaabe, and Animosh, the boy shaman of the woodland, and the great mongrel detectors of disease on the reservation. Chagall listened closely and then laughed when the meaning of the words shaman and mongrel diagnostician were translated, *chaman indien*, *chien bâtard*, into French.

Nathan continued the stories about his relatives the traders who had established an ethical union with natives on pueblos and reservations in the Southwest of the United States. The stories about the early traders were always compelling, and the visual scenes were interrelated with generations of other traders and the connection and collection of native art at the Galerie Crémieux in Paris.

Chagall told several stories about the great theaters in Russia, circus clowns, the natural tease and dance of horses, and the nostalgic wisps of visionary scenes in the window mirrors of passenger trains. Aloysius was touched with the poetic ideas and insights of the artist, the actual perceptions of presence, of shadows and motion, and the intensity of his reflections on visionary art. I reminisced about that critical moment fifteen years earlier when my brother had sensed the extent of various perspectives and dimensions of images reflected in the window of an art gallery in Minneapolis.

Chagall paused, turned toward his daughter, and declared that he had always aspired to paint "an art of the earth and not merely an art of the head." Bella translated the declaration of aspiration and earthly art several times that afternoon to be certain that we had clearly perceived the concepts of terrestrial and artistic passion, but not wholly sensual.

I pointed out, however, that the head and the mind were both ethereal and earthly. Painters were sensuous poets, and the traces of literary images and painterly scenes were derived as they have always been from the very same mysterious passions of evolution and native stories of presence, chance, and trickery.

Aloysius mentioned his new portrayals of *mutilés de guerre*, the painted masks, broken faces, blue ravens, statues, and bridges over the River Seine. Chagall was moved by the images of blue ravens, and by the abstract depictions of wounded soldiers and the war. He was silent, tearful, and turned suddenly toward his wife and daughter. Bella indicated that her husband was always troubled by the images of war, and the terrible misery, waste, and mutilation of land, face, spirit, heart, and memory.

Chagall could have indicted states and empires, associations and communities for atrocities against Jews. He was an artist of fury, compassion, and religious ceremonies, but never painted the figures of fascism. Aloysius repeated the very same words, *terre, visage humain, esprit, coeur, mémoire,* and then he embraced the word *liberté* three times.

My brother had decided earlier not to present a scene of blue ravens as a gift to Chagall. He was there only to appreciate the brilliance of the artist, and not to solicit comments on the abstract motion of blue ravens, wounded soldiers, and the River Seine.

Nathan formally invited Marc, Bella, and Ida to the exhibition of the new blue raven *mutilés de guerre* series, and at the same time to celebrate the publication of my selected war stories, on Saturday, October 25, at the Galerie Crémieux.

Corbeaux Bleus
Les Mutilés de Guerre
Nouvelles Peintures
Par Aloysius Hudon Beaulieu
et
Le Retour à la France

Histoires de Guerre
Par Basile Hudon Beaulieu
Samedi 25 Octobre 1924
GALERIE CRÉMIEUX

Blue ravens were the solemn prefects of the *mutilés de guerre* on the River Seine. The wounded soldiers gathered overnight in ghostly camps on the bloody shores of the *zone rouge* tributaries to warn the successors and to search for the strays. The sunrise and seasons were diverted by the war, and the rivers became the steady stream of death. Broken bodies, shards of mighty country bones, and the tow of unnamed heads, hands, and bloated shoulders in uniform ran ashore in the heavy rain.

The rivers nurtured no secure memories of the dead soldiers, only fragments afloat with thousands of other reflections. Yet the faces of warriors looked back forever with a natural radiance. The Somme, Meuse, Marne, Aisne, Oise, and Seine River have carried for many generations the blue bones of soldiers out to the stormy sea.

Aloysius painted twenty original blue raven scenes of statues, monuments, fountains, camouflage masks, broken bones, hideous faces, and the *mutilés de guerre* on the River Seine. The portrayals were painted for the exhibition at the gallery. The perspectives and style were distinctive, and not the same as the first series of blue ravens and bridges.

My brother was swayed more by native ledger artists and hide painters than by the geometric creations of cubist painters. The faces and contours were fractured, turned back on the wily muse of deceptive representations, and altered in the new portrayals, and yet there were elusive traces of blue ravens, conspicuous soldiers, and warrior names, tricksters, and many other figurative scenes.

The hues of blue created a sense of natural motion and figural impermanence. The *gueules cassées*, or soldiers with broken faces, and stacked limbs, blue bones afloat, contorted wings, slanted beaks, models of congruity breached, creased, and the common cast of art perspectives were distorted, otherwise the cues of cubism and the avant-garde were always present in native scenes of the blue ravens, but not the obvious painterly geometry.

Aloysius had painted mostly on half sheets of rough wove finish paper, about two feet wide, but he painted four weighty scenes on full sheets of watercolor paper for the *mutilés de guerre* series and exhibition at the Galerie Crémieux. The paintings, about two feet by three feet framed, were four variations of gruesome abstract scenes of soldiers with broken faces.

In one portrayal, *Blue Ravens and Fractured Peace*, my brother painted four enormous blue ravens, and with huge elaborate beaks, crowded close together in a row across the center of the wide paper, wings askew, and each raven wore a great oval blue peace pendant. The images painted on each pendant were the fractured, broken faces of the *mutilés de guerre*. Crushed cheeks, jaws, bony eye sockets, noses sheared, caved frontal bones, cracked smiles, huge circular scars, nasal cavities covered with thick globs of grafted flesh, and grotesque angles of teeth, lips, and tongues. The peace medals or pendant scenes were painted for the exhibition on a full sheet of wove finish watercolor paper.

Medals of Honor, the second portrayal of the *mutilés de guerre* and hideous wounds, was a blotchy blue wash with awry traces of connected scars, wounds, cavities, and distorted faces afloat, sealed with oval, twisted images of military decorations, Medal of Honor, Distinguished Service Cross, Victory Medal, and the Army Wound Chevron. Ignatius Vizenor, the name, was painted in faint rouge over the elongated eagle on the medal of the Distinguished Service Cross.

Aloysius used only natural blue pigments, and wild honey as a binder to paint the waves in two river scenes. He painted enormous river waves in the *ukiyo-e* woodblock print style of *The Great Wave off Kanagawa* by Katsushika Hokusai. The waves reached across the wide sheets of watercolor paper.

The Great Wave on the River Seine pictured the blue bones of soldiers on the crests of the waves. The blue hands, femurs, thighs, skulls, collarbones, and shards of facial bones protruded and tumbled with the waves. Each bone was touched with a trace of rouge. Two blue ravens were portrayed on the wing in the trough of the waves, and with bones in their claws.

The primary feathers of the blue ravens were painted in the same contours as the crest of the waves. The vane of the feathers flowed into the waves, and the natural blue wash merged feathers with the heavier blue pigment that outlined the mighty waves. The bones were numbered in the hundred thousands, and the numbers were blurred in rouge on the waves.

More than four million soldiers died in the war, and millions more dead civilians.

Alfred Dreyfus, that name of honor in *Dreyfus in Natural Motion*, was printed in distinct outline rouge and the letters were curved in the shape of a fish with dorsal and caudal fins. Dreyfus was in motion upstream with other names submerged in the River Seine. The entire large sheet of watercolor paper was a blue wash with streams of delicate blue hues of underwater currents, and slight beams of rouge sunlight reached through the shadows of the Pont Neuf. The surface of the river was a narrow blue ripple at the very top of the scene, on the deckled edge of the paper.

Alfred Dreyfus, Émile Zola, Georges Picquart, Anatole France, Henri Poincaré, Georges Clemenceau, Basile Hudon Beaulieu, John Clement Beaulieu, Paul Hudon Beaulieu, Lawrence Vizenor, Ignatius Vizenor, Ellanora Beaulieu, Pierre Chaisson, Guillaume Apollinaire, Blaise Cendrars, Nathan Crémieux, and many other citizens and soldiers were distinct names painted in the shape of common fish in the current of the River Seine.

Aloysius included his own name in the shape of a sunfish in the shadow stream of the Pont Neuf, and the name of our favorite uncle, Augustus Hudon Beaulieu, who told us about the venal prosecution and scandal of the military court, and he railed against the priestly bigotry and unjust conviction for treason of the loyal artillery officer Alfred Dreyfus.

Augustus had reminded us several times, and especially after he had been drinking with the priest, that we were born in the same year that Alfred Dreyfus was demeaned in a public courtyard at the *École Militaire*.

Dreyfus served almost five years in isolation at a prison in French Guiana. He was exonerated eleven years later, and we were eleven years old, and promoted to major in the *Armée de Terre*, or French Army. The stubby noses of the names of soldiers in the river stream were touched with rouge.

Ferdinand Walsin Esterhazy and other names were painted in faint and indistinct blackish letters in the ghastly shape of dead fish and other dreary creatures in the current of the river. Esterhazy and the names of other dishonorable military creatures were gasping for air at the surface of the River Seine. I could imagine the deadly hiss and wheeze of the creatures painted streaky blue with the huge wide mouths of bloated carp.

Major Esterhazy deserved to wheeze to death forever in an abstract portrayal painted by my brother. The major betrayed his country and then by deceit allowed the conviction and degradation of an honorable military officer only to conceal his own debauchery and treachery. A French military court ruled that Esterhazy was not guilty of espionage for the German Empire.

Édouard Drumont, the publisher of *La Libre Parole*, a socialist and antisemitic newspaper at the time of the betrayal of Dreyfus, was painted by name in the shape of a transparent scaly snake. The snake was shriveled in a simulated gasp at the very top of the underwater scene in the portrayal. Dumont published *La France Juive*, a nasty jingoistic tirade against modern art and the exclusion of Jews from France.

Aloysius painted sixteen more blue raven scenes on smaller standard sheets of wove watercolor paper for the *mutilés de guerre* series. Nathan had already started to frame the pictures, but he would not mount the series in the gallery until the morning of the exhibition. He wanted the entire new series of blue raven pictures to be a surprise display.

Aloysius painted *Apollinaire in Flight*, the scene of four blue ravens perched on top and around the rough stone marker and the grave of Guillaume Apollinaire at *Cimetière du Père Lachaise* in Paris. The ravens had enormous watery blue wings with intricate patterns, waves of blue hues on the mane, and very sturdy claws similar to human hands with traces of veins. The crowns of the four ravens were covered with gauzy bandages, a semblance of the actual wounds of the soldier and poet. The gauze was created with a slight wash, and then faintly outlined in blue with a wide soft brush.

Four raven claws held bluish paper scrolls, and on each scroll the title of a poem in rouge, *Le Pont Mirabeau*, *À la Santé*, *Zone*, and *La Maison des Morts*, published in *Alcools* by Apollinaire. Naturally this was my favorite painting in the entire series because the scenes and composition of the portrayal honored a great soldier, art critic, and poet. Apollinaire died on November 9, 1918, two days before the armistice and the end of the First World War. The poet was buried only about two months before we arrived for the first time in Paris.

Aloysius created *Totemic Wounds*, an incredible totem of blue broken faces, a monument to honor the *mutilés de guerre* and the soldiers with monstrous head wounds. My brother painted only two vertical totem scenes in the entire series. The totem pictures were about two feet high. The *mu-tilés de guerre* totem was painted at the center of the Champs de Mars be-tween the mighty Eiffel Tower and the *École Militaire*. The painted totem was located near the actual site of the Paris *Exposition Universelle* in 1889, and in 1900.

Three giant blue ravens were painted and posted as honor guards at the base of the monument. My brother painted rouge chevrons on the cocked primary feathers of the ravens. The blue beak of the raven on the crown of the totem was fractured, and only the lower bony shard of the beak re-mained as a hideous scoop. The totem was painted wound by wound with the broken blue faces of soldiers, the grotesque cheeks, jaws, noses, fore-heads, and massive scars mounted and interconnected on the totem as a spectacle for tourists at the Eiffel Tower and cadets at the nearby *École Militaire*.

Blue Horses at the Senate, the second vertical totem, was a similar por-trayal of native and *mutilés de guerre* warriors between the gardens, circular pond, and the French Senate in the Jardin du Luxembourg. The painted faces on the totem were blue ravens and native warriors who had resisted the military crusade and federal detention on reservations. The blue ravens and warriors were mounted and portrayed on the monument with the tor-tured and broken faces of wounded soldiers.

Aloysius painted and connected the blue ravens and broken faces of sol-diers on the totem to the semblances of Tecumseh, Chief Pontiac, Geron-imo, Little Wolf, Sitting Bull, Red Cloud, Crazy Horse, and Chief Joseph. The names of the warriors were painted in various hues of rouge and caught in the nearby trees and shrubbery. The name *mutilés de guerre* was painted seventeen times in faint blue and in motion around the monument.

The native warriors were original and visionary portrayals, of course, be-cause my brother never pretended to paint or depict scenes of authentic-ity. The soldiers were painted from visual memory of the masks and broken faces of the *mutilés de guerre*. The signature faces and features of soldiers and warriors were fractured and ghastly on the totem, an avant-garde por-trayal and not merely the guises of naturalism.

The *mutilés de guerre* were teased as gargoyles and prey only by chil-dren, and sometimes pious speculators teased the presence of war demons. Consequently most wounded soldiers on the river ducked their faces in the presence of children. Some of the carved stone gargoyles were animals, dogs, goats, monkeys, wolves, but most of the figures were fantastic creatures that diverted water on cathedrals, a grotesque ornamentation that once represented evil monsters, and that curse of representation was delivered to the wounded soldiers of the First World War.

Aloysius painted four native warriors on marvelous blue and rouge horses in the ledger art style of natural motion. The horses were in natural motion at the background of the totem near the gardens of the French Senate. The entire scene was vertical, and the wispy blue wash of the watercolor paper merged with the totem of warriors and broken faces, and appeared to float in natural motion with the blue and rouge horses.

The portrayals of the two totems concentrated on the blue ravens, the soldiers, and horses, but not the presence of tourist or cadets at the *École Militaire*. Naturally, there were always tourists near the Eiffel Tower and the Jardin du Luxembourg. My brother explained that the scenes were visionary and ambiguous, and not depictions or renditions of public events.

The portrayals of blue wounded soldiers and native warriors were revolutionary because the scenes were elusive and ethereal representations, otherwise the picture would have been an excessive mockery. Native visionary or avant-garde artists would never paint only to anticipate the praise of cultural realism or the care and conceit of authentic cultural memory.

Saint Michel trounced the devil with a sword and the sturdy wings of an angel in the sculptural exhibition at the monument and fountain in Place Saint-Michel near the Île de la Cité and the River Seine. My brother transformed that tourist square with two nude war widows, *mutilés de guerre*, and blue ravens.

Saint Michel the Blue Raven was the only portrayal in the series that my brother painted at night. We walked around the fountain and square many times and noted the poses and gestures of the seven sculptures. The muscular devil at the feet of Saint Michel might have captured more tourist attention than the other smaller statues on the crown of the columns.

Aloysius mostly painted in the morning light, but he could not create the scenes he wanted for *Saint Michel the Blue Raven*, so he decided to paint at night in the faint light of a single table lamp. The scenes of the blue raven and war widow saints were heavier, and the hues of blue were darker than the other portrayals. The wash was a faint hue of blue, and the course of water in the portrayal was created with a bloom or backruns on the paper. Late at night he painted the visionary sculptures near the fountains with a darker hue of blues.

Aloysius painted the four columns of the monument with mushy hues of rouge, and the two winged dragon fountains were transfigured into two blue and nude war widows. The nude statues pointed toward the conversion of the four statues of virtue into blue ravens on the crown of the columns. The statues of virtue, prudence, power, justice, and temperance were deposed by painterly mutations of the *mutilés de guerre* into four wounded soldiers with huge blue raven wings, elongated beaks, and with one enormous claw that reached over the columns.

Saint Michel was always ready to fly and slay the devil in the liturgy of many faiths and religions. Michael was a crusader in Judaism, the spiritual warrior and tricky angel of death in Roman Catholicism, an archangel in Protestantism, and a creator, prince, and patriarch in Mormonism. Saint Michel the winged archangel was fully engaged in a monotheistic duel with the husky devil at the fountain, but the figuration of celestial creatures and magical flight were much more memorable in native stories. Yes, more memorable because the imagined characters were transformational in trickster stories and never represented in sculptural monuments. Stories, and the continuation of creative scenes of transformation and natural motion, were the most honorable sources of cultural memory.

The trickster was an ironic native saint, an elusive character in the best visionary stories. Tricksters were androgynous saints, wild beasts, pests, creators, healers, demons, the necessary contradictions of nature, and in constant motion or transformation in the marvelous scenes of native stories. Native tricksters were more reliable in the end than the winged saints of monotheism and monuments.

The trickster saints were elusive representation in visionary stories, and monotheistic saints were either obvious ironies or the unintended ironies of pious concoctions and doctrines of theologians and plucky politicians.

Saint Christopher and many other saints have been sidelined in holy history, a serious demotion in the hierarchy of the priests, but tricksters were never ousted in native stories, and persisted as teasers of arrogance and piety. The blue ravens were stories of evasive tricksters and forever abused the masters and mavens of naturalism with the testy delights of irony.

Aloysius portrayed the statue of Saint Michel at the fountain as an androgynous creature with a touch of rouge on his navel and the enormous wings of a blue raven. Michel stomped on the devil, and the brute underneath his left foot on the rocky fountain mound was the semblance of the pompous Kaiser Wilhelm II.

The Blau German Emperor wore a Prussian Garde du Corps metal helmet with a nasty eagle perched on the crown. My brother touched one wild eye of the emperor with a black tear. The Kaiser in the portrayal might have been reviewed as a mere caricature, not avant-garde or serious art, but the face of the emperor was fractured, nose severed, one eye gouged, cheek craters, crooked teeth exposed, and creased with scars. The emperor in the picture displayed the wounds and mutilations of the war.

Aloysius created a marvelous scene of blue ravens perched on *Le Pâtre et la Chèvre*, or the Shepherd and the Goat, a sculpture by Paul Lemoyne in the garden of the Palais Royal. Seventeen blue ravens converted the sculpture into a war memorial. *Blue Raven Mutilés* was a portrayal of the broken faces of soldiers outlined in faint hues of rouge on the extended wings of the ravens.

Eugène Delacroix once lived at Place de Furstenberg, near the Abbey of Saint-Germain-des-Prés in Paris. Aloysius created an abstract blue raven statue, *Natchez Liberty*, in the small square to honor the Natchez natives and the warrior leader Great Sun.

Delacroix painted *Les Natchez*, a passive romantic scene of a native man and woman with a newborn child, and that became the connection and intense cause to honor the natives outside the early residence of the famous artist. Delacroix was aroused by the native culture he read about in the romantic novel *Atala* by François-René de Chateaubriand.

Delacroix portrayed the inactive natives with romantic Roman noses, and painted the same nose on the robust woman bearing the tricolor in *Liberty Leading the People*. Liberty was painted brave, and walked over the dead in a revolution, but the two natives were passive, a sentiment of tragedy.

The Natchez were at war in the early eighteenth century with the colonial French. Commander Sieur de Chépart had ordered the Natchez natives to leave a particular section of land, but they resisted and were ultimately defeated by the French and native Choctaw. The colonial governor designated the land as a plantation for the cultivation of tobacco. Great Sun and hundreds of Natchez natives were captured, tortured, and enslaved on plantations in the Caribbean. The French sold many of the native survivors into slavery.

The blue ravens on the statue honored the warriors who had been enslaved by the colonial French. Great Sun wore a feathered crown, and my brother painted similar feathers on the crown of the statue and touched the barbs with rouge. Great Sun, the name, was painted in rouge on the base of the statue. Several names of soldiers with broken faces, and names of *mutilés de guerre*, were painted on the huge leaves of the *platane*, or plane tree.

The French presence at the source of the *gichiziibe*, the great Mississippi River, was not the same as the colonial cruelty at the other end of the river. Our ancestors were *voyageurs* fur traders not colonialists, and the union was by trade, stories, and songs, and not by slavery, otherwise we would have resisted the colonial occupation of the French.

Aloysius painted *The Danton Strategies* as a similar portrayal of the bronze statue and stone monument of Georges Danton, the revolutionary, with warriors at his side, near the Métro Odéon on Boulevard Saint-Germain. Danton was a green statue of insurgence and blue in the original portrayal of the series.

Danton faced north and pointed forever in the direction of the Cathédrale Notre-Dame de Paris. My brother painted a handsome row of blue ravens with huge wings cocked in various angles on the extended right arm of the strategic revolutionary. Auguste Paris, the sculptor, created a determined gesture that became an eternal ironic point of direction and destination. The painted blue heads and broken faces of soldiers were stacked at the bottom of the monument, between the muscular legs of Danton.

The *Fontaine des Innocents* was one of the oldest fountains in Paris. The fountain, once named the *Cimetière des Saints-Innocents*, was located in Les Halles near the Théâtre du Châtelet. Aloysius painted blue broken faces on the six curved steps that surrounded the fountain. The faces were distinct and painted with alternate traces of black and rouge eyes on the stone steps.

Natives were created in trickster stories, a more humane and ironic analogy to nature and other creatures than the solitary and separate creation stories of monotheism. I was raised on trickster stories, and resisted the dominion of churchy or federal separatism. Trickster stories encouraged a natural sense of native presence, and surely provided that necessary source of pluck and guile to endure the absence of irony on federal reservations.

Augustus and my parents told original and elusive stories about tricksters, and in different styles. The stories my uncle told were more political as the trickster would tease and outwit federal agents. Honoré, my father, told more elusive trickster stories about natural reason and the sentiments of animals and humans. Father Aloysius Hermanutz was a pensive listener, and smiled over the tease of the trickster in stories, but the stories he told were about piety, devotion, sacrifice, salvation, and godly virtues over demonic temptations.

Augustus teased the priest to consider that trickster stories provided visionary surprises, ironic humor, and delight in the face of fear, war, and ordinary contradictions. My uncle declared that stories about evil were the tedious cutthroats of irony. Divine and patriotic stories were never trustworthy in the face of a fierce enemy in war, so the only stories that created a sense of presence were about ingenious tricksters who fractured and outwitted the contradictions of tragic monotheism with guile, creature transformations, and with gestures of humane irony. Native tricksters created avant-garde art.

My first written stories about the dance of the plovers were visionary trickster stories. The most inspired and deceptive plover dances were a variety of feigns and guises as evasive entertainment, and not a predictable pattern or liturgy.

Aloysius created blue ravens as tricksters in elusive portrayals of the *mutilés de guerre*, and the broken faces of soldiers. The scenes at statues and monuments were fractured and grotesque to alter the common sentiments of heroic stature and countenance, the obvious evasion of naturalism and monotheism.

Blue Ravens and Fractured Peace, *Medals of Honor*, *The Great Wave on the River Seine*, and *Dreyfus in Natural Motion* were the four large portrayals by my brother. He painted two vertical totem scenes, *Totemic Wounds* and *Blue Horses at the Senate*, and fourteen other blue raven portrayals that included *Apollinaire in Flight*, *Saint Michel the Blue Raven*, *Blue Raven Mutilés*, *Natchez Liberty*, *Danton Strategies*, and *Fontaine des Innocents*.

A wide blue-and-rouge banner with our signatures as artists announced the exhibition, and was posted on the display window of the Galerie Cré-mieux. Aloysius painted a small raven with a broken beak on the right side of my forehead, and a larger blue raven with a fractured wing and touched with rouge on the back of his left hand. Naturally, visitors to the gallery observed the raven on my forehead but never inquired about the beak or the reason. The gesture seemed rather ordinary, and associated with the exhibition, of course, but my reasons were related to trickster stories about the *mutilés de guerre* and political masks of the Great War.

Copies of my new book of war stories, *Le Retour à la France: Histoires de Guerre*, were on display in the window, and stacked on a table at the entrance. The *Corbeaux Bleus: Les Mutilés de Guerre*, twenty blue raven portrayals, were framed and the showcase art of the gallery. The four large watercolor paintings were mounted in a row on the back wall of the gallery, and the two vertical portrayals were displayed on easels near the entrance.

Nathan provided wines, cheeses, baguettes, *petits sablés*, coconut and chocolate macaroons, and other desserts. Most people arrived at dusk, and before dinner, in groups of artists and curators. Marie Vassilieff, Daniel-Henry Kahnweiler, Berthe Weill, Moïse Kisling, Sylvia Beach, Adrienne Monnier, Marc Chagall, his wife Bella, daughter Ida, and several student artists were the first to examine my book and view the blue ravens by Aloysius. A mysterious art professor and collector had arrived earlier in the day from Germany. He examined the twenty portrayals that afternoon, and returned for the formal exhibition for a second review of the blue ravens.

Pierre Chaisson and the wounded veterans from the Square du Vert-Galant arrived later at the gallery. The veterans had painted elegant blue ravens on their cheeks to honor the creation of blue ravens and Aloysius. My brother was moved by the gesture, and was ready to paint blue ravens on the cheeks of anyone in the gallery. Marie, Sylvia, Adrienne, Moïse, Berthe, and most of the art students were decorated with blue ravens that night at the gallery.

Several weeks later my brother presented to each of the wounded veterans a small original portrayal of broken blue ravens with the *mutilés de guerre* in the shadows of the Pont Neuf on the River Seine.

The wounded veterans hobbled around the gallery, examined the art, drank wine, gobbled the macaroons, and teased my brother about the success of his pictures. They talked to the gallery owners and other artists about the horror and brilliance of war and broken blue ravens.

Olivier Black Elk, Coyote Standing Bear, André, and Henri arrived with another group of artists. Aloysius commented at the time on the incredible coincidence of two native pretenders and masked soldiers in the gallery at the same moment. The native feign of a romantic presence, and the disguise of a broken face. The cruel connections were ironic and obscure, but the agony of that moment was never forgotten, and became one of my best trickster stories of endurance. André and Henri had returned from several years of exile and avoidance in Sète, a commune on the Mediterranean Sea near Montpellier.

Nathan introduced the native veterans to the gallery owners, the other artists, and to our friends. The gallery was crowded, and the conversations were lively, spontaneous, and serious comments were appreciated more fully with a sense of native irony.

The four larger watercolor portrayals were priced at fifteen hundred francs, and the smaller pictures at twelve hundred francs, a few hundred francs higher than the series last year, *Thirty-Six Scenes of Blue Ravens and Bridges on the River Seine*. The franc had lost value in the past year, and was worth about half as much converted to the dollar. Our expenses were the same, and we had never made as much money, so we were not directly affected by the financial crisis in the country.

I overheard one art collector comment that the blue ravens were tourist scenes. My response to the critical comment was direct and concise, that tourist art was not about the *mutilés de guerre* and broken faces of soldiers. Tourist art was a romantic promotion, the commercial nonsense of nationalism, not the scenes of wounded soldiers, and the masks that cover fractured faces and gestures. The art collector looked around the gallery, and then turned to explain that his comments were inconsiderate. I ordered the young collector to have his cheeks painted, and later he actually engaged André and Henri in conversation. He was nervous, of course, and told tourist stories about his family in Boston, Massachusetts. André and Henri appeared to listen to the stories, but the pleasant artistic expressions of the metal masks remained the same.

Daniel-Henry Kahnweiler returned several times to consider *Dreyfus in Natural Motion* and *Natchez Liberty*. He told me that the references to

French colonialism, the commerce in slavery of natives, and the biased and wrongful persecution and conviction of Alfred Dreyfus were subjects considered much too risky to present or even discuss at an art exhibition.

Kahnweiler was born a Jew in Germany, and that became a double persecution during the Great War. France was his choice of residence, with absolute loyalty, and his primary language of art, literature, and culture, but he was persecuted and forced to leave his home and gallery in Paris. Kahnweiler confirmed once again that his collection of incomparable cubist and avant-garde art was seized and sold at auction by the police. Not an easy conversation that night at the gallery, but he was never hesitant or unclear about his critical sentiments on colonialism and empire slavery.

Nathan raised his voice and announced my reading of sections from *Le Retour à la France: Histoires de Guerre*. He had translated my collection of stories and the Galerie Crémieux published the book in French. I was hesitant to practice my French, and instead read the short sections that night in English, and Nathan read the selected translations in French.

The gallery was silent. I could hear my breath. Marie smiled and waited for me to read. Every person in the gallery waited for me to read, but the silence was a hindrance. I had never read to a crowd, and was very nervous.

André bowed his head and touched his mask with one finger. That gesture of respect as a veteran relieved my anxiety, and that reminded me to begin the reading with the dedication of my stories to the *mutilés de guerre* and to the courage of André and Henri.

I read three concise stories from the book. The first scene was written about my arrival on the *Mount Vernon*, a troop ship, at Brest, France. The second concise story was about the utter destruction of Château-Thierry, and the last story was a scene about camouflage and combat near the Vesle River at Fismette. I concluded with my recent imagistic poem, "Prefects of the River Seine."

Brest: The Mount Vernon and other troopships delivered newly trained soldiers and then immediately returned with the casualties, the badly wounded in the war. Suddenly the wave of red sails and excitement of our arrival had ended, and every soldier on the dock stared in silence at the wounded. Medical vehicles were loaded with wounded soldiers, hundreds of desolate soldiers with heads, hands, and faces bound in bloody bandages. Many of the soldiers had lost arms and legs.

Château-Thierry: The Germans had bombed the bridge over the Marne River at Château-Thierry. The ruins of churches, farms, and entire communes became a common sight as the trucks moved in a column on the narrow roads west to Villiers-Saint-Denis and Château-Thierry.

German artillery had exploded the roofs, collapsed the walls of houses and apartments, and cracked louvers exposed the private scenes of the heart, bedrooms, closets, kitchens, furniture, and abandoned laundry on a rack. Broken crockery, and the legacy of lace curtains set sail for liberty. Familiar shadows were disfigured at a primary school, and children searched for the seams of memory. The scent of ancient dust lingered in the favors of the country.

Vesle River: Aloysius painted the blue wing feathers of abstract ravens on the cheeks of the infantry soldiers. The spread of primaries created the illusion of a face in flight. Yes, every painted soldier returned safely from combat that night. Blue was a secure color of peace, courage, and liberty. The soldiers saved the paint on their faces, and later my brother retouched the feathers.

Aloysius lead the way through the forest muck in leaps and bounds with each burst of lightning and explosion to secure a natural mound in the center of huge cracked trees. Our strategy was to fall asleep there despite the weather and artillery, to become a native presence in the folly and deadly chaos of the war. My brother was a warrior beam, the face of malice in every flash of lightning.

The artillery bombardment ended early in the morning. The trees around the mound emerged in the faint traces of light as black and splintered skeletons. We were native scouts in a nightmare, a curse of war duty to capture the enemy.

The Boche reeked of trench culture, and we could easily sense by nose the very presence of the enemy. An actual presence detected by the cranks and throaty sounds, and by the very scent of porridge, cordite, moist earth, biscuits, and overrun latrines at a great distance. Some odors were much more prominent, urine, cigarettes, and cigars, that moist morning. Officers smoked cigars, so we knew we were close to a command bunker. The most obvious scent of the enemy was the discarded tins of Wurst and Schinkin, sausage and ham, and the particular rations of Heer und Flotte Zigaretten and Zigarren.

The Great War could be described by the distinctive scent of mustard gas, chlorine, urine, putrefied bodies, cheesy feet, machine oil, and by cigarettes, Heer und Flotte, Gauloises Caporal, and Lucky Strike.

I paused and turned toward the display window. Two children had pressed their faces against the glass. I waved and motioned with my hand to enter the gallery, but the children ran away.

PREFECTS OF THE RIVER SEINE

Mighty blue ravens
prefects of wounded memories
seasons of war
and the *mutilés de guerre*
mustered on the ancient tributaries
down to the River Seine

Soldiers gather overnight
ghostly camps on the *zone rouge*
warn the successors
and search for the strays

The early sunrise broken
stream of bodies
shards of country bones
crushed cheeks
noses sheared
bloated hands and shoulders
come ashore in uniform

The Somme and Meuse
Marne and Aisne
Oise and the Seine River
headwaters of the *mutilés de guerre*
generations of blue bones
blurred forever on the waves
out to the stormy sea

No one in the gallery that night dared to applaud the images of war, wounded soldiers, or the *mutilés de guerre* at the end of the reading. My brother saluted me, and repeated some of the images of wounded soldiers, children, and the river, *shoulders come ashore in uniform, seams of memory, streams of bodies, generations of blue bones,* and *out to the stormy sea.*

Marie was teary.

André touched his mask with a finger and bowed a second time to me. Henri came forward and touched my cheeks, a gesture of respect. Kahnweiler silently clapped his hands together. Moïse, the soldier and painter, aimed his pipe at me, and then he poured another glass of wine. Augustus, my uncle, came to mind that night in every word and gesture.

The German art collector had closely examined each portrayal several times, and yet he never said a word about the blue ravens, the composition, or the style. Once or twice he touched his right ear, and rubbed the bristly white hair on his chin, but never uttered a word to suggest his mood, assessment, appreciation, or critique.

Nathan was about to negotiate the sale of the two vertical portrayals, *Totemic Wounds* and *Blue Horses at the Senate,* when the German collector rushed forward and shouted that he would buy the entire collection of blue ravens, twenty paintings. Conversations in the gallery were hushed, almost a ghostly silence. Suddenly the private negotiations over two portrayals became a public transaction of the entire exhibition of blue ravens.

Nathan directed the mysterious German to discuss the unusual declaration at the back of the gallery. The collector had not revealed his name to anyone that night. Aloysius was summoned later to the discussion, and then the sensational announcement was made that the *Corbeaux Bleus: Les Mutilés de Guerre,* the entire twenty blue raven portrayals, had been sold to a single collector.

Aloysius announced that he would accept commissions to paint similar scenes in the series. He had already agreed to paint two more vertical totems, and that was the necessary condition to negotiate the sale of the entire collection of blue raven portrayals.

Nathan was surprised only because the portrayals sold on the night of the exhibition. He was convinced that the entire blue raven series would have sold in a few weeks time. The German collector paid in cash that night, and actually had the series packed the next day for immediate shipment to a gallery in Berlin, Germany.

Nathan invited friends and veterans to a celebration of drinks and dinner at the Café du Dôme. André and Henri were grateful to be invited, but they could not face the curious spectators, and they could not eat or drink with a mask. André tried to explain that the sight of their broken faces would distract the company.

Aloysius rightly refused to accept the defense of a grotesque wounded face as a reason to avoid dinner with friends. He insisted that André and Henri show their wounded faces, then and there, and that would resolve any concern about spectator avoidance. Everyone consented to circle the veterans at the Café du Dôme.

We told the story of the blue ravens sale over and over with variations, and each story became more elaborate and ironic. The German, in the last stories, was a spy for the exiled emperor, and would secure and destroy avant-garde savage art and especially the scene with Saint Michel and the Kaiser, or the art collector was a *metis* native and veteran of the war, or the collector was a secret buyer for the British Museum. That story was quickly shouted down as arrogant and elitist, but the story that lasted the longest that night, and had the most convoluted variations, was the art collector as colorblind gallery owner who had no idea what he had actually acquired in the name of blue ravens. Aloysius was teased in every story, and he deserved to be teased for several days about the sale of *mutilés de guerre* and blue ravens.

André and Henri raised the metal masks and used a fork to eat sausage and mashed potatoes, and sipped wine from a large spoon. My brother teased the veterans that there was not much chance to overdrink with a spoon of wine at a time. André raised the mask and laughed, and everyone at our circle of tables drank wine with a large spoon that night.

Nathan told another story about the collector, that he was so eager and concerned about acquiring the entire series that he paid three thousand francs more than the actual cost of the entire series, and my brother was paid seventy percent of the total amount. The money news generated many teases, slight tributes, and some ironic envy.

Marie toasted my brother, toasted the veterans, praised the compassion and integrity of great gallery owners, and then turned directly to Nathan. She touched his gentle face, and he blushed, so the others reached out and touched his face even more. The circle of veterans raised spoons of wine to honor his dedication to native art. Nathan turned rouge, more than the slight touch of rouge in the portrayals of blue ravens by my brother.

Aloysius told the veterans that he was not a schooled artist, but a native visionary painter, and he would not have been recognized as widely without the interest and support of the gallery, and my stories would not have been published in translation without the generous and direct assistance of Nathan Crémieux.

Marie insisted that the stories be continued at her atelier at Le Chemin du Montparnasse. Nathan paid for the dinners and ordered a case of wine delivered to the atelier. The stories were in natural motion that night at the Café du Dôme, and resumed at the atelier with even greater character and irony.

Augustus, my uncle, convinced me that the best stories were created and revealed in the most spirited situations and natural places. Natives continued the stories of our ancestors in natural motion at the headwaters of the Great River. The stories continued at the livery stable, government school, reservation hospital, Orpheum Theatre, Château-Thierry, Square du Vert-Galant, Café du Dôme, and Le Chemin du Montparnasse.

I imagined the presence of my uncle that night and we anticipated the sites of our best stories. Most of my stories had been published, and the site of memory was the Galerie Crémieux. Misaabe told stories in his cabin on Bad Boy Lake, and even the mongrels were enchanted. Odysseus was a great singer on the road, and his stories on a summer porch, at the livery stable with his horses, and over dinner and absinthe were truly memorable.

I presented signed copies, with a dedication to the memory of Augustus Hudon Beaulieu, to the veterans and friends that night at the Café du Dôme.

Marie told marvelous ironic stories about expatriate artists and sculptors, and the stories were always captivating and memorable in her atelier. The banquet stories of Amedeo Modigliani, Juan Gris, Fernand Léger, Blaise Cendrars, Pablo Picasso, Georges Braque, Béatrice Hastings, and others were not only visual memories, but opera scenes and singable. I told many versions of native stories by visual memory, and the atelier was a spirited site of art and trader stories that night.

André must have been inspired with the mood and sprightly humor, the natural irony, and liberty in the beams of the atelier, because the stories he told that night were poignant, momentous, and catchy. He had created a character named the Façade Man, and his stories were forever connected to the sites of ateliers, cafés, art galleries, and the River Seine.

Façade Man covered the caverns on his face with a metal mask. He could not remember the origins of his face, the curve of his jaw, the natural pucker, tease, and gestures were only faces created in stories, not by memory.

Façade Man had no sense of age by the natural wrinkles of his face. The grafted skin was lumpy and hard, ageless. He had no visual memory of his own face, no favor of form or natural color in the morning light. Only some animals and birds were aroused with his sense of magic in a metal mask.

Façade Man collected masks, and wore a different mask every day, masks of countenance, and he imagined the stories of the mask, the presence of the mask in public. He wore the masks of shamans, carnival dancers, ceremonial masks, tragic and comic theater masks, and even various gas masks. The many masks of demons and the demented, and with sprouts of wild hair, were not as sinister or as ominous as the ordinary military gas masks.

Façade Man never found a trace or memory of his face in a mask, but he found a profound sense of presence in some masks. Gas masks brought him comfort when he could not bear the mirror image of the hideous cavity on his face. The gas mask tormented more people than his own broken face. The mask that saved his memory, and became a connection to the world was a twisted wooden mask, a false face, and a mask similar to the masks of the False Face Society of the Iroquois.

Façade Man served in the military with a native soldier, and learned how to carve masks. The spiritual power of the false face masks was derived from the way the masks were carved from a live tree, and the tree continued to live after the release of the mask. The mask was the memory of the tree, and the mask became the memory of his original face. The carved mask was his spiritual liberty. The mask scared some people, mostly children, but most people were more curious than scared. The wooden mask created a sense of age, motion, and liberty for the Façade Man.

Marie invited me to stay for the night. I was ecstatic, of course, to be intimate once again, and to touch her sensuous body. The stories never seemed to really end that night, as most of the veterans and our friends had

just wandered away. André and Henri removed their masks and slept overnight on the floor of the atelier, and with a secure sense of presence.

Marie moved closer, rested on my chest, and our breath was natural, a
secret union. We heard the laughter in the room below, the murmur over
wine and the last stories, and that human sound created a natural sense of
solace.

>>> <<<

I read book twenty-four of *The Odyssey*, the last in the book of adventures
by Homer. I was at the window in the early morning light. Marie was asleep,
a gentle spirit nearby, her face radiant in the rouge light. Paris was my best
story, and no other place would ever be the same.

*I should have said that you were one of those who should wash well, eat
well, and lie soft at night as old men have a right to do; but tell me, and tell
me true, whose bondman are you, and in whose garden are you working?
Tell me also about another matter. Is this place that I have come to really
Ithaca? I met a man just now who said so, but he was a dull fellow, and had
not the patience to hear my story out when I was asking him about an old
friend of mine, whether he was still living, or was already dead and in the
house of Hades.*

*Believe me when I tell you that this man came to my house once when I
was in my own country and never yet did any stranger come to me whom I
liked better.*

About the Author

Gerald Vizenor is a prolific writer and
literary critic, and a citizen of the White Earth
Nation of the Anishinaabeg in Minnesota. He is
Professor Emeritus of American Studies at the
University of California, Berkeley. Vizenor is
the author of several novels, books of poetry,
and critical studies of Native American
culture, identity, politics,
and literature.